In Praise o

'It's wonderfully written, in
the end of the Second Worl
of guilt, memory, love, responsibility and deceit with flawless
clarity and insight'.
– A. L. Kennedy on
The Element of Water, The Telegraph

'Stevie Davies is one of our most consistent and continually
undervalued writers whose unsentimental, quietly revelatory
novels have cropped up on the Booker and Orange shortlists ....
Into Suez ... presents the most fully realised fusion of her personal
and political histories to date.'
– Alfred Hickling on
Into Suez, The Guardian

'... curious and empathetic ... [her] lightness of touch and saving
humour guard against any trace of earnestness ...
She helps a reader understand manifestations of evil so that it is
not out there, to be scorned, vilified and only attributed to others,
monsters, but potentially discernible in oneself.'
– Barbara Prys-Williams on
Arms and the Girl, The New Welsh Review

'Stevie Davies's fusion of past and present is masterly ...As always,
Stevie Davies writes with prose of unaffected clarity, and a calm
like the still surface of Lake Plön, where the Germans scuppered
subs and sometimes drowned themselves. As she dredges up the
history, it is a revelation.'
– Nicolette Jones on
The Element of Water, The Independent

'Resonating with poignant imagery, this outstanding novel examines the best and worst of human nature.'
– Emma Rea on *The Element of Water*, *The Times*

'It's impossible to convey here the complexities and beauties of the story, which gently pries apart knots of prejudice and pain that endured long after the war ended – many of which are with us still.'
–Carrie O'Grady on *The Element of Water*, *The Guardian*

EARTHLY CREATURES

Stevie Davies

HONNO MODERN FICTION

First published in Great Britain in 2024 by Honno Press
D41, Hugh Owen Building, Aberystwyth University, Ceredigion, SY23 3DY

1 2 3 4 5 6 7 8 9 10

Copyright: Stevie Davies © 2024

The right of Stevie Davies to be identified as the Author of the Work has been asserted in accordance with the Copyright, Designs and Patents Act 1988. All rights reserved. No part of the book may be reproduced, stored in a retrieval system, or transmitted in any form, or by any means, electronic, mechanical, photocopying, recording or otherwise without the prior permission of the copyright owner.

A catalogue record for this book is available from the British Library.

Published with the financial support of the Books Council of Wales.

ISBN 978-1-916821-01-9 (paperback)
ISBN 978-1-916821-02-6 (ebook)
Cover design by Ifan Bates
Text Design by Elaine Sharples
Printed by 4edge Limited

This is a work of fiction and no resemblance to persons living or dead is intended or implied.

*To Julie Bertagna and Frances Hill,
dear friends, peerless writers*

I desire a violent, domineering, fearless and ferocious upcoming generation ... able to bear pain ... show no signs of weakness or tenderness. The free and magnificent predator must once again glint from their eyes.[1]

> Adolf Hitler to Hermann Rauschning, 1934

Long nights now. Short days ...
– Burn the houses down, my brothers! ...
Every village – is now a fire!
Everything flames. Locked in their burning
Cowsheds, how the cows are bellowing -
– Ah, poor creatures ...[2]

> Aleksandr Solzhenitsyn, *Prussian Nights,* 1947

Off with your steel helmets! Throw your rifles away!
Enough of this murderous enmity!

Do you love a woman? So do I.
And have you a mother? A mother bore me.
What about your child? I too love children.
And the houses reek of cursing, praying, weeping...

You were brave men. Now throw away national pride.
The green sea is rising. Just take my hand.[3]

> Gerrit Engelke, 'To the Soldiers of the Great War', 1916–18

PRELUDE
East Prussia, 1944

> Wild geese are rushing through the night,
> With shrill cry northwards faring.
> Danger awaits! Take care your flight!
> The world is full of murder.[4]
>
> Walter Flex, 1916

Storks, in their thousands, prepared to abdicate their high thrones. They peered down from chimney stacks and churches. Raising their heads, the creatures clattered their bills, spread huge wings, rose and soared in circles above the villages of East Prussia.

It was time, it was high time: the birds must abandon Europe without delay. So immemorial wisdom dictated, but with fresh urgency, for the storks could see from their vantage point what the human herd below avoided: Russia surging across the map from east to west. Southwards the flocks prepared to migrate, over the shrinking German Empire, across Hungary, Romania, Bulgaria, Turkey, cruising above the Bosporus to ride the thermals over Egypt, and follow the Nile down to the safety of breeding grounds in Africa.

Everywhere Magdalena Arber wandered, that halcyon summer and early autumn, she came across folk staring upwards, ruminating. You could hear what they did not say: *Will you ever return home, beloved creatures? Shall we?* In that peaceful season, the lush pastures of East Prussia had never seemed as fruitful. The villagers continued to eat their fill, while Europe famished. Wading through waves of green, Magdalena felt faint earth tremors: the reverberation of a distant earthquake. On the main arteries, a westward trickle of refugees became a denser flow.

Now along the river valleys trekked strange cattle, driven east to west, breeds no one had seen before. In their thousands the animals gathered on the plains. On no account go near them, Magdalena was warned: these beasts are not a herd, you see, they're unrelated to one another. They've reverted and are wild animals now: they'll take you for an enemy. The cattle stampeded through the land, trod down fences, broke into gardens and stripped bushes and trees.

Uneasy news travelled by word of mouth, east to west. Border towns – Memel, Tilsit, Schirwindt – had been burned and bombed to ash. The rumble of distant artillery troubled your dreams; the eastern horizon glowed blood-red. The Russian front was coming, Stalin was coming! Terrified villagers abandoned their homes to join the flood of migrants...

...only to return and take up where they had left off.

For a deep, somnolent quiet had resumed. False alarm! Everyone exhaled. Our armies must have driven back the Slavs. The Russians are subhuman, everyone agreed, they cannot win against our Aryan might and manhood and technical know-how.

The wild geese took to the air, for their westward migration.

A first thick frost rimed the pastures. No grass remained for the alien cattle to eat, and they starved. They stood still, their stomachs distended, and when the snow fell, so – with a final defeated bellowing – did they.

Magdalena knelt to the child who was not her child, dressing her warmly in double layers of woollens and coats. She packed a rucksack, wrapped the crossbar of her bike in padding, and said, calmly, 'Dearest love, we need to go. But don't worry, Magda will look after you.'

1
Lübeck – Spring 1941

The Master of Mercy will protect him forever, from behind the hiding of his wings, and will tie his soul with the rope of life.[5]

The Jewish Prayer for the Dead

The moment she unfolded the letter and saw the official stamp at the head of the sheet, Magdalena knew: this was it! The imperial eagle spread the black symmetry of its wings on its swastika perch.

The call had come, she was under orders from the National Socialist Labour Service, flying the nest to make her contribution for Germany. Miss Magdalena Dorothea Arber was summoned to perform her war service as a village schoolteacher in East Prussia.

At last! Goodbye to lovely old Lübeck; release from the cosy cage of childhood and her family's dangerous equivocations. Nineteen years old and called to perform the kind of duty she valued most – brain work, rather than digging up spuds on a farm or assembling parts in a factory. Forming minds; taking culture to stinted children in the great fertile plains of the east. Bookish, greedy for knowledge, a lover of languages, Magda had yearned to study at university but the doors were closed to women. Never mind: this was a good second best.

And ... amazingly ... in East Prussia!

That unseen and poetic land had called to her forever: her dead mother's birthplace had been Königsberg. Magdalena knew East Prussia through the history books and a few photos in the family album. Primeval forests stocked with wild creatures: she was mad about animals, there'd be elk and bison, bears and foxes, wolves and beaver, chamois and lynx and deer and boar and storks! There'd be vast wheatfields undulating as far as the eye could see and ancient forests. East Prussia was on an edge, a frontier. It was *over there!* A far country that was also, reassuringly, German to the core. To the east lay Asia, the Slavic races. Lithuania, Ukraine, Latvia, Russia. Imagine!

Magdalena could take her young pupils to view the Teutonic Knights' castles and fortresses from the thirteenth century. They'd be the children of farmers and hunters, horse breeders, foresters and fishermen. Her pupils could teach her about their myths and customs, mysterious and ancient. She could take them to the white sands of the Baltic Sea shore with its trove of amber. Lagoons, rivers, lakes. They'd be *her* children, Magdalena loved them already!

Yes, and Dorothea her mother, somehow an abiding presence in that unknown land, seemed to be calling.

Magdalena went haring round the house to share the news, only to find preoccupied murmuring coming from the kitchen. She paused at the ajar door to listen.

Dad was telling Auntie Ebba about his last conversation with ... whom? The blackout was down and they were seated by candlelight at the rough old beechwood table. The halo of light cast by the candle picked out the table's whorls that remembered the original tree and its wounds; the stipple of pretend runes she and her cousin Clem had dug into the wood ('It wasn't me, honestly, Uncle Max – it was her!'; 'No it wasn't, Dad, it was him!')

Dad was speaking, Ebba listening. Through the gap, Magdalena could not see her aunt's face, only the fingertips of one hand tracing irregularities in the wood, round and round.

'...said he should have gone to Turkey with Erich in '37 while he had the chance. Erich begged him ... he pleaded with him...'

'Erich?'

'Auerbach.'

Magdalena heard the tears in Ebba's voice. 'Oh yes, of course. How did Hans-Martin ... how did he seem?'

'Calm, wry – matter-of-fact. Relieved almost at taking his life in his own hands. Thwarting *them*. You know how he is. Master of irony to the bitter end. Jested that he'd missed the boat when it came to Turkey. *And now they want to put me on the train!*'

Hans-Martin? Oh no, it was Dr Süsskind Dad was talking about. Dear Dr Süsskind who had been in their lives forever, scholarly, kind, austere. He couldn't help being a Jew and anyway he was exceptional. He'd been protected up till now by friends high in the Party. A complicated qualm overcame Magdalena. What train did they want to put Dr Süsskind on? But Magdalena knew. Of course she did. And instantly denied it to herself. No, that can't be right. International Jewry is one thing and must, she understood, be curbed. But not culled. Dr Süsskind is a good Jew. And anyway he's old. How could he labour in a work camp? Must be a terrible mistake.

A good Jew? A good *person*. Other people shocked Magdalena often, but not as grossly as she shocked herself.

'Shouldn't we go in and ... be with him, Max?' asked Ebba.

'He said no. Categorically. For our own sakes. They must come and find the body themselves when he doesn't show up at the station. Doesn't want us involved in any way. He asked me to take his books and manuscripts, Ebba, and preserve them if I possibly can, without danger to myself. And this ... and these...'

Magdalena heard a soft jingling as Dad began to turn out his jacket pockets onto the table. Watches, a string of his dead wife's pearls, rings, fountain pens, cigarette case came into sparkling view in the candle glow.

'Oh, bless him. Such a tender spirit. Hide them. Where have you put the books?'

'It's all right. Don't worry. Well hidden. With the others. He says he's glad Deborah isn't here to suffer this, it's easier this way.'

'Shall we ... do you mind if I...pray for him, Max?'

Pause. Magdalena could imagine the expression on her atheist father's face. And the love.

'All right. You say whatever prayer seems...'

Ebba's hand reached across Magdalena's line of vision, to take her brother's hand.

Ebba prayed.

'God, full of mercy, who dwells in the heights, provide a sure rest upon the wings of the Divine Presence, within the range of the holy, pure and glorious, whose shining resembles the sky's, to the soul of Hans-Martin Süsskind. The Master of Mercy will protect him forever, from behind the hiding of his wings, and will tie his soul with the rope of life.'

There was silence.

This was the Hebrew prayer for the dead, Ebba said. A rough translation. As a pious young Christian woman, she had learned the language to help with her Bible studies.

Magdalena listened while her father, voice breaking, said that Hans-Martin had tried to comfort him for his coming loss, saying, *Do not torment yourself, my friend. This is my escape. You are innocent of all this.* But Dad had replied, *Not one German is innocent. Not one of us.* To which his friend had responded, *Ah, but, my dear Max, I am a German too.*

Magdalena made to creep away, hugging to her chest the summons to war service and her own contradictions. Two kinds of crippling shame struggled within her. For much of her life she'd veered wildly between the National Socialist ideals – honour, submission, loyalty to Leader and Fatherland – and her home world, divided as it was between her father's old-fashioned humanism and her aunt's unflinching Protestant faith.

Her shoe squeaked as she turned, and they registered her presence.

'Is that you, Magda?'

Magdalena advanced into the candlelight, apologising for the interruption and ... oh, but ... seeing the tears on her father's face ... maybe this wasn't the time. The motion of the door caused air to rush in and out of the kitchen, twisting the candle flame. Light faltered on the faces of her father and aunt.

'What is it, Magda? Has something happened?'

'I have my marching orders, that's all. I'm being sent as a teacher to East Prussia.'

*

Magdalena wasn't at home when they came for Dr Süsskind.

Returning from having her documents stamped, she glanced up at their neighbour's lovely house, attached to her home and identical with it. She'd always felt as if the red-brick houses with their crow-stepped Gothic façades and rust-pink roofs held their arms around one another all along the row. They stood together in the terrace, all for one, one for all. In the sunlight, the red brick glowed. But Dr Süsskind's ruined front door, off its hinges, left a darkly gaping mouth into a cavernous interior.

The Gestapo had come too late, Ebba told her. The Veronal had done its job; their friend had slept the sleep of the just. Thank God. For God, full of love, would never condemn suicide in such a case, whatever anyone told you to the contrary. She gave her niece one of her penetrating looks.

'Oh no,' Magda hastened to say. 'I would never condemn ... there are times ... and circumstances...'

Ebba had been kneading the dough when the men came. She'd heard the pounding on Hans-Martin's door as they broke it down; the bellowing when they discovered that their prey had flown, and they tossed out the corpse onto the pavement. After looting the home, they'd dumped Hans-Martin's remains on the lorry with other human trash.

But our dear friend had seen and heard none of this barbarism, Ebba said quietly; our friend was safe, bless his heart.

Magdalena did not know what to say. Swallowing the qualm, she turned away, to go and sort her clothes: decide what to take with her on her adventure; darn or turn any garment that looked shabby.

A memory popped into her mind of a birthday, her fourth or

fifth perhaps. Dr Süsskind had appeared at the door, pulling along a toy tortoise on a string. *His name is Ferdinando, Magdalena my dear, and he has told me he would like to come and live with you.*

Anyway, she thought, never mind that. A dress but which one? As she only had two halfway decent ones, it wouldn't be much of a problem.

Also, books and paper. A parcel of textbooks had arrived, handsome-looking volumes, quite new off the press. She was saving this trove for the long journey east. But how on earth to transport the whole lot? Oh, it was all right, she'd be taking the bike, with its panniers and basket. One day Magda would write her own books – children's stories first perhaps, based on her work at Alt Schönbek – animal fables, modernisations of Aesop – and perhaps illustrate them herself. It was her life's ambition. Why not? Oh, and she would definitely take the blue silk blouse for best. And as well as skirts, trousers for walking and riding. Would she be able to ride one of the famous East Prussian Trakehner horses? And which shoes? Not that there was much choice. She'd never been interested in clothes but obviously you didn't want to affront anyone's eyes.

Halfway up the stairs, Magda seemed to register a dizzying silence from next door. It stopped her in her tracks. Dr Süsskind was gone. Really gone. He would never come back. He did not exist.

Retracing her steps, she went back into the kitchen and said, 'Auntie, I'm so sorry.'

*

Preparations were soon in full spate. Magdalena would be taking the bike on the train, she told her family. And that was that.

The dear old bike! It even had a name: the Auroch. A lumbering, heavy and unpredictable beast, antediluvian. The handlebars reminded Magda of the curved horns of the extinct species of cow that once terrorised the primeval forests of Europe and which science was trying to breed back into existence. She might even see one of the new aurochs in East Prussia! Nobody else had such a bike or ever would have.

'Oh no, Magda, you don't want to be encumbered with that hulking great thing,' Dad objected.

She put her foot down: 'The Auroch is coming with me! For it is axiomatic,' Magda informed her father and Auntie Ebba, '*axiomatic,* that the Auroch and Magda Arber cannot be parted!'

Father ridiculed the nineteen-year-old's self-consciously educated diction, picked up of course from himself, and her arrogant tone, picked up from her role as standard-bearer in the Band of German Maidens: '*Axiomatic!* Don't be ridiculous, Magdalena!'

Yes, but the girl would do it anyway, ridiculous or not, as Ebba knew. Magda read the expression on her aunt's face: it said, *I'd give up if I were you, Max dear, save your breath, she's going to do what she's determined to do. In any case she'll be safer over there. No air raids, remember. Plenty of food and plenty of churches.*

Dad's haunted face replied, *She's so young, Ebba. The Auroch! Axiomatic! I ask you! Thinks she knows it all. She knows nothing. She's all over the place. And her bike is just a heap of junk.*

Ultimately Max, surrendering, limped out and pumped the Auroch's tyres. He oiled the chain; tightened everything he could see that might benefit from tightening. He wheeled the uncouth machine round the garden and out of the gate. Magda and Ebba, observing from a window, winced as they saw him mount, push off and wobble along the road. His right leg, broken in the camp, had not been properly set at the time and, over the years, the damage had been compounded by arthritis. Magda was relieved to see her father dismount, for surely that must be it: the Auroch would be passed as adequate.

But no.

Dad was testing the tyres again, between thumb and finger, shaking his head. His sister and daughter could see him scratching his head, wondering if he'd maybe tightened some of the parts too much; he accordingly loosened, just a touch, what he judged he had over-tightened. Magda reckoned that the machine was now more or less as it had been before Dad began to tamper with it.

The Auroch was a homemade contraption, a mongrel. Clem, oily handed, had patched it together from parts salvaged from ex-Army bicycles. Men's bikes, of course – but Magda was athletic for a girl, Clem had observed, and could cope with that. The thing was a clanking, grotesque horror, his uncle had objected, the moment he clapped eyes on the finished article. And the handlebars appeared to be upside-down! It had no *unity*, he'd told his nephew. A reliable machine couldn't be assembled willy-nilly from bits of rubbish! Whatever was Clem thinking of?

Clem had grinned and winked, and said, rather patronisingly, for at sixteen and three-quarters he had also caught the tone, *Don't you worry, Uncle Max, I wouldn't have offered it to Magda if it wasn't strong as a horse, she'll be fine, you'll see, she's no weakling.* He'd patted his uncle on the shoulder, causing him to flinch, humiliated, and complain about Clem's bad grammar.

Coming indoors, Max now announced that he'd done his best with the thing but frankly it could not be called a bicycle. It was a hotchpotch. A mismatch. A contradiction in terms.

But Magdalena adored her machine, she'd mastered it from the off, and mastered her father too, and he knew when he was beaten.

*

Magdalena stood in the hall. Her father was seated at his study desk, just visible between the open door and the jamb.

She'd always known not to interrupt him in the study. Not to clatter downstairs singing at the top of her voice. Not to chase the kittens along the hallway. The scholar of the Enlightenment needed, not mere quietness but unqualified silence. Magda would take off her shoes and skate along the hall in her socks, before bursting out into the pandemonium of daylight to join her friends. Then beetle off down to the beach at Travemünde, to swim half the day and nestle the other half in a beach-basket in a pile of giggling pals. Through early childhood, her parents had always trusted her. Now her father scarcely trusted the motherless Magdalena out of his sight. And she was nineteen, for heaven's sake!

The air in Max's study was dense with smoke and dusky with the brown leather-covered books that rose up every wall to the ceiling. Antiquarian books in French, Italian, English, Latin and Greek, some made from the skin of dead lambs. The study smelled of a rich composite: vellum, nicotine, antiquity. And an occasional tang of brandy. Her father was the author of half a shelf of these books. But although he still researched and wrote, the great book on Voltaire begun ten years ago had stalled when, after his incarceration, Max Arber had ceased to be publishable. There could be no market for books on eighteenth-century France. And besides who would publish Francophile Max Arber, even if he could pretend to make his ideas tally with National Socialist thought? Germany's armies had rolled into louche, effeminate Paris last summer – strolled in, rather. The French army had just laid down arms and run away. Pitiful. In any case, there was no market for books on any subject by authors who'd once stained their copybooks. Relegated to a menial job at the Institute after his protest and his stay in the re-education camp at Dachau, Max Arber had forfeited worth and dignity – in his own eyes too.

And frankly you are lucky to be employed at all, Dr Arber. Even as a porter.

Magdalena feared for him – and she also feared him. The new world belonged to the young. Anachronisms like her dad endangered themselves and their families.

Nicotined fingers reached for another cigarette in the lamplight.

Max lit up. Sat back, coughed, took a deep drag, blew a smoke ring. Magdalena watched it tremble up through the air, passing beyond the bubble of lamplight. Opening a drawer, he rummaged around, taking out what looked like, but surely couldn't be, a toothpaste packet. He seemed to be studying it. Was he worried about his teeth again? His teeth were awful.

Few nights now remained to Magdalena at her childhood home. Tomorrow she must do the rounds of neighbours and friends, bidding farewell – the friends of her childhood, whom she'd known forever, a Band of German Maidens sisterhood really, and all scattering at more or less the same moment. Most had been conscripted as mere farm labourers.

Magdalena made friends easily. She had a sense of community, helping others, putting her shoulder to the wheel. Seeing new things and people, enlarging her acquaintance, and putting into action her National Socialist commitment to aiding the community. Now there'd be a chance to escape feeling undermined by her family's contempt for the Leader. In East Prussia the ground would not be constantly shifting under Magda's feet. She only dreaded going east for Dad's sake. She wouldn't be able to keep an eye on his vagaries. Sloppy about the blackout when Ebba was out, he'd been taken to task by the block warden. He neglected to perform the *Heil* salute; smiled wryly when he should be straight-faced; made no effort to appease Mrs Koch the notorious informer with the simpering smile; tuned in to the BBC, a criminal offence.

Good God, Magdalena had been tempted to denounce him herself when her adolescent passion for the Leader first set in!

No, no, Dad would be all right, Magda reassured herself, he'd have to be. Her own life was just beginning. To be let loose! To realise oneself! To do something for her Fatherland in its time of crisis, using her training to maximum effect! This posting was Magdalena Arber's destiny and she embraced it.

Tried to embrace it. A door in her mind kept blowing open, however hard she tried to lock and bolt it. Beyond the door, something obscene was at large.

She turned her mind away.

By the front porch stood Magdalena's rucksack and the case Dad had locked, strapped and labelled. Typically, he'd got everything ready way in advance of departure. Magda's summer jackets hung on the peg. Ebba had brushed them and strengthened the buttons. Magda would have to wear most of her clothes on the train to avoid carrying too much luggage – and it was warm. The Auroch's panniers were already crammed full.

Dad's face was gaunt; he looked ten years older than his actual fifty-two. He dragged his leg and she was sure he suffered pain there, despite his denial. He mumbled and muttered to himself in the street, which for every reason he shouldn't do. His friendship with Dr Süsskind had been dangerous but now Dr Süsskind was gone. Years back, Dad had parted company with the dad who used to jounce her on his knee, dance her round the kitchen, read aloud to Mum and herself, performing all the voices – excelling as a wildly warbling Brunhild, a martial Siegfried and an army of Nibelungen dwarves. His audience would roll around laughing till it hurt, and beg him, *Don't! don't!*

And then suddenly he didn't.

All this was like a film Magdalena had once seen, rather than a memory of her own. She knew Dad had once been larger than life, daringly original, a distinguished teacher and scholar. Upright, witty and authoritative. She knew that as a Social Democrat he'd taken political risks, spoken out according to his conscience, or the ethic of his old-fashioned scholarship, for they seemed to her to add up to much the same thing. Ancient Rome and Romance languages and Voltaire: the day-before-yesterday's idealisms. However, all that had been before.

Before Mum's death.

Before his bereaved sister and nephew moved in with them.

Before the camp, Auntie Ebba had said, without elaborating, her face tautening into *that* expression.

What happened exactly at Dachau, apart from the broken leg? No one would say. The shame, presumably. Hobbling ignominiously home, with a soiled name. Shame could kill you. And Dad had obviously done himself some kind of injury there. If you asked for further explanation, Ebba would shake her head, purse her lips, flap her hand and turn away. Widowed brother and sister, having lost half their worlds, had joined forces in one household. It made sense for all four of them.

Magdalena lingered at the study door, in a niche of time, capturing her father in the sepia perspective between door and frame, loving him, fearful for his safety.

She tapped on the door and stepped through.

'I'll leave it behind, Dad, if it's really going to trouble you.'

He swivelled, looked at her over his specs. 'Leave what behind?'

'The Auroch.'

He hesitated.

'Just say, Dad. If it bothers you very much.'

Turfing Goethe and Schiller off the chair, at which they mewed crossly, she sat down. The desk was littered with papers and files and Dad's typewriter, a handsome Torpedo model bought when the household was flush with money. Dad's English fountain pen, the pride of his writing life, lay on top of the blotting paper. He'd brought it home from Oxford on his last visit, years before the war. Magdalena picked up the pen and weighed it in her hand. He was still holding the toothpaste box.

He looked into her eyes. His face said, *Magda, you are my one ewe lamb. I cannot lose you.*

And it was precisely for that reason that her father now capitulated to her wishes: she saw that clearly. The floor of his certainty yielded, its walls sagged inwards. Her heart twisted. To have been loved like this, child and woman, was a rare gift. He had spread himself across the loss of a mother, keeping that loss drowned in the vast reaches of the unsaid.

And for months in the wake of Dorothea's death, the articulate and voluble girl had been struck literally speechless. She'd lost her voice. Dad had spoken for her, giving her his full attention.

Nowadays, in Dad's mind, there was reason for anxiety whichever side of a choice one opted for. Wherever he looked lay minefields of equivocation. Magda understood that Max Arber's generation of scholars, steeped in antiquity, could fail to grasp the obvious. They over-thought the least thing, making what should be automatic a source of conflict. How, for instance, could it hurt him so much to raise his hand in the customary salute? Just do it! The salute, Magda thought, is an everyday courtesy that binds you all together in one body. It says: *We are one great German family, we speak a common language under our Leader, we are rooted in a common territory, we share a common destiny.* What shocked Max and Ebba appeared to Magdalena and Clem – oh dear – what other word could you use? – *axiomatic.*

'No, my love,' Dad said decisively. 'I won't ask you to leave your bicycle behind. You may need it. And say you ... I don't know ... needed to get away from someone or something ... and I'd persuaded you to leave your bike behind ... how could I ever forgive myself?'

In the yellow lamplight, she caught sight of the text on the toothpaste box: *Doramad Radioactive Tooth Cream*, promising to shine your teeth blindingly white.

It seemed all of a sudden as if their roles had reversed and the daughter must take responsibility for her father, his broken heart, his broken will.

'If it's going to add to your anxiety, Dad,' Magdalena said sympathetically. 'I'll gladly leave it. Just say the word. I don't want to be worrying about you worrying about me, we don't need that, do we?'

'But *will* you be careful, love?'

'You know I will. And East Prussia is a very safe place after all – perhaps the safest place in Germany. Nobody is bombing it. Besides, I don't have a choice, do I? I've been ordered to go and go I must.'

Her father straightened up in his chair, his dignity ruffled. 'For instance, Magda, you will be on your own and there are always sharks around.'

'Sharks?'

'Men may ... had you thought of this? – take advantage of you.

You're inclined to be headstrong, to put it mildly – you know that – yes, you *are*, don't shake your head. Fundamentally you have a good heart and conscience. But you're painfully naïve, like so many in your generation. Young men – soldiers, for instance – will take you up and use you and drop you like a rag, if you're not careful. Do you know how to fend them off?'

'Of course I do!' She squirmed.

'Well then, what would you do, if a man came up to you ... like this...?'

He sprang from his chair. Grasped her shoulders. Towered over her. Magdalena pulled back, laughed with shock and not because it was funny, it was not funny, the look in his eyes, the panic rising.

'Stop it, Dad. What are you *doing*?'

Releasing her, he took a step back. 'You see. You have no idea. None. If this happens to you, ever – listen now, Magda – this is what you do. You don't freeze. You knee the swine in the groin. You know what the groin is, don't you?'

'*Pardon*? Yes, of course I know what a ... groin ... is!' It was a word you absolutely did not want to hear from your father.

'I'm serious, Magda, I've never been more serious in my life. You knee him hard in the balls. Like this.'

Together they rehearsed the kneeing in the balls.

'Hard, that's it – then you run. You bellow at the top of your voice and you take off and you run like hell. If he catches you, you ram your fingers in his eyes. Or better still a key. Like this.'

Preposterously it came over Magdalena, the memory of *The Nibelungenlied* and Dad playing all the parts while his audience died laughing. How King Gunther tumbled Brunhild's shift as he claimed his marital rights, and how Brunhild bound him hand and foot with her belt, carried him to a nail and hung him on the wall, leaving him there to squirm and moan all night while she snuggled down for a nice cosy sleep.

But what her father was counselling, she knew was not a joke. Magda's sexual knowledge was not exactly limited: it was non-existent.

The thing with Peter Schneider had been limited to hand-holding and chaste goodbye kisses. Pecks, really. Peter was in Poland now. And besides on the whole she preferred the company of girls.

'I will remember, I promise,' she assured him seriously, quietly, to soothe him. 'Thank you, Dad. I will be careful. I won't put myself in dangerous situations.'

'For my sake.'

Magdalena took both his hands in hers. 'For your sake. And for Mother's. And Auntie Ebba's. And Clem's. And mine – yes, I know, especially for mine. And don't forget, I'll have the Auroch for a fast getaway.'

'Well, that's true.' He grinned with one half of his mouth.

'You do have to start believing in me though, Dad.'

'Well, I do, of course. I know you'll be happy and do good work in Alt Schönbek. I shall be proud – and Ebba too, here she is. I was just saying, you'll be proud of our Magda too, won't you, when she's a teacher like her beloved Miss Heller?'

'It goes without saying. She is our shining girl.'

Ebba had brought coffee. She set down the tray on the desk: it was the last of the real coffee, saved for a special treat. 'And she'll be fine, you'll see,' she assured her brother. 'What's this doing here?' – picking up the toothpaste box from where it had dropped.

'Oh, I bought that years ago. It was a bit of a novelty then.'

At the pharmacy, Max hadn't noticed the swastika decoration at both ends, which nowadays of course was commonplace – on cakes, on shoe polish, on tins of paraffin. He'd kept the box, he said, as a trinket of the times, a piece of memorabilia for when all this – he didn't say what – was well and truly *over*.

'So are we to understand,' asked Ebba, bridling because there was no excuse for waste in this day and age, when there was so little in the shops, 'that you have kept a tube of perfectly good toothpaste stowed away in your desk drawer for years, Max? Will it even be usable now?'

'No, dear. I just kept the box. A *memento mori*, if you like. Patriotic toothpaste. Radioactive. Very healthy.'

2

> This is the truth which bound me to Thee:
> I looked for Thee and found my Fatherland.
> I was a leaf astray in boundless space.
> Thou art now my homeland and my tree.
> How far I would be scattered by the wind,
> If Thou wert not the power that girds the roots.
> I believe in Thee, for Thou art the nation.
> I believe in Germany.
> For Thou art Germany's son.[6]
>
> Baldur von Schirach,
> 'To the Leader, Adolf Hitler', 1939

The following day, Magdalena's last-but-one in Lübeck, the blow fell from which Clem's mother and uncle might never recover.

Ebba, up with the lark, was busy, and at her happiest when busy. She double-checked Magda's documents: identity card, passport, call-up papers, Band of German Maidens membership. Then she reopened the locked case, to put in a little surprise. *No peeping, mind!*

Clem, on his way out to work, bent to appraise himself in the hall mirror, slicking back his pale hair from his forehead with the heel of his hand as he turned his head this way and that. He looked unusually spruce, even for him.

'Admiring yourself again?'

Clem didn't stop to banter with his cousin; he kissed her hair before opening the door. 'See you later.'

There would be no later, not in the sense his family understood it.

Ebba had saved some precious pork, she said, for Magda's sandwiches tomorrow. And some tomatoes. Would Magda like to take an apple? Two apples? And one for luck? Was there much fruit in East Prussia? She should take the vacuum flask with a warm drink because you never knew with trains these days, and what with so many changes, some of the connections might very well fail.

'Auntie Ebba?'

'Yes, dear?' Her aunt, catching the emotional note, stopped in her tracks. 'What is it?'

'Just. I need to say. You are so lovely,' blurted Magda. 'Always so endlessly kind. And patient, even when I've been a pain. Thank you for all you do for me. And for your guidance. Thank you for being ... a mother to me.'

Tears swam in their eyes. Easy tears for Magdalena, who could cry and laugh in a breath. Not so for Ebba, who turned away, stood still, turned back, took her niece in her arms and held her.

A round of farewells took Magda much of the day. She came home laden with gifts she couldn't possibly take with her. You'd need a herd of Aurochs to carry it all. She lolled with her feet up, weary of preparations, wanting to be gone and yet dreading it, fondling the two little tomcats, Goethe and Schiller, in her lap.

'I'll miss you, you two naughties. Be good for Dad. And don't make messes on the kitchen floor. Right? Right.'

They coiled in her lap, purring, until Goethe elected to climb up Magda's front, clawing at her woollen jumper, and draped himself round her shoulders like a furry scarf.

'Oi! Get down! Oh no, not you too!'

Wherever Goethe was, Schiller wanted to be too, and the argument could get fratricidal. She wrestled the kittens back on to her lap and held them apart.

The front door opened and closed. That would be Clem.

Then the shriek.

Scattering cats, Magda leapt up, rushed into the hall, and there on the doormat stood a tall soldier in field grey uniform.

Her aunt was sobbing. 'Clem, *why*? You didn't have to do that!'

Father, pausing on the staircase, swivelled his head and was silent.

A nightmare had come in the door in place of his nephew, who had joined up before his time. Voluntarily. Secretly.

Magdalena, rushing to Ebba, guided her into the seat by the telephone. *Auntie, it's all right, it's all right. Breathe! That's it – come on, breathe!*

When Magdalena looked up, her father had come downstairs and now stood on the bottom step, stock still.

He marched straight up to his nephew, raised his right hand and snarled with savage sarcasm, *Heil Hitler!*

At which, incredibly, Clem snapped to attention.

Shot up his hand. *Sieg Heil!*

Uncle and nephew faced each other a foot apart, signalling from opposite worlds, arms in the air.

Clem, at not yet eighteen, was tall and muscular. Hair bright as brass. Creamy-complexioned. The authorities had been more than happy to accept him. He'd returned home wearing the coveted uniform, in the simplicity of his soul, proud of his manly devotion to duty. Only the expression in his eyes betrayed a plea for the approval indoors which he was sure of out of doors. Now he glowed with pride at his welcome, for Clem could be innocent of irony. Stupid, stupid, to spring this on them. Magdalena felt sick to the stomach.

There was unacknowledged violence between man and boy.

It flashed through her mind yet again that Dad was a terrible danger to himself, cloven as he was, unable to accommodate to things as they were, and must be. He stood a head shorter than his nephew. Clem was a danger to Dad. But then so was she. The house was wrenching itself apart.

'Well, there you are then.' Dad dropped his hand. 'You've made your choice, Clemens.'

'The Leader called me and I have answered!'

'What's done is done,' Max said to Ebba, crouching to her. 'Don't cry, love. He won't actually go for some time. There'll be training and so on. *Won't there, Clem?*' he growled. 'Perhaps the war will end before he's put in action. He will be careful for his mother's sake, *won't you, Clemens?'*

Clem assured Ebba that, yes, he'd be going to Braunschweig first for training. Obviously, he'd be as careful as any German soldier could be. But on the battlefield he would do his duty as a man must, she could be sure of that, he'd not be found wanting, the nation needed heroes. On and on he burbled. He raised his weeping mother and, taking her in his arms, rocked her, looking over her head at Magdalena.

'Just ... a bit of a shock,' Ebba managed. Dried her eyes, blew her nose. 'You never said, I had no idea you were even thinking ... you might have discussed ... and both of you, our children going like this ... into something ... very dark...'

What Ebba didn't say, but they all heard, was the word *impiety*. Her child had chosen to turn away from the Christian Light.

'But it's better like this, isn't it, Auntie,' Magda soothed. 'We're both going to do our bit for Germany. I know you don't see eye to eye with us but we have to serve, don't we? Not always in the way you would prefer. We'll all miss each other, of course we shall,' Magda went on. 'But Clem will come home on leave – won't you, Clem? And I will too. Before you know it. And the War really won't go on much longer.'

Oh yes, he would have leave, obviously, Clem answered, and he'd always look forward to coming home and being together and so on. But the thrill of adventure enthralled Clem: you saw it in his bearing. He couldn't wait to get away and be a proper soldier rather than a common or garden Hitler Youth leader.

Magdalena's father slipped into the study, closing the door behind him.

Within two days they'd both have flown. Magdalena knew what her father was thinking. What would become of his adored children in the alien and bloody east?

And – a different implicit question – what would they become?

3

> I saw you coming through
> the green woods; but then over
> the pass on the frontier
> you turned and left me...
> I fear for your safety in all
> the dangers that surround you...
> I think of the host of proud
> officials who throng the capital ...
> who can say there is justice
> under heaven?[7]
>
> Tu Fu (712–770),
> 'Dreaming of Li Pai'

There was a man in the bedroom. A desperate man. She heard his ragged breathing. Magdalena struggled up in a panic, switched on the lamp.

Her father, in his dressing gown, was standing at the bottom of her bed. What was it? In the dim light he looked terrible. A stroke? Had Dad suffered a stroke or a heart attack? He was clutching at his chest.

'What is it? Daddy, whatever is it?' Magdalena scrambled up. 'Are you ill? Shall I call the doctor?'

'Oh no, I'm perfectly all right, don't fuss. There's just not much time left. And your mother would want me to...'

'Would want you to ... what?' Mum was never mentioned by name. The denied, inexpressible longing for her presence and the knowledge of her absence surrounded them like the air they breathed.

Magda squinted at the clock: 1.20. Today she was travelling. To her mother's homeland. Was that what had brought him? She had to be on the train by six, and then a journey of over twenty hours.

'Sorry to wake you, dear.'

'It's all right. As long as you're not ill?'

She patted the bed and he sat down. Magda arranged the quilt to cover his knees. Her father took her hand.

'Something I need to say ... should have said, long before.' He scrambled for words – Max Arber, the orator, who used to captivate audiences of students and scholars, and put them under a spell. 'Thing is, darling, I blame myself. No point in saying this to Clem, dear Clem, because ... hook, line and sinker ... he's ... Anyway, he's ... taken the bait, as how could he not? He was always so soft and they hardened him. They rob the mothers of their children. And today, when Clem came marching in at the door like that, I knew he'd gone. Nothing to be done about it. We can only hope he'll be lucky – and survive. But you – Magdalena – darling – I feel you haven't completely gone.'

She rubbed her eyes, stifled a yawn. 'Gone where?'

Two opposite things were obsessing him, he said: the obligation to call one's soul one's own, to resist what he saw as delusion and brutality and lies; the need to camouflage oneself, to keep one's head down, hide in the herd. Two kinds of safety, neither of which was safe at all. He was sure Magdalena understood and had intuited something of the same. Hadn't she?

It was too late for all this ... maundering. Questioning one's own motives was fine when there was leisure for airy-fairy philosophising. But this, Magda blearily felt, was not the time for picking at the scabs of moral scruples. Light was pricking through a pinhole in the blackout. Dawn of a day which required action, not spiders' webs of cogitation.

It was like seeing someone knit a garment and then unravel the knitting.

And start the futile process again.

Magda glanced at the clock. On and on Dad droned. Tears leaked down his face, but bizarrely out of one eye only, as if a duct were blocked.

Half an hour had passed. Day advanced.

'Do you know what I felt when Clem appeared in that uniform, Magda?'

'Well, I think you and Ebba were shocked because Clem had signed up before he needed to? Without discussing it with you first, and taking your advice? And because of course you love him and you don't want him to die?'

'Those were not my first thoughts. All that came later.'

'Oh? What then?'

'My first thought was: *They've come for me again.*'

'But *they* hadn't, darling Daddy. And in any case, who are *they*? You're not a Communist or a Jew, or anything like that.'

A quick stare. A frisson of anxious contempt ran across his face. She stifled a yawn.

'Am I boring you, Magdalena?' Coldly.

'Of course not, Dad.' Patiently.

'Because, if I am boring you, let me know now...'

'Dad, you are not boring me. You could never bore me,' she lied. 'You just gave me a shock, that's all, and I'm a bit nervous about today. And there are things we don't see eye to eye on but, you know, we've been into all this and frankly...'

'Sorry, love, I'm sorry.'

'It's fine, Dad. I want to hear what you want to say, of course I do.'

More verbosity. About how evolution had gone into reverse. Going back to barbarism and savagery. Blood and soil. Recidivism to the condition of predators in the jungle. Atavism. He twisted the cord of his dressing gown, plaited and unplaited the tassels. And his one ewe lamb would see this one day, he insisted, see through the lies and unreason and injustice, because she was his child, and her mother's daughter. The veil would rend.

And yet ... and yet ... if and when she did see through it all, Magdalena must cover up this enlightenment! Promise him! Or she wouldn't stand a chance. She must survive, at all costs. He knew that temperamentally she was resolute. What she felt, she showed, she lived. Oh yes, he could read her like a book.

You believe you can, she thought, and shifted impatiently.

When he had rambled to a pause, Magdalena said, 'I'll still be me, Dad. Don't worry. But with more experience. And I want to contribute something. Have a responsible profession. Be someone!'

She had always ignored the fact that a girl or woman could seldom or never *be someone*. Sure, you could march with the Band of German Maidens, holding the banner – and she had. She'd had no objection to marching and saluting, and she liked to be in charge, but, if Magdalena was frank, the interminable meetings had started to bore her. Blah blah blah, the endless verbiage and self-importance. The language was always the same, a repertoire of obligatory phrases endlessly repeated. A dead language. The death of language, her father had quoted his friend Victor who said, *Words can be like little doses of arsenic.*

Clem, always an energetic member of his youth group, loved the comradeship of camping, marching, singing, flag-waving, athletics. Magda had cheerfully participated but didn't overdo it. And presumably Dad had seen that. As a woman, your ultimate calling, and it was a noble one, she supposed, is to bear children. But one was a realist: young men were dying in their millions for the Fatherland. There'd be a shortage of husbands when peace came. Meanwhile, she'd do her bit for the higher good.

Magda was willing to marry and have babies – but, oh please, not yet! Not for a long while.

She made as if to get out of bed. But her father had not finished his warnings. It was as if he'd opened a door in his breast, to let her see the livid, pumping heart walled up in there.

'Dad, I need to get ready.'

'The camp, you see, Magda. The camp.'

'I know, it was awful for you. But I need to get up.'

'Magdalena, you really don't know.'

'I don't. You've never explained. You ... protected us from it.'

'Mistreated,' he muttered, rubbing his eyes with his knuckles. 'The things I saw.'

She was dumb, frozen. Something was coming. It was coming. She'd seen it coming for a long while. The horror buried underground. Perhaps she would have to know now, in which case the world could never be the same.

But now was not the moment. 'Dad, I need to get ready.'

'Mistreated,' her father repeated, rather as a question than a statement. He turned over his hands and scanned the palms. 'No, not mistreated: maltreated. I got off lightly. Very lightly. With my leg. Many of them ... abused, abased. Obscene. Called it education, it was barbarism. It was a return ... a return to...'

They were hardened criminals probably, Magda thought, who were treated roughly. And Dad had been put in amongst them, he'd got out of line, he'd done nothing wrong, not like criminals. It was his blindness to all the Leader had done for them all, probably, that had got him into trouble. And the friendship with Professor Süsskind especially. Not that Professor Süsskind wasn't a ... decent ... Jew but he was, well, he was ... and anyway ... oh dear, the poor man, the lovely man ... and Dad does blurt, she thought, he gives himself away, or his face gives him away, the irony...

She could feel a tic twanging away under her eye. There are always a few bad eggs, she thought. Even in the best system. She blenched, even so, and swerved her eyes away, not wishing to see into the cavity where the red, aghast heart was exposed and visibly pulsating.

'Don't let them corrupt your *language*. The inner language you speak to yourself.'

Well, Magdalena thought, and slid out of bed, I'll speak my own truth, in my own words. I always have and I always will. I hope I'll always call a spade a spade, a bad egg a bad egg. And if I see bad things, I'll speak out. End of subject.

So keep your head down, he begged her, following her to the door, out of the bedroom, along the corridor to the bathroom. *You are intelligent, Magdalena. You may see things that ... well, you don't like. It may come over you to show your feelings or protest. Or even to flout the rules. Yes, really, it might. But don't. Don't do it. I am saying, Do as I say, not as I once did.*

4

Do you know the land where lemon trees bloom?
Within dark foliage golden oranges glow,
Softly the wind blows from the heavenly blue
Quiet the myrtle, high the laurels grow.
Do you know that land?
    There, oh there
I long, my beloved, to go with you.[8]
              Johann Wolfgang von Goethe, '*Mignon*', 1796

From Lübeck to Rostock, Rostock to Neubrandenburg, Neubrandenburg to Königsberg, Königsberg to Alt Schönbek Magdalena would carry her worldly goods eastwards, stuffed in the bulging rucksack, which she hoped to God would not split open, and the rest in her bike panniers.

She wrestled the Auroch onto the guard's van of the Rostock train, with the aid of soldiers practising gallantry to maidens. There'd be new people to talk and listen to. All the way to Königsberg, she'd be travelling second class, a luxury Ebba had insisted on. With her adorable books. And her packed lunch. There'd be plush seats and room for your legs, despite the fact that transport nowadays was crowded to the gills.

Having stashed the Auroch, Magdalena found her seat, smoothed down her skirt and placed a couple of set books in her lap. Children's books nowadays were so alluring. Gorgeous red cover, a picture of a naughty fox. *Trust No Fox on his Green Heath*, the work apparently of a girl of eighteen. Oh the envy! Still time for me though! Magda thought, watching the last passengers scramble on to the train and doors slam all the way down the platform. She'd dearly love to write a book. A children's book, yes, but dealing with geography and history. And teaching a lesson or fable. Her children (for the unseen youngsters were already *her* children) would learn where they came from. She'd connect modern Prussia with its deep past – the conquests of the Teutonic Knights in the thirteenth century, the castles, the monuments – poems and songs and stories.

She'd take her children on trips to the great monuments. Like the Pied Piper – except, come to think of it, the Pied Piper led the children of Hameln to a desolate cave, never to be seen again ... whereas Magdalena Arber would lead hers into the heart of civilisation!

The train started, they were off.

In this glory of early light, Lübeck's copper spires and red roofs gleamed. British air raids were not unknown: they'd hit the Dräger works, the factory that produced breathing equipment and gas masks. Apart from that, bombs had fallen in small numbers and, it seemed, randomly. Thank heaven, she could leave Dad and Ebba in relative safety: the city could hardly be high on Churchill's list. What was there to bomb in an ancient Hanseatic city? Some factories. Ancient churches. Wharfs and warehouses. Offices. Homes. Nothing of military or industrial significance, surely: well, there was the armament factory, but at a distance from the city and besides she had the feeling that Lübeck would be safe.

The British after all pride themselves on *decency*.

Farewell to the jingle-jangle masts mirrored in the Trave, to the round towers of the Holstentor, to childhood itself. Magdalena enjoyed every sensation: the rattling rhythm, white plumes billowing past the window as they got up speed, unknown faces that flowered for a moment, a sense of purpose and destiny.

Travelling east, alone! Such a thrill! Even if it was just to serve as an infant teacher in a village school in the back of beyond, this was freedom and adventure. A chance to be something more than a breeding machine. Plenty of time for all that. For now, in these extreme circumstances, Magdalena was needed – and not only that, but also employed in a task worthy of her. She was all set to bring urban knowledge and culture to the backwaters of rural life; and in return, she'd learn their history and folk customs. And perhaps help with the grain harvest in the breadbasket of the Empire. Magdalena hugged the children's book to her chest.

As the locomotive gathered momentum, its rhythm triggered an earworm. *Travelling-Eastwards! Going-to-Mother!* Relentlessly round and round, faster and faster, *Going-to-Mother* sounded in Magdalena's head with rising excitement. Steam clouds gusted past; ghost-smoke brushed the pane. And then the slackening as they neared one of numerous small stations on the line: *Nearly-home-now, Coming-to-Mother.*

Folk got in, folk got out. The sun rose higher in the sky: a beautiful morning. Magdalena relished scenes as transients became fleeting acquaintances. When she told her neighbour where she was bound, and why, out came a surreptitious slice of sausage from the woman's large basket. A strong, capable woman, legs planted apart, she was the farmer, now that her husband was away at the front.

'Oh, I couldn't! Are you sure?'

'Come on, try it, dear, do. And tell me what you think.'

'But have you plenty?'

'Go on! Enjoy it.'

She did, and sucked her fingers afterwards for the strong, spicy taste. Nowadays everyone was stingy with food, you didn't hand it round, you squirreled morsels of your ration away for a hungry hour. Far from quelling appetite, the sausage awakened it. Her mouth watered. Then – a real treat, a rarity Magda hadn't seen for months, the farmer's wife smuggled to her – wonder of wonders! – a square of marzipan.

She sat beholding this treasure on her open palm; then nibbled like a mouse, to make it last. The other passengers studiously averted their eyes. Would anyone notice if she licked her fingers again? Probably. She did anyway and dried them on a handkerchief.

Magdalena amused herself by nicknaming everyone in her compartment and providing a story for each.

Adorable Sausage-and-Marzipan Lady, way up at the top of the list.

Mr Threadbare, self-effacing smile, hunted look, thin, big nose, elbows pinched in to waist, shirtsleeves, paper collar.

Emperor Wilhelm II: mustachios of yesteryear, much twirled, great harrumphing.

Mr My-It's-Hot, beetroot red, rotund, woollen jacket, strangled by his tie.

Mr Mushroom: moss-green uniform whose runic decorations Magda could not construe, Party badge, deep in a book on … what was it? … German fungi.

At the next station a new passenger took the place of the abdicating Emperor, announcing herself to all and sundry as Call-Me-Lili.

Oh dear, a blabbermouth, said the passengers' expressions. A newspaper barricade went up. Round the newcomer's shoulders lay an unseasonable fox fur, drenching one in sweat, as Call-Me-Lili complained, but you have to suffer for fashion's sake, don't you? Off came the fox and a navy hat with twin feathers. Lili chatted away, hardly pausing for breath, all the while caressing the fox pelt on her lap like a cherished pet.

A soldier, an Army doctor. The good-looking young lieutenant flirted long-lashed, bloodshot eyes at Magda. He confessed to the world that he'd had a few last night, asked politely where Magdalena was bound (the compartment listening with approval to her answer) and dropped off to sleep, arms folded.

Another stop. A lass plumped down beside Magda; wriggled annoyingly, pulled at her skirt and sighed, before confiding in an all-too-audible whisper that her suspender belt was digging in frightfully! It was! It itched like crazy! Her mum *made* her wear it. A mediaeval torture instrument! Honestly!

Whilst pretending not to have registered these embarrassing confidences, the passengers exchanged glances.

When Suspender Belt disembarked, in came a mother and daughter, angelic, fair haired, blue eyed.

Ah, what a perfect little princess!

You couldn't look away. The ravishing child was perhaps four or five. She was wearing a blue, embroidered dirndl to match her eyes, and her pale hair had been lovingly plaited and coiled around her head like a crown.

'And what might *your* name be, little miss?' asked Lili, bending forward to woo the child.

Stare. Little finger inserted into puffed-out cheeks. Pop!

'Her name is Rosmarie,' said the mother. 'Isn't it, angel? Answer the nice lady.'

Stare. Finger inserted into nostril. Screwed round, clockwise and anticlockwise.

'Rosmarie is rather shy,' the mother explained hastily. '*Take it out*,' she hissed.

'What a charming name. Would you like to stroke Foxy, Rosmarie?' Lili asked her.

Stare. Shaken head. Audible *Ugh*!

'I *said*, take it *out!*'

'Foxy is so sweet,' Lili crooned. 'Aren't you, Foxy? All soft and cuddly-wuddly.'

Magdalena saw what the child saw: a stuffed head hanging over its owner's knee, malign glass eyes, legs and paws dangling obscenely, as if caught forever in the moment of death.

Lili clearly wasn't one to heed hints or take no for an answer. She thrust the fox head at Rosmarie, waggling it in her face.

The child, burying her head in her mother's bosom, let out a siren wail.

'Don't be frightened,' said Lili. 'He's such a nice foxy-woxy.'

And so it went on, wearying everyone, until Magda wanted to burst out, *Oh give it a rest, you ass.*

Midday: the train slowed; jolted to a standstill. It stuck fast in a grove of birch trees, with a gasp, before shunting backwards and halting again. After a while the soldier lit up. Although the compartment was labelled a non-smoker, no one had the heart to object. If a youngster was travelling east to protect his Fatherland against Slavic hordes, who could begrudge him a smoke? Soon several others lit up and others took out their sandwiches.

The guard looked in: rerouted back towards Neubrandenburg, they'd lose some time, not too long, he hoped, to allow the military to pass through. Someone opened the window. In the quiet, you could hear the birds in the birches and the rustle of foliage. Fug cleared, and you smelled the herbs growing beside the track.

During the extended pause, Mr Mushroom slapped his book shut and announced that his name was Vogel.

'And your name?' He pointed with his forefinger at each in turn. 'And yours?'

Dr Vogel, benignly interrogating his fellow passengers, soon had them all in his sights. All but Mr Threadbare, who Magdalena and everyone else could see was feigning sleep. The eyelashes were fluttering on his young, hungry face.

Static for half an hour, the locomotive took off again, charging forward as if to catch up with itself.

Mr Vogel plucked the unread book from Magdalena's lap: 'Let me see if I guessed right!'

Congratulating himself on his correct guess, he returned the book, a classic modern text, an educational masterpiece written by a young woman, not nineteen years of age. 'Ah yes, you are a teacher, young lady!' He congratulated Magdalena fulsomely on her mission. She flushed; murmuring that she was only too glad to be doing her bit.

'Only I haven't seen you reading it!' Chortling, he reached out his stubby fingers. He wasn't going to chuck her under the chin, was he? No, he refrained. 'Is it just for show?'

'No indeed – I've been thinking!' She returned his banter.

'Thinking! Oh my dear young lady – no good will come of that!'

Well-fed, sun-tanned, Dr Vogel turned out to be a loquacious know-all of the kind Magda generally disliked; finger in every pie; wanted you to know that he was acquainted with greatness. But his uniform? Some kind of forestry official? She tried to make out the badges on his jacket.

Dr Vogel knew a lot about trees and forests. Cattle and livestock. Big game. He'd shot lions and tigers in Africa. Also elephants, crocodiles, hippos, rhinos, you name the animal, Dr Vogel had shot it! Not to mention bears, wolves, elk, boar, in our own magnificent German forests.

'I might even have shot that fox you're so fond of, Mrs Keller!'

But he quickly reassured young Rosmarie, who screwed up her face and looked ready to cry, that this was not cruel – no, no, the animals did not suffer, they were not permitted to suffer, there were German laws against animals being made to suffer. If you're hunting, hit them with your first shot – *bang!* Nice clean kill! That is the Aryan way! Germany, he reminded the compartment, was the first nation in the world to protect animals and nature. Our great Leader holds out his arms over all earthly creatures.

Magdalena looked down at the book in her lap, conscious for the first time of the full title: *Trust No Fox on his Green Heath and No Jew on his Oath*.

'For Nature,' Dr Vogel was saying, flailing out his arm and catching his threadbare neighbour a glancing blow, for which he did not apologise, although the victim unaccountably did apologise, 'Nature is our holy law!'

The warhorse is our comrade!

Our great Leader calls himself a wolf!

A true German will share his rationed bread with a squirrel in the Tiergarten on a Sunday morning. Isn't that so? Anyone who mistreats animals is our mortal foe.

'Have you fed the duckies in the park, little miss? Of course you have! I'm sure you love duckies, don't you?'

'She does,' said the mother. 'We often feed the ducks on the river, don't we, Rose?'

'Yes but—'

'Well, and I expect you eat ducks too! You wouldn't say no to a nice juicy piece of fried duck breast, would you, Rosmarie? Of course you wouldn't! Eh? Our great Leader, of course, never eats meat. In his graciousness, he allows us feebler mortals to consume animals. But in his serene tolerance, our Leader does not insist that the rest of us confine ourselves to vegetables. And we have laws on the humane slaughter of livestock, pets, animals of all description. You may not drown kittens. You may not boil lobsters alive. I'm sure you know that.'

'But...'

'Shush, dear ... I said *shush!*' the mother hissed, bright red, fanning her face with a magazine. 'Don't keep saying *But!* It's rude.'

This was sheer provocation, Magda thought as the child bubbled out, *'But but butbutbut...'*

'In point of fact,' Dr Vogel went on, addressing the entire compartment, 'so passionately do we Germans feel about the health and wellbeing of our animal companions on this earth that – I will give you an example – the Ministry of the Interior reprimanded a scientist for cutting up earthworms insufficiently anaesthetised. Think on that! It's a fact. One of his students reported him, and he was told by the highest authorities that it would not be tolerated.'

A giggle rose in Magda's throat, and the young soldier snoozing in a corner seat emitted a convulsive snort, opening one eye. Magda throttled off her laugh. The soldier closed his eye.

The Army doctor remarked mildly, phrasing it as a query, that *some* might feel the earthworm complaint was going a bit far? Anaesthetic, after all, was a precious commodity.

All eyes were fixed on Dr Vogel and his Party badge. Who was he exactly? He had not mentioned an affiliation or a rank.

The young doctor, slamming into reverse, wisely backtracked: of course, he himself assented to the principle of justice to *all* animals, great and small. It was a matter, he opined, equally of, erm, science and morality. He had sometimes been called upon to act as a vet when there was none available, for instance when a horse was lamed or a dog run over.

The little girl gave it as her opinion that worms were slimy disgusting wrigglers.

The Marzipan lady, leaning forward, advised her that earthworms enrich the soil; they're great blessings – the more the better – and besides they're all God's creatures, as the Bible tells us. And if you cut one in half, then you have two!

Magdalena asked herself: well, actually, why should one not feel for the lowest species? There is so much pain in this world, she thought, and we – as a species – are selfish beings. She considered for a dizzy moment the plight of earthworms, earwigs, flies: how far down the chain of being would you have to descend before this concern became ridiculous? Or impracticable. How would you administer an injection to a frog, say, or an earwig?

She would have to ponder these questions if she was to teach the children of Alt Schönbek things valuable for them to learn.

'Our Imperial Hunting Master, Marshall Hermann Goering, has forbidden the use of traps on his domains! No buckshot may be used. Clean killing, that's the German rule.'

Inserting her thumb in her mouth, Rosmarie twiddled a strand of hair and stared out of the window. She did not repeat her *But*.

However, Dr Vogel did.

'*But* – and there is always a *but*, is there not? – our young friend is quite right – animals must be culled,' he said. 'And hunting game is beneficial both for man and forest – and also, let it be said, for beast. We cull the weak to improve the species, so that only the purest, strongest, most perfect specimens survive. By this we prove our mettle as a warrior race.'

'All this is tremendously interesting. You are a zoologist perhaps?' The army doctor offered Dr Vogel a cigarillo.

Herbert Vogel, it turned out, was employed by Dr Heck as one of his research and acquisition group. *The* Dr Lutz Heck, illustrious keeper of the Berlin Zoo? Yes indeed! Vogel had been sent on what one might call a fishing expedition! He was on the first leg of his quest to inspect and inventory eastern zoos, firstly visiting our own dear immortal Königsberg, then the Rominten game reserve, thence to the ex-Polish territories. And beyond. Who knew how far the map of Germany would ultimately extend? Tremendous plans for the east! he exclaimed, tremendous! The vast primeval forest there was, properly speaking, German forest. The ancient animals were bona fide German animals.

The afternoon wore on. Now they were past Danzig and dusk was falling. Magdalena's excitement ebbed as exhaustion took over. She closed her eyes, kept drifting off and jerking awake.

Someone muttered the word, *Yid*.

Someone else muttered, *Sure of it! The bottle nose! The hooter, the schnozzle, the conk!*

Someone muttered, *Ha! How did that one get in?*
Not allowed in our compartments.
They'll have to wear a label before long. A badge.

Who were they whispering about? Mr Threadbare: that was who. Because of his nose?

Life-unworthy-of-life, life-unworthy-of-life.

Magdalena's head toppled forward and as she tried to rouse herself, she saw through half-open eyes that her lap was awash with red. Her period? Oh no! Please, no. The shame of it, the shame. How could she even get up to go to the toilet and clean up? Drape her cardigan over her skirt?

But no, it's all right. Oh my God. Just the scarlet book on her lap. Which suddenly Magdalena took against. As if it had actually stained her skirt – or soaked an indelible stain of her own to the surface.

You couldn't blot out the offence. Of the title, *Trust No Fox on his Green Heath and No Jew on his Oath*.

I would have trusted Dr Süsskind with my life, she thought, oath or no oath. And he trusted Dad and Ebba with his.

Down she plunged again, into a torrent of sleep. A blanket of ashy dusk had fallen and a man was leaning over Magdalena, far too close, she smelled his armpits and his breath, saw his Adam's apple. She gagged. No, it was all right, just a guard coming round to check the blackout. Two small lamps burned above the seats, yellowing the faces of the travellers.

When she woke again, Magdalena caught herself murmuring a line of a Goethe lyric ... *God's is the Orient, God's is the Occident* ... Had she spoken aloud? Evidently she had. For Mr Threadbare's lips were moving, he recognised the poem and breathed the words: *Northern and southern lands/ Rest in the peace of his hands.*

The young man's eyes gleamed for a moment before he closed them, and Magdalena closed hers.

A jolt. Pitch black night out there.

The Marzipan lady, the soldier, the doctor and Lili had vanished as if they had never existed; Rosmarie's mother was in process of hefting her lax, unconscious daughter towards the exit.

Goodbye, goodbye: out into the dark.

The melancholy threadbare man sat crouched into himself, round-shouldered, arms cradling chest, as if to take up the smallest possible space and to beg for mercy if he was proving too visible.

Magdalena pulled herself together. Rubbed her eyes, sat up straighter. Which station had the train reached? No knowing. When new passengers boarded, she asked where exactly they were. Accents had so markedly altered now that she needed to ask twice before grasping the answer. Forty minutes from Königsberg, all being well.

The further east the locomotive had travelled, the riper, richer, had grown the language at stations, more – in a curious way – antiquated. It was like a journey into the heart of Germany's remote past. Travelling back and back to origins. She was fascinated. By the time Magda and the Auroch had alighted at Königsberg, she'd be rrrolling her Rrrrs with the best of them.

It was one in the morning when they approached the city's magnificent station, like a railway cathedral, though dark as sin in the blackout. Magda would have to curl up on a bench in a waiting room, to catch the first train of the morning.

*

'Thank you ever so much for helping me with the Auroch,' she said to her fellow passenger as, having set down his own case, he hefted the bike from the wagon.

'Helping you with the *what*?'

'Oh, I call my trusty old bike the Auroch.'

Dr Vogel threw back his head and guffawed. 'Well I never! Good name! If only you knew! Suits it down to the ground. And where did you acquire your "Auroch", Miss Arber? Must admit, I've never seen a bike quite like this.'

'Nobody has! It's unique! My cousin Clem's a budding engineer, he put it together out of the old parts of clapped-out bikes before he joined up.'

'Ah, you must be proud of your soldier-cousin, Miss Arber.'

He trundled the Auroch along the dark platform in the stream of passengers.

'Oh, we are. Very proud. Could I just say … I was interested in what you were saying about cruelty to animals, Dr Vogel. You really made me think.'

He stopped in his tracks, pleased. 'Just what a German zoologist wants to hear! What especially caught your attention, if I may ask?'

'Well, actually, it was what you told us about the earthworms. It set me wondering – how far down the chain of being should we go? For instance, can a spider feel pain?'

'Astute question, Miss Arber. Well, what I always say is this: we should proceed with due reverence, *as if* we knew these creatures could feel pain. Some animals, of course, are self-evidently pests – vermin. These are not *German* animals and must be ruthlessly exterminated. Even so, let us be merciful,' he added piously, 'in all our dealings.'

Mercifully ruthless? Is that what he meant? Ruthlessly merciful? Did animals know their nationality? That would be ridiculous, he couldn't mean that ... Was he talking about love, extending the circle of our loving care? But not to non-German animals? Dr Vogel had not spoken the word *love,* but surely that was what he meant. There was such scope for suffering in the world. Magdalena had never taken full account of this before, by considering the plight of the lower animals. She'd grown up familiarised with calls for violence – the marching and the flags and the slogans and the war songs. It flashed through her mind that there may be a tender side to the National Socialist belief system – a compassion that, once peace arrived, might be allowed to come to the fore.

And perhaps East Prussia, her mother's childhood world, would prove a place where that love – that web or net of all being – could be cultivated.

Dr Vogel might be a bigmouth, a windbag, but even as he mystified her, he'd stirred something within her. In the semi-darkness of an alien platform, in the early hours of the morning, her world was expanding. Magdalena was glad to have bumped into an expert on modern zoology – and evidently Dr Vogel was interested in her. He turned to her, surprised at her intelligence. Yes, she thought, I am *astute!* Perhaps he sees me as a cut above the common run of young women.

She thanked Dr Vogel and wished him well in his quest. 'Here's a waiting room ... I'll park the bike and wait for the first train.'

No indeed, Dr Vogel would not dream of allowing the young lady to do such a thing. He would never forgive himself. One must sometimes courteously and decorously act *in loco parentis.* Magdalena should accompany him to his hotel, where he would arrange for her to sit in comfort in the lounge and take refreshment.

He would hear of no protests but swept the Auroch along, with Magdalena in tow.

She trotted along behind, before asking herself, *What am I doing?*

Where am I going? No, I'm not going with you. I'm not a child. She stopped dead. The flow of travellers jostled her as it flooded past and she was knocked off balance.

Dr Vogel continued along the dim platform, pushing the Auroch with one hand, like a hostage, waving his case with the other, as if to herd his protégée forward.

The passenger with the fraying sleeves paused fleetingly at Magdalena's elbow, looked into her face.

'You all right, miss?'

'Oh yes – thank you, yes.'

'Is something bothering you?'

'No, truly. But thank you.'

'Sure?'

'Yes.'

He nodded, shouldered his bag, and scurried past, head down, a rabbit with hounds at his heels. He made for the stairs and lost himself in inky blackness.

*

Who was he?

Awareness dawned. There'd been whisperers in the compartment; she'd heard them through the twilight of her doze. Persons who conversed in nods and winks, or *sotto voce*. They were the know-alls who tapped their noses and leant forwards to exchange whispers. And this was not surprising, for one overheard them everywhere. Was this gentle stranger the person with the alleged bottle nose, the conk, the schnozzle, they'd been whispering about on the train? Yes, Magdalena thought, offended, and this man was afraid, and yet he stopped for me.

Offended, yes, but also affronted – as so often – by herself and her shifting, inchoate allegiances.

At the exit Dr Vogel was waiting for her to catch up. Was he one of the whisperers? Of course he was. They thought a Jew had got into their unpolluted carriage, passing himself off as a German, as a human being.

He turned his head. 'Aren't you coming?'

'Actually, Dr Vogel, I'll wait at the station, thanks, if you don't mind. Please would you give my bike back?'

'Did that fellow bother you?'

'Oh no. He was being helpful.'

'Flouting the travel laws, they all do it if they think they can get away with it. Well, it won't go on forever, you can be sure of that. Wait and see.'

Yes, Magdalena thought, Vogel is one of them, the nose-tappers, the winkers and nodders, the righteous back-stabbers.

'I reproach myself now,' he added. 'Should have asked the guard to check the fellow's papers. They are forbidden to share a carriage with us. Come along now, Miss Arber.'

'I'm staying here, Dr Vogel, at the station. I'm not going with you. Thank you anyway.'

Anodyne words poured from his lips, for Dr Vogel had been wishing only to help Miss Arber, take her to safety and shelter until she could proceed on her way – dangerous times, the station being no place for a young lady to be stranded alone at night. He shook his head. But if the young lady insisted? ... she did insist? ... really? Most unwise, in his view. But if she could not be persuaded, Miss Arber must allow him to park the bicycle and chain it up.

'I can do that myself. Thank you though.'

'The least I can do.'

'No, really.' She gripped the steel key in the palm of a sweating hand.

'The key, please, Miss Arber. Thank you ... there we are. One day I shall fill you in about the true auroch!' He secured the bike; straightened up. 'And maybe introduce you to an auroch! I hope you do not imagine ... for under no circumstances...'

'Oh no, I don't ... imagine anything ... of course not,' she gabbled. Was she being rude? 'It's just that I need to take care of myself. Start as I mean to go on. My father would...'

Instant capitulation.

Mr Vogel saw Magdalena to the waiting room, lit by a single bulb, hot and stuffy with the day's trapped air and musky with sweat. An elderly man dozing in the corner roused himself and squinted at his watch. Above them, the Leader's all-seeing eye sternly observed, as if through a window, to ascertain what mortals were getting up to in the shadowy realm below.

Magda shouldered off her rucksack; sank down on a bench. Wondered whether to apologise; didn't.

Had Miss Arber all she needed? Could Dr Vogel arrange a hot drink for her? He was sure the station office could provide one, at his request. Just say the word. No? She had enough water? Something to eat if she should feel peckish? He could arrange a cushion for her comfort? Say the word.

'No? Then I will say good night.'

But it was not as simple as that.

Dr Vogel's valediction droned on without remorse: he wished Miss Arber well under several headings – the remainder of the journey to Alt Schönbek; her profession; her future life.

At the exit he startled her by turning to trumpet a *Heil Hitler*! – not the informal version usual in a private situation, but a blast. The elderly man and Magda struggled to their feet and returned the salute.

And Dr Vogel was gone...

...only to reappear with no less an official than the deputy stationmaster bearing a cushion, a flask and a note of the departure time and platform of the first train of the morning. He had agreed to appear in person to escort the young lady to the train in good time. She was not to worry at all, she would be looked after.

'Your father should be nearly as proud of his courageous daughter as he would be of a son,' Dr Vogel declared, handing her his card. Should she ever find herself visiting the wildlife sanctuary at Rominten, mention their meeting and show the card to the wardens, who would be delighted to show her round.

And greetings to her father.

5

> General, man is very useful.
> He can fly and he can kill.
> But he has one defect:
> He can think.[9]
>
> Bertolt Brecht,
> *War Primer*, 1955

Greetings to her *father*? The geezer couldn't know who her father was. Good thing too.

It was if a ghostly version of Dad had risen between them like a cloud of blue-black cigarette smoke, to send Dr Vogel on his way. Not that it had been a case of needing to call on her newfound 'kneeing-in-the-groin' skills: there was surely nothing remotely sexual in the man. He reserved his passion for the animal kingdom. And, goodness, Dr Vogel was an antique! – late thirties at least, maybe forty – and tending to flab.

Also pompous, prolix and peremptory.

Maybe he mistook Dad for some high-up with a similar surname, and was worried he might get into trouble for trying to divert his daughter from her chaste path?

Only Dr Vogel's wide and deep knowledge of biology and zoology attracted Magda, subjects that had thrilled her ever since she'd been made responsible for the pet axolotl at infant school. That pink fishy being with legs and fins, remember him? – Old Axli, waddle-walk-sculling round his tank, perpetually hopeful of finding a way out; peering out through the glass with what seemed limitless curiosity. Miss Heller had chosen Magdalena as guardian of this comical salamander because she was one of the few city girls quite happy to cut up ... oh dear God, of course ... shrimps and earthworms for Axli's tea.

Unanaesthetised earthworms.

And suddenly in the waiting room she began to laugh. It was 3 o'clock in the morning, and Magdalena Arber was in fits of laughter.

The thought of Miss Heller quenched the laughter. Miss Miriam Heller was the teacher who'd taken Magdalena to her heart after Mum's death, chatting with the monosyllabic child to try to awaken her voice. Taking her out on the heath to witness the lapwings' songflights, as they rose, rolled, spiralled and zigzagged into the blue. Holding Magdalena's hand as they walked to view the wild orchids, single stems with pale blue bells, disguised, Miss Heller had said, as insects, to delude the real insects into trying to mate with them – weren't they clever? Through this evolutionary trick the orchids disseminated their pollen, the teacher had explained.

Crouching, Miss Heller had looked into the child's face: *It is our secret orchid, Magda dear, isn't it?*

Yes, breathed Magda, *yes it is. Our secret. Thank you.*

The pedagogue who'd replaced Miss Heller had a grating voice and a poker face. She'd swallowed the textbook and regurgitated it in undigested gobbets.

I shall never teach like that woman, Magdalena thought as the local train rattled along into the countryside. I shall teach from the heart, like Miss Heller.

*

East Prussia was greenness and deliquescence, red brick farmsteads and cottages with steep thatched roofs; forests, lakes and rivers. Black and white cattle grazed the lush fields as they'd been doing for thousands of years, ruminating in a landscape that had never changed and she felt never would. The train, aged and ramshackle, chuntered deeper into the countryside. Local passengers got on and off, stood and chatted in the aisles in sometimes impenetrable dialect.

Magdalena's was the second-to-last stop. She jumped down on to an empty platform and retrieved the Auroch.

The quiet of the platform when the train had left.

The overarching stillness of the sky.

For the first time Magdalena felt lost. All around lay pastures and meadows, encircled by forest; she made out a couple of distant farmhouses with long barns. There was no traffic on the lane, which abruptly vanished into forest. So presumably she'd need to cycle the rest of the way. But in which direction? There was no one to ask until a horse-drawn cart appeared.

Excuse me! The way to Alt Schönbek?

Come on up. Yes, the farmer, Mr Kallweit, could carry her halfway there, and the bike too, plenty of room, no trouble, hop up, that's the way, mind the churns. Tree canopies met over their heads, plunging them into a cool, scented tunnel of green shadow. Once Magdalena had introduced herself as the new schoolteacher, the farmer insisted on taking her the whole way. The least he could do. Magdalena would find the warmest of welcomes at Alt Schönbek, for the headmaster and the other male member of staff were away at the front; there was only Mrs Daschke left at Rosa House.

Mr Kallweit spoke in short bursts, with silences between.

'Our children,' he said, 'used to go barefoot. Now they have shoes.'

'That's good to know.'

Later on, he confided, 'Five sons I've got, five, all but one away at the front. There used to be six. No young men to speak of in our neck of the woods now.'

'That must be hard.'

'Ah well ... their poor mother ... well. We pray.'

Silence.

Later: 'Very few young horses either, come to that, apart from the stud – and the cart horses and old biddies like my Nelke here.'

'Warhorses.'

'Baggage horses. Aye.'

The clopping of hooves; creaking of leather and rattle of wheels.

Then: 'We many of us keep geese. You can send one home to your parents in Lübeck, can't you? They'll appreciate that.'

'Send a goose?' She laughed. 'A whole goose?'

'Aye. Through the post.'

Running out of the forest, the cart emerged into sunshine. A stream; a boggy field brimful of dazzling marsh marigolds as far as the eye could see. Farm buildings, long barns.

'Those labourers in the field ... see them over there? Poles, decent workers mostly, have to chivvy them a bit. And here we have the stud,' Mr Kallweit said. 'The Laulitz estate. A lady farms it. Miss von Laulitz. There she is, see, over there! On horseback. Nearly there now.'

*

'And I love it here!' Magdalena wrote to Dad and Ebba. 'I've landed on my feet so DON'T you be worrying about me. Only take care of your dear selves for me and Clem. I am safe and shall keep safe (*Dad, take note!!*) And Clem will take care of himself. He promised me faithfully. Have you heard from him? Post is going to take four or five days to get to me. I'm hoping he has been in touch and is well.

'I'm lodging in the attic of Rosa House with Ruth Daschke and her twin girls. The whole village is relieved to have me here. Just three days here and I've been welcomed by so many lovely people – farmers, foresters, the baker, they just pop in to greet me! I'm showered with invitations and welcome-presents! You'd never *believe* in a million years the cake I've guzzled! I already have to breathe in to do up my belt. Home-made, of course. Cakes we've not seen in the west for ages. I'm going to find out how to send you some – so you needn't be too envious.

'And we had Klopse last night – Prussian meatballs – and oh the sauce – anchovies, capers! Out of this world. Are you drooling?

'Mrs Daschke – Ruth – has had to teach 103 children all on her own – yes, 103, all age groups, can you imagine? – so no wonder she's over the moon to have even a grass-green know-nothing apprentice like Yours Truly to share the work. Mr D died on the second day of the war, in Poland, so sad. She doesn't speak about him.

'I like her very much – she is in some ways an idiosyncrasy on legs! She's what Dad would call an autodidact – no formal education to speak of – taught herself Greek and Latin (yes, really!) and pulled herself up by her boot-straps – she's very proud of that, and rightly. At 5 foot nothing, she walks tall. Can be very odd. (You'd like her). (Whoops, I didn't mean that the way it sounds!)

'Ruth's little girls (twins, 6 years old) sneak up to my room to talk to me – they bring me bunches of wildflowers – daisies and cornflowers and poppies. Well, when I say they come to *talk,* one (Flora, the younger by almost a day) is nearly mute apart from grunting noises, makes signs, she's lopsided, there's something wrong with her legs and her left hand is a claw – and sometimes her sister Julia has to interpret, but I'm learning to get the gist of what Flora is telling me. Well, I think I am. And she's lovely! And I love her! Apparently, the doctor insists she would do far better if sent to an institution in Königsberg for further diagnosis, but Ruth won't hear of it. She says: *over my dead body!* Tiny little person but fierce as a lioness, at least on this subject.

'In point of fact, I don't think Flora is stupid. She just has different qualities.

'There are many languages, Dad, aren't there? You've taught me that. The body speaks, it has its truth. The face speaks. The tilt of the head. The hands. They all have a language. And so I have the sense that Flora is speaking to me and wants me to understand, and that it is my job to decrypt what she is saying, by listening with the whole of me. Does that make sense?

'There are a few ladies in the village best avoided, according to Ruth. Chief among them a Mrs Struppat, if that's how you spell it.

Proud of her roots, and will fill you in thunderously on her lineage back to ... well, not Adam and Eve because she objects to them on racial grounds. But the Teutonic Knights. Not sure how she worked that out because the Teutonic Knights were monks, weren't they? Anyway, she has a gang of daughters, all over five foot seven, magnificently endowed, so Ruth says. (Chiefly endowed with tongues.) Oh, and apparently Mrs Struppat heard of some woman sending the Leader an 80-page letter and getting a reply – so she has written him a hundred-page letter and is awaiting his answer and fuming because he hasn't found time in his crowded schedule to respond.

'Her friend, who is also a deadly rival – and the two of them lock horns (if females can be said to lock horns?) – is a Mrs Braun who comes to help out at the school, especially with toileting. She is big on hygiene and purity.

'Met some characters on the train! There was a little lass who disputed *everything* that was said, mainly by yelling BUT! Made me laugh, she was an original, and I hope the world won't beat the spirit out of her. Although I'm guessing it will have a go. Our opinionated little Julia here reminds me of her. There was also an official employed by Dr Heck (Lutz Heck, zoo man) who helped me with the Auroch when we got off at Königsberg, promised me a visit to the Imperial Marshall's estate, no less! – and said they were using a system of back-breeding (?) to resurrect extinct wild animals. Also a sweet old soul in the waiting room who'd been a pastor in earlier life. Auntie Ebba, you would have liked talking to him.

'Anyway. Teaching. Well, if I'm honest, it's a bit hair-raising. So many children, from all round the area, and different levels even within the classes. I'm preparing half the night. Those new textbooks I brought with me are, for reasons I won't go into, not all that easy to work with. I'll work round them. Yes, I know, I <u>know</u>, Dad! – I obviously have a lot to learn! I don't want to boast (never let it be said!) but the children do seem to take to me! I make them giggle. I try to sugar the pill. And I've started as I mean to go on –

i.e., by sparing the rod. My plan is to make knowledge palatable so it slips down like cream. At least that's the idea. You did that for me, Dad.

'And I've been remembering Miss Heller. Do you know what happened to her? She was very kind to me. Is there any way you could find her address? I'd like to write, and maybe visit when I come home on leave.

'Now then, you will be astonished to learn that most of our children have never even been on a train! They've never visited a city or seen the sea. In this day and age! I plan to take them on railway excursions to the seaside and to Königsberg. Won't their eyes pop out of their heads when they clap eyes on the castle and the cathedral and Kant's monument? Today I'm teaching them the history of the Teutonic Knights and how they rode east to conquer this land from the pagans, built glorious monuments, established civilisation and so on.

'Here's hoping the inspector of schools Mr Excorn (appointment with him the day after tomorrow, oh dear) will like my ideas. Press your thumbs for luck! Harder, harder!

'Just looked out of the window and saw ... a swish Mercedes in the square! What's that doing here? Carts and tractors are our staple – and anyway there's no petrol. At Mrs D's, electricity in winter will be rather fitful apparently. Some folk draw their water from wells in their gardens and have outside privies but we are lucky – running water and a decent bathroom and toilet. When you go into the poorer households, it's like living history. Everything here is peaceful. No air raids from west or east.

'Ah, yes, I'm craning my neck, and I realise it's the doctor in the Merc. Whoops, he's coming here. Ruth used to regard him as a personal friend but now she loathes him. And I sense she fears him. I don't know why. He's going up in the world apparently. Ruth bristles like a hedgehog at the very thought of him.

'Anyway, I send you my love and blessings – and instruct you again (now that my profession is to instruct others and they *have to listen*!) to look after your health, my darlings, and to keep safe and not to worry one little bit about your ever-loving

'Mad Magdalena, who misses you more than she can ever say.'

*

Magdalena began to read through what she had written so far. Through the open mansard window she heard the doctor's car door close. Now he was speaking in a hearty voice to Julia who'd paused in her jumping and clapping game to reply – to the effect that she did not know where her sister was. She had no idea. Out, probably.

Julia knew perfectly well where Flora was. What was it about the doctor that Ruth didn't trust? The chap was hardly going to kidnap anyone! All Ruth would say was that Old Littmann had got above himself. Too big for his boots. She'd preferred him when he used to get a bit tiddly, and sing. She also seemed to hold it against Dr Littmann that he knew no Greek. *Well, I don't know any Greek either!* Magda had admitted. *And you don't hold that against me! ... Or do you?* Apparently that was a different kettle of fish.

Well, anyway, they all knew the drill. Arrival of doctor: concealment of daughter.

Magda turned to look across at Flora lying on her back on her bed, wafting one leg in the air – absorbed in its motion in and out of her eyeline. Eyelines, rather, for one eye had difficulty in focusing, so she must be seeing double. What was it about Flora that was so endearing? She gave you back so much, that was part of it. A sense of her trustful presence alongside you. So strange, given that Flora was labelled mentally subnormal ... and that Magdalena was a newcomer to her little world.

Flora began to croon to herself, cooing and blowing little whistling sounds between her teeth.

Laying down her pen, Magda went over and perched on the bed. She put her forefinger over her lips to signal that they were going to be ever-so quiet. She lay down and took the small body in her arms.

Dr Littmann rapped on the front door and was admitted. His voice was full of unction and bonhomie. He'd brought an offering.

'Flowers for you, dear Ruth,' he boomed, 'and what about a nice cup of coffee? I'm parched.'

6

> Truly, those who can make you believe absurdities
> can make you commit atrocities.[10]
> Voltaire, *Questions Concerning Miracles*, 1765

Never in her life had Magdalena seen such a desk as Mr Excorn's. Solid oak, it bristled with stripped antler horns stuck on at the front and sides, together with carved dog heads and a green leather top. You would not want to bump into this desk: its prongs looked keen to gore you if you ran against them at a wrong angle. Biedermeier, according to Mr Excorn's secretary-wife, as she ushered Magdalena in and laid out papers on her husband's desk: late nineteenth century. The thing looked as if it had just staggered indoors from the forest, a long-lost mongrel composed of tree and beast.

There was a fusty odour in the room – something organic like leather, or did it come from the giant candles in the corners? Presumably these were purely ornamental and never lit.

Mr Excorn appeared, a round-faced, balding man wearing spectacles, the left lens black. A war wound presumably, but, judging by his age, not sustained in the current war. Magdalena stood to return his salute.

'Very pleased to welcome you, Miss Arber. I trust you had a reasonable journey? Yes? Very good. Do sit down. And you are lodging with Mrs Daschke, of course. Comfortable? Good. You've been here, let me see, just under a fortnight? That's right. And now tell me about yourself.'

East Prussia was a revelation, she told Mr Excorn breathlessly. It really was.

Elbows on the desk, he jiggled his thumbs together, faster and faster, as Magdalena revealed how she had read and read all her life, just devouring books, wanting more and more knowledge, obsessed by poetry, philosophy, history – and how she would like to offer something of the same passion for knowledge to the children under her care.

Light glinted on the lenses of Mr Excorn's round spectacles. His one visible eye stared without blinking. Down came the guillotine as she should have known it must.

'Stop there, Miss Arber. Firstly, there is no such thing as knowledge.'

'No such thing as...?'

'Not in these woolly, outmoded terms. *Knowledge* is not a word we use. I counsel you to drop it. It is a dead word. The professors of so-called *knowledge* are an extinct breed. In amongst your literary ramblings, you may have come across Nietzsche? No? He will set you right: *O Voltaire! O humaneness! O nonsense!*'

Oh. Bad start. Deplorable, judging by the sourly triumphant expression on Mr Excorn's face. She had an image of Dad being dropped from a great height, an extinct species unaccountably persisting. Dad the professor. Dad the lover of Voltaire. Dad the dad. At the same time, Magda was confounded by the order of her own error. Why on earth did I come out with all that gush?

How to undo the mistake, make clear her intention to toe the line?

'However, I expect you are just suffering from nervousness,' he suggested forgivingly.

'I *am* feeling nervous,' she hastened to agree. 'I'm sorry. It's all so new. I just ... wanted to give you an idea of how I *personally* came to teaching. And of course I know,' she caught up with and overtook herself, 'I mean, I am *aware*, that the individual is nothing, except in so far as ... I just thought...'

'Well, I am here to guide you, Miss Arber, so never mind. You have received all the appropriate training and,' (glancing down at her papers) 'I see that you graduated amongst the top five students of your class in Kiel. You strike me as an enthusiast. Good. But enthusiasm must bow to discipline. Let me ask you: do you drive a car, Miss Arber?'

'Well, yes, I can drive, Mr Excorn, I have a licence ... but my family doesn't own a car, so I may be a bit rusty.'

'But let's suppose you have a car. Shall we? A modern People's Car, say. Now, you wouldn't want to drive it up a tree, would you?'

'Definitely not.' Was he going to smile, was this a joke? Apparently not.

'Or off a cliff?'

'No, sir.'

'So where would you want to drive your car?'

'On the road?'

'On the road. And which side of the road? The right side – exactly. Not the wrong side. For instance, you would not elect to drive into oncoming traffic on the Autobahn? No, I thought not. Because?'

'Well, I'd cause a crash.'

'And?'

'It's against the law.'

'Precisely. Now let us consider the Autobahn. Did you design and construct this highway yourself, Miss Arber? ... No indeed. Who built the road?'

It clicked. She saw belatedly where the catechism was going. 'Our great Leader built it.'

'*Now* we are getting somewhere!' Mr Excorn beamed, sweeping with his cuff imaginary dust from the surface of the desk. He was treating Magdalena like a class of six year olds; seemed to be in his element. 'And are these youngsters, whom you have come all this way to educate, your own children?'

'Oh no, sir, the children belong to our great Leader. They are cared for on our Leader's august behalf by their parents and educated at his behest by ourselves.'

'Very *good*. Impressively said. *August*. And you, Miss Arber, whose daughter are you?'

She came straight in with, 'I am the Leader's daughter.'

'Correct. We prepare our pupils for their destiny in a Darwinian world of struggle. We don't want milksops, deviants, degenerates, dissidents, lunatics, cripples, parasites ... contaminating the race. You are following?'

'Oh yes.' She was beginning to dislike him cordially.

'Good. So, tell me, Miss Arber, what do we want our children to become?'

She thought for a moment. The right words, the right words? Got it.

'Quick as greyhounds, tough as leather, and hard as Krupp steel,' Magdalena recited. 'To quote our great Leader.'

The stock answer was irrefutable. But Mr Excorn's one visible eye shot her a piercing look. Perhaps, despite the fact that Magdalena had assented to the doctrine, impatience or irony were leaking through her tone of voice.

'Let's say you have two charming little kiddies in your classroom. We'll call them Otto and Liesl, shall we? Dear young souls, honey-coloured hair, big blue eyes, six years old. Let's say chubby Otto is shy and lazy, he won't play at soldiers with the other boys, he lisps, he is effeminate. And little Liesl is still inclined to suck her thumb and whine. Your vocation, Miss Arber, is to mould Otto and Liesl into the makings of a manly warrior and a resourceful mother.'

Magdalena, in the spirit of the catechism, hastened to assure Mr Excorn that she would stick rigidly to the curriculum. Would encourage sport, marching, drill, athletics, cross-country running, ball games. She claimed to be looking forward to fulfilling a leadership role in the regional Band of German Maidens.

Her mentor still did not look wholly impressed. Magdalena felt as you might when a dog comes sniffing at your crotch and not much liking the scent you're giving off. The two stuffed stag heads on the wall looked on as if they'd broken through from the forest to observe her lacklustre performance. The wild boar curled both horn and lip.

You have to be two people, Dad had counselled. Let one protect the other.

'Any questions you'd care to ask me at this stage?'

Yes, she thought, she'd like to ask him about the textbooks. The vileness of some of them, how they made her feel sick to the stomach, no civilised person could tolerate, let alone teach, such depravity...

...but no, you can't possibly ask him that, she reproved herself: for God's *sake*! You'll get yourself sent back to Lübeck in disgrace ... or worse...

...because you have already seen things and they are coming to the surface all of a sudden, like moles burrowing through the earth, yes, like moles, they are coming to the surface ... coming up now...

...and Dad (his forehead cloven, one side oddly young-looking, the other ploughed into furrows of anxiety) had cautioned, *Don't give yourself away, speak your own truth but only ever to yourself, my Magda*...

...and she had shrugged off his counsel, in her boundless excitement about travelling east, to pursue her profession, to be free of glum Dad and virtuous Voltaire and the Christian forbearance of Auntie Ebba.

But, yes, I *shall* ask, I don't care! she thought. What a poor sap I shall be if I don't raise this. Excorn can just put it down to my naiveté. I shall say, *I can't teach that filth about the Fox and the Jew, I can't even bear to look at it.*

Mr Excorn again asked if she had any further questions, perturbed at her silence. His eye, peering over the frame of his glasses, searched her.

Somehow a brainwave saved Magdalena from herself. She mentioned that, oh yes, she'd like to ask about a project that had occurred to her. By lucky chance Magdalena had met a leading zoologist, Dr Vogel, one of the famous Dr Heck's research team, and discussed with him the latest developments in National Socialist biology. Dr Vogel had kindly invited Magdalena to visit the Imperial Marshall's estate at Rominten.

In fact, she had Dr Vogel's card here, with a handwritten note on it. She handed it over.

Would Mr Excorn advise her? Perhaps she'd be permitted to take a party of the oldest pupils on a visit to Rominten, to ground them in National Socialist science? Might that be allowed? Did Mr Excorn feel that the children would glean useful ... she paused, swerved aside from the stigmatised word *knowledge* and settled for *experience*?

The school inspector looked from the card to the apprentice's face and back again, with an appearance of wonderment. He smiled. He appeared to revise his estimate of Miss Arber. His visible eye crinkled up.

*

Escape, escape, hissed the Auroch's tyres, bowling over ruts in the road, clearing the little town, making for open country until Mr Excorn's domain had been swallowed up in distance. Don't look back. You have twenty miles and the whole of the rest of the day to yourself. You have a packed lunch in your rucksack. You don't have to account for yourself to him for another month. You are a free woman.

At the forest edge, Magdalena braked, skidded to a halt, leaned the Auroch against the silver trunk of a birch and walked in. The remnant of ancient forest closed its trees behind her. She could no longer see the road or the bike.

Quiet. Peace.

Was it quiet though? In the glade, she rested her back against a beech and listened in to shiftings in the undergrowth, throbs of birdsong. Comings and goings. Everything is growing, everything is decaying, she thought, in its own time. Nothing keeps still, even the trees are not still, they are humming with life. Look for signs, one of the old Alt Schönbek foresters had said when he accompanied her class on a walk. You will know about the past by reading signs: the forest remembers. Study the bark of trees stripped overnight by elk; scuffs of earth kicked up by foraging wild boar. Clues and traces of lives foraging in the leaf litter. Moss, fern, lichen and fungus sucking their living from exposed tree roots.

Magdalena pulled out the bundle of sandwiches from the rucksack, poured coffee from the flask, sat back and let out a deep breath.

Just be, she advised herself; just be. Like the birds. Like this millipede, travelling over the debris at quite a lick. It marched like an army on manoeuvres, each pair of legs attached to a single segment of the body. Placing her forefinger in its path, Magdalena watched the creature hesitate before climbing straight over and continuing on its quest. We are young compared with you, she thought, you are millions of years old; we are an afterthought. Brown in the shade, glossy orange in the light, the thousand-legged wonder snaked along, disappearing under a mossed log.

There is something about Mr Excorn, Magdalena thought, taking a bite from the sandwich, something which...

...no, you can't think that! He is harmless enough.

But you do think it! More than that, you know it. It is *knowledge*. You've known things for years that you've mostly ignored or side-stepped. You kept a dark cupboard in your mind and stuffed all the filth in there. Since you were sixteen, or fifteen even, or even before that, all of you girls together worked on corporate avoidance, the whole class averted its complicit gaze from ... the unspeakable thing.

She and Angela had been coming home from school. Pandemonium in the square: crowds of people in fits of hilarity. Bystanders braying with laughter, mirthlessly, as though not to be exploding might count as being caught with your trousers down. *Hee-haw, hee-haw.*

Look, said Angela.

An elderly man was running round the fountain – dodging and swerving.

The poor soul. Nobody lifted a finger. Angela had gone white, she shook, seemed to miss her footing, righted herself, and was found afterwards to have peed her pants. In a public place! Peed her pants!

Magdalena sat in this dim forest as in a chapel, remembering, half in and half out of a shaft of light pouring through the canopy, a light which seemed to fizz for it was full of circling insects, and the light climbed up and up in a liquid pillar to the rent in the leafy ceiling. The timber echoed. Magdalena could hear the running man's cries, hounded by a mob, mainly Hitler Youths, having a whale of a time, never enjoyed themselves so much ... and bystanders gaped in frozen shock...

...for his beard was on fire! They had lit his beard! And as he ran he grabbed at his chin with both hands to put out the flame, and a lad whacked the terrified hands away with a baton, and they all brayed with laughter again, *hee haw hee haw* and they called out, *Run, Rabbit, run!*

But, no, it was, *Run, Rabbi, run!* that they cried.

And nobody took his part. The poor soul.

The moment you saw something that turned your stomach, you made sure to unknow it. You swerved and beetled off as fast as you could go. Folk turned away, made themselves scarce. Heads down, Magdalena and Angela quitted the square. Angela was in tears, the back of her dress was stained, the shame, the shame, she knew this man, she was ashamed and afraid.

Home. Nothing said. One day Angela did not turn up at school.

Oh, unfortunately we are all stone-blind, we are deaf and dumb, we have entirely lost our sense of smell. And for that reason we can't taste anything – we swallow whatever is put in our mouths untasted. *Ye are the salt of the earth: but if the salt hath lost its savour, wherewith shall it be seasoned?*

We only see what you tell us to see; at least, we say we see it when you catechise us.

Mr Excorn isn't the worst, no, not by a long chalk. He is average. Ordinary. Banal. But.

Something about Mr Excorn, Magda thought, not to put too fine a point on it (taking a sip of artificial coffee, it had no taste and the sandwich had no taste but you had to eat), without beating about the bush ... come on, spit it out...

A bird high in the foliage blew its bugle-call.

The fact is: something about Mr Excorn *stinks*.

You could smell it in his room. Or was it the bearskin rug with a ghastly flattened face and a stuffed tongue sticking out of long-dead jaws, that had been trampled on by the feet of Mr Excorn and the feet of Mrs Excorn, and for all she knew by half a dozen little Excornlets? Or was it Magdalena's own sweat, from pedalling the twenty-two miles on the Auroch from Alt Schönbek in baking heat? Had she just been smelling herself?

My human smell, she thought. It happened sometimes that you caught a whiff of it, sniffing your own armpits or in a momentary awareness of bad breath. The cruel streak that is in you, the cowardice, the shallowness, the *Schadenfreude*. Not because you are specially wicked, for you aren't.

Once Ursula Zimmermann had come running down their road, snorting with laughter, spluttering that she'd left a present in an old Yid's garden. *I left the old fart a turd!*

And we all tittered, Magdalena remembered, even though Ursula Zimmermann was gross, she was crude, we thought her beneath us. But still we laughed, although I knew immediately who was meant.

Magdalena had felt weird in her stomach, looking down from her bedroom window at Dr Süsskind when he came out with his shopping bag the next morning. But I told myself I'd had to laugh, everyone was laughing. I was a bad taste in my own mouth and I could not spit myself out.

Temperate, stoical, Dr Süsskind must have seen the end coming, even though he missed the chance to leave for Turkey. Having lost his wife and one son, the other son having emigrated to Palestine, what did he have to lose? Friendship, his philological studies – and perhaps also, as Dad had said, the feeling that he was German.

Once Magdalena had crossed the road to avoid him. And he'd seen.

Dear Daddy, she thought now, you are one in a million dads, you have shielded me in a very complex way. It has cost you. She longed to have him beside her. To take his hands in his. To thank and reassure him; share counsel for the road, which was going to be a different road from now on.

Otto and Liesl would need to be shielded, as Magdalena had been shielded. A tall order. For they must be protected by their teacher from what she was required to teach them. Their spirits would need nurture, they must be offered the sustaining milk of human kindness, she must find that in herself, while at the same time appearing to stick to the rigid curriculum. It should not be beyond her powers to ... well, yes, equivocate ... but equivocate in a decent way. Was that even possible? Wasn't it a contradiction in terms?

It had not been Dad alone who protected Magdalena, not just Auntie Ebba, not only the childhood friendship of Kristel and Anne, or Miss Heller. (Where was Miss Heller now, Magda longed to get in touch with her, she would find her somehow, there must be a way, she wanted to knock at a door and the door would open, and she would ask Miss Heller whether she remembered Magdalena Arber, the girl with the axolotl? The mute girl who had been given back her voice? Her teacher would be greyer now but not old, not old at all.)

Shakespeare and Emily Brontë had protected her. But also Goethe, Schiller, Hölderlin. Lessing. Rilke. German books have been your fortress, arrayed around you, one resting on the heart of the other. Not like a house of cards. For they are inside you too, known by heart.

And Auntie Ebba with her Christian faith, which, although Magdalena did not exactly share it, had taught you how to love, and therefore how to stand.

Pines, slender and tall, reached high above Magdalena, inclining inward so that they met at their branching tips, a green cathedral scented with resin. It was a comfort to be here, calling your soul your own.

And there was the person who came before all these, whose name Magda rarely spoke, even to herself. One day – soon, yes, soon – she would take the train and trace the house in Königsberg, on the island of Lomse, her mother's birthplace, a visit she was endlessly conscious of deferring.

*

7

> The moon hunts petrified women
> from their blood-spattered doorsteps.
> Grey wolves have forced the gates.[11]
> > Georg Trakl, 'On the Eastern Front', 1914

Latching the front door of Rosa House, she heard the hum of voices from Ruth's parlour. Maybe there was a card game in progress, although if so they were playing in an unusually sober mood. Parties could get uproarious and last into the early hours, especially if husbands or sons were home on leave. Then neighbours gathered in a tight knot of belonging, as if the little community were reassuring itself, *Look, everyone, we're alive and together, in this moment! We're not being bombed! It will all be over by Christmas! Celebrate!* There'd be singing, accompanied by Renate Schmidt on her accordion. Wine and brandy would be liberated from depleted cellars. Mountains of rich cake would be baked: 'bee sting' cakes topped with honey and cream, pepper nut biscuits, luscious marzipan concoctions. Tables would groan with luxuries not seen in the west for months.

Tonight there was just an intermittent murmur coming from Ruth's living room. Magda wouldn't interrupt. She felt, not tired exactly, but as if she were flying above her own head. She'd lived a year in a single day.

Pausing in the hall, Magda listened out for the youngsters, but the house was quiet. Probably they were asleep already, teeth brushed, prayers said and the 'Lovely Words' repeated, with which the little family closed each day. It's past their bedtime, she thought, and climbed the stairs to her attic. She loved the sloping ceiling, the room's asymmetries, the tilt of wooden floorboards like a listing boat. And oh, the aerial view over red rooftops, trees and meadows full of cornflowers, poppies, buttercups. Home.

Everything was just as she'd left it. The piles of books, a petticoat discarded on a chair, the open curtains.

The splash of red on the crowded little desk was the textbook, *Trust No Fox on his Green Heath and No Jew on his Oath*. On one side of the cover was the caricature of a bloated, hook-nosed, thick-lipped swindler; on the other the smarming, wily, lethal fox. Beside the book lay the pad with Magdalena's jotted notes on how in God's name to present this compulsory filth to her children.

For filth it was. And the Magdalena who came in from the forest was not quite the same woman who'd abandoned the task.

Well, she would refuse to teach it. Not overtly. Best to dissemble, like everyone else. Burn the book and play the innocent. *Oh dear, I'm afraid I mislaid that book, Mr Excorn, I left it on the train, how careless of me.* Or would she find the courage to say (because deceit could only work as a delaying tactic, she'd be supplied forthwith with a replacement copy), *As a matter of fact, I burned that book, Mr Excorn: it was obscene, it was a lie from beginning to end*?

What would Miss Heller have done in this situation?

Magda shut the book in a drawer and went to sit down on the bed. Good thing she looked first. A ruck in the quilt, the faintest of breathings, gave away a small presence.

Oh, it's you, she thought. You're here. There was a sweetness to knowing that Ruth's children considered her as family.

'I've found an angel in my bed,' she whispered to the child.

Flora opened her eyes, reached her good arm to draw Magda down. Kicking off her shoes, Magdalena laid her head on the pillow.

'A darling little angel, having a lovely nap in Magda's bed.'

Eyes smiled into eyes, heart-meltingly. Magda was content to lie there stroking the little girl's wispy fair hair back from her forehead, although it was warm, far too warm, in the attic room, where the sun had beaten down all day on the roof. Folding back the quilt, she blew on Flora's sweaty forehead to cool it.

How dared they call her unfit?

Magdalena knew, lying here with the child in her arms, that Flora was perfect.

But what was the little girl doing here? She seemed peaceful. Her fingers stroked Magda's cheek and she smiled.

The last of the sunlight glowed palely through the open window. 'But where's Julia, Flora?'

Flora waved her arm. Uttered something unintelligible.

'What? You don't mean ... over there? ... in the wardrobe?' Magdalena tried to rise but the child clung. 'Let go, darling, I'm just going to look.'

Flora's arm flopped; she said something that sounded like 'Make-suring?'

'Yes, my sweetheart. Make-suring.'

You see, Magdalena reminded herself, she understands and can communicate. She really can. She tiptoed to the wardrobe.

The door was partly open. Julia's face appeared in the gloom. She scrambled out.

Finger on lips, authoritative: 'We've got to shush. Doctor's here.'

It dawned on Magdalena in a rush. It was not just the doctor who was downstairs. It was the State. It was the Law. They got into your home through the main entrance. They had the right.

Now they were three-in-a-bed. Magdalena was astounded. What was Ruth thinking, hiding the twins from the doctor in her assistant's bedroom? Did she imagine that nobody would come looking in here? A self-serving query wriggled up from the depths: didn't Ruth reflect that this might look bad for Magdalena, implicate her?

Implicate her in what? Unworthy to think like this.

And what about Julia? Magda could hardly credit the discipline that had kept a child of six in a cupboard, holding herself still and composed, silent in a dark space that smelled of shoes and mothballs. A girl who had said only the other day, *I don't like moths, they might go up your nose.*

Magda lay on her back with one twin in the crook of each arm, their heads resting on her shoulders. She thought back. Of course, as she'd stowed the Auroch, she'd vaguely noticed the black car. Dr Littmann had parked further down the road, by the public house. So she'd assumed he was visiting Renate's family.

She kissed the girls' foreheads alternately, and they snuggled up close. They were drowsy (after all it was past their bedtime) – and, now that an adult had arrived, Julia could cede responsibility for Flora.

The girls' mouths went lax, their breathing deepened. One lost consciousness, and then the other.

*

Footsteps. Voices. Farewells. The front door opened and closed. A car engine started up. Sounds of a bolt being shot. Footsteps came running up the staircase.

*

They managed to carry the girls to their own bedrooms, without waking them. Then they tiptoed downstairs to Ruth's parlour.

He'd always been a decent man, Dr Littmann, Ruth said querulously: she'd felt she could confide in him, thinking of him almost as a family friend, you know? He'd once treated her husband without payment. And he was not stingy with his time; he listened; never let you down. In fact he'd always been kind and sympathetic to Flora, whom he'd delivered. Still was kind, come to that. All the way along, until recently, he'd held back from adding Flora to the list.

'He's had his thumb in the dam,' Ruth said. 'That's what I think. In the end you can't hold it back ... the flood.'

Ruth's hands shook as she received a glass of wine from Magdalena. Her face was white.

'The list? The flood?'

'He says there's a list, yes, an official list of the mentally and physically subnormal. And new rules.'

'What new rules?'

'Rules we're not supposed to know about. Nobody knows about them.'

'But we do?'

'I'm not an idiot, whoever else is. And the thing is, he doesn't necessarily agree that the feeble-minded are leading pointless lives,' Ruth explained. 'Or didn't. He's a Party man now, isn't he?'

It was as if Ruth were putting up an emergency defence against her own doubts. It was her finger that was in the dam, but it was too late, and the flood was rising, as Ruth was beginning to acknowledge. 'But now he feels someone with Flora's limitations would be better off in a caring institution – and I burst out, I could hardly contain myself: *Dr Littmann, with due respect, I am Flora's mother! Who can be more caring than myself? What is more essential than a mother's love?*'

'Oh no, he said, he didn't mean that, if I would just let him finish...

'... and he seemed testy and a bit flustered – got on his high horse – never seen him on quite such a high horse before, he was rattled and red in the face, and perhaps *he* was worried about being put on a list too, if he stretched his neck out any further...

'Let me *explain*, he said. What is being offered is the kind of *technical* and *specific* care that is based on *medical science*, which with the best will in the world hardly *any* mother can provide. And besides – and at this point he leaned over and kind-of dropped his voice – (who did he think was listening? the cat?) – it would be better in the long run not only for Flora but also for me and Julia if I let her go now.'

'As opposed to...?'

'As opposed to refusing to let her go.'

'Why?'

They stared at one another, dumbly. Magdalena saw a small, plump, conservative-looking woman of forty who had risen to her full five foot nothing to oppose a man on his high horse ... had resisted him at the fullest stretch of her powers, and whose pallid face in the aftermath was written over with lines of anger, lines of abhorrence, lines of terror.

Magda crossed to the table, cut some bread and cheese for Ruth, handed her the plate. 'You need to eat. Please eat something.'

Ruth shook her head, held out her glass. 'Just top me up.'

'Eat first.'

'I can't.'

'Try.'

Ruth took a couple of bites and Magda topped up her glass.

They sat side by side on the couch.

'He says she is an interesting case,' said Ruth tonelessly, looking straight ahead. 'And there's something else.'

'Tell me.'

'Some damn busybody has been asking if there aren't laws dealing with *mistakes like Mrs Daschke's malformed kid.*'

'No, surely?'

'Yes. And it doesn't take a genius to guess who that might be. Biggest mouth in the village? Blondest beast? Progeny of Wagner and Brunhild? Any ideas?'

It was a pithy description of Edith Struppat.

'So what shall we do?' asked Magda. It was *we* now. She must follow through on this. The child's two carers must take hands and put a ring round her. 'There must be something we can do. Someone we can appeal to for help?'

'I don't know,' said Ruth. 'The pastor perhaps. But ... Magda! ... I don't trust the pastor!' She gave a shout of shocked laughter. 'What have I just said? If you can't trust your pastor ... but, for God's sake, old Jacobeit's got *Mein Kampf* on his damned altar! ... well, not literally! But I bet it's in the vestry. Surprised he doesn't chant it instead of the Creed. I would have asked Mr Poppendick of the

Confessional Church but he's been banned from public speaking – so what could he do? But, Magdalena, listen, this is my bottom line: I shall never let Flora go. Never.'

Then they will snatch her, thought Magda, and there will be nothing we can do about it. She saw the same thought running round Ruth's mind. And if you refuse to give Flora up, they'll have *you* down on another list. You're probably on it already. And what will Julia do if anything happens to you? We are just women. What power do we have?

Are we though, Magdalena asked herself? – just women? Is that all we are?

'Ruth. We are teachers. It cannot be beyond us to prove that Flora is actually ... well, intelligent.'

She saw the look on Ruth's face.

'Yes, actually, I do mean intelligent! I've sometimes suspected – seriously, haven't you? – that Flora kind-of leaves it to Julia to interpret for her? Which Julia does, magnificently – she's a force of nature. She lives full-tilt for both of them. But maybe little Flora passively complies – almost lazily – but understands more than she shows, or at least has some inkling. And sounds come out which are not just noises.'

Ruth stared. She was certainly wondering: what can this inexperienced newcomer know? About my child, who is made of me, flesh of my flesh, and whom I've known intimately for six years, plus the eight months before that, and she has known for all of five minutes?

And yet. And yet. Perhaps the outsider's perspective is clearer. You may be too close up.

Magdalena, seeing Ruth revising her first instinct, went on, 'We need to – I don't know – bring this intelligence out? Show them – demonstrate to them – that she is not ... altogether devoid of reason?'

Ruth's face retorted, as clearly as if she had spoken the words, 'But it's not *Flora*, Magdalena, who is devoid of reason.'

And that, the face said, is the insuperable problem.

*

She did her best over the next weeks to help Flora, who shuffled around after Magdalena, hanging on to her skirt. Then they all caught colds and Flora had to be put to bed with earache. Ruth didn't want to call Dr Littmann, from whom nothing more had been heard. Perhaps he'd succeeded in intervening with the Scientific Committee. In any case, it was safer to keep their heads down.

Magdalena's throat was raw, not only with the cold, but also through talking too much, taking over Ruth's classes on top of her own, and having to shout to be heard. A hundred children. Half the night she was up preparing lessons, and all day she taught, not one class after another, but juggling classes.

Arithmetic to the six year olds; German to the sevens; local history to the eights; geography and zoology to the nines and tens. And then the eternal gymnastic exercises, and the drill, of which she was heartily sick, until Mrs Braun and Mrs Struppat drafted themselves in to take over the marching.

There was nothing she could do for Flora except free her mother to nurse her. The work was madness, and left Magdalena fit for nothing. She'd only just got used to the dialect of some of the pupils. They regarded her high German as a kind of foreign language with comical features.

By the end of the week Magda was so hoarse that she could only whisper. This was a disadvantage when you needed to discipline lads playing around in the earth closets, only six metres from the schoolhouse, or swarming over the school benches in muddy shoes, shouting *Giddy-up*! Some of the ten-year-old boys were nearly as tall as Magda, and muscular from helping with heavy work at home. It was not that she was physically afraid of them. Yes, she really did want to hit the little brats. But no, she was damned if she was going to use the switch supplied by the authorities for punishment. The object hung on a hook beside her desk, impotent. They knew Miss Arber wouldn't use it.

Instead, Magda made the lads clean the schoolroom, which they did with a surprisingly good grace.

Mr Excorn, visiting to check on progress, prior to sitting in on a session so that he could assess Miss Arber's techniques, raised an eyebrow when Magdalena put it to him that corporal punishment should rarely or never be necessary. He mentioned milksop teachers and ill-disciplined pupils, his brusque manner implying a potential blot on her copybook.

So what did Miss Arber think the switch was for? Decoration?

She opened her mouth to retort and closed it again. The twenty-year-old teacher – for last week Magdalena had celebrated her twentieth birthday – was convinced that her methods were working. The children loved her and showed it. On her birthday, she'd entered the classroom to find it full of flowers. They lay in scented rainbow mounds all over her desk; in vases at every window. Parents had sent in honey cakes and sausage, cheeses and vegetables, more than she and Ruth could ever eat.

Rather than arguing, Magdalena swerved, to run past Mr Excorn her proposal to take all the pupils on focused educational visits where they could study aspects of the topics on their curriculum. Hoarsely, she unfolded her plan.

For instance: zoology and agriculture. Pigs, for example! After all, more or less every family in this deeply rural area, however poor, kept a pig behind their cottage, along with a few chickens and occasionally even a cow. So the children already had practical knowledge of husbandry, which could be used and built on.

Her idea was to visit the Laulitz farm, a walk of about a mile and a half through the forest. Magdalena had sounded out Miss von Laulitz, who was more than happy to welcome them, the more the merrier, and had promised to help in any way she could. The six-year-olds would count pigs and piglets, adding up and taking away and multiplying and dividing and so forth, she extemporised. The sevens would learn the technical terms for farming and breeding. The eights would be introduced to the history of agriculture in East

Prussia. The nines and tens would study the anatomy and life cycle of the animals.

Then they'd all march home to Alt Schönbek and write up their findings. She sat and waited expectantly.

'I see. And what other visits had you in mind?' Mr Excorn asked.

'Well, a trip to Königsberg on the train, to introduce the children to the castle and cathedral – the Teutonic Knights and the history of East Prussia? My own mother came from Königsberg originally, as it happens. And then I wondered about the visit to Rominten Sanctuary which I mentioned at our first meeting?'

'Ah yes.'

'Perhaps, if you still like the idea, you might wish to write to Dr Vogel?'

The instructor's jaw was working as if chewing the cud of this proposition. He hadn't mentioned the matter of Magdalena's heretical avoidance of set textbooks: raising the idea of Rominten Game Reserve might help them bypass the problem.

Good, if so, because *Trust No Fox on his Green Heath* had been ash in the grate for some time now.

'I shall indeed write to Dr Vogel. A first-rate connection – and in keeping with our Leader's advanced thinking on scientific education.' He glanced up at the mandatory portrait. 'As you know, Miss Arber, Rominten is Imperial Marshall Goering's estate, run on the most modern – and at the same time the most ancient – principles. So doubtless the Imperial Marshall's office will need to be consulted. I shall also write to the Chief Forester. Please leave this with me. Do not attempt it yourself.'

He wants the kudos, Magda thought. Good. She'd impressed him after all and now he'd leave her alone for another month.

Don't count on it.

'There is one matter, however, which I must take up with you. I have received a rather troubling letter.'

He drew from his file an official-looking envelope and flapped it.

'It concerns your commitment to your role in the Band of

German Maidens. It seems you have twice sent excuses for non-attendance.'

Apparently problems of distance, lack of transport, tonsillitis, full-time work and the limitations of a home-made bike on a twenty-mile journey cut no ice with Dr Excorn. His eye beetled at her, with a sort of glee. Oh how he loved it. You are a fly and my fat thumb is about to squash you, the look said. Here it comes.

She was required to attend the three-day Moot of regional Youth Leaders this coming Saturday. In Königsberg. No excuses. And Miss Arber must not only attend but also perform her role with conviction, bearing the flag, delivering an address and taking her turn to supervise marching and singing.

Her shoulders sagged.

'I do realise that you have been unwell,' he conceded. 'And I make allowances. But consider this, Miss Arber. Our heroic soldiers – many of them younger than yourself – are storming east against hordes of degenerates – for Operation Barbarossa has begun, when we shall overcome the Slavic hordes, Commies, Jews – for our sakes. Let's imagine a scenario!'

Let's not, she thought. How pleased Excorn was with himself. He loved these little allegories. Of Otto and Liesl. Of Autobahns and cliff edges.

'So – Miss Arber – let's say there's a young soldier on the Eastern Front. What shall we call him? Friedrich! What if this soldier woke up one morning in his foxhole with a bit of a sniffle, and a nasty cough? Oh dear, thinks our soldier, I'm not feeling well at all, unfortunately I won't be able to defend the Fatherland today, I'll stay here nice and cosy, coddling myself. Eh? No, exactly. You get my meaning. And, seriously, we owe our heroes an inestimable debt, do we not? And we must do our utmost to deserve their sacrifice, it is the least we can do.'

Hoarsely, Magdalena agreed. She had a cousin in the field herself. More like a brother really. Very close. She'd been hoping Clem might be able to see her this weekend ... in Königsberg ... on his way to the front.

'Ah, yes. We all have someone. I have four sons and one stepson in the field.'

His eyebrows worked. Then his expression softened and he said, 'Well, well,' which seemed to indicate that the conversation was over and she was about to be released, to set up the classroom for her assessment. Mr Excorn shuffled his papers, tapping them against the desk to align them; made ready to rise, and did rise, but sat down again.

'At our first meeting, Miss Arber, you were forthcoming enough to tell me something of your own personal development. I may have appeared somewhat severe. Did you understand *why* I came down rather strongly on you?'

'Oh yes. Of course.' She took a risk. 'You wanted me to travel the right way up the Autobahn. And not drive off a cliff.'

He actually smiled. He thought highly of her aptitude, Mr Excorn assured Magdalena, and her zest for learning and teaching. He got up from his chair, came round and perched on the edge of the desk. What was coming next?

'So, in return, let me confide something about myself. You will have wondered about my partial blindness. Well, in a word, I lost my right eye at Verdun, and half a lung. Shrapnel. That was the end of my war.'

'Oh no. I *see*. I'm so sorry.'

'I'd been at the front a total of nine days. Invalided out, half blind. My condition was far worse than as you see it today. One eye had to be removed, the other was doubtful. Ultimately, I came home to find – anarchy – civil strife – poverty – famine – sickness. Neither work nor worth. Obsolete – shamed – betrayed, we all were. My mother died of influenza. But – now then, Miss Arber – there is a big *but* coming! Our Leader arose – guided us out of the Valley of Humiliation – repudiated the monstrous Versailles Treaty – fed the hungry – restored the economy. In the Leader's Germany I am of *use*. I have a part to play – minor, yes, but not without honour. I owe – we all owe – our Leader a debt of gratitude which can never,

never be repaid. We must all fight with passionate fanaticism. With whatever weapons we have at our disposal. As one body.'

'As in the Bible: *We are all members one of another?*'

'Well, ah, if you wish to put it like that,' he said, doubtfully.

8

> Do you know the land where the assault guns bloom?
> You don't know it? You'll get to know it soon![12]
>   Erich Kästner, 'Do you know the land', 1928

The light shifts, Magdalena thought, and you glimpse what was never shown before, although you might have guessed it. Someone vulnerable has been hunkering in the dark behind a public façade, addressing you through a loudspeaker as if you were a public meeting. The stranger takes a cautious step out into the light, to expose a fragment of his inner self. He lays bare the bones of his history. You witness excruciating early pain; private helplessness; poverty and hunger; fear; humiliation. Impossible simply to scorn Mr Excorn.

And yet, since learning his history, Magdalena found she feared Mr Excorn *more* than before.

The inspector sat at the side of her classroom, to assess the quality of the apprentice's teaching. With one arm slung over the back of his chair, his posture was relaxed and genial, his good eye roaming the children's faces. They were learning about Frederick Barbarossa. Magdalena had brought a picture of the bust of the twelfth-century king, modelled in gold. The class liked the thought of Barbarossa's red beard, his golden hair and milk-white teeth, his broad shoulders, his tendency to blush, his charisma. She fed them morsels of description that might bring him to life in their imaginations.

The little ones were asked to draw pictures of Frederick on Crusade, which they began zestfully to do. The older children were to write a poem about his myth, for Barbarossa, said Magdalena, was said never to have died! He's only sleeping in a cave on a mountain, according to the story – and the augury said that when the ravens ceased to fly around the mountain, Barbarossa would awaken and restore Germany to its ancient greatness.

'And,' cried Mr Excorn, taking over, swivelling in his chair, 'I have news for you, children! Do you want to hear it? All of you? Very well. The ravens have left the mountain! Barbarossa has awoken!'

He began to clap his hands. After some uncertainty, the class joined in.

Mr Excorn stood up. The class stood up.

Mr Excorn gave the salute, clicked his heels, raised his arm, held it high. A forest of hands went up. Magdalena raised hers.

All together, the children shouted *Heil Hitler!*

Mr Excorn, taking over from Magdalena, came forward, and she was glad enough to have her place usurped. He spoke of the rising of a great Leader. Of Operation Barbarossa. Why had our great Leader named the invasion of Russia Operation Barbarossa? Yes, little girl. What's your name? Hedwig? Well done, Hedwig.

Did Magdalena have a map to hand? Good. And a pointer? Good. Now then, lad in the front row – yes, you. Your name? Well then, Paul Nikoleit, can you point to Germany on this map?

Paul came forward and indicated the territory in red.

Trace the borders for me, Paul, with this pointer – that's the way.

Ah, but I have news for you. Those borders, my young comrade, are already out of date. Due to Barbarossa!

Here is Germany. Or rather, here *was* Germany on 22 June of this year!

And ... here *was* Germany on 29 June! – you see, it's got bigger in a week!

And here *was* Germany on 9 July! – bigger still! – Can you read the name of the city, boy, second from left, front row, curly hair? Yes, Minsk! On the Tuesday Minsk was in Russian hands – on the Wednesday Minsk had fallen to Germany!

And here (everyone look where I am indicating) can you see these other cities? – Smolensk! Moscow! We'll soon have those in our pocket! Hurrah for Operation Barbarossa! And so Germany grows and grows, children! And Russia shrinks and shrinks!

At each victory, Mr Excorn led the class in Hurrah after Hurrah. They drummed their feet and pounded their desks and bellowed.

Magdalena was exhausted by the time he left.

What if she never saw Clem again? *I lost an eye and half a lung in the war.* Clem too was seventeen, ardent, avid for adventure, comradeship, glory. *I lasted nine days in the trenches.* Clem's hardly grown up, she thought. He was woven intricately into her patchwork past. A desperate need to hold her cousin in her arms – always more a younger brother than a cousin – came over Magdalena. And somehow keep him.

Meanwhile there was the first of the school expeditions to organise.

*

Flora lay in bed, vacant, whimpering, green snot dripping from her nose, hand clasping her ear, not getting better. Not getting worse: or so Ruth insisted. Or, if she was getting worse, that was because the condition was coming to a crisis. The doctor must on no account be called, she insisted, abrasively. There was no need. Earaches? – she'd had earaches herself all the time as a child and you just had to sit it out until the drum burst and the muck poured out.

When Magdalena pointed out Flora's sky-high temperature, Ruth nearly bit her head off.

Ruth could no longer teach. Before leaving the school, Mr Excorn warned that he had no option but to note in the records that Mrs Daschke was out of action as a result of the illness of her feeble-minded child. And that this imposed extra strain on the apprentice teacher who, however, had insisted she could cope. And that this state of affairs was uneconomic, a perverse waste of resources, and could not be allowed to continue long.

Ruth knew better than to beg and plead with the inspector. You might as well have entreated a brick wall to look kindly on you. She forced a smile, forced herself to fawn, and said brightly that she was confident Flora was just about to turn the corner. She would shortly – very shortly – be able to resume her full duties.

She nursed her sick daughter, broken-heartedly.

Magdalena looked in before she left for the farm visit. Through the gap between door and jamb, she could see Ruth sagging in her chair, where she had spent the night. Flora lay with her mouth gaping open, uttering a feeble, intermittent wail, the breath growling in her lungs.

The child needed a doctor.

*

The stream of chattering children walked two by two along the fringe of the forest, down paths whose mud had baked hard in the heat. Passing occasional timber houses belonging to the foresters, they waved and called out, since everybody knew everybody at Alt Schönbek. In the absence of Ruth, Renate Schmidt brought up the rear, while Edith Struppat and Mrs Braun patrolled the line, ensuring, with their customary brusque efficiency, that there were no stragglers. Renate, kindly and cultured, had a lovely singing voice. Magdalena and Ruth often heard her singing her daughter to sleep in the evening, through an open window.

Now Renate raised her voice. She sang – and every child joined in – about wandering. Whenever the golden sun laughs in the sky, Renate Schmidt sang, she must wander the world, in quest of the blue flower. Until she found the blue flower, Renate would never give up her wandering, never, and neither would the children. Somewhere in the midst of the impromptu choir walked Julia, hand in hand with her best friend Karin. Yes, there they were, swinging their arms, looking into each other's faces as they sang about finding the blue flower.

Julia had been difficult lately, with her twin out of action and her mother preoccupied. Well, *difficult* was a feeble word for the way Julia could behave when thwarted. She looked happy now, swinging along with Karin. There was a feeling of holiday.

And here was Eva von Laulitz's estate. She and her elderly pigman were waiting at the gate. A tall, impressive woman in, perhaps, her late thirties, Miss von Laulitz was dressed in riding breeches and high boots, spattered with mud. She was loud, confident, commanding, running the estate herself, not married and not intending to marry. And she was not going to apologise to *anyone* for that! Why would I want to subject myself to one of *them*? I am a one-off job, her demeanour implied. I come of an ancient family and this you can tell from my grand manner and my awe-inspiring accent.

In an odd way Miss von Laulitz seemed to Magdalena, who liked her at once, a double throw-back – to the Weimar time when women might have boyish hairstyles and mannish ways. And, as the last sprig of a noble family, in the absence of males, she managed the great estate she could never personally own, on what seemed the basis of a benevolent feudalism. Magda had never met anyone like her. Her workers – prisoners of war, forced labourers, elderly locals and wives – were her loyal children; she the matriarch of the fiefdom.

Miss von Laulitz ('Call me Eva') shook Magdalena's hand warmly, happy to show off the estate. Hers was the largest in the region, worked in part by foreign labourers, mainly Poles but also a couple of Ukrainians, one Norwegian and even an English prisoner of war.

'Over there, with the wheelbarrow, name of Bert, captured in France, salt of the earth. And next to Bert, Alf Hansen from Tromso. Splendid chaps. And our Poles – they are family.'

Magdalena stared, at Miss von Laulitz rather than at Bert and Alf.

There were brick pigsties for fifty breeding pigs, a cowshed with eighty dairy cattle and stables for working horses. Only two were left, the remainder having been commandeered for the war in the east. The barn was monumental. Awe-inspiring. A cathedral of grain. It would house the harvest of wheat, rye and oats for threshing in winter. There was a forge with tractors, managed by a Polish engineer; a vegetable garden and farm cottages. Miss von Laulitz housed and fed her workers well. They worked hard, she said, and deserved no less.

She pointed out with pride the immense, towering manure heap. 'Nice and ripe and stinky,' she said to the children. 'Write that down, *ripe and stinky*. Very important for...?'

'Fertiliser! Ripe and stinky!'

'Exactly. And now to the piggery! My pride and joy!' she announced, waving the children on.

The grunting and shrieking were symphonic. The children joined in with gusto. In the farrowing barn, one sow had only just produced a litter; another had recently been put out to pasture with her seven piglets, all suckling noisily at her teats except one, the runt, trampled by his brethren as he struggled to find a place at the feast.

'The good old sow's name is Bolshy,' said Miss von Laulitz. 'Say hallo to Bolshy, children!'

'Hallo, Bolshy!' they caterwauled.

'Well, yesterday Bolshy was in a bad mood, wasn't she, Rudi?'

'Looking for trouble,' agreed the pigman.

'And she got fed up with being milked,' said Miss von Laulitz. 'I mean, properly fed up, she'd had enough, wouldn't you in her position? Wouldn't you, Miss Arber, if you had seven babies all trying to suck at you? I can tell you, I would.'

Laughter, raucous or stifled, from the children, who observed their teacher curiously, to see how she was taking the banter. Magda grinned and played along.

'Well, Bolshy has quite a temper on her. Good breeder though, the best. One year she gave us a litter of fourteen, only two duds. This time just seven, she's getting on a bit now. Runty-boy – the little grey fellow, see him, bit of a sad sack? – well, I wish you'd seen him yesterday. Runty came creeping round to his mother's head, in case there was a spare teat on her *face*! Bolshy took one look and dug her snout underneath his belly – and she launched him in the air. Flew up high! Never seen that before. A piglet-rocket! Didn't hurt him but a devil of a shock. How we laughed.'

'Do it again, Bolshy! Do it again!' chorused the children.

The whimpering runt struggled in the heap of his seething siblings. Half-buried, less than two thirds the size of the largest, with nothing going for him, the piglet was squeezed out of the pile. Round he limped to take another abject look at Bolshy's face.

'Doesn't learn, does he?' said Miss von Laulitz. 'Watch now ... watch! She's going to...'

Maddened, the sow caught the piglet in wide jaws. She bit down hard.

The scream died in an instant. The baby's head and mangled forelegs lay in a pool of blood; the mother chewed his life back into herself, blood running down her cheeks.

Most of Magda's brood did not seem nonplussed, though they'd yelped and recoiled at the moment of execution. For country children, the pig-slaughter was a major event in the economy of their homes. They'd hold the bucket for the draining of the precious blood. Magdalena felt sick to her stomach. She swallowed hard and reminded herself that she enjoyed pork as much as anyone.

'Mother Nature doesn't tolerate waste,' Miss von Laulitz told them. 'Bolshy will eat up every scrap of the carcase, if we let her, and replace the energy she's lost farrowing and feeding. Do you blame her?'

No, of course not.

'You didn't expect that, did you, Miss Arber?' said the pigman. 'The little fellow would never have amounted to anything. Waste of milk, if he could ever get hold of a teat. Nice quick end. Back into the breed.'

Later, the children were led off to the wildflower meadow for their picnic, supervised by Edith Struppat, Mrs Braun and Renate. Magdalena accepted Eva's invitation to have lunch with her indoors.

The last she heard was Edith's booming voice explaining to Cassandra Braun that pigs were *Aryan* animals with *pure* blood so when we *Germans* eat them, their *pure* blood enters our *pure Aryan* bloodstream ... and when she heard folk calling the Yids dirty swine, it made Mrs Struppat's German blood boil because pigs are *clean* animals! ... whereas Yids! ... hold your nose!

'Yes, I know,' said her companion.

Magdalena stopped in her tracks; turned and gaped.

Miss von Laulitz took Magdalena's arm; grinned.

'Come and eat. Let's get to know each other.'

She mentioned that you could hear a whole load of *pure shit* talked nowadays if you bothered to listen.

9

> Blessed he who, from the world,
> Without hate withdraws,
> Holding to his heart a friend,
> And with him adores
>
> What, unknown to men,
> Or never visualised,
> In the breast's labyrinth
> Wanders in the night.[13]
>
> Johann Wolfgang von Goethe,
'To the Moon', 1789

An ornate tiled stove reached to the ceiling in the living room. The structure towered above you like a pale green palace, with ornamental pilasters and baroque mouldings. Bookshelves were filled with antiquarian books, floor to ceiling, and the walls were hung with oil paintings. Portraits of East Prussian nobles, eighteenth and nineteenth century beings, bemedalled and moustached or, quill in hand, pursuing the life of the mind.

And, look, at one end of the room Miss von Laulitz had a harpsichord and a spinet. A cello in its case stood against a wall.

How Dad would have revelled in the Laulitz library. The sight of the books made Magda feel hungry. For print. For wisdom. For music that had nothing to do with martial parades. For knowledge and emotion that had been distilled, collected and preserved over time, passed down from generation to generation.

Everything here was archaic, in the magnificent building with its pillared entrance; timbered gable; stone-flagged floors. Through it all ran a theme of partially arrested decay. The house remembered its one-time opulence and the power of its owners. It stated, *I am still here, we are still here, despite all. Despite the little corporal. I shall be the last to depart.* It was the remnant of a feudal Prussian world of a landed aristocracy, a network of princelings whose threads still just about held. Ruth had related in forgettably complex detail Miss von Laulitz's distant relationship to the great families, the Dohna-Schlobittens, the Lehndorffs.

'Do you mind if I browse your books, Miss von Laulitz?'

Her host did not immediately respond. She seemed to be sizing up her visitor.

'Please do. They're not all mine though – I'm keeping them for someone. A friend. Excuse me just a minute.' She'd go and ask about lunch, she said, and then: 'Enjoy truffling around, Bookworm. Take home anything you want. But run it past me first, if you don't mind, Magdalena. And I'll wrap it for you.'

She'd wrap it for me? Why would she...?

On her way out of the door, Miss von Laulitz added, 'Some books got a bit burnt a few years ago – know what I mean? – let's say I don't want any tell-tale soot to come off on your nice clean outfit.'

Magda took down a leather-bound volume of Hölderlin's collected poems, an edition published nearly a century back. A beautiful book to hold in your hands: red leather covers, imprinted with gold. What Dad always did with a rare book was to sniff at the pages. She opened the volume carefully and breathed in the subtle earthy, woody scent. There were inked comments and a burn mark, as if a smoker had dropped an ember on a page. *Never, never write on a book!* Dad had scolded her, catching Magda doodling on the end-papers. She couldn't agree less. Traces of earlier readers brought strangers suddenly close, as if someone kin to herself had just closed the book and turned away into the past.

Here was a whole shelf of Goethe. She eased out an early edition of his lyrics. The poems' titles were, many of them, ringed in pencil. Magda leafed through, pausing at those she most loved, a choice she seemed to share with the reader holding the pencil. Each word of the last two stanzas of 'To the Moon' was individually underlined. The phrase *Without hate* had been ringed in ink.

Blessed he who, from the world,

Without hate withdraws...

Without hate. How did you banish hate, free yourself from its claws? Hatred was held to be compulsory for enemies east and west, who must be slaughtered before they slaughtered you; and for the stigmatised enemy within. Hatred begat fear, which begat hatred, which begat fear ... on and on, how could the cycle be stemmed?

And within oneself, embroiled in the dark treacle of this medium, hatred seethed for the haters.

A flash of memory. Not thought of him for years: the hating man who'd popped up in Dad's study one Saturday – a year or so before the war it must have been. She'd listened at the door. Someone seemed to be cursing. In a high-pitched voice and an elite accent, her Dad's visitor was turning the air blue with malediction. She'd caught phrases like *a raw-vegetable Genghis Khan! ... a teetotaling Alexander! ... a womanless Napoleon! ... a turd-faced stunted moron ... a parvenu! ... born in chicanery, blackmail and swindle!*

She'd remembered the volley of abuse word for word – especially the fruitier epithets – and the change of tone when the rant had turned darkly elegiac, a lament for *long years filled with hate, hate at lying down, and hate at rising, hate through the long hours of bad dreams...*

She'd tapped and peered round the door, out of sheer curiosity. The visitor, a meagre middle-aged man with a receding hairline that made his forehead seem immense, had a paper in his hand. Had he been reading aloud then? He subsided immediately Magdalena entered.

'Meet Fritz,' Dad had said. 'Dear friend from Munich. Dr Friedrich Reck-Malleczewen. You've got one or two of his children's books on your shelf, I think, Magda. He's been reading notes from his new Gothic novel.'

'Just call me Fritz. Delighted to meet you, gracious lady.'

Gracious lady? A common-or-garden lass in BDM uniform?

The visitor had held out his hand and smiled and was charming. He'd entertained them over dinner with tall tales of the literary world. But Magdalena had not been charmed. He was a snob and she disliked that. Still flush with the remnant of National Socialist idealism, she'd seen something in his eyes and heard it in his voice – as if he'd shown her a boil, putrid, pus-filled, and the boil was the rage at the secret centre of his inner world. Perhaps she'd suspected then – but shied away for Dad's sake – what she realised now: the object of Reck's hatred was the Party, the mass madness of Germany, Hitler himself, '*bobbing corklike on a sea of sewage.*'

Like the Arbers, the hater was an exile in his own country. So was there such a thing, she wondered now, as righteous hatred which I should espouse? Ebba would say no, we are taught to love our enemies.

But the poet, whom Magdalena revered, insisted, *without hate*. This was the condition upon which rescue depended. Goethe's elegy maintained that you could find blessing if you had a friend to retreat with from the sadness and complexity of it all.

In the labyrinth of the breast.

But wasn't withdrawal from the world into private fellowship a kind of desertion? It took courage even to confide your suspicions to anyone not in your own family; a wincing and fraught courage, even to acknowledge your misgivings to yourself. How did Magdalena know she could trust Miss von Laulitz? She felt she would.

But she might not.

Should not, even.

What had Miss von Laulitz (she could not possibly call her Eva) meant about her books having been burnt? Nothing in this immaculate library was even singed.

And then she saw.

There was a book behind the Goethe lyrics. She removed more to disclose a row of hidden books. Forbidden books. Heinrich Mann and Hemingway, Remarque, Kafka, Zweig, Helen Keller. It was like coming upon old friends. So that was what Miss von Laulitz had meant about the burning. Forbidden friends, friends incinerated at Nüremberg as being Anti-German, amid music, singing, incantations and 'fire-oaths' by the German Student Union louts, as being examples of loathsome Jewish intellectualism.

Hastily Magdalena rebuilt the façade.

Closing the Goethe and reshelving it, sealing the gap in Eva's defences, Magdalena murmured the last two verses to herself. She'd had the poem by heart ever since ... ever since when? From schooldays perhaps? ... from Miss Heller, who read poetry to the class in her contralto voice, sounding every note, as in music. Poetry is close to music, Miss Heller had taught. No word in a poem, she'd explained to the children, was insignificant. A poem's every pause is a link in the rhythm, in the weave. Listen to the pauses. Listen to what is not said. Poetry is not mortal, as are poets, Miriam Heller had taught. Through these marks on the page, we hear a living voice. Listen; just listen.

But had Magda actually met this poem before Miss Heller's time? Had she heard her mother reading it – Dorothea who'd loved poetry, and had reams by heart, and had been taught by her own mother, who was taught by ... and back ... and back?

When Magda went home to Lűbeck, she would look for Miss Heller and tell her she remembered it all – the axolotl, the secret orchid they'd visited together, a violin and a candlestick ... in a strange and lovely room, with kind eyes welcoming her at a bad time, in firelight ... arms reaching out ... but wherever was that? She would tell Miss Heller that she was, in some sense, her child. She'd gone a bit wrong in her teens but she'd circled home. And that she was intent on passing on to her own pupils that listening wisdom.

*

Miss von Laulitz was back with a maid, bringing lunch. She was talking to her in a foreign language. Polish?

'What's that you're reading, Magdalena? Ah, yes.'

'I couldn't possibly borrow books like these.'

'Why not?'

'Well, these are rare books, Miss von Laulitz: they're priceless.'

'For goodness sake, I keep telling you, call me Eva! Come over on your bike and read here at weekends if you don't want to remove them. But honestly, take what you want. I know you'll bring them back.'

Miss von Laulitz added matter-of-factly that this particular volume did not belong to her, it was Leonie's copy. Her friend. She lit a cigarette, coughed, and stubbed it out. Her hands had a tremor.

'Anyway, you're always welcome to browse and borrow books – hers or mine. Why don't you treat me as your librarian, Magdalena?'

'Oh my goodness, thank you so much. I'd love to come and read. I'm starving for books. I mean, good books. Real books, decent books, if you know what I mean.'

'I miss her.'

'Your friend?'

'As long as she's safe. That's all that matters.'

'Your friend did the underlinings, and ringed the special words?'

'What do you mean? What special words?'

'Look.' Magdalena fetched Goethe down again and leafed through to the lyric.

Eva took the book in her hands; read; traced the words with her fingertips; carried it to the window. *The breast's labyrinth.* Her face was working. *Without hate.* Closing the volume, she reshelved it, turned away. No more was said on that subject. They took the bread and cheese outside and ate on a bench, in the shade of an oak, and Eva drew Magda out, studying her face attentively.

'So now I'm going to interrogate you, Miss Magdalena Arber, schoolteacher from Lübeck. What did you notice about my books?'

'That there are a lot of them?'

'And?'

'Well, that they're often early editions? Rare books. It's a priceless antiquarian library.'

'Come on, I know you saw others. You truffled about a bit. I watched you!'

'Oh dear.' Magda's face flushed. 'I couldn't help noticing...'

'It's all right. I trust you. What's life *worth,* if you don't trust your instincts, ever? But, Magdalena ... don't mention the name Leonie to anyone, please. That's private.'

*

Later, leading the column of children home, Magda imagined what she might and should have said, glimpsing the depth of this woman's emotion for the unknown friend, who loved poetry, and had been forced to leave, and may not be safe, or – if Magda had guessed right – may not even be alive.

She should have said more clearly, *Leonie has left you not just one message, Eva, but many. They are in the underlinings.*

'Well, Miss Arber!' Edith Struppat came up behind; tapped her on the shoulder as if making an arrest. 'How are you liking our little community and your work here?'

'Very much, thank you.'

'And are you enjoying your work with the Band of German Maidens? I gather there's to be a Moot at Kőnigsberg next week? I'm sure you will be looking forward to it no end.'

Deep breath. Smile. 'Oh yes, Mrs Struppat, no end. I'm to be a flag-bearer.'

'What a proud role for you. A sacred calling. My daughters have all acted as flag-bearers. Have I told you about my daughters?'

'Oh yes.'

'*Seven* daughters! All pursuing their womanly work for our Leader. We must not let the Leader down. Between ourselves, and with the best will in the world, Mrs Daschke could have been more assiduous in that area.'

'Oh no,' Magda came back quickly. 'I'm sure that's not the case. Mrs Daschke is tremendously *assiduous*,' Magda intervened.

'Passionate about all her duties. Of course as a widowed mother, she can't always be free to...'

Mrs Struppat's eyes were like a ferret's, small and too far apart. 'Well,' she said, 'I can imagine that the ... simpleton child ... must take a great deal of time and effort.'

'Flora is a lovely little girl,' Magdalena choked out. 'She is making good progress, in her quiet way. Only she's not very well at present. Tonsillitis.'

So this was how they spoke about Ruth and Flora, was it? The ferrets of Alt Schönbek, sniffing for prey.

Magdalena went on, resorting to her teacherly voice, 'Yes, Flora is making real progress. And as for the Band of German Maidens, I'm employed to fulfil that duty, of course. I'm more the age for it. As you know, the Leader likes the young to lead the young. Don't worry about it at all.'

Mrs Struppat said she was relieved to hear it.

Now, full-throttle, she filled Magdalena in on the achievements of the seven daughters, all but one married and each playing her part in the gigantic wartime effort for the Fatherland. Between them they were proud mothers of thirteen children. Only the youngest Struppat, Dagmar, was as yet unmarried. A fortnight ago, Mrs Struppat had attended the consecration of the latest babe, born to Irmgard and Ernst. Another boy, would you believe? Named Viktor. What an occasion! They'd hung a Rune of Life flag in Irmgard's living room, white on a blue background – and the proud father was granted leave from the front for the occasion. The witnesses had gathered in a circle and Ernst bore Baby Viktor in on a Teutonic shield he'd made himself out of cardboard covered with a special blanket!

'My goodness. That sounds ... Do excuse me, Mrs Struppat, I must just make sure we don't lose anyone...'

Magdalena called to the children not to straggle and that they were coming near to the place in the wood where the wild strawberries grew. Mrs Struppat reinforced this message by bawling Magda's words after her like a human loud hailer.

'Yes,' she continued. 'As I was saying, a bona fide Teutonic shield, made of cardboard, such as the Knights of old used to dedicate their infants ... a black cross on a gold cross, with the imperial eagle. My daughter had knitted a version of the Teutonic Knight's helmet, with crocheted wings coming out, and the baby was wearing this helmet on his head, can you imagine? So sweet. The blanket was made of undyed wool with a long red fringe and it was embroidered, of course, with oak leaves and various runes and swastikas and so on. Also...'

'And your son-in-law made this blanket? ... Keep up with your partner, Heini!'

Mrs Struppat chortled at the very idea. 'Whatever next? No, it was Irmgard's task to sew the blanket and knit the helmet! Obviously a new-born baby could not be expected to wear a tin replica. Not good for his head. Of course you have not had babies, Miss Arber, so you may not know about the fontanelles? The soft part of the infant skull. Ernst attached the blanket securely to the shield. And then he ceremoniously opened his son's Book of Life and wrote his name and birthdate on the first page, with a poem of his own devising, while we all saluted.'

'Your son-in-law is a poet, Mrs Struppat?'

'First and foremost, a *soldier*, of course. But for great occasions Ernst (in his leisure hours) composes. You are fond of poetry, I know, Miss Arber.'

'Oh yes.'

But not of gibberish, Magdalena thought, or people shouting in my ear. Big and buxom, square-jawed and humourless, Mrs Struppat was relentless in the marching of her feet and the marching of her mouth.

Renate was starting the children off again with a hiking song. Perhaps the Struppat would be overwhelmed by music and drop off like a leech.

No. She hung on firmly to her monologue, whilst turning up the volume. 'I learned Ernst's poem off by heart, if you would like to hear it? Let me see, how did it go exactly? ... Forgotten now but the last two lines were, *One day thou wilt understand, my son/ Thoroughly all thy breed!* Well, something like that. Mystical, you see – you're not supposed to know exactly what it means.'

'So ... an enigma?'

'An enigma! Just the right word!' She clapped Magda on the shoulder.

'Ernst is so good to Irmgard, you can't even begin to imagine. He brought her several pairs of shoes from Prague, two furs from Poland and nine pairs of silk stockings! She gave me one pair. Ernst didn't mind. Plenty more where those came from, he said. Yids don't need stockings where they're going. Look at my legs!' Mrs Struppat stopped in her tracks and thrust forth a silken leg. 'Of course Ernst has gone back to Prague now. And he's been promoted! An officer, forsooth! Did I tell you about my other daughters?'

'I'm afraid we'll have to keep that for another time, Mrs Struppat. We're nearly there now...'

At which, Mrs Struppat turned, clapped her hands and bellowed to the flock, *'Nearly there!'*

In the pause to allow the children to pick woodland strawberries, tiny but delicious and fragrant, to take home to their parents, Magdalena went back over the conversation with Eva. For now, however, its quiet tenor and the sensation of Eva's charisma were lost in the blast.

10

> A visit to the asylum. There I encountered a woman whose only tic consisted of continuously murmuring 'Heil Hitler'. At least it's a fitting, topical form of insanity.[1]
> Ernst Jűnger, *First Paris Diary*, 1942

Beneath the flagpole at the Königsberg Leadership Moot, young men had been performing their songs of death. They sang of wild geese rushing through the night ... the grey-winged migrants overhead, the grey-coated legions marshalled below ... maybe never to return.

'Danger awaits! Take care your flight!

The world is full of murder.'

So the East Prussian soldier-poet, Walter Flex, had written on sentry duty in the Great War, before perishing and inseminating the soil with the blood of his race, as he'd proudly predicted. The dead-to-be of a second world war sang Flex's words to a martial tune.

Magdalena was suffering from murder fatigue. From marching fatigue. From furious boredom. Her feet hurt. Her throat hurt from issuing orders. During the Moot she'd been criticised for poor leadership qualities; ordered to shout her commands with attack, with conviction. Was she a mouse or was she a she-wolf? Let the Slavs hear you roaring as far away as the steppes of Lithuania and Russia! Again! Come along, give it attack! Again!

Magdalena wouldn't mind if she never saw another flagpole.

A fellow Leader, an apprentice teacher from Köln, seemed to suffer from a similar inhibition: Marianne Günther. They'd exchanged rueful glances and addresses. Clandestine friends might be all around if you only knew how to signal to each other. Or they might not, so be careful with your signals. Yesterday evening Marianne had confided that she'd had to attend a BDM meeting in Masuren. She was so shocked. The poor Poles had been turned out of their farms, and made to serve the new German owners, who were ashamed.

'I don't see how they can do this to people.'

'They're people like us.'

Only a handful of words had been exchanged but they were heresy. The two of them intuitively trusted one another. For what is life worth, how can you live with yourself, and with your neighbours, if you can trust no one? Eva had asked this question. Despite this, Magdalena reminded herself that even this open-faced, comradely young woman from Köln, a fellow teacher, who loved books and cycling and nature, might denounce you, if only to save herself.

You have to have friends though.

Nevertheless, be on your guard, take care, take care: the world is full of murder.

Magdalena, Marianne and the one hundred and ninety-eight other regional BDM Leaders were a sideshow compared with the four hundred and fifty Hitler Youth Leaders assembled in Königsberg. Blond heroes avid for glory, the young men marched as one, each vying with the other to demonstrate prowess. Dauntless young butchers-to-be. Martyrs-to-be. As she continued to stand to attention, Magdalena's hope sagged; her arm wilted with holding the prolonged salute. When would it end?

Clem would be passing through Königsberg Station on his way east, and she couldn't bear to miss him.

She thought of the wingbeats of the wild geese, the wraith-like honking calls you heard as a flock flew overhead, away and away. She'd read Flex's work: he carried you on the current of his melancholy intensity. And he could really write, which caught you off guard and made you susceptible. Then you plummeted down to earth, through the gap between emotion and truth. An army is out to kill; a flight of migrant geese is out to live.

At last. The swastika was about to ascend. The lads sang of holding the flag high ... the ghosts of the dead marched alongside them ... the day was breaking for freedom and for bread...

Now the air began to reverberate. A screeching whine. A flight of planes.

Whose? Theirs or ours? Ours, surely? There'd been no alarm. You were not supposed to look up, away from the business in hand. But you did glance up, with a flinching sensation.

But no, it's all right. Messerschmitts. Volleys of cheers went up.

There'd been no bombs to speak of here. And none had fallen on Magda's family in Lűbeck which, if it should be attacked, would go up like a firework, because it was built of timber, a pyre looking for a match – but why would anyone attack harmless Lűbeck? They wouldn't. Lűbeck would not be a target. Don't even think of it.

And surely the English prided themselves on being *decent*. They liked the word *decent*. They would never sully themselves by bombing women and children.

You were not allowed to think like this. You were not supposed to know that the enemy cared about decency. You were forbidden to listen to the British radio, on pain of escalating penalties. But you did if you could, or you talked to someone who'd heard from someone who kept a clandestine radio in his loft.

The planes circled Königsberg, a V formation. Everyone was hurrahing. Magdalena found herself cheering too.

When the planes had departed, the anthem began again from the beginning. The five hundred boys sang as one boy, one single boy who was the son of the Leader, a boy who would be proud to die for the Leader, one single Leader who incorporated millions of folk, he was the folk and the folk were the Leader, so that each boy represented an atom of the Leader, and Magdalena Arber was an atom too, a lowly girl-atom, having no choice or very little, she was just there to breed new atoms, and the Messerschmitts were protecting Magdalena Arber and all her fellow atoms, by command of the Leader, who held his wing over the people, and so she hurrahed with the rest. You are confused, she told herself, terminally confused, and, when you come down to earth, you cringe and cannot make yourself out.

And now you are hollering the Horst Wessel song, she reflected. And – she glanced aside – Marianne Günther is raising her voice too or at least her lips are moving, and we are all thrilling to the massed voices of German boys and girls together, for we are the future. They sang that millions of people were gazing at them, full of hope ... that slavery would not last forever.

She'd not seen Clem face to face since he left for training. He'd be sharing the compartment with his pals, in high spirits. And don't worry, she reminded herself, they aren't going straight to the killing fields, there's further training to come, in what had been, less than two years ago, Poland.

Now, as the Chief Youth Leader was issuing a final dose of doctrine, Magdalena thought: perhaps Clem's train will be late, and I can still make it if I run like the wind.

Was Clem still the person he'd once been? But who was that? He'd been made of mercury, flowing in various directions, as young folk did, as she herself was still doing. Magdalena was haunted by Dad's shocked face when Clem appeared in the doorway like the ghost of his future self, a cocky ghost, dressed in his uniform, a carapace over the soft body.

Soft, gentle, tender: that was how Magdalena remembered Clem as a child. When Mum died, his presence had brought her unexpected consolation, allowing her to cradle him in her arms and rock him. In so doing she'd rocked her unmothered self and was able to comfort him when he lost his father, leaving Clem forever off-kilter, radically uncertain.

Clem's voice had broken late. At summer camp an older boy had tried to make him eat three live toads, so Clem had whispered to his mother, but he couldn't eat the toads, he couldn't!

'Alive, they were alive!'

But why, why would someone do that?

To make a man of me. Because I'm a milksop and a mummy's boy, that's what I am.

In time Clem had escaped persecution: he'd shot up tall and his voice fell. Bonded at last to comrades, a man-in-the-making, no longer a pariah, he'd swagger home from the Youth Meeting, slandering Jews and gypsies at the top of his voice.

His mother had pleaded, Stop it, Clem, they're just people.

Some of them may be *people* all right, he'd conceded. For all I know. Well, yes, old Süsskind seems decent. But the rest of them, *Pfui*, and he'd held his nose.

What does Clem think now about eating live toads? Magdalena wondered. Mr What's-his-Name ... Vogel ... would have had something to say about *that*! Perhaps he'd have ruled that Clem could eat the toads as long as they'd been anaesthetised first.

Right, this is it. They're winding things up.

Any minute, she'd bolt. If only she'd been able to bring the Auroch with her on the train: she could have made it to the station in three minutes flat.

Here we go: Magda took to her heels, waving to Marianne. They had each other's addresses. She shouldered her way through the applauding crowds, sprinted down side streets to the station, where she spoke to a guard, hardly able to get the words out for breathlessness.

Oh yes, train delayed, miss. Should be coming in on Platform 4.

*

She was babbling, she was jumping up and down, she didn't know what she was saying, only that she could have wept for joy as Clem stepped off the train, straight into her arms. He lifted her off her feet, whirling her round.

He was the same, beautifully the same. Her kith and kin – and she could not help but feel that he looked handsome in his uniform.

Hand in hand they stepped out of the station into the afternoon, and something that had been missing – something you had to subsist without, there was no choice – was restored. Home. The feel of his palm against her palm, the shape and substance of a familial hand which could not have been anyone else's hand, she'd have known its touch if she'd been blind. Clem brought with him the ramshackle tenderness of their makeshift family.

There were messages and gifts in his kitbag from Auntie Ebba. And advice from Dad, although Clem couldn't remember exactly what. Don't do something or other, but also make sure you do something or other else. Clem had stopped off at Lübeck on his way, without warning Max and Ebba.

When he'd appeared at the door, the two of them had burst out crying – and sobbed their hearts out when he left.

'They love you so much,' Magdalena said.

'Yes,' he said simply. 'But it would be better if...'

'If what?'

'Oh, nothing. Never mind, Lena.'

They would have a whole hour together. A mortal hour. Don't squander it, don't let the sand sift through the hourglass too soon, live in the now, we have each other now, Magdalena thought: each grain of time is precious.

In the restaurant, the baby-faced soldier and the BDM girl in collar and tie were ushered to a window seat and served real coffee. Magdalena could hardly bear to let go of her cousin's hands to lift her cup. Ten minutes were spent already.

'I need to tell you something,' Clem said. 'Now don't get all upset, Lena. Everything's dealt with now. It's all behind them, as long as...'

'What is?'

'Well, it's Uncle Max.'

'Is Dad ill? What's the matter with him?' Her cup jangled into the saucer; coffee slopped out.

'It's a blackout infringement. He left a light showing through the kitchen window. Although of course, being Uncle Max, he denies it. Have you ever met anyone as self-righteous as your dad? Self-righteous and totally wrong. He told the block warden it was a trumped-up charge. To his face.'

'And?'

'Well, he had to spend three days in a police cell.'

No.

Her head swarmed with anxieties. Dad would have said: *Don't tell Magdalena, she doesn't need to know*. But surely a blackout offence was not considered so serious that you'd need to be detained? Surely it counted as an oversight, punishable by a fine. So the fact that he'd been taken into custody must mean ... what did it mean? Was it because Dad kept denying the offence to the warden or the policeman? Was it ... some kind of warning, from above?

'How is he?' she asked in a small voice.

'One can only hope he's learnt a salutary lesson.'

Salutary lesson? Joy was withering in her heart. Clem was just eighteen and Dad was fifty-two. It was Dad who should talk about *salutary lessons*. Nowadays boys Clem's age knew it all, they were initiates, masters of the hour, they had the lingo, and looked down on poor mortals who still spoke the old, time-honoured language.

'His braces were taken away.'

'Why?'

'Oh, it's what they do, Lena,' he said loftily. 'Just procedure. Everyone in custody is treated the same – equally. Which is as it should be.'

'But how did he ... keep his trousers up?' she mumbled.

Magdalena felt the scorch of Dad's humiliation. Felt how his pride must have crumbled, as it had crumbled before in the camp. He'd shambled home from Dachau cowed, infused with self-doubt, a twilight soul. And then the demotion so that he was not only answerable to his juniors but also was abased – reduced to a porter trundling a trolley. Now Dad was being dealt another salutary lesson. By a pipsqueak he'd jounced on his knee and who had swum on his fatherly back as he breast-stroked out into the sea at Sylt. And

Ebba had said, *Do be careful, Max – not too far out –* and Dad had said, *Our darling is safe with me.*

Cock of the walk, Clem smiled with one side of his mouth. 'Don't take it to heart, Lena. Mum has put herself in charge of blackout duties from now on.'

'Good.'

Magdalena looked away, at the heraldic plaque on the oak-panelled wall, on which the black Konigsberg eagle, unfurling his wings, stuck out a long, spiky tongue at his enemies. Tears filmed her eyes for Dad's impotent resistance to a world Clem believed he did not understand.

Magdalena thought: *Dad does understand it, he understands it all too well, and that's the whole problem.*

She took in the anxiety in Clem's lopsided grin. To have an uncle you love, who stands in for your father and cherishes you like a son, is something to be grateful for. But to have an uncle who is flaky, who blabs bitterly from time to time, has a salute like a limp fish, and trails an iffy reputation behind him like an unsavoury tail – that was not what an ambitious young man wanted in a close relative.

'Someone needs to keep an eye on Uncle Max,' Clem said. He tapped his fingers on the table. 'It affects us all. Bound to.'

'I'll be going back for a fortnight in July – after the trip to Rominten.'

'Rominten? You mean ... *the* Rominten Heath? Tell!'

He took the bait.

Clem sparkled into life. Of course she understood why. The idea of visiting the famous estate – perhaps to see the great Hermann Goering in person – was an intoxicating thought. In the cinema everyone cheered the newsreel film whenever the Imperial Marshall's flamboyant figure strode into view, flying his honours like a child's balloons – Chief of the Air Force, President of Prussia, State Forester and Hunting Master of Germany – and all the other colourful titles she'd forgotten.

Clem was ecstatic at the thought of a visit to Rominten Heath.

And more than a little envious. Maybe Lena would hear the great man speak – even be noticed by him, the flying ace, so grandly larger than life, in his mediaeval hunting gear and his jewellery, but popular too, genial, with the common touch. You saw him chatting and jesting with ordinary folk, scattering cordial charm.

She filled Clem in on the chance meeting with Dr Vogel on the train, and his connection with Dr Heck and the Berlin Zoo – and how he'd given her a standing invitation to Rominten. She told him how taken Dr Vogel had been by the fact that she'd named her bike the Auroch. He'd been involved in back-breeding cattle, to create the living likeness of the extinct German aurochs.

'No? Really?'

'Yes, really!'

'So he admired my handiwork? He really did?' Clem was a boy again, beaming from ear to ear.

'He did! I told him you'd built it yourself from scratch, out of bits of old military bikes.'

'You told him about me?'

'Pat yourself on the back, Clem: he was impressed. Joked that the machine was an Aryan beast as fierce as Dr Heck's aurochs and bison, and that you'd practised an engineering version of back-breeding! So anyway my teaching mentor, Mr Excorn, was thrilled to think I'd been invited to Rominten Heath. Downside though, Clem, he wants to come along when I take my children – presumably he'd like to share a little limelight.' She pulled a face. 'I prefer to take my children on my own – open the door to nature, the forest and the animal kingdom, in my own way.'

Clem shook his head. 'You haven't changed, have you, Magda? *In my own way!*'

'Well, I don't know,' she said slowly. 'I think I have changed actually, Clem. The more you see, the more you ... wonder.'

'Wonder? Meaning?'

'Well, question.'

'It's not our place to question,' said Clem piously. 'I am a German soldier, Lena. I've made a sacred vow. My life is devoted to the Fatherland. It's not my life anymore. I don't go around *wondering*, let alone *questioning*.' The parrot phrases came tumbling out, as if from one of her infants who'd learnt phrases by rote for a test. 'And I advise you to keep to the rules. The rules are there for a reason.'

Magdalena heard, as clearly as if he'd spoken aloud and at length, what her cousin did not say. He was doing his best to be affectionate and brotherly. But Clem could not quite hide his suspicion that his cousin was nearly as flaky as her father, despite the regulation BDM tie and beret and ochre jacket; despite her profession as teacher. He felt he'd overtaken her, as a male will always overtake a female on the public stage.

A true German man knows everything one needs to know; he bends his will to the greater will of the Leader. She read his face quite clearly. Magdalena was only a girl, and not only that but also a girl tainted with her father's wishy-washy, effeminate, Jew-loving intellectualism. Leaning back in his chair, Clem clicked his fingers at the waiter, for the bill. The old man came scurrying.

A quarter of an hour remained. Deep breaths, Magdalena thought: get close again. You'll regret it afterwards if you don't. As they walked back to the station, she asked about his friends.

'Oh Lena, the best of the best,' Clem said, reviving. 'You know you can rely on one another one hundred per cent. We are brothers. There's nothing we would not do for each other, nothing. You can say hallo to them ... but hang on a moment ... what's this? I can smell something! A son of Israel, no less!' he barked.

He swerved directly into the path of two hurrying passers-by, civilians, halting them in their tracks. You saw how tall Clem was, and at the same time how ludicrously young, with his milky complexion and freckles, as he loomed above the strangers.

'I *beg* your pardon!'

'Oh no, sir, of course not, no,' Clem jabbered, 'of course not. Oh no. I didn't mean you, sir – I meant that fellow over there – he's gone now.'

The stranger thrust his rage and his identity card into Clem's face: *Georg Buchholz, Deputy Head, Labour Service, Königsberg.*

Too late Clem realised his error – his gross, crass, unpardonable error. An error that could affect the whole of his life. How had he not spotted the Party badge? It was glaring like a furious eye from the coat of Georg Buchholz, high official of impeccable lineage and reputation.

'How dare you? And where is your salute?'

Clem slammed to attention.

'Keep your hand up, you clown! How dare you lower your hand? Name?'

Citizens going about their daily business scurried past, giving the confrontation as wide a berth as possible. Clem's chosen victim sauntered round him, surveying him from every angle.

Would Private Arber-Thiessen agree that he was a disgrace to his illustrious uniform and unit? ... 'Speak up, boy! And pass me your documents without lowering your right hand.'

'Truly, sir, I didn't mean you...'

Clem's left hand fumbled out his identity card, his right hand quivered.

Was Private Arber-Thiessen aware that slandering a pure-bred National Socialist as a subhuman ranked with the most egregious of offences?

Did he know there was a penalty for failing to greet a fellow German with the salute?

Did he know anything at all? Well, did he?

'I'm fanatical about ... as the Leader wants...'

Magdalena thought: keep your stupid mouth shut, Clem.

'So you're a fanatic, are you? Do you even know the meaning of the word? Ah! I think I see a policeman over there...'

Magdalena understood – and now it must surely be dawning on Clem – that the victim of public insult must strike back hard, with fangs and claws.

Mr Buchholz's wife came swiftly forward. She soothed, 'The foolish youth will take a major lesson from his mistake, I'm sure?'

'He will, I vouch for him.' Magdalena took her cue from the wife's emphasis on age and inexperience. Frankly her cousin looked about fourteen in his present state of confusion. She could feel Clem cringe as she put her wing over him. 'Clemens has not long joined up. He wants to do the right thing, don't you?'

'Yes.' His hand was still in the air.

Magdalena ploughed on. 'He is desperate to get to the Eastern Front, giving his all for the Fatherland.'

'And who might you be, miss?'

'Magdalena Arber, from Lűbeck, sir. Private Arber-Thiessen's first cousin. Doing my war service as teacher at Alt Schönbek School.'

'All I can say is: let us hope your puerile relative will not find himself firing on his own side on the battlefield. *Heil Hitler!*'

With that, they were gone.

Clem lowered his hand.

Clem pushed back the lock of hair stuck to his sweating forehead. His lips quivered; his eyes with their invisibly pale lashes were tearful. Why be sorry for the idiot? The corrupted idiot. Why be embarrassed for Clem? But part of Magda felt for his humiliation, as if it had been her own. The shamer shamed.

And then again, she was mastered by fear for Clem, fear of him.

'The train,' Magdalena said. She made no comment on what had just passed, as they plunged towards the station.

On the concourse, Clem begged, 'Don't tell anyone at home, don't tell Uncle Max, don't, Lena. For pity's sake.'

'Learn your lesson, Clem.'

'But promise.'

'I do promise – for your mother's sake. She would never sleep again.'

On the platform, gathered outside the open carriage door, Clem's comrades were laughing, slapping each other on the back, in high spirits. There was a bottle of good Cognac waiting for the last leg of the journey.

'You never told us, Clem! Your cousin's a film star!'

Clem began to cheer up, or at least to perform a version of cheerfulness. Without looking into Magdalena's eyes, he pecked her on the cheek in farewell. She heard his loud laugh inside the train, as if he'd dumped the load of his shame on her and left it behind in Königsberg.

Doors slammed all the way down the platform. As the train moved off, the lads leaned out and waved, but she couldn't see Clem.

*

The rustic train hobbled through the Prussian countryside. In bright sunshine, the fields lay green and golden, stretching as far as the eye could see, until they met the darkness of the forests. In the meadows, cattle waded in lush grass that came up to their stomachs. How many shades of green were there in this world? You felt you'd never had occasion to ask such a question before coming east. And the vast, impersonal blueness of the overarching skies. Turquoise lakes, rivers of silver. Red brick farmsteads.

It was peaceful, slumbrous. There was relief in the return journey to Alt Schönbek. The train slowed, swayed, and from the window Magdalena watched a woman in a headscarf turn the crank handle at a village well, until the bucket emerged and she could decant the water into her own bucket. A pair of storks sat sentinel on the massive fortress of their nest, surveying the world below. They had been doing this for thousands of years, season by season.

The train stopped dead, but something in its machinery continued to tick.

Immemorially, the headscarfed woman had been turning this handle. She would continue to do so, day by day, summer and winter, whether in the blaze of sun or in the deep Prussian snow when the water threatened to freeze and ice must be smashed.

Endlessly, the boys were rounded up and sent east. The wild geese migrated. The world was full of murder – over there, beyond the horizon.

A breeze had got up and you saw it stir the ripening corn in acre after acre of rich fields. The cereal flowed, but never in one direction. The wind, at variance with itself, tossed the stalks in eddies and ripples.

The little train began to amble on its way.

What could Magdalena do for Clem, who was so astray? He would have to grow up in his own time – and perhaps had been taught a *salutary lesson* by today's fiasco, curbing his insolence. Or at least the incident might help him conform to the regulation insolence practised by the pack of his brethren.

But my father, she thought. Her heart twisted in her chest. Dad, arrested. She saw him in the police cell, minus his braces.

Nothing was more important than getting home to him, and saying, *I see now, Dad, I am beginning to see.*

11

Siegfried killed a strong young tusker, an enormous lion, a wisent, an elk, four mighty aurochs, a great boar ... You'll never see a better hunting outfit: he wore a surcoat of costly black silk and a splendid hat of sable, and you should have seen the gorgeous silken tassels on his quiver...[15]

Anon, *The Nibelungenlied*, c. 1200

Later, the memory of Rominten would retain the dark and tainted, but gilded, aura of a dream. Or rather, a film. Yes, a film. The leading man was the world-straddling Master Huntsman in his finery. Huge and globular, the Imperial Marshall strode into the glade with his retinue, raising a gracious hand to guests and cameras. An amenable flippancy accompanied – and capriciously undermined – his every grandiose gesture. *I am a comic act, a charlatan, a porcine waddler, but I will murder any one of you who acknowledges it.*

The circle of honoured guests, including Magdalena and her children, stood where they had been positioned, an audience waiting to be captivated.

Sunlight filtered through the sway of the trees and pooled in the clearing, washing to and fro on the pine-needled ground. Magdalena's ten hand-picked pupils – five boys and five girls – waited patiently, immaculate in their Hitler Youth uniforms. She'd been required to select children primarily for blondness and bearing – the boys for tallness and the girls for prettiness. But also, and in practical terms equally important, they were chosen for the ability to stand still and retain their urine. Julia must go with you, she cannot miss this opportunity, Ruth had pleaded. Poor Ruth, who seemed at times half deranged by dread and sleeplessness. And though Julia was neither the blondest nor the most reliable of pupils, and despite the fact that one disliked special pleading, Magdalena had complied. Who could refuse Ruth anything, now that her life had shrunk to the sick bed of the weaker twin?

The train ride through mountains and valleys had been sheer poetry. Finally, there was a wooden arch, bearing a swastika, runes and SS-signs engraved 'Rominten Heath Nature Park'. An official limousine had met the children's train, carrying the party to the imperial hunting estate, set in one hundred square miles of the game reserve. Silent with awe, they'd been driven over the Deer Bridge, past the Royal Hunting Lodge, built in the Norwegian style from fir wood, a galleon sailing on a sea of ancient forest trees.

Into the enchanted sylvan world, the children had been led by boys of the Hermann Goering Division with their white collar tabs, to the glade where a beaming Chief Forester in full array was waiting, flanked by Dr Vogel and a group of scientists. The Chief Forester had crowned the five girls with floral garlands, and fixed sprays of fir on to the boys' shirts.

'Stand tall, you honoured boys and girls! For you are The Leader's children and the Imperial Marshall's guests of honour!'

Magdalena felt Julia's excited hand creep into her own; squeeze and let go.

The antlered kill had been laid out on the ground for the Imperial Marshall's ritual inspection – a row of six revered creatures, sacrificed to a higher god. The children, offspring of foresters and farmers, were familiar with the sight of dead prey, but these were of formidable size. The stags' eyes were half closed. Excess blood had been wiped from their wounds. Their faces, to Magdalena's eye, appeared soft and tender.

But each face, as Dr Vogel explained to her, would be stripped from the decapitated head, the bone macerated, degreased, dried and sunned, so that the skull with its branching rack could be mounted on a wall, a testament to the hunter's peerless power. The horn, by the way, is deciduous, he pointed out – was Miss Arber aware of this? – like tree branches.

'Antlers are shed year by year. There is something – I don't know: what would you call it? – *mystical* about this German forest world. Some power, long hidden, is being resurrected. Do you feel that, Miss Arber – you who are so sensitive to wildlife and nature? You do? I felt that you would. German science and German mysticism, as you know, go hand in hand now – thanks in great part to our Imperial Marshall.

'Later I shall ask you about the wonderful mechanical Auroch you introduced me to! You see, I have remembered! And maybe there'll be a viewing of the living aurochs we've bred!'

But now everyone must keep quiet. Green-suited foresters, in plumed felt hats and high boots, came marching into the glade, positioning themselves in a semi-circle. Musicians blew their antique hunting horns. In these forests, Magdalena thought, the Romans had been vanquished by the Teutons. Bison and auroch had roamed. Royalty had hunted; heroes had fought.

The Chief Forester now addressed the onlookers.

'Six of the noblest stags in the world, bred in the most royally German of primeval forests, cared for by the most expert of German foresters, are laid out before you. For the last time, these red bucks have bellowed their mating status; clashed antlers and injected their sperm. These creatures have done this for Germany, and will live on through generation after generation, forever evolving in majesty, in their royal progeny.

'The German animals before you have shown themselves worthy of being killed by German hunters!

'The antlers of these master-stags are of nearly unequalled mass and grandeur. They've all been carefully measured and documented – and nobody here,' the Chief Forester guaranteed, 'will be surprised to learn that the Imperial Marshall shot the greatest of these, the stag named the Matador!'

Magdalena looked at the Matador. He lay with the underside of his head on the ground, as if sunk in a pensive quandary.

'And in a minute' – the Chief Forester indicated the path – 'the Imperial Marshall will appear to claim his trophy!'

The dead stags waited. The foresters waited. The men with the cine-cameras adjusted lenses and angles for the last time. The honoured guests waited. The children waited.

But Julia Daschke did not wait.

Without warning the child broke ranks and went skipping off round the circle, blithe, devil-may-care, a law unto herself. Magdalena saw too late that she should have held on tight to Julia's hand. She should have foreseen.

All eyes followed the skipping dancer. Aware of her audience, Julia began to show off, twirling and leaping. Her coppery hair rayed out in the sun and her floral crown came adrift.

It was all right, everyone was laughing and clapping. They think it's planned, Magdalena realised, and made ready to grab Julia when she got round.

'Hold my hand, and don't you dare let go,' she hissed.

Julia smirked.

The musicians blew their horns.

And 'Siegfried' arrived with his entourage. His outfit was sumptuous, displaying the girth and glory of a mighty prince. A white silk shirt billowed along his arms, topped with a green leather waistcoat, buffed to a high shine. A hunting knife was stuck in his belt. In his high boots he strode forward with a curious daintiness for one so great.

Cameras rolled. The Imperial Marshall examined the kill, checking the stags' antlers with knowing fingers, commenting on their endowments and scrutinising the measurements supplied by his foresters. He handed his gun to a retainer; another passed the Imperial Marshall his personal cine-camera.

'Prepare to be shot!' Magdalena heard witty Hermann quip, as he stepped with a stalker's delicacy towards the cameramen, filming the filmers, to everyone's amusement.

Now he spared a few minutes for the little angels, patting each on the head, greeting Julia as a dear little nixie, a water-sprite escaped from the River Rhine. Magdalena saw the shine of gold rings on the big hand that stroked Julia's cheek and pinched her under the chin. A waft of perfume drifted from the handkerchief with which he wiped his forehead. He had a few words for any child who dared speak to him.

'Yes, little man, you may hold my hunting knife just for a moment, if the gracious lady your teacher permits?' He drew it from its scabbard, the hilt bulging with jewels. 'Careful now, that's the way. Would you like one of your own?'

'Oh yes please, sir!'

Laughter all round. Then off Siegfried swept, with a farewell salute and a final grin. Magdalena saw his face change in the moment of turning away, setting hard.

They heard a limousine start up. That was it. What now?

'A feast is laid on for the Imperial Marshall's special guests,' said Dr Vogel. 'Venison and wild boar sausage. And you will never have tasted any meat as excellent in your entire lives.'

They sat on rustic benches near tables groaning with food. As the children gorged and chattered, Dr Vogel smiled upon them, glad to have been able to arrange the visit. He chatted indulgently with Magdalena, enquiring about her work, feeding her titbits of news of Dr Heck's work in the Berlin Zoo. To her relief, his attention was constantly diverted by colleagues, releasing Magdalena to listen in to the voices of Hermann Goering's elite guests – the anatomist from Posen, the SS general with a chestful of medals, the zoologists.

Magnificent occasion! Splendid beasts! And how generous of the Imperial Marshall to make time for us all, since Rominten is now his HQ for the war in the east.

It will all be over by Christmas ... the actual fighting, that is, bar the mopping up ... breadbasket of the east ... oilwells ... industrial plant...

We'll crucify Comrade Stalin!

'Ah, Miss Arber, isn't it? Dr Vogel mentioned you. My name is Hallervorden. What dear little children – and this is the maiden who danced so charmingly for us! And her name? ... How do you do, Miss Julia! Your dance was most graceful.'

Julia's mouth was stuffed with venison. Her reply was unintelligible. The speaker drifted off.

What will they call Russia when it's conquered?

Some very good brains came in from Buchenwald last week...

We ate some of the most delicious strawberries ... superabundant in the Warthegau...

Magdalena vaguely wondered about the brains.

Ah! Białowieża! Primeval forest. The Imperial Marshall's sacred land. The last true European wilderness ... Bison, elk, aurochs ... and how do we know that there are no mastodons roaming in its dark viscera?

It is every German's dream.

What kind of brains were delivered? she wondered as she moved round offering bread to her charges. For scientific anatomisation, presumably.

And had mastodons actually lived in forests? She urged the youngsters to eat slowly and not shovel the food in, for there was plenty to go round. Finish, she suggested hopefully, when you have had enough.

She especially didn't want anyone to throw up on the train.

We get some wonderfully interesting specimens. Children, especially.

There was wonderful material among these brains, beautiful mental defectives, malformation, and early infantile disease.

Oh yes, our new institute in Posen is shaping up remarkably well. We've a crematorium in the basement ... two wagons of Polish ash were taken away just yesterday ... outside my office, the robinias are blooming cheerfully...

That was one of the anatomists. He'd been pointed out as Dr Hermann Voss, who was turning the old Polish city institution into a centre for German science. She was struck by the look of ... what would you call it? ... woe? that settled on his face whenever he stopped speaking. For, oh, he missed Leipzig, he couldn't help admitting to a colleague, and often would sit at his open window to commune with the moon, and its essential loneliness.

Oh yes, we sampled the bison. Decidedly chewy. Strange taste ... pungent, savoury, a bit like cheese – you know, that Austrian smoked cheese, forget the name – but there's a musky kind of sweetness. And the flesh is bright red!

Well, of course, an animal tastes of whatever it eats ... wild garlic and sorrel ... ash bark and linden seeds ... plants that only grow together in primeval forest ... and then you get an explosion of taste on your tongue...

Smoked bison's lung! Now there's a dish!

They have no shoes, they are uncivilised.

Dr Vogel was back, with the Master Forester in tow.

'This young lady-teacher named her bicycle the Auroch! If you saw it, you'd understand why!'

'Do you have aurochs at Rominten?' Magdalena asked.

'Well, we introduced twenty-two of the Heck back-bred aurochs. But you won't actually see one today, Miss Arber. No sooner had they arrived, than the aurochs got down to the serious business of destroying the habitat. Yes, really! They tore the trees apart! They ransacked the deer fodder. They'd chase you down, Miss Arber, as soon as look at you. So we keep them penned in their own area, where – I can tell you – they're not happy! Once we've fully secured Białowieża, most of them will be introduced there. It's their native habitat, you see. They'll be, so to speak, going home.'

'Like us, of course, the aurochs are fiercely German, in need of living space,' said Dr Vogel with a twinkle. He clapped his hands. 'Would you children like to visit a mighty forest one day? A forest that makes even Rominten seem like a garden?'

'Yes, sir!'

'Well, children,' said the Master Forester, 'our armies have captured such a forest! How long do you think it took?'

'A year, sir?'

'No!'

'Five years, sir?'

'It took five days flat! That is what a German army can achieve.

Now, I want you to imagine this forest. Dark, full of black bogs, aspens and alder and birch and elm, all ancient ... a charnel house of rotting oaks hundreds of years old... *What is a charnel house? you ask, little girl with the wondering eyes* ... ah, forgive me, I'm using grown-up words, you don't need to know that ... let's think of ... of gingerbread houses instead ... shall we? ... there may be a gingerbread house, mightn't there, and Hansel and Gretel, and a wicked witch, who knows?'

'I would stick her in her own cooking pot and boil her alive!'

The Master Forester had sent their childish imaginations helter-skelter down a diversion, in his effort to distract from the charnel house of his metaphor. Magdalena was suddenly weary. The children had eaten their fill. She glanced at her watch: not quite time, but the limousine would surely be ready.

As she led the children, walking two by two, hand in hand, away from the glade, guests waved and called out in farewell. And the children, charmingly, waved back, returning the good wishes in a chorus.

'You did well, Magdalena,' whispered Dr Vogel. 'And I'm sure the Imperial Marshall was impressed. I was proud of my protégés. I shall report in glowing terms to your mentor. And my greetings to your respected father.'

He would visit the school at Alt Schönbek on his next trip to East Prussia, Dr Vogel promised, handing Magdalena into the car. Would she like that? Oh good! Nothing was more important than to cultivate the minds of the coming generation. He'd gladly address the children on any zoological topic of her choice, linking science with folklore. No hurry to choose: think about it and let him know.

Magdalena sank back into the plush upholstery. His face had come a fraction too close and she'd felt his breath on her cheek. Dr Vogel had called her by her Christian name. She hadn't recoiled; in fact she'd smiled into his face. Why had she done that? Why did she keep smiling and agreeing when she felt like throwing up? Embarrassment? Probably. Or was it the flattered need to ingratiate herself further with a mentor who might assist with her future career? As the car took off, she shivered.

The good-looking young SS driver grinned at her in the mirror. 'You all right, miss?'

'Fine, thank you.'

'Good. Have a comfortable journey. We've plenty of time. Have the children enjoyed themselves at Rominten?'

They chatted on and off throughout the drive. The driver was originally from Hildesheim: nice enough place to grow up. But now, with the SS, he could see the world.

He was the right age. His eyes said he liked her. And Magda knew he'd ask to keep in touch and see her again. As was perfectly natural. She wasn't specially tempted, but it made her wonder: could a man like Vogel have designs on her? He was middle-aged, despite his plumply unlined face. You thought of him as a kind of nomadic husband on an elastic leash, attached to a Lady-Wife ... Magda could see Lady-Wife in her mind's eye ... she'd earned the Mother's Cross of Honour by producing a quiverful of bona fide Aryan children.

Perhaps Vogel made a habit of waylaying young female acolytes on his travels; told them tales about anaesthetising the earthworms; marched off with their bikes on dark station platforms; enticed them with invitations to Berlin Zoo or Carinhall. And at a certain point the acolytes would feel they could not say no.

Or this suspicion might be entirely unjust.

'My name is Werner,' said the tall youth, pushing a scrap of paper with a unit address into her hand. 'It has been a pleasure to meet you, Miss Arber. And I hope we'll meet again.'

*

On the train, the children passed out. Up since the early hours, they'd effervesced with excitement throughout the eventful day, wolfed a heavy meal, seen the big fat man and the dead stags – and now it was home time. The compartment seemed to sough with the rhythm of their breathing. Julia had laid her head on Magdalena's lap and was so deeply asleep that she couldn't be roused when they arrived. She had to be carried on to the platform. Mr Kallweit's cart was there to meet them and to drop each child at home. Everything had gone like clockwork. A thick veil of dusk had fallen over Alt Schönbek and a sickle moon was waxing.

Magdalena and Julia were the last to be dropped off. Julia, now wide awake, skipped up the steps to her home, found the door open and raced in, calling for her mother.

No voice replied. The rooms were dark. Flora's bed was empty.

Julia searched under the bed and in the wardrobe; thundered downstairs to the living room and kitchen; ran back again upstairs to her mother's bedroom, up to Magdalena's attic, down to the basement.

'Julia – darling – it's all right, look, there's a note from Mummy. She's gone to the hospital about Flora's poorly ear. She needs the nasty stuff draining out of it. Mummy will be back soon.'

'When is soon? When?'

'I don't know, perhaps tomorrow, but she has sent you a big hug and a kiss – don't cry now – Mummy asks you to be a good girl for Magda and not to worry. Come here, love, let me give you Mummy's kiss. I am here, I am here.'

Julia stamped her foot. 'I – want – Flora! I – want – Mummy!'

Magdalena poured milk for Julia, her hand trembling. The past day had degraded into a folksy carnival in the woods, mummery, flummery, where costumed performers cavorted in garish colours under an artificial light. Like actors in Dad's one-man *Nibelungen* show, but less talented than Dad, who played for laughs. The day behind her was dust and ashes.

'The milk's off, ugh, I can't drink it,' said Julia, shaking her head, handing back the glass.

Magdalena sniffed. 'It isn't off, darling. It's fine. Let me taste it.'

The milk really was not off. The cream at the top was thick with fatty goodness.

'Would you like to try again? Or shall Magda drink it?'

Julia took the glass, grumbling, but showed her trust by drinking it all off in one swig. She allowed Magdalena to undress and wash her, to kneel for her goodnight prayer and the 'Lovely Words' she repeated with her mother every night. Magdalena had heard them so often that she had no trouble remembering them:

Night night, sleep tight.
Always love you and kiss you.
Be my best friend.
Look forward to seeing you in the morning.

The words must be spoken slowly and in the correct order, like a blessing, every single night of the twins' lives. In the weave of these words, the child would be held and safeguarded, though words were frailer than links in a daisy chain.

Once Julia had dropped off to sleep, Magdalena reread the note. Flora's temperature had shot up, she was burning, her cough was like a dog barking and there was a livid rash all over her body. In panic, Ruth had called the doctor from Renate's phone. He'd come at once. Flora must be admitted to hospital as an emergency. If her eardrum were not lanced and her sepsis went untreated, there was no hope of survival. No option. Ruth would accompany them. Did not know when she'd be back.

'Please, Magda, take care of Julia for me.'

Howling in the night.

Magdalena shot out of her first sleep, taking it for the whining of a siren, there must be a raid, but no, it was human wailing, and she rushed in, lifted Julia and brought her back to her own bed, where somehow or other the child's presence was a comfort.

12

Into every house I enter, I will enter to help the sick, and I will abstain from all intentional wrong-doing and harm.[16]
The Hippocratic Oath

Look here now, boys, if you're going to kill all these people at least take the brains out, so that the material can be utilised![17]
Dr Julius Hallervorden

Julia's face filled Magdalena's view for three days, eclipsing almost everything beyond the bounds of that horizon. Refusing to sleep in her own bed, the child homed in on her sister's room and occupied Flora's place. She linked her arms softly round Magdalena's neck, giving and calling forth tenderness. Tired and fraught as she was, Magdalena was captivated. *This must be how you'd feel towards children of your own.* There was much Julia did not say but which Magdalena clearly heard.

When Julia wet the bed in the night, Magdalena would be alerted by whimpering sounds. The child wouldn't be properly awake, just tossing around, dreaming. Magdalena lifted her, stripped the sheets and nightgown, wiped the rubber under-sheet and remade the bed, laying Julia back in fresh sheets. She'd dump the bundle in the copper to soak till morning.

Julia, taking comfort and courage, and seeing that little mutinies and soulful sulks had no effect, seemed to relax. She played with Flora's doll, Helga. In the wild hurry of departure, Ruth had picked up Julia's doll instead.

Renate put her head round the door: Ruth had phoned to say she'd be home shortly.

How had she sounded? How was Flora? Was Flora being discharged and coming home with Ruth?

Renate couldn't be sure. Poor Ruth was upset and gabbling.

When was shortly? Magdalena had temporarily taken over Ruth's mothering; even wore the floral apron with the large catch-all pocket. Willingly, yes, of course, and out of affection as well as duty. At the same time, half her heart clamoured for freedom. The summer break was Magda's own time; she needed to go home, to reassure herself about Dad and Ebba. Just to occupy the familiar spaces of childhood. I can make a difference now, she thought, to Dad – and I can listen to him as I never did before. I can take wisdom and fortitude from Ebba.

But how can I bear to leave you? she asked herself, looking into the blue-green trustfulness of Julia's eyes. She crossed and recrossed the invisible divide between the two incompatible halves of her spirit. For she couldn't bear to leave the child.

Meanwhile she boiled up two kettles, poured the steaming water on the sheets and, once it had cooled down, pummelled them. Fed them through the mangle. Then out into hot sunshine.

The garden was a riot of colour, lilies and lavender buzzing with a drowse of bees. Magdalena spread the sheets on the warm grass to bleach and dry in the scented air. Julia helped by spreading pillowcases on the hedge; then sat on the cherry tree swing, with Helga on her lap, quite placid, and for that reason not quite herself.

'Come on, cherub. Sit on Magda's knee and see how high we can swing, you, me and Helga.'

Julia climbed up, craned her neck to observe a pony and cart approaching – and then: 'Look! They're back! Mummy, it's Mummy! They're back! Flora! Put me down, Magda, put me down!'

In a moment Ruth was at the gate, gathering her daughter into her arms, thanking Magdalena, laughing, weeping. Julia clung, then wriggled to get down.

She raced out of the gate into the street. Stared right and left, wailing Flora's name.

'She's coming later,' Ruth told her. 'Don't worry.'
'When? When?'

Ruth had been forced to leave Flora at the surgical ward of Königsberg Hospital, to have her ear drained and the sepsis treated. She hadn't been allowed inside the ward, because of infection, they're very careful, but the Sister was kind and explained everything.

It was all right, she assured Flora's twin, perfectly all right: their darling was definitely beginning to recover, she'd be home in no time. Ruth would be called to collect her, and they'd all be together again like peas in a pod. Ruth looked exhausted. Dark rings round her eyes.

'How has she been?' she asked Magdalena that evening, once they'd got Julia into bed.

'Well – pining, of course, Ruth, for you and Flora. Not quite herself. But she'll be so much better now you're here.'

'They've never been apart – all their lives. They've been like this.' Ruth clasped her hands, lacing her fingers together. 'Even when they're not looking at each other, they are present to one another.'

'I know. They cleave to one another. And now they're cloven.'

Ruth took her hands in both of hers. 'Thank you, Magda, for everything. I hope you know what it means to us. You're like a sister to me. I'll be forever in your debt.'

There was no debt, none in the world, Magdalena assured her. In a couple of days, allowing for things to settle down (Renate could come in, she would be glad to help if Ruth needed someone), Magda felt she could leave for Lűbeck. And return to find the Daschke family whole again. And this time she would really pull her weight in helping Flora to overcome her difficulties. She would teach her to speak clearly and perhaps – why not? – to read simple words, starting with her own name. And to count. And to walk better. So that nobody would say, ever again, *Here comes the idiot Daschke girl*.

An official letter arrived two days later. Ruth tore open the envelope. Stifled a shriek.

Flora had been removed to Tapiau Provincial Asylum, for investigation of *other aspects of her health*. Ruth was assured that they had all the appropriate medications at Tapiau; the infection was being treated, and Flora's temperature was beginning to come down. There was no cause for alarm.

Alarm? No cause? Together they read the letter over and over. Magdalena thought: Ruth is being deceived. But would a hospital deceive a mother? It was unthinkable.

The doorbell sounded. Dr Littmann. 'May I trespass, ladies?'

He settled down in an easy chair, accepting a cup of coffee, as if he had all the time in the world. He glanced round the room, admiring the flowers; asked after Julia. Magdalena, keeping Ruth company on the couch, noticed how relaxed the doctor appeared, or wished to appear, crossing one leg over the other, dressed in a tweedy jacket, casually elegant these days, as if he had come up in the world. You could hardly help but respond to his broad, avuncular smile.

'I know you've been contacted by Tapiau – that's the letter in your hand, if I'm not mistaken? – so I'm here to fill you in. I absolutely don't want you to worry, Ruth. In fact I forbid it! While your little Flora is at the facility...'

'But why have they taken her there? Why? How long will it be?'

'As long as it takes, I'm afraid, to give her the best possible chance to recover fully from this nasty infection and set her on her feet. This disease, make no bones about it, was life-threatening. And I won't conceal the fact that you should have called me earlier, a good deal earlier. But Flora is making good progress, I could see that when I looked in. While she's with us...'

'Who are *us*?'

'While she's with us, my dear Ruth – that is, at the Tapiau neurological clinic to which I now have the honour to be affiliated – because of my specialist research, yes, my twin research, and we're working in tandem with the great Dr Voss of Posen! – have you heard of Dr Voss? – no? – ah, you have, Miss Arber! You've *met* Dr

Voss, my goodness me ... met him personally ... at Rominten? You were invited to Rominten? With your pupils? What an honour, you'll have to tell me about it ... but anyway, setting that aside, where was I? – we at Tapiau...'

How grand the doctor sounded, pluming himself upon his scientific standing, launching his convoluted sentences that led nowhere. Magdalena studied him, a middle-aged local general practitioner who could hardly get over how high he was flying, so late in life. Magdalena remembered Ruth describing Dr Littmann as being on his high horse. And here he was, yes, balancing on his steed, rather nervously.

And actually, she thought, the steed was an ass.

'We at Tapiau are taking the chance, while we have your little mite with us, and are treating her sepsis ... to conduct tests on Flora's overall health, including of course her mental health. You will be glad of this in the end, I promise you that, Ruth. Yes, truly, you will. Now, don't look like that, my dear! Have I ever let you down? Now, have I?'

Ruth's suspicious face contradicted her: 'No.'

'Exactly. And now I'm going to have to get a bit technical, so forgive me!'

Advanced experiments were being conducted by a team of neurologists, in which he himself had the honour to participate. The outcome might well turn out to benefit Flora as well as the race as a whole. German science in the present day had reached undreamt-of heights. Scientists had access to research material and data they never had the means to compile in the past. They now possessed, thanks to the genius of the Leader and his promotion of German science, machinery unsurpassed by and indeed unimaginable to earlier generations.

'But how is my Flora?' Ruth broke in. 'Is she distressed? Is she upset about her doll? – I left the wrong doll with her! Is she asking for me? Flora needs me, you don't seem to understand. When can I visit?'

He sat forward, put down his cup, assured Ruth that Flora was comfortable. She was content with the doll that went with her. In any case she was kept nice and sleepy; was fed as much as she needed.

'But…'

'Look here, I will come back,' Dr Littmann assured Ruth, rising from his chair, taking her hand for a moment, with a kindly smile, 'as soon as there's anything of significance to tell you. I promise. And meanwhile, do not distress yourself. Young Flora is in the safest of safe hands. We ask that relatives defer their visits, to give our patients a chance to accommodate.'

The polysyllable *accommodate* jangled round Magda's head. And the phrase *nice and sleepy.*

Accommodate? How was Flora expected to do that? She didn't even have her familiar doll with her. Magdalena ran to fetch Helga, begging the doctor to give it to Flora when he next visited.

'Yes, yes, Dr Littmann, please,' said Ruth. 'The doll's name is Helga. You will give it to her, won't you?'

He raised his eyebrows, assented, took the doll and vanished.

Now that her mother was home, Julia followed her around the house, grabbed at her clothing, grizzled, and knocked on the door whenever Ruth secluded herself, constantly asking where Helga was. On two occasions Ruth lost her temper and raised her voice. *Give me a moment's peace, can't you?* Magdalena heard her telling her daughter to *grow up!* In response Julia staged a tantrum, throwing a glass at the mirror. Ruth went storming off. *Now look what you've done!*

Magda heard Ruth sobbing in her bedroom while Julia sobbed in the kitchen. She soothed Julia, brushed up the shards of glass, wrapped them in newspaper, took the child into the garden and pushed her on the swing.

Ruth emerged with red eyes and begged her daughter's pardon. Julia smacked her mother's arm, more out of a sense of justice than a desire to hurt. When Ruth offered the other hand, the child kissed it instead.

Magdalena had the ridiculous idea that she should make it her business to take the train to Tapiau, wangle her way in and see with her own eyes how Flora was faring amongst the data and the unsurpassed machinery.

Perhaps I should do that, she thought. Before I go home to Lűbeck. Maybe I owe this to Flora. I let her down.

As too often in her life, Magdalena had promised more than she'd accomplished, preening herself on the thought that she, a loving and loyal teacher (as Miss Heller had been to her), could draw out Flora's hidden intelligence. She would prove to the powers-that-be that Flora was not feeble-minded, not subnormal. The moment she'd settled on this plan, she deferred her action. For what do I know, she thought, about the mind? And who was Magdalena Arber to quarrel with the experts? This critique seemed to originate outside herself, spoken in a tone of reproof, a male voice of authority. We are at war, the internalised voice said. This is a global crisis. Germany is fighting not only for its honour but also its life! You have your humble allotted place, and an obligatory contribution to make. Just get on with it.

In any case, what had idealistic Magdalena achieved so far for Flora? Visited herself by a nasty cold, she'd thought, *Oh poor me! I've got tonsillitis! I've got no voice! I have to do all this preparation and marking!* She'd been sorry for herself for having to add Ruth's pupils to her own. Then there was the excitement of the farm visit and Rominten. When Flora had got ill, Magda left her to Ruth to nurse.

But what else could she have done? After all, Magdalena was just one person. What can one woman do? She needed to see Dad and Auntie Ebba, and pour it all out, and be open to their advice.

And Dad would speak merciful words: *You can't take the whole world on your shoulders.*

Ebba would say: *Listen to the still, small voice. Then you will know.*

Taking a deep breath, Magda did her best to comfort and compose Ruth, and to nurture Julia, giving the mother a chance to rest. She offered Julia a lovely walk in the forest – they'd take a picnic and climb trees – just the two of them – wouldn't she love that?

They could go to Miss von Laulitz's farm and see the piggies! What about riding there on the Auroch? She could pad the bar with a coat for Julia to ride. It would be the best fun. What about it?

Julia shook her head. 'Only if Mummy comes.'

She stuck her thumb in her mouth. Magdalena removed the thumb, which Julia restored when Magda's back was turned. The child's plan, Magda saw, was to stay and guard her mother, in case she tried to escape again.

*

Within two days, back came the doctor, as good as his word, with assurances of Flora's continuing improvement, and requesting ('now I think of it, since I'm here, Ruth'), to examine Julia's head, with a view to possible X-ray.

'*Julia's* head?' demanded Ruth, shrinking into herself. 'You want to examine *Julia's* head?'

Dr Littmann proposed to take the elder twin to the X-ray department at Tapiau for a brief visit – 'Just brief, you know – a quick in-and-out job' – to gauge whether her skull matched in any respect the unusual features detected in Flora's cranium.

'Now listen ... *listen*, Ruth, and don't start working yourself up into one of your states! It will be the business of half an hour's visit – in my car – you can come along with us for the jaunt.'

Different as the Daschke twins appeared, they may well have started out from a single fertilised *ovum* – monozygotic. Flora's cranium exhibited an interesting homoplastic osteoma, or exostosis. A lump, or bump, to the layman! Dr Littmann and his eminent colleagues wished to see whether there might exist, or might *once* have existed, a similar, or indeed identical, osteoma or exostasis – or possibly the undeveloped *potential* for such – on the viable twin's cranium. A feature that had been missed earlier.

'Viable? The viable twin? Did you say viable?'

The dormant volcano in Ruth's head exploded. She flushed,

jumping up from her chair. No, Magdalena thought, seeing the expression on her friend's face; that is not the way. We have to use our brains here. She laid a hand on Ruth's wrist but Ruth shook it off. For a moment Magdalena thought – and perhaps the doctor imagined too, for he drew back – that Ruth was about to strike him.

Both her daughters were viable! Are you viable? Am I? What about God? Is God viable? Is Jesus Christ? And Ruth must have Flora home. Now, today, not next week.

'Only if you want to endanger her survival, Ruth.'

Ruth sank back down in her chair.

Dr Littmann smiled ruefully at her outburst, which after all was hardly unexpected. He congratulated Ruth on being a devoted mother, but one whose heart (despite her vocation as a teacher) had a tendency to overrule her reason. And the emotions of ladies can be hysterical.

'Release my little girl,' demanded Ruth, but then in a quailing voice: 'please.'

All in good time, Flora could be released. It was not up to him, in any case. His tone was frigid. Dr Littmann had had enough.

To accelerate Flora's discharge, Ruth would be wise to allow the doctor *manually* to examine Julia's skull? He could do that now. Ruth was welcome to remain in the room while this procedure was undertaken. And Miss Arber too, by all means. It would take only a couple of minutes.

Sweat beaded on Ruth's forehead. 'No, and I want her sister back home immediately.'

'Alas, that will not be possible yet awhile.'

'I see what you're doing!' Ruth lost all control. 'I see it all – you don't fool me! You've taken one daughter, and now you're trying to take the other one – to advance your own career – in some way – I shall complain, I warn you, I have rights, I'll go directly to the Leader, our Leader will listen to a mother, the Leader knows how to value mothers ... and then what will you do at your beloved Tapiau?'

'My goodness me,' Littmann said. 'I'm afraid you are not well, Ruth.'

'I am well. I can *see* now.'

He shook his head, standing to his full height, ready to depart with his immediate wish unfulfilled, but not prepared to leave without shooting an arrow back into the mother's heart where it might fester, and perhaps produce the desired effect.

'Not at all well,' he repeated. 'Mentally. You know that really, my dear Ruth.'

'Mrs Daschke to you! I want my daughter home, Dr Littmann, and I will have her.'

'Excuse me, *Mrs Daschke*! Speaking now as your own physician ... I would say this: your mind is ... well, how can I put it? ... not functioning appropriately in the real world. I can give you something to help.'

'What, like a nice dose of arsenic?'

'This behaviour is frankly pathological.'

'Pathological!' Ruth spat. 'Yes, good word. Pathological. But not pathological on my side. I want my daughter back. Now. And I will have my Flora back if it kills me. Oh and, by the way, you took an oath. The Hippocratic Oath. Would you like me to remind you of it in Greek?'

As Littmann turned towards the door, Magdalena saw Ruth wheel round symmetrically in the opposite direction, clamping both hands over her mouth, as if to cram the words of revolt back into herself. *What have I said? What have I done?*

Too late. The words had rushed out in a mob, penetrated the enemy's ears, registered in his brain: they could never be unsaid.

Where would those words go next? Out through his hand, ink on paper, a version would travel along the web of authority, attested, signed for, rubber-stamped. What would they trigger if transcribed and sent to some committee of something or other with inconceivable consequences?

Magdalena asked herself this as she showed Littmann out.

'I'll be back to check on Mrs Daschke,' he promised. His usually sallow face was red. His Party badge was level with Magda's eyes.

'May I have a word, Dr Littmann?'

He glanced at his watch.

'It won't take a minute.'

'Very well. I must be at the Institute within the hour, but I can spare you five minutes.'

Magdalena walked with him to his car.

'I just wanted to say, Dr Littmann, that in my opinion – in my humble opinion – Mrs Daschke is experiencing deep grief, natural grief, as I'm sure we all would in her circumstances, I mean all mothers, and I imagine many fathers too? Not sleeping, you know, and the worry, and of course, her husband is … he gave his life in Poland for the Fatherland … the wound is still so raw, and she has carried on valiantly with her work, so I do hope… And maybe I could put it like this – the fact that Mrs Daschke can speak to you in this way, from the heart, as it were – which seems, well, out of order, and disrespectful – it actually shows how much she believes in you.'

This brainwave, which had occurred to Magdalena as she spoke, seemed to pique Littmann's interest. He peered amusedly into her face.

'How so?'

'It shows she trusts you, if I may say so, as … one of the oldest friends of her family. She trusts you as I might trust my parents, for instance, to bear with me if I were … under huge pressure … and burst out in my … well, my rage of grief. She knows you, of all people, will not condemn her…'

He reached for Magdalena's hand and held it. He said he hoped that, if *he* were ever in trouble, he might have a friend as eloquent to speak for him.

'But try to bring your colleague down to earth, Miss Arber,' he advised quietly, bending his head. 'Nobody can throw accusations and insults around like that. But nobody. My dear young lady, this behaviour is a form of suicide.'

This last word numbed her. His left hand was still holding Magda's right. Feeling its tremor, he squeezed gently.

'Forgive me,' he said. 'But I can see that you understand what I'm saying. You are wise beyond your years, Miss Arber. I can overlook the scene we've just witnessed, just this once.'

'Thank you.'

Give me back my hand.

'Let us agree to excuse this regrettable scene ... although the threat to complain to our great Leader ... well, there cannot be any more of *that*. And besides, it is wide of the mark. Our Leader has initiated, and takes the greatest interest in, our genetic research. It is not a side issue but germane to his plans for the new Europe we are creating. Perhaps you can use your powers of persuasion to settle Mrs Daschke's mind and counsel her to cooperate? When I visit again, I hope we can discuss progress. You and I.'

*

'Whose skull is safe in this world?' Ruth raged, raved, as she grasped the neck of the bottle, to pour the red liquor down her gullet.

13

> Their voices, my God, their voices! Again and again, I am overwhelmed by all that they betray. Their deadness ... The stinking corpse of a *vox humana!*[18]
>
> Theodor Haecker, *Journal in the Night,* April 1940

Dr Goebbels was attacking Magdalena's new radio, lashing it with his fury, but the radio was fighting back. The crackling effect was reinforced by blizzards of interference, for it was one of the cheap models nicknamed *Goebbels' Snout.* The best you could say for this flimsy fabrication of Bakelite, cardboard and cloth was that it made a noise. The vulpine face and rigid gestures of the Imperial Propaganda Minister were all visible to your mind's eye. The wagging forefinger, the pumping arm, the rancorous stare.

His voice came and went, and perhaps the interference was worsened by a high wind gusting outside. A noun screamed from the radio set but its verb was cancelled. A phrase snarled or snorted out at you.

Marianne Günther sat cross-legged on Magdalena's bed, drinking coffee and nibbling a pastry. After a while they gave up trying to listen and switched off.

'Such an endearing chap,' Marianne said, deadpan. 'Imagine being married to him! Did you hear the joke? How long will the war last?'

'Until Goering fits into Goebbels' trousers?'

'Ah, you knew it!'

'Anything you want to know about Hermann's trousers, I'm an authority. Green breeches. Ten yards of fabric per leg.'

Magdalena launched into a description of Rominten. She let go of her burdens and was young again. You didn't have to embellish your story. The challenge lay in finding words adequate to describe what she'd witnessed. Marianne's eyes widened. They laughed till their stomachs hurt.

Marianne chatted away: she liked her teaching post in Gertlauken, her pupils, the warm kindness and hospitality of the villagers. In so many ways she was blest. For a start, she had electric light and a proper bed to sleep in.

Paula, her friend from Köln, had no bed! Imagine! No bed! She had a choice of a hammock and the floor. Paula's advisor – no, not Mr Excorn, he was a dry old stick but he'd probably have done something about it – Paula's couldn't care less. Said it was just a detail. A detail! Marianne would like to know how this geezer would cope without a bed – and someone dismissing it as a trivial detail! Whenever she could get away, Marianne had taken to cycling over to take Paula out in the woods, where they'd wander and sing, and Paula would become carefree again, for as long as the visit lasted. Or else Paula came to stay with her and slept in Marianne's bed.

'But there's always this terrible ... I don't know, Magda ... undertow, isn't there?' Marianne said, looking down. 'We can be as carefree as we like ... but our families in the west are being bombed ... and our brothers are fighting and dying in the east ... and other things that can't be said. It feels unreal ... living here in peace and plenty... But what can we do?'

Magdalena reached across and took her friend's hand.

Marianne went on, 'Perhaps it won't be long till Goering fits into Goebbels' trousers. Perhaps he will take a slimming cure. We win the war and everything calms down ... And some of the painful things that trouble us are... Anyway, Magda, I met a sergeant at the lagoon!'

'A sergeant?'

'On the steamer to Pillau. On leave from the east. He swore that Russia will fall before Christmas, they're just smashing through Stalin's lines, it's almost too easy. Knife though butter, he said. And it was this chap's birthday, there was wine and the young soldiers were singing, terrible racket. I go to the lagoon whenever I can. I swim naked, the beaches are so huge and the dunes are softer than you can imagine, the water's very warm. East Prussia is so beautiful.'

'But you didn't swim ... naked ... with this sergeant?'

'Not likely! He stayed on the steamer, they were all sloshed. The dunes are amazing – grains of sand fine as silk, it's nearly white. And you can walk miles along the spit without seeing a soul. You look out to the Baltic ... and it's turquoise, and so still, and you feel you are on the edge of ... I don't know ... eternity. Does that sound silly?'

'No, not at all.'

'You have to come, Magda, let's go together. Lovely eyes my soldier had, long lashes. He wasn't very tall. Asked me to write to him.'

'And will you?'

Marianne shook her head. 'Nah. Have you met anyone?'

'Well, I had a lift from an SS driver. Werner. He was due to go to the front and wanted me to correspond. You feel a bit torn, because they must be so lonely out there – exposed to such danger.'

'And? Did you swap your address?'

'No.'

They were both addicted to the freedom to be themselves, to ride out into the countryside, and feel the beauty of the green world, the peace. And also to connect with people, on their own terms. Marianne's parents in Cologne were dead set against her moving out of lodgings into a flat of her own, but she was going to anyway.

'What about you, Magda?'

'I've loved the teaching – and the people – and the countryside. But it's not easy. There's something very wrong here at Rosa House, Marianne,' she confided. 'Will you promise never to speak about it to anyone? Even your parents?'

Marianne said nothing. Her lips were tightly closed; she placed a finger over them.

'Let me show you our little Julia.'

They tiptoed into Flora's bedroom, where Julia was fast asleep.

It was hot in the room and she'd kicked off the bedclothes. Her hair was damp. Magda stroked it back and bent to kiss her forehead. The child did not stir.

'I love her,' she whispered. 'Almost like my own.'

'Dear little soul. How old is she?'

'Seven. She won't sleep in her own room any longer,' Magdalena whispered. 'Since her twin sister was taken away. And I think her mother is ... very upset. I don't know what to do, Marianne.'

'What about the doctor? What does he say?'

They crept out, leaving the door ajar, in case Julia woke.

'Ruth won't let him in. So he insists on talking to *me*, privately. He paws me. It feels like a betrayal.'

'The doctor? She won't let the *doctor* in? Why though, Magda? Surely a doctor ... should help? He ... paws you? Mind you, they all paw you, given half a chance.'

How to explain to Marianne? How to phrase the radical questions that had opened out under Mrs Daschke's roof: who owns a child? Who has the right to determine her future? A mother or the State? What is meant by a defective child?

And perhaps Magdalena ought not to share any of this. How did she know that Marianne Günther could be trusted? Joking about Goering's trousers was one thing, everyone did it. This was different. I have reached an edge, Magda thought, above a void. Balancing there is a matter of sheer mother-wit. To lean on another person might be a risk – a tipping point, perhaps.

Surely though, if I can trust anyone, I can trust Marianne, she felt: she's sincere, she's lovely. And although she's careful with words, she thinks for herself. The intimacy that had sprung up at Königsberg did not feel trivial.

She led Marianne back along the corridor. Passing Ruth's bedroom door, they couldn't help glancing in. Hunched on her bed in her petticoat, hands on knees, Ruth, caught in the glow of the paraffin lamp, was staring at the wall. The cigarette between her fingers held a long column of ash.

'Are you all right, Ruth?'

No reply. The ash fell.

'Can we get you anything? Are you hungry?'

Ruth swivelled her head. She rose, came to the door and closed it in their faces.

'Oh dear,' Marianne whispered, taking a step back. 'What shall we do?'

'I don't know. It can't go on. It's dangerous.'

'If she's drinking ... she needs to eat,' Marianne said.

They brought up a tray of sandwiches and coffee; Magdalena took it in. The smell of alcohol hit you, and a fug of smoke. A bottle of Kirsch was two thirds empty. Ruth seemed to have been drinking it straight from the bottle.

'You need to eat something, love. Please try and eat,' Magda cajoled. 'Look, and there's real coffee, Marianne brought it. For Julia's sake. For Flora's. Will you?'

What are tears called that can't be shed? What happens to the trapped salt water when its volume mounts, threatening the line beyond which it cannot be contained? Ruth was crying in this way. But she accepted the plate of sandwiches they'd cut up small, into triangles, as for a convalescent child after debilitating sickness. She stubbed out the cigarette and began to nibble. Sipped the coffee.

'Don't watch me, Magda! I'm not a child.' And then Ruth bethought herself, and added, 'Sorry, dear, don't mind me. I'm feeling a bit ... well, you know. Thank you for the food.'

Magdalena closed the door, reconsidered, and opened it a crack; peered in. Ruth was still eating. That was good. She saw her put the cup to her lips.

Back in her own room, Magda began to outline the gist of the story to Marianne.

'There may be things amiss,' Marianne carefully conceded. She paused. 'In fact, there probably are. There are mistakes and errors, aren't there, in all systems, even the best.'

Pause.

'Although the doctor may be right, mightn't he? He may have everyone's good at heart. After all, he's a *doctor*.'

Pause.

'Maybe this one's a rogue. He pawed at you, that's disgusting. What is wrong with these men?'

Pause.

'We can't change the system. We can only do our best to live according to our consciences, in our small, private spheres. Listen to the still small voice. That's what I tell myself.'

Pause.

'And then again, Magda. You want to go home, don't you? You need to see your parents, and you should, it's your right – and they need to see you. If we have divided loyalties, we have to somehow or other apportion ourselves, don't you think?'

The last thing Marianne said, straddling her bike, backpack on her shoulders, squeezing her brakes, was, 'You need to be so careful.'

*

So perhaps it was like a maths problem, this apportionment. That might be one way to see it, at least. But this was no simple theorem. How do I cleave myself down the centre and go two ways at once? Where is the centre anyway?

Magdalena got ready for bed. A sudden shower of hail came rattling down on the roof, out of what had been moments ago a cloudless sky. The hailstones were large, making a violent to-do overhead.

Abruptly the bombardment ceased. The dying sun revived. Magdalena stood at the loft window looking out as the intense greens of the treetops faded into a common twilight.

She climbed into bed, drew a sheet over her head; began to relax. Tomorrow Magda would say to Ruth: *I must go home for a fortnight, to see my parents. What can I do to help you before I go?*

*

She awoke late; had slept through the night and felt refreshed. The birds had already concluded the most climactic parts of their morning chorus, generally a bedlam that roused you at first light.

But someone human was singing. That old lullaby by Matthias Claudius about the moon rising, the gleaming stars, the hush in the woods, the white mists on the meadows.

Magda listened. Two voices, mother and child.

And then – magically – a voice joined in from outside, the trained and powerful mezzo soprano of Renate Schmidt. She stood out there on the gravel and held a descant.

The three sang the lyric right through to the last verse with its sombre warning, 'Cold is the breath of evening.'

Mother, child and neighbour admitted, with Matthias Claudius, that they only ever saw half the truth; that at their best they knew little about reality; they made things up, vainly chasing phantasms.

They asked for a gentle death and ended by pleading for God's blessing on the next-door neighbour.

The child held the melody, the mother varied upon it and the friend varied upon that.

Not since she had first arrived at Alt Schönbek had Magda heard Ruth singing. A lovely alto.

She leaned out and waved from the mansard window. Renate waved back, took a bow, blew a kiss and continued on her way.

Barefoot, Magdalena ran downstairs and threw open the kitchen door. To her astonishment, Ruth was standing at the basin in her apron, quite herself. She was washing the sudsy dishes, head turned, smiling, to greet Magda, offering her eggs for breakfast.

It was jolly well about time she pulled her blooming weight, Ruth said. Magda had been a tower of strength to both of them. She thanked her from her heart.

She and Julia, Ruth went on, drying her hands, fetching the eggs from the pantry, had formulated a plan of action. They had something to ask of Magdalena.

Julia came rushing to Magdalena and embraced her.

'When you go home for your holiday, can I come with you?' she asked. 'Please, please, Magda, please say yes! So that Mummy can go and bring Flora home. I'm not letting go until you say yes – and that's that!'

14

> We have not come here for human encounters with those pigs in there. We do not consider them human beings as we are... We have the power. If those pigs had come to power, they would have cut off all our heads... The more of those pig-dogs we strike down, the fewer we need to feed.[19]
>
> Johann-Erasmus Freiherr von Malsen-Ponickau,
> Head of Munich Auxiliary Police,
> *Motivational Address* to
> SS Guards at Dachau, April 1933

Over the bridge the baker's cart drove at a smart pace, leaving Alt Schönbek behind. Along the road through the forest they rattled, passing the Laulitz farm as they emerged into the light. And was that Eva herself over there, riding her horse across the meadow?

There was still time to turn back.

Why in heaven's name had Magdalena consented? Compassion for Ruth and tenderness for Julia should not have been allowed to take precedence over prudence. You felt squeezed into a narrow space between windowless walls that closed in – and then you wanted out.

At any moment she and Julia could double back. It was not too late. She could say, *I'm so sorry, Ruth, I can't take Julia with me after all.*

Even when they'd reached the station and boarded the Königsberg train, Magdalena told herself that the Rubicon had not been crossed; she could still get off at one of the little stations, about-turn, take Julia home to her mother. She could admit they'd made a mistake: *I don't know what came over me, Ruth, it's too dangerous, I'm so sorry, this is a crazy plan, there has to be another way.*

Ruth would not yet have left for Tapiau.

Up to now, Magdalena had been circumspect about defying laws and customs. She'd had major doubts about the regime, of course she had, but she and her doubts seemed perpetually stuck in a swing door, circling endlessly, so that however hard you pushed, you knew it was safe to carry on round. The door would deliver you back to the anonymity of the conformist world.

For who could dare to say, straight out, to himself: I have been born into a filthy, insane, evil society, ruled by madmen, I will not tolerate it?

Well, her father had dared to stand up and say so. Out loud. In 1933, he'd paid for it in the camp at Dachau. He'd spared her the details. She remembered overhearing scraps. The word *heinous* which Magda had not understood at the time. The phrase, *within an inch of our lives,* she had.

Did Magda remember, or had she made it up, opening the front door to a broken man, so broken that she had not been entirely sure that this was her father at all, unable to lift his broken leg over the threshold, uttering a broken cry of pain, black in the face, black and broken, and Mrs Süsskind helping the broken father up and laying him on the couch, and saying to Magdalena and Clem, *Go out and play, you two – he'll be all right, don't worry, just needs a good rest.*

Julia, in the jacket Ruth had fashioned for her out of an old sheet dyed bright blue, sat on the train with her legs wedged against Magda's, hand clasping hers. Her small body rocked with the rhythm. The child looked collectedly out of the window as they travelled away from her home. She'd never been away from her mother in her life, for longer than a few days – and yet Julia's spirit had arisen in all the vitality of the lass who'd taken off at Rominten to dance around Siegfried's clearing.

She's a brave one, thought Magdalena, marvelling, looking down on the child's stillness amid all the clatter and hissing. Her daddy was dead, her twin missing, her mother embarked on what must surely be a wild goose chase, and possibly a catastrophe – but Julia

Daschke confided herself to Magdalena's care, apparently without a qualm. She had accepted the surrender of the doll Helga without making any fuss. She'd stopped wetting the bed. She'd let Ruth go, though her mother was her harbour and haven.

And as for Ruth: it had been like a resurrection. Overnight some change of heart as powerful as an electric shock had jolted her out of her state of alcoholic breakdown, inspiring a burst of resistance. She'd bustled about, clearing up the bottles from her bedroom, getting the house spick and span for Flora's imagined return.

And I'm playing my part in the wild goose chase, Magda said to herself. She did not know whether taking Julia away from Alt Schönbek for a fortnight was even permitted by the powers-that-be. Was Dr Littmann a power-that-was? She could not forget his last words on Ruth's attitude: *My dear young lady, this behaviour of Mrs Daschke's is a form of suicide.*

It was as if he'd infiltrated Magdalena's mental space, trying to enlist her. Even now her heart was in her mouth, looking round with incoherent nervousness – but for what? She was breaking no law. Littmann had no right – and actually had asserted no right – to examine Julia. What I am doing is perfectly ordinary, legitimate, she told herself. I'm a sort of auntie. And here they were on the dear old train clanking along with the farm people. Ordinary folk going about their day-to-day business. What was wrong with a teacher taking a child away on her annual holiday?

Even so: am I being a complete fool?

No, because I am able to talk myself out of situations, Magdalena reminded herself. Act dumb. Lie if the truth calls for it. I've found a key. I'm learning to hate. The art of hatred. Yes, to hate.

But more than this: to hate intelligently.

They were passing through an idyll: vast silvery fields of ripening, rippling rye, with a blue dazzle of cornflowers. The arms of a windmill gently turned; a wayside cross on a hillock stood out against the horizon, the relic of an earlier war. There was no going back.

At Königsberg Station Julia insisted on carrying her own luggage as they struggled through the crowds.

'Ah, what a poppet your daughter is,' exclaimed an elderly passenger in the carriage. Everybody beamed at Julia.

'She's not my mummy, actually,' Julia corrected her, but quite courteously, and – thank heaven – without adding anything rude like *You silly sausage!* 'She's Magdalena.'

'Ah, your big sister? You do look alike.'

'No. Keep guessing!'

'Let me think! Your cousin perhaps?'

'Not my cousin!'

'I'm a close friend of Julia's family,' Magdalena put in, since Julia, wriggling, was rapidly tiring of the interrogation. 'And also her teacher.'

She thought: there's no word for what I am to Julia and what she is to me. As the train gathered speed, and passengers came and went, she remembered the eastward journey months ago, with the Auroch. Only months? It felt like a year. How odd that Magdalena recalled most of the passengers in the carriage that day – the lady with the rabbit – no, fox – cape; Dr Vogel of course; the gurning girl with the itchy corset; people you glimpsed in passing, never expecting to meet them again.

And the starved-looking soul, the object of mockery, whose aim in life seemed to be to vanish into himself, the nondescript chap with the paper collar – who'd mimed the Goethe poem – who'd dashed along the dark platform but slowed down to ask whether she was all right – *he* asked if *she* was all right! – recognising the attentions of Vogel to herself as he took the Auroch into protective custody.

The young man was a Jew, or suspected to be a Jew. Jews are not allowed to travel with Aryans. Jews might infect us. By merely looking at me, she thought, he might have been arrested for – what was it called? – race shame.

The passengers had sniffed him out with their snouts, rooting round for buried filth.

I suppose I knew who they meant when I overheard them whisper about someone's nose? The strange thing was, I never said to myself the word *Jew*. I mean, out loud within myself. And perhaps this humane Jewish person observed the vile book on my lap. Surely he must have seen it and read the title? He must surely have thought: she is one of *them*.

And yet he stopped for me.

*

In the blacked-out street, you could scarcely see a yard ahead. The only light in Lűbeck came from a clouded moon, glimmering on rainy surfaces. Julia, after her long day, walked as if in her sleep. Magdalena held on tight to her hand; she would have carried her but for their bulky luggage. Nearly there now, surely?

Was this her home? Or the one next door? Walking through ink, nothing was familiar. Surely, yes, this was right. The curve of the terrace seemed to say so.

'Here we are.'

'Where?'

About to say *home,* Magda, just in time, swallowed the word. 'Where we're going.'

She'd not been able to get through to Dad on the phone. How to avoid frightening him by ringing the doorbell at two in the morning? He'd think *they* had come for him.

Perhaps however he was awake, in his study writing, as he often did during sleepless nights. About Voltaire, about Diderot, about Èmilie du Châtelet. In that case Dad would hear, without panic, a gentle tapping on the door. For *they* wouldn't knock like that. But if he and Ebba were fast asleep upstairs, they wouldn't hear a thing.

She tried the gentle tap: nothing. But when she knocked again, the door opened a cautious inch. It was dark inside. She could just make out her father in his dressing gown, with one of the kittens, lantern-eyed, in the crook of his arm.

'Daddy, it's only me,' she said.

He snatched them in. Putting out his head, he glanced both ways up the road before shutting and locking the door and drawing the black velvet curtain across. Now he switched on the hallway light, a single, dim bulb casting a faint glow on the three of them.

'This is Julia, Ruth's daughter,' she explained, voice muffled as he clasped her against him, and she breathed in that smoky, homely scent of her father.

'Ebba!' he yelled up the stairs, 'Magda is home! Wake up! It's Magda!'

'Hallo, darling,' he said to the child, bending to her. 'Have you come to see us?'

Julia said nothing. She stared at the stranger. Then she reached one finger to touch his bristly cheek and asked uncertainly, as if using guesswork to challenge the laws of nature, 'Are you my granddad come back?'

Back from the grave, she meant.

'I'm Magdalena's daddy, dear. And I'm so very glad to see you both. And amazed! All of a sudden the two of you just pop up out of the blue! Did you fly on your wings, angel?'

'No,' said Julia, seriously. 'We came on the train.'

'You must tell me all about it. Perhaps tomorrow when you've had a lovely rest? I've heard all about you, you know, Julia.'

Ebba was flying down the stairs in her nightgown, hair in a net. She caught Julia up and held out her hand to her niece, tears pouring down her face. 'Magda, You're home!'

Everyone was crying, and Julia joined in at the top of her voice.

'We're just happy, sweetheart, that's why we're crying!' Ebba sobbed, kissing away the child's tears. 'It's all right, it's all right. Safe now, safe. What a long old journey for you both. You must be worn out. Do you like pussy cats, Julia? This is Schiller. I don't know where Goethe is. Oh yes, here comes Goethe! Goethe is the big fat one! Hates to be left out. Would you like a nice drink? Would you like to call us Uncle and Auntie?'

*

Julia lay with her mouth open, a doll in one arm. Magdalena tucked the thick hair back from her face, behind her ears, kissed her forehead. They hadn't said prayers or their Lovely Words. Exhausted as Magdalena felt, there was an odd sense of blessing, being there with the child, under her family's roof. She perched on the bed with one hand on Julia's bare shoulder, listening to her even breathing.

Her old room, kept fresh and aired, remained as it had been for the twenty years of her life. The doll's house that had been her mother's, with the peg-people carved for Magda by Clem's young hands and dressed in tiny clothes sewn by Ebba. How Julia would love the doll's house. The scent of lavender in the room came from the sprig beneath the pillow. Magdalena's desk was as she had left it, with the sunken inkwell and a sheet of green blotting paper laid out on the lid. The peacock and the parrot in red and blue cross stitch gazed down open-beaked as they'd always done from the sampler on the wall.

It took a while to recognise the noise that woke her. Julia, in her element, was galloping Blitz, the old rocking horse, for all he was worth, across the creaking floorboards towards the window: a girl-Napoleon, one hand on the reins, the other urging on her regiments.

'I love him, I love him! And we're going to see the river and the boats and we might go on a boat and we're going to eat the ham and sausage and cake we've brought, a picnic, and Auntie says she's never seen such a feast! And we're going to play ball in the park. Get up, get up, Magda, come *on*!'

'I can't until I've had a hug and a kiss. And don't be stingy with them, Julia. I need a proper morning hug.'

'There we are then. Is that enough?'

'Yes, I suppose so ... it will do for now.'

*

Father and daughter sat together on a sunlit bench beside the water. Breeze rustled the foliage of the lime trees; butterflies spiralled in couples. Were they mating or fighting? You couldn't tell. Julia played ball with Ebba and showed her the dance she'd performed at that place, she couldn't remember the name, with the dead stag and the big fat man with the knife.

'Come on, Julia!' called Ebba. 'Come and chase me!'

The two hared off together. Ebba's forty-four years had halved, and then halved again. She was proposing that they climb a tree, what did Julia think of that?

'Ebba's not actually going up that tree, is she, Dad?'

'She used to climb anything with a trunk. A few years ago, mind. Ebba!' he called. 'For goodness' sake be careful!'

His sister flapped him a dismissive wave.

Magdalena shrugged off her cardigan to soak up the sun. Her father shed his jacket and was down to his shirt and braces. He rolled up his sleeves. Terribly thin. There was nothing to him. Look at his spindling arms. They looked as if they could snap at the least pressure. Well, Dad had always been, as he liked to recount, *a slender young man*, according to the friends of his student days. But his present condition was nothing to do with slenderness. No one here got quite enough to eat. The coupons didn't stretch. He needed fattening up. Shockingly, he and Ebba set aside a considerable portion of their meat and fish ration for the cats. No point in remonstrating. Goethe and Schiller were important in the brother's and sister's existence and economy. They gave joy, simply through being. They were mortals like us, our innocent dependents.

Magdalena felt a rush of renewed guilt about living so well in the east while folk here went without.

She had so much to share with Dad. She started with the difficult story of Ruth and the twins.

The tic beneath his eye was twanging. Grave-faced, Dad said nothing for a moment, then, quietly, 'I have the feeling that you are ... aware.'

'Yes.'

'Boundless depravity,' he murmured, as if to himself. 'Boundless.'

But the little girl came skipping up. Had they seen her doing her bunny-hops? Had they been watching? And her cartwheels? No? Should she do a cartwheel to show Uncle? Would he like to see a handstand against a tree? He would?

Off she sped.

'We can speak about that matter in due course,' said Max.

And Magdalena thought: he is more collected than when I left. What has happened to collect him?

'But first,' her father said, lighting up a cigarette, 'I'll tell you about my socks.'

'Your *socks*? What about them?' She looked down at his feet.

He'd been neurotic before his week in detention for infringement of blackout regulations, her father confessed, about his socks. He knew how ridiculous that sounded. But so it had been.

And the root of this anxiety – because all anxieties have roots – was that, in his earlier *protective custody*, so-called, amid infinitely worse persecution (and yet he'd fared undeservedly far better than others), he'd had his socks confiscated by a guard. For some non-existent misdemeanour. It was the day before they broke his leg, so perhaps that was one reason why it loomed large in his memory. But there was another.

What was he going to tell her? Some violence up to now dammed behind speechless darkness was coming through, it was coming. It could not be stopped, it was heinous, and yet he was calm.

'Trivial as the sock business was, I've been ashamed ever since, and never mentioned it to anyone, even your mother or Ebba. I stole a pair of socks from a fellow prisoner. Mine had been stolen, my feet were chafing, the blisters were hurting, so ... I stole someone else's. This man was about to be discharged, going home the following day. He possessed two pairs, a fact I remember using to salve my conscience.'

'Oh, *Dad*.'

Magdalena's eyes filled with tears. She took his hand and kissed it. He didn't snatch it away. He put his other hand on her lowered head. He'd never spoken in detail about his *re-education*. Was it that he now acknowledged Magdalena as an equal? She'd never felt as close to her father as she did there, on the park bench.

And he'd just remarked, matter-of-factly, *The next day they broke my leg.*

'This is how one's moral compass can be breached. Well, I should rather say, this is how *I* allowed myself to be corrupted. This sock business – how can I put it? – created a window in my vanity, and I was never quite the same after that.'

'You don't need to ... you mustn't ... please don't carry that with you, Dad, for another minute. Put the damn socks down. It was ... a moment of weakness. How can you say you are corrupt? You are my guiding star. Don't you know that? In any case, I'm pretty sure that Voltaire would have done the same.'

Smiling, he ruffled her hair. That might have been true of Kant, or let's say Rousseau, her father acknowledged, yes, Rousseau would have filched the socks and the shoes, and a pair of trousers (but we'll get to the trousers in a minute!) and then he'd have lied through his teeth – but Dad could not believe it of his good friend Voltaire, no, never!

'So you're saying that Voltaire wasn't actually a human being like us? He was some kind of secular saint?'

'Good answer!' He chuckled.

'I remember Mum used to say: frankly, we're all much of a muchness when it comes down to it.'

Her father even recalled the chap's face. He was a Communist factory worker from Hamburg who'd been caught pasting up leaflets.

'Please could we just drop the socks, Dad? Now that you've confessed, I absolve you! *Ego te absolvo.* Go, my child!'

'Darling!'

'Well? What about it?'

'I accept the absolution. Any penance for me?'

'The tiny sin was remitted long ago,' she told her father. 'You've overpaid. You have credit.'

Last month he'd been deeply afraid, Max said, to be arrested again – and Ebba, even more so. Particularly as the block warden was making it up about the blackout – or whichever snitch denounced him (he thought he knew who *that* might be, and always be alert for snitches, you're never safe from snitches, the cockroaches are crawling around everywhere).

He paused to ask her, 'Is there anyone at Alt Schönbek you suspect as a possible informer, Magda?'

'I'd say Mrs Struppat. But she's so *stupid*.'

'Stupidity doesn't rule out cunning. It's a qualification for the job. Be on your guard.'

Anyway, with regard to the blackout, it was either an informer, or someone in authority wanted to scare him. The blackout was not defective.

Not in any respect.

Clem had scoffed; he'd pointed out that his uncle lived with his head in the clouds. Yes, maybe so, Max didn't deny that he wasn't always very practical. But in this instance Clem was mistaken. The blackout was perfectly in order. Not a gleam of light could have got through.

And Clem ... but never mind that.

For a while neither Max nor Ebba had believed one could actually be taken into police custody for a footling offence. He hadn't quite taken in the reality until he turned up at the police station at the appointed date, with a bag containing necessities – change of clothes, books, pen, pad, and so on – and was led down to the cells, where he was deprived of his watch, tie and braces, hairbrush, books, pen and spectacles. Without his glasses, well – it was a very stranding thing.

'I was so worried about your braces when Clem told me,' Magdalena said.

'You go in a philosopher and you come out a poor bare forked animal. Although...'

'Although what?'

'Well, the trousers took over from the socks. No contest. What I did to keep them up was this – I pulled at a bunch of threads just here – see? – and wove it round this button. Best I could do. You walk differently, you shamble, you keep groping for your dignity. I begged for my glasses and a pen and paper. *You're in prison, you don't need glasses.* However. One morning – I've got to tell you this, Magda, it made a strong impression – there was this scrabbling noise. I looked round and a hand was thrusting something through the hole in the door. My glasses and a stub of pencil, wrapped in two sheets of paper. Yes, really.'

'Who was it?'

'Never saw his face, never thanked him. Well, that was it. I was free of the misery of uncharted time. I wrote in minuscule letters. A coded diary. That helped me more than I can say, Magda. It wasn't only having these staples of life, it was that someone had gone out on a limb to give them to me, in this world of monumental conformity. I'll show you the pages when we get home.'

'Bless him. What were you going to say earlier?'

He'd started writing a new book, her father told her. He'd put aside the Enlightenment tome in favour of something more like a journal or diary. Did Magdalena remember Fritz Reck who visited a few years ago? (called himself Reck-Malleczewen, pompous old so-and-so!) Well, Dad had got the idea from him. Reck, he said, kept a journal as a testament of resistance.

'Oh, you mean the hating man?'

He laughed. 'Yes, the hating man! You do remember! You overheard him quoting from the journal. He keeps it hidden in the woods on his estate in Bavaria – in a tree, believe it or not! A different tree every night. And there are others – a dear friend of Ebba's, Theodor Haecker the philosopher, he calls it his *Journal in the Night*, keeps it in a dining-room cabinet – and others – Victor

Klemperer the philologist in Dresden, the dearest man – Friedrich Kellner in Mainz, you've heard me speak of him? – because the important thing, Magda, is language. Language that challenges the corruption of language. Do you see what I mean? Of course you do. So anyway there I was in prison bereft of braces and dignity but armed with a stump of pencil and bits of paper – and found I could testify too. And it seems to me that all these diarists form a hidden network of resistance. I'd always thought myself too dry and pedantic to keep a journal of this sort – but prison taught me better.'

Dad would tell Magdalena where he stowed the journal, so that if anything happened to him, she could find it.

'But nothing must happen to you, Dad.'

'Nothing must happen to you either, Magda.'

'Don't keep listening to the BBC, Dad. Don't. Just don't. Ebba knows exactly what you're doing in the loft. It eats away at her. Dad, if something happens to you, it happens to us all.'

Later he told her about Dachau. Some details. So that she understood that if she got out of line, these were the inevitable repercussions. He told her about the badges. Red for politicals. Green for criminals. Black for asocials. Violet for Jehovah's Witnesses. Pink for homosexuals. Yellow star for Jews.

And white armbands labelled 'Moron' for idiots.

The Jews and the idiots did not last long, he said; and said no more.

Her heart thundered.

Whereupon a door fell open in Magda's memory. Miss Heller's apartment in Sankt-Lorenz. She stepped back in, as she had done on that blessed day, all those years ago, when Miss Heller had reached out with love and compassion to the mute and motherless girl.

In this memory-room, Miss Heller's parents and her grandmother were revealed, grouped in an attitude of waiting. They turned their faces to the door as the child and her teacher entered, and rose, and embraced Magdalena. They sat her down by the fire. They made no effort to coax her to talk, for Miss Heller had explained that on the whole Magdalena did not speak, just at present. There was a music stand and a violin which the child was allowed to hold. She touched the strings, felt the resonance within the curved golden-brown body, listened to the hum in the instrument's heart. When she blew air over the strings, Magda heard a secret voice inside.

While the table was being laid, Magda looked round at oil paintings and ornaments such as she'd never before witnessed, like the seven-branched candlestick, gleaming silver in the firelight. The candlestick was very old, Miss Heller told her: it had been passed down from generation to generation. Her father, the rabbi, smiled and said that the candlestick was thousands of years old, you could put it like that.

'I had thought of looking for Miss Heller while I was here. My old teacher – you remember,' Magda said to Dad. 'But...'

She knew from his face that Miss Heller would no longer be there in her family home at Sankt-Lorenz. That she was long-gone.

That night the air raid siren got them up and out. Magdalena had expected the shelter to be underground. But the Winkel Tower was an extraordinary construction, tall and pointed, Gothic-looking like the ancient city, with sloped walls a metre thick, which any bomb was supposed to slide off. For a couple of hours they sat on the second floor, Julia asleep in Ebba's lap, waking to call for her mother and Flora – *Where are they? Where are they? And where is Daddy? Where?* – screaming with all her pent anguish until the All Clear sounded.

She sobbed all the way home and would not be comforted.

And the next night.

And the next but one.

No bombs fell.

*

'Going home!' Julia skipped along. She'd clung to Ebba, then to Max, then back to Ebba, but consented to let them go. Now she was in riotous spirits. She informed passers-by that she was going home to Mummy now, and her sister, she was going on the big fast train!

At Lűbeck Station, the forecourt had been cordoned off. Why was that?

The answer soon became clear to the thwarted passengers, who complained that a smell was advancing towards them. A stink of unwashed flesh. The smell was marching in the direction of the exit. Foreigners.

For they were not us.

Julia held her nose and expressed the view, quite loudly, that they were pongy people, at which a young SS man shepherding the column of forced workers chuckled.

'Never a truer word, little miss!' he said, causing Julia to bounce up and down, shrieking 'Pongy people! Stinky-pooh!'

'That's enough!' Magdalena yanked at her hand. 'Stop that at once. There is no smell.'

She said it again, louder, but not so loud as to be publicly audible above the din of her fellow travellers.

The forced labourers, men and women, were said by some to be from Poland and France. Others suggested Ukraine or Belgium or Denmark or Holland, for we'd conquered the whole blooming lot; gone through them like a knife through butter. Or Norway, Luxembourg, Yugoslavia, or even Greece.

But wouldn't they be swarthy if they'd come from Greece? They're not swarthy.

They couldn't be Danes, someone said: *Or Norwegians. Not blond enough. Probably Poles, they look moronic.*

Look, there's a blond one there. Poles can be blond.

Maybe they're Jews?

Nah, they wouldn't bring Jews to Lűbeck. We're trying to get rid of them!

Apparently they're Croats. Someone just said.

What? Goats?

Croats.

Or just rats! Get it? Rats!

The crowd tittered. It set Julia off.

'They're pongy rats! Pongy rats!'

And Magdalena, who doted upon her, was visited by an urge to strike the child. A phantom arm rose and suspended itself over Julia's head.

It's not the child's fault, she rebuked herself. It's the swamp she's growing up in. And this is the way it happens. It's normal. It happened to me, even though I had the home I had, with Dad, and Ebba, and Miss Heller. If it happened to me ... who escapes scot-free?

The forced workers had been cooped up in carriages for days. As they came out of the station, they screwed up their eyes against the brilliant sunlight. When the last of the phalanx had emerged and departed, the passengers were admitted to the station.

Later, on the train, Magdalena thought: there was no smell. None whatever. Except our own bad breath. Plenty of that in here.

You breathed more cleanly in the countryside. The air was clearer, fresher.

Disembarking at Königsberg, Magda and Julia got straight on to the stopping train, and off they went. It was not yet dark. They chuntered along through a deepening twilight in which trees flattened into dark silhouettes and stars implied their presence though the sky was still blue.

'Nearly home now,' she said to Julia, kissing her tired head. 'Home to Mummy!'

15

> Who knows the burden that weighs
> upon the shoulders of women?[20]
> Ernst Jűnger, *First Paris Journal*, 1941

Even in the first passionate moments of greeting, as Julia rushed across the threshold, radiant to be home, and shouting her mother's name, Magdalena sensed Flora's absence. She put down the bags, shrugged off the knapsack, and looked round the hall and stairwell. No little red coat on the peg, no orthopaedic shoes by the door.

Oh Flora. Darling.

The little soul, whose image Magdalena had suppressed all this time, rose on a tide of memory. Tears swam on her eyes. So Ruth has failed, she thought, as the mother appeared, running on bare feet, and scooped Julia up, kissing her, whirling her around.

'You're home! You're home!'

Magdalena saw Ruth's failure confirmed in the haggard face, even in its moment of jubilation. She hugged mother and child and they swayed together.

'Put me down! Put me down!' cried the squirming home-comer. 'I want to go and see ... all of it!'

Julia thundered upstairs and they followed. Overjoyed to see and touch her toys and clothes, the wanderer clutched her favourites to her face and sniffed at them. Their familiarity gleamed with a transient gloss of novelty. She examined everything, to ensure all was just as it should be and where it ought to be, in relation to everything else. Running her fingertips over well-known surfaces, Julia named items of particular value as if conducting an inventory.

She didn't enter Flora's room and did not mention her name.

Having checked that major aspects of her world were in order, Julia began to give a full and hectic account of her adventures. She told Ruth all about Auntie Ebba and how she could do handstands against a tree, she really could! – and how Auntie didn't mind if her knickers showed – even though she was *old,* and even though she had a cross above her bed, but it was not a crucifix because Jesus was not hanging on it, nobody was hanging on it, it was just a cross. And about Uncle Max, who was so *funny,* and he could draw and paint, he'd done this picture of her and Magda in pen and ink.

'It's for you,' she said quite bashfully, thrusting the pen-portrait into Ruth's hands.

'Thank you, love – it's very good.'

'Does it look like me?'

'It does. Very like. It's a lovely picture.'

'But what do you *really* think of it? Do you adore it?' Julia's voice was thick with disappointment.

'I do, of course I do. It's a good likeness, isn't it?' Ruth looked from the sketch to the sitter and back, nodding.

For goodness' sake, Magdalena thought, show some enthusiasm! You're even trying not to yawn! Had she been drinking? Nobody had spoken a word about Flora. Nobody raised her name from the sealed mouth of her absence.

And she thought, *Flora no longer exists.* But that was unthinkable, and she dismissed it.

'Do you like the way Auntie Ebba did my hair?' Julia asked breathlessly, palms planted on Ruth's knees, bobbing her face to and fro into her mother's. '*Do* you?'

'I don't know, darling, I didn't see it.'

'It's there, it's there! In the picture! There! Look!'

'Oh yes, plaits on the top of your head. Very nice. Clever Ebba.'

'*Auntie* Ebba! We call her *Auntie!*'

After the initial flare of excitement, Ruth's fire burned low. She struggled to respond to the loud, prancing, dancing, demanding reality of Julia, who trailed her mother from room to room, rapping on the bathroom door when Ruth was inside.

'Come out! Let me in! I want to see you!'

'Don't do that, dear,' came Ruth's thin voice.

Magdalena led Julia away to help put away her things.

Wouldn't you think a mother would be comforted by having at least one child safe and sound beside her? She wasn't. After the first wild joy, it had been an effort for Ruth to smile. It came forcefully to Magdalena that Ruth was ill. She'd been ill for a long time now. I'm not a nurse, she thought – and I don't want to be. If only Ebba were here, to advise.

Twice Julia skipped past Flora's door, without looking or commenting.

Perhaps if Julia denied her sister's existence, she lost the sense of loss. The mind did that for you. In Lűbeck the child had been made much of by Dad and Ebba, who of course had never known Julia as a twin. To them she was a singleton, a one-off. The links of likeness were being uncoupled.

One of Flora's dolls had been taken to Lűbeck and lost. Julia hadn't seemed to mind. Perhaps the talisman had shed its magic and what remained was a mere bundle of matter: cloth and thread.

Magdalena turned to Ruth: 'What happened, Ruth?' And, softly, 'Where is Flora?'

Ruth shook her head. 'Later, Magdalena.'

The three of them sat down to a late meal. Ruth was not eating. She filled her glass and lit a new cigarette from the butt of the old one. After staring for a few minutes, Julia knelt up on her chair, flapped at the smoke, and attempted to feed her mother from her own plate. Mothering her mother, as if working in her intuitive way to remedy whatever had gone awry.

She offered a forkful of fried potato. 'Mmn, come on, Mummy, eat up, it's so nice, it's delicious, open wide!'

Ruth grimaced, shook her head, pursed her lips, giving it to be understood that she had eaten already. Julia, her bounty spurned, jabbed the fork at her mother's mouth. Ruth swerved her face and the fork accidentally grazed her chin.

'Don't do that, please, Julia.'

'Eat then, it's good for you.' She pushed another forkful at her mother's lips. 'Have this piece ... come on, open up.'

Jab, jab.

Ruth leapt to her feet. Her chair toppled back and her glass tipped over. 'Stop that! At once! Cut it out! Now!'

It was not Ruth who shouted this. No, but it came out of Ruth's mouth.

Stunned, Magdalena had a sense that the mother was about to strike the daughter. She shot out her arm, to shield both mother and daughter against this disaster. 'No, Ruth – no, don't ... she's only trying to...'

'Don't you tell me what to do!'

Julia now intervened to stage one of the most dramatic tantrums of her life. Exhausted from her journey, the excitement and disappointment, she lost all control. The storm went on and on. She ended up in the cellar, rolling round the coal heap, where Magdalena chased her down and gathered her up, accepting a coating of coal on her white blouse.

'Mummy doesn't mean anything unkind,' she crooned. 'Mummy's just very...' She hesitated, casting around for the anodyne word. 'Very tired, you see. She has a lot on her mind.'

'Well, so have I got a lot on my blooming mind! A lot, a lot, a *lot!* So there! And she hasn't seen me for a year! And she doesn't care! And you be quiet, Magda, if you haven't got anything sensible to say!'

Tears made channels down her soiled face. The two of them sat side by side alongside the coal heap, and both sobbed. By and by Julia's small hand crept across and took hold of Magda's.

'Let's be kind and gentle, shall we?' said Magda. 'It's probably not the best idea in the world to roll round in the coal heap.'

Julia grinned through the tears and snot. 'Anyway you've got a big black nose!'

'Yes, and so have you. We need a bath. Shall we have a bath? Together?'

'All right.'

'And you must apologise to Mummy for being a pig. Promise me now, love. You can't behave like that, Julia, you just can't.'

Julia snorted and oinked but seemed willing to apologise.

There was no one to say sorry to, for Ruth had slammed out of the house, and perhaps that was best, to allow her to recover.

They cooperated in boiling up kettles of water and pouring it into the tin bath. Julia got in first, had a good soak and scrub, and Magdalena towelled her dry. Tipping the black water away, they repeated the process for Magdalena, after which Julia towelled her dry. Magda plunged towels and clothes into a bucket of soapy water.

'Don't forget now, say sorry to Mummy.' She had an uncomfortable sense that by taking over the work of care from Ruth, she was somehow being elbowed into a false position.

'Let me whisper,' said Julia, mouth close to Magdalena's ear.

'What do you want to whisper?'

'*She's not my mummy.*'

Julia sat back to assess the effect of her triumphant denial.

'Don't be ridiculous.' Magda's heart sank like lead. 'That's enough.'

Her head throbbed. She was sick of it, sick! She'd done everything she'd been asked to do – against her own judgement. The net result of her compliance was to be used like a ... wet nurse! An unpaid wet nurse! And this, after having been exposed to who knew what danger by a woman she'd lived with for only a matter of months. She missed Dad and Ebba, especially Ebba, with her wisdom and practicality. But also Dad, with that new closeness. All Magdalena wanted was some peace. What was this mayhem to do with her anyway?

She longed to curl up in her bedroom and read a book; to nod off over the book and wake up ten hours later. And go round to Eva's and browse for a whole morning amongst the rare books. And ask

Eva about her friend who had run for her life, having underlined *Without hate* in the Goethe poem. The girl Eva loved.

I want my freedom, Magda thought. Perhaps she should do what Marianne had done, and ask around for a rented flat of her own?

Ruth opened the front door.

Here we go, Magda thought.

But Julia could be heard pattering down the stairs and saying – from the heart – sorry.

Ruth accepted the apology; said she was sorry too.

Julia was put to bed.

Magda heard Ruth saying the Lovely Words, in a softened voice. Thank God for that.

*

At breakfast the next day, Julia made no attempt to feed Ruth. Instead she started on Magdalena. Her mother observed dispassionately, or so it seemed. She sipped her coffee, elbows on the table, miming tranquillity; then switched on the radio.

Martial music flooded the kitchen, celebrating our victorious advance on Kiev, on Minsk, on Leningrad! Watch out, Kharkov and Dunbas, your oil is about to flow into the Fatherland! Watch out, Moscow! The wheatfields of the Steppes are ours. Praise for our indomitable boys and our incomparable Leader! More martial music.

And dearest Clem: where was he in all this? Had he killed anyone yet?

Julia kept on with her redirected campaign, ignoring the patriotic noise.

It was not a case of a child simply offering unwanted crusts of her bread. This campaign was determinedly self-sacrificial. Julia nibbled her way round the best bits of a slice of rye bread and butter and insisted that her victim eat the luscious centre.

'Come along now, for goodness' sake,' she chivvied. 'Eat up, Magdalena, do. Don't you want to be nice and chubby and cuddly?'

'Well, cuddly perhaps. But aren't I cuddly already? And Mummy is the cuddliest of us all,' she ended lamely, accepting a fragment of the bread and returning the rest and adding, 'Though obviously, not chubby.' Her words fell into the embarrassing void of Ruth's silence.

'Now eat this, please,' Julia continued. Ignoring her mother, she nevertheless directed the whole charade at her. 'This will do you good now, Magda,' she said authoritatively. 'It will help you to grow up big and strong.'

'Erm ... Julia, I *am* grown up, in case you hadn't noticed!'

'That's what *you* say, my girl!'

Having divided lean from fatty bacon on her plate, the child offered a forkful of the best to Magda.

'No, darling. Enough of that. It's not funny anymore. Eat your meal,' said Magda.

Ruth got up from the table without a word and wandered to the window, where she stood, arms folded, looking out.

Was something dead inside Ruth? Did she notice, did she not mind, that Julia had gravitated to Magdalena, and was blanking her out? Or was she too far gone to care? They needed a doctor – but the available doctor was the last thing they needed.

Just get on with it for the moment, Magda counselled herself. She would tackle Ruth when the child had gone out to play with her friends. Magda would put it strongly, insisting: *This cannot go on, Ruth. I am not a nursemaid. I am your colleague, lodger and friend. I have a life and an important job to do. You owe it to me to explain where we stand.*

Meanwhile, there was plenty of food to go round – more than enough, unlike in Lűbeck where everything was *ersatz* and 'one-pot', with little meat available, and that little diverted by the Arbers to the cats. There was plenty on Julia's plate to allow her to share some without going short herself.

Magda watched the child earnestly dividing her food, making finicky calculations, head on one side, cheeks rather flushed. She thought: *You are trying to strike a bargain with the universe, that's what you're doing.* What happened in a little person's mind – deep down where there are no words for things – faced with a world that has eaten its own tail?

Magdalena struck her own counter-bargain, accepting initial offers but refusing more, explaining that she and Mummy had more pleasure in seeing Julia enjoy her food. She accounted it a success when the little girl gave in and gobbled the rest herself.

Magda was vaingloriously conscious, as she directed this little performance, of demonstrating to Ruth how the situation could and should be managed by a competent parent.

*

Ruth would talk about her journeys to Tapiau, now that Julia had gone out to play with Hans and Klara on the swing. Magda kept her eye on the little group. She was aware of the bossy voice of Julia directing play.

At first, said Ruth, the hospital receptionist had refused point blank to admit her. According to this automaton, rules were rules; procedures were procedures. Infection control was priority; family visiting strictly forbidden. Mrs Daschke's wasted journey was regrettable. Best to go home now (and the woman had helpfully pointed to the door).

Mrs Daschke could write a letter if she was concerned.

Well, Ruth had already written letters and been fobbed off. She was going nowhere, she told the woman, and demanded to speak to someone in authority. She named her daughter. Where was she?

Two porters were called. They escorted Mrs Daschke out of the door.

Ruth sat down on the steps.

Back came the porters and marched the mother to the gate. They were not unpleasant and did not handle her roughly. They were just doing their job.

She understood that but she was also doing her job.

Back stalked Ruth through the main door and reported a second time at the reception desk. With some asperity.

Back marched the porters and removed her, this time with somewhat less patience.

One of the men, however, circled back. He murmured: 'For your own sake, dear lady ... go home...'

Ruth walked into town, spent some time drinking coffee in a cafe, debating what to do next and deciding to reconnoitre the asylum grounds. Perhaps there were other entrances. A beautiful Gothic place, Tapiau, she said – white buildings with red roofs and spires. Vast, idyllic-looking place, with trees and fields on two sides. She tramped round the perimeter until the weather turned.

'At each high window I thought: *Is she in there? Or there?* My whole body ached in every cell,' Ruth said. 'You had taken Julia and *he* had taken Flora.'

Magdalena gasped and swallowed. She'd been persuaded, against her better judgement, to take Ruth's daughter out of harm's way. It had not been an easy journey, and she'd put herself at risk. Magdalena had invested heart and soul in caring for the little girl and loved her like a daughter. And now this!

She held her peace.

Ruth had given up when, out of a blue sky, it started to rain. She'd caught the next train home. Oh the empty house, her childless, empty home. She'd never missed her husband so much. She thought she would die of that emptiness.

However, she'd found the antidote, she said: rage!

'Rage,' Ruth observed, straightening her spine, 'is the great redeemer. Yes, you heard right, Magda. Rage. You'll think it's not very Christian perhaps ... although Christ upset the tables of the moneychangers in the temple, didn't he? He wasn't being milky mild *then,* was he? No, my Jesus struck out against impiety. He didn't say, *Oh dear, I don't think it's very nice to turn my Father's temple into the house of Mammon!* And when the disciples were shooing off children, what did he say? Did he say, *Clear off, you little brats?* Or did he say, *Suffer the little children to come unto me, and forbid them not, for of such is the kingdom of Heaven?* Did he bow and scrape to the Pharisees? He wasn't a milksop, his Mother wasn't a milksop either, not her.'

Magda thought, and did not say, *No, but He was crucified*.

'However,' Ruth added, 'you also have to have the wiles of Satan. God knows, *they* have. I simmered down. I took counsel of my soul. I waited a couple of days. I scoured the house from top to bottom. I washed all Flora's bedclothes.'

Then Ruth travelled a second time to Tapiau. For this visit she'd selected her clothes carefully. She wore her grey work suit, to indicate professionalism, her black felt hat with the feather, and she carried her husband's leather briefcase, containing documents.

'They take us for idiots,' she said. 'It's their Achilles heel. Not that they know anything about Achilles. Or anything else for that matter.'

Ruth had loitered at the main gate to the asylum. When a stream of hospital staff had come through, she slipped into the group and swept past reception, into the arteries of the hospital. Nobody had asked for her identity card. An advantage of small stature, Ruth had always found, was the ability to dive beneath the surface of a crowd. Clasping the bundle of papers to her chest, she'd stalked along with her nose in the air as if she knew where she was going. Massive place, miles of corridor. Eventually she'd found her way to Anatomy and Pathology.

'And, lo and behold, guess who now lords it in a plush office with his name plate in gold script and a personal secretary clacking on a typewriter in a vestibule! Can you believe it? I could hear him droning in his office with a handful of cronies.'

While Ruth had been confronting Dr Littmann's young secretary, the meeting began to break up and his door half-opened. One of the cronies had been holding the doorknob, swaying the door to and fro, while they finished their jovial conversation.

'And?' Magdalena asked.

'The cronies left. Littmann ushered me into his swanky office. Leather chairs. Box of cigars. Fur rug, bear's head and all. Shelves groaning with books. Oh please. He doesn't even realise...'

She paused.

'Realise what, Ruth?'

'That I know *Greek*!' she burst out. 'And Latin! Yes! These people are barbarians!'

What did Homer have to do with anything? Magdalena asked herself.

'This jumped-up rustic provincial nobody, who used to be known as a bit of a soak, ask anyone ... and don't look at me like that, Magda ... they'll all tell you ... although he was decent enough in those days, we called him by his Christian name, imagine that ... he wasn't above holding the bowl for you to be sick in ... yes, really ... a simple family doctor who didn't aspire beyond... Well, anyway, he informed me that my Flora had been *transferred*. Without my say-so, without my knowledge. *It's better this way, better for her, better for you*, he said. Formal letter on its way.'

'So did he say where she'd gone?'

'No. But I found out. I'm not stupid, Magda. I will have my daughter back if it's the last thing I do. Whatever else I may be, stupid I am not.'

'Of course not. But how did it end?'

'He wondered if I was tired of living?'

'Oh *no*, Ruth. Don't you realise what he was saying?'

'And he mentioned the *viable* twin.'

'No. Ruth, we need to...'

'Next time, he would not protect me. *Protect* me? Did you ever hear anything like it? But do you want to know something, Magda? They are more afraid of mothers than mothers are of them!'

'Really?' Magda asked faintly. It was beginning to dawn on her that the doctor who coveted Ruth's daughters for his own ends had nevertheless shielded Ruth. From herself; from himself; from the Gestapo.

'Oh yes. He has put his big fat foot in it. They need us to smile and comply. But there's one thing mothers won't tolerate, Magda – the ill-treatment of our children. It happened before ... the doctors were sterilising their patients, for God's sake! There were rumours that they were being starved to death. But Our Leader stood with the mothers over that. All that stopped.'

No, it won't have stopped, thought Magda. It's gone underground.

Her father's warnings echoed, from his time in the camp: white armbands labelled 'Moron' for idiots and how the Jews and the idiots *did not last long*. Keep out of trouble, do not step out of line, he'd pleaded. They will squash you under their thumb like a fly. And what they want to do, be sure they do it – in secret. Orders come from the top, from the very top, do not forget that.

You're too like me, Magda, Dad had said, shaking his head. Or as I used to be. It's all my fault. Be more like Ebba. Keep quiet. Don't stand out.

Ruth had been ejected, this time by an SS guard.

She'd placed herself squarely in the path of an oncoming tank. And Magdalena had helped to facilitate this. There was no doubt in her mind that Ruth would be run over.

16

> I grieve for the girl born to me ...
> whose piercing cry I heard resounding
> through the boundless aether
> as if she were being forced,
> though I did not see it with my eyes.[21]
> *Homeric Hymn to Demeter*,
> seventh/sixth century BCE

It was time, it was high time. The storks knew this. The knowledge forked its lightning in their brains, it shimmered in their bellies, agitating their hearts to thunder.

Away! Away!

Abandoning their nests, rising on six-foot wingspans, the stork army assembled in marshy fields and pastures. You could not hear yourself think. In the peaceful August countryside, the clattering of their bills sounded alarmingly like machine gun fire. The storks, said the grandmothers of Alt Schönbek, had fed full this summer. A good auspice for us, as long as they are not crossed. Lizards and frogs, birds and fish, snakes and snails, voles and mice, abundant this summer, had been loaded into the gullets of the young. Mother and father, loyal life partners, had crammed their offspring with thousands of creatures freshly killed, and the fledglings throve.

There'd been no need for the stork parents to tip runts out of the nest during this halcyon season. Oh, they are clever creatures, folk agreed: no doubt about that! Arithmeticians, these birds are – they calculate the food situation and, in case the sums don't add up, the parents chuck out weak or infected chicks.

Never harm a stork, warned the grandmothers. It's a sin. It brings a curse down upon the people. Your babies will die. Your crops will be blighted. Your houses will burn down. The Stork Mother is implacable. Do not tempt her in any way.

Are you listening? demanded the grandmothers. Don't stand there grinning and tapping your noses. She is lethal. Have you ever experienced famine? We have. Famine can come again, with a vengeance.

The young storks were fit and fat, having doubled, trebled, quadrupled in size and weight, ready for a ten thousand-kilometre flight. They rose in a thunderclap and stormed through the skies, southwards.

September, October: harvest. Everyone came out to help. Grandmothers, as they lent their aid to the work, spoke of the Rye Mother, who must not be offended for fear of appalling retaliation, and of the Corn Mother, just as easily riled, who must be propitiated at all costs. The grandmothers were not laughing when they spoke of deaths the Rye Mother had imposed.

And don't say, *Yes! yes!* like that, and wink at one another. Harvest, when we reap the good of the earth we've toiled over all year, is our most vulnerable season. You think nature bends to our will? When the horses drag the reaping machine round, starting at the outermost edges of the field, the Corn Mother is driven back to an island where her power is concentrated. She retires into her anger until we have confined her in the last sheaf.

Beat her out, thrash her, thresh her, plait her into a corn dolly, to seal up her rage.

*

Soon after dawn the whole community was out in the fields, and Magdalena with them. It was now or never. The weather held. Mr Excorn had exhorted Magdalena and her fellow teachers to 'show willing, in helping with the harvest so as to appear involved in the community and food production for the nation.'

Appear involved?

How cynical. Of course they were involved, and not for show, or to impress the locals! With her mentor's permission, Magdalena closed the school for a week.

Now the Auroch came into its own as a bicycle for two. Magdalena blessed Clem for his skill and care in marrying parts from extinct bikes into this powerful machine. She padded the crossbar with an old dressing gown and tied it on securely. Julia adored the wild way Magda pedalled as they set off at crack of dawn to Eva's farm, alongside cornfields pinkish-golden in early sunlight. They sped along forest tracks, beneath leaf canopies arched into dark green tunnels. Ruts in the path jiggled Julia up and down: *Faster! Faster!* The Auroch, heavy as it was, was capable of good speeds.

Eva's estate, the largest in the region, was like a village in its own right. A road bisected the farm, flanked with labourers' cottages, continuing past the courtyard, past forge, stables and a meadow for the horses. Through the arable fields and pastures wound a broad lane, bordered by ancient oaks and beeches. It rose on a breast-like swell, kinked, and curved past three silver poplars. From the kink you looked down on the immense panorama of the estate and beyond.

At this point, Julia would shout, *Go! Go!* – and Magdalena could let the Auroch glide down the slope, freewheeling all the way.

Slave workers began to arrive – the Poles now joined by a few Russians. Their guards lounged around watching, firearms slung around their necks, relieved no doubt to have this cushy job, far from the killing fields. Eva housed them in farm cottages and an empty barn, where they slept on palliasses stuffed with straw. Nobody tried to escape. Where would you go? And besides, you could have no more humane a master than Eva.

In the afternoons, when most of the smaller children went home, Eva allowed Julia to curl up on her bed and gave her the run of children's books from her own youth. Julia played with toys passed down through generations of von Laulitz youngsters: miniature chess sets and tiny wooden dolls in crinolines with the original hair and ribbons. Prussian soldiers in full regalia with legs that marched. Julia would write adventure stories about the august persons peering from the ancestral oil paintings on the walls: noblemen in white wigs and chestfuls of insignia, ladies whose high hair was topped with outlandish arrangements of feathers, pearls and roses. Julia loved it all. She was in love with – and in awe of – their owner. Magda felt a version of the same double emotion.

Eva slipped a brown paper package into Magda's rucksack: *I can see you're ravenous, enjoy the cake! Keep it to yourself, mind.* Magda peeped: George Orwell, Nelly Sachs, forbidden books.

'I shall eat this cake *all* by myself, Eva, and *nobody* else will get a look-in,' Magda reassured her. 'You can be sure of that.'

Eva laughed. 'Yes, I know,' she said casually, turning to go. 'It's all right. Don't worry. Oh, and by the way, I had a letter!'

'You did?'

Eva nodded. She was shrugging on her jacket ready to return to the fields. Although she was not smiling, a painful joy glowed in her face.

'Came by hand. Hands, rather. Primitive postal service.'

Magda made sure not to ask where Leonie was, whether she had safely escaped to Switzerland or Spain. But she was *alive* – at least had been when she wrote the letter. Leonie, Magda suddenly thought incredulously, is ... something like ... Eva's other self. She remembered the beautiful verse from the biblical *Song of Solomon*: *A garden enclosed is my sister, my spouse; a spring shut up, a fountain sealed.* Yes, her spouse, her beloved, whatever you want to call it, though there are no words in any language. She stowed away this perception to mull over later. There was so much you didn't know about life, growing up in your bubble of dogmatic ignorance, that no one ever taught you. I'm green as grass, Magda thought. However did I come to earn Eva's trust? I could never aspire to count as her friend.

And Leonie is Jewish, Magda thought. But I already knew that.

She followed Eva out into the field, with a sense that she would like to put a caring arm round the tall, dominant woman and, grass-green as she was, shelter her.

Out in the fields, they all toiled together. Magdalena liked to work alongside the Norwegian prisoner of war, Alf. His German was flawless. He had a gaunt, kind, ironic face. Alf helped Magdalena get the hang of the back-breaking work. At the end of the day, you cycled home singing but you crawled into bed at night. In the mornings Magdalena tottered downstairs like an aged person, stretched her arms in the doorway, breathing in air that was cooling with the season.

So much to learn about the earth. It turned out that Miss Arber, who'd bestowed herself so generously upon Alt Schönbek to cultivate the minds of the rustics, was a bit of a dunce. She had to be shown the simplest things. About soil and shit; about oats and wheat and rye, reaping and threshing and gleaning and storing; about animal fodder; about potatoes and beet. About the food of the peasants, which she now recognised as the food of the gods. Rye was a never-say-die stalwart: you could sow and reap it twice a year. As the season yielded its declining warmth, rye's arms could reach up above ground. Beneath the cowl of snow the buried roots would thrive, grasping the earth in their claws, never-say-die.

Every bite of the pumpernickel bread, so brown it was nearly black, carried into your mouth its mineral tang. Eva's farm was teaching Magda's tastebuds a novel sensuality. Farm work aroused and transiently sated appetite. She rolled the sweet bitterness of the heavy rye bread around her mouth and gorged on the dark, thick caramel of molasses. Soon after eating she was ravenous again.

Everything was about food, wasn't it? What am I but a stomach on legs? she thought. I wake, I eat, I work, I shit, I sleep: round and round I go. Her parents' generation had suffered famine after the Great War, in the 'Turnip Winter'. As a small child – sitting in a tram on her father's knee – Magda had seen folk on the platform keel over: malnourished, Dad had explained. Nobody had come to their aid. *Waste not, want not*, her family had repeated, over and over. *Eat up every crumb now, Magda*. No one had minded when Magdalena wet her finger to glean every last particle of food from her plate. But as a city girl, growing up in relative plenty, she'd taken food for granted, standing in the butcher's and baker's queues, having her bacon sliced, weighed and wrapped, being handed her loaf over the counter. The slaughtered pig bleeds for my bacon; the wheat-field is harrowed for my bread. Every child knows *that*. But you know nothing until you carry the knowledge in your belly.

Magda never seemed to stop thinking about food. She saw now why the armies had been sent east to that massive Russian granary. We must devour our enemies.

Clem was over there, helping with the devouring. There'd been a letter this morning.

'Easy as pie!' Clem crowed. 'Ivan is a pansy! Ivan is a girl! He surrenders in hundreds of thousands – comes haring out of the woods with his hands up – *here I am, take me, take me!* The Leader told us we just had to kick in the door didn't he & the whole rotten structure would come crashing down. How right he was!

'My god Lena,' Clem wrote, 'the grub I've guzzled since I came east! Unbelievable! Aubergines & luscious melons – fish & flesh – plums & pears, eggs & potatoes. It's all I can do to waddle along after a meal! Folk can't do enough for us. They *want* to feed us! They welcome us as liberators. You see they believe they'll get to keep their own crops now that the Commies have been driven out. No more parasites. No more useless eaters, no more commissars & collective farms & all that bilge. Folk offer us their own beds but we say gallantly, thank you but we wouldn't dream of it – we'll sleep here on your floor.

'That's the thing Lena – wherever we Germans go we set a good orderly example & decent people love us for it.

'Been raining recently,' Clem remarked in a postscript, '& when I say raining I mean cats and dogs! When it lets up you've got a quagmire. Hope it stops soon. Couldn't move the truck yesterday. Send me more of that cake! I think I can find space in my belly to stuff it in for pudding. On second thoughts don't. I'll drop in on my way to Mum's – I've got a leave coming up – & I'll scoff some with you so get baking.'

She was not sure exactly where Clem was: he wasn't allowed to say. Ukraine? Lithuania? She longed to have him with her. Safe. Close. He'd been proud of being *blooded*, as when he came proudly home from the hunt with his dad, a brown smear of blood still visible on his forehead. He wouldn't wash it off, whatever Ebba said: women didn't understand hunters, he'd informed her, batting her hand away when she came at him with a flannel.

If all Clem had to worry about was the weather, that couldn't be so terrible, could it? And if Ivan was surrendering, the danger was so much less, wasn't it?

Hardly a drop of rain had fallen in the Alt Schönbek region since a week of summer downpours. Magdalena's pupils were all out helping bring in the harvest. The big boys had already missed weeks of class: at ten and eleven years old, they'd had to take over the roles of the men of the family. Fathers, uncles and brothers were falling at the front. Neighbours had lost sons. You could not help but realise, despite the triumphal broadcasts, that there were losses in the east. But Clem sounded buoyant. He had nothing to complain of but the weather.

Ruth was subdued. She came to help with the reaping; said little; got on with the work as she had done for many seasons. Folk asked Magda, *Is our dear Mrs Daschke all right? Is she ill? She's not herself. Can we do anything? What is the news of little Flora?* Ruth was a bit short with people when they enquired, so they spoke to Magdalena instead.

Magda would shake her head. *No news. But we are hopeful.*

*

At home with Ruth, a stressful calm prevailed. The letter predicted by Dr Littmann duly came. It told them nothing they did not already know: Flora's infection had been successfully cured and she'd accordingly been transferred to another institution whose facilities would 'better meet the patient's needs'. They neglected to say where. But Ruth knew, having spotted the word Gütersloh on the secretary's desk at Tapiau when she visited Littmann's office. *They don't seem to credit that schoolteachers are practised in reading upside-down,* she'd observed dryly.

By and by she filled Magdalena in on the journey she'd taken to track Flora down. She'd taken the train to Gütersloh Sanatorium. Flora was no longer there. She'd been there, yes, but shortly after her arrival had been transferred again.

The head nurse had taken the time to sit down with Ruth. She hadn't fobbed her off. She'd assured her that she understood why Mrs Daschke had travelled all that way and why she was anxious. She had children of her own.

She'd consulted Flora's notes, which simply read, *Transferred for tests*, and the date.

'But don't worry, Mrs Daschke,' she'd said. 'She's in the system. We'll track her down.'

She'd called up the ward, and a young nurse appeared.

Oh yes, the young woman had cared for little Flora. Such a sweet girl! They had good hopes of her. She'd sat down whenever she could at Flora's bedside and played with the dolly she loved so much.

'Helga, wasn't it?'

And seeing that Ruth beamed through her tears, and her hands trembled, the nurse had gone on to describe the home-made doll.

'Yes, yes, that is Flora's doll! It is her most precious possession.'

'Did you sew it yourself, Mrs Daschke?'

'I did – I did!'

And little Flora, they'd reported, had seemed content and settled, despite the change of place. She was now in a transit centre, and would shortly be moved to one of three institutions, depending on the results of the examination they were conducting. *We have high hopes that little Flora can be taught to speak!*

'Taught to *speak*?' echoed Ruth. Tears had poured down her face.

'Under expert care, of course, using the most up-to-the-minute methods. But I must caution you. This will not happen overnight, Mrs Daschke. I only say: *we have hopes.*'

'But why,' Ruth had asked, 'may I not see her? Surely a mother ... and I am a teacher by profession...'

'Oh no, with due respect, a mother is the last person ... a scientific approach requires what one might call emotional neutrality ... and this is a highly specialised method of treatment. As a teacher, you will understand this. And, no, I cannot tell you where the transit centre is. And you must on no account go chasing round the country looking for it. That will not be tolerated. And, Mrs Daschke, it is more likely to harm than help your daughter. *However*, once the treatment is – let us say – advanced, you'll be notified and welcomed with open arms, be sure of that, and your little Flora will be restored to you.'

'Do you mean, she'll be discharged and come home? For good?'

'Of course! What else would I mean?'

'I thought ... I was afraid...'

'What were you afraid of?'

'I was afraid ... I'd never see her again...'

'Goodness me! Where is your faith? Leave your daughter in the care of the National Socialist Health Service.' The head nurse had replaced the documents in the folder and the folder in the filing cabinet, nodding to the young nurse to return to her duties. 'And trust us to offer the best and most modern treatment.'

'But when will I be told where she is?'

'You should hear within two weeks. Mrs Daschke, trust us. What are we for, if not to heal those who suffer? We have taken sacred oaths.'

*

'Sacred oaths,' repeated Ruth to Magdalena. 'The Hippocratic Oath, she must have meant. I looked it up. *I swear by Apollo the Physician, by Asclepius ... and so on ... by all the gods and goddesses ... I will abstain from intentional harm or injustice.* Or did she mean some other oath? God knows, there are plenty of oaths about. Oaths are two-a-penny. However, a doll! You can't make up a doll! I keep coming back to that. A handmade doll, unique in the world! Flora has her doll with her. That's the material point.'

'So – you were satisfied?' asked Magdalena. They sat at table, and Ruth was eating again, which was perhaps one answer to the question. She spread a slice of rye bread, smothering it with butter and molasses, and nibbled it.

'They were human, that was what I felt. And when they said about the doll ... now, *that* was the moment, you see ... I knew Flora must have been there. It was a trace. The first genuine trace.'

'I'm so glad, Ruth. You seem much more yourself. Are you coming to the farm today?'

'I'll follow you a bit later. Mr Excorn wants to see me but that shouldn't take long. And, Magda ... just a minute—'

Ruth flushed and reached out her hand.

'Magda, forgive me for how I've been. I'm so sorry. I've been behaving like a madwoman. In a bad dream. Taking it out on you. And you cared for Julia and put up with me and my – ravings. You are the one person ... the only person guaranteed never to let us down. I can never thank you enough. Never. You've been like a sister.'

The door to escape was closing. It would not reopen. Magdalena knew that. She took the hand that was reaching out to her. And at least Ruth's drinking had levelled off.

'Nothing to forgive, Ruth. Nothing in the world.'

'Yes. There is.'

'Really. But all right, don't look like that, if it makes you feel better, of course I forgive you. With all my heart. Will you promise me something though?'

Ruth grinned. 'Depends! I expect so. Give me a clue.'

'When I was in Lübeck, my father – who knows what I'm like, because he's like it himself, and suffered for it – headstrong, a bit of a know-all – he has really made me think – Dad begged me to keep my head down. Not stand out in the crowd. In any way. And I promised. Because I saw what it would do to him, and everyone I love, if I were arrested. Ruth, would you do the same? You've been taking horrific risks.'

She would do her best, said Ruth. She'd been aware of Edith Struppat rooting round, sniffing for information about Flora. *How was I feeling? Where had I been? And she wanted me to talk to a pal of hers whose son had been at Tapiau.*

'Why?'

'I don't know. And I'm not going to find out.'

'You must survive, for both the twins. My father was in Dachau KZ, '33, Ruth. He *saw*.'

By and by, as they sat, and their loving talk flowed, shafts of low light increased in the kitchen and pooled on the floor, where crumbs Julia had dropped from her plate cast improbable slant shadows.

They spoke about how there could be no such thing for them as political resistance. How they were not the stuff of which martyrs are made. How they had to live for the living, and keep those they loved alive, and warm, and fed, and safe, and cherished. They agreed that all they could do was to open out and safeguard a space for their families and the closest of close friends. How they were being watched. All the time, watched. They were trapped on a vast sticky web. Every time they moved, the web quivered, and the watchers on a million nodes felt the vibration, and the arachnids homed in on prey.

Once they had Flora safely home with them, they'd lock and bolt the door of their joint world.

It was an oath of sorts. The two women sat bent forward, each holding both the other's hands, speaking freely and without embarrassment or concealment. Tears fell and they wiped them away.

It was getting late. Come on, Magda thought. We need to put our skates on. And next week I have to go on BDM service to Joniec and Ploehnen. At least Marianne will be with me. We managed that well.

'But would you do something for me, Magda?'

Getting up, Ruth went over to her bureau, unlocked a drawer and took out an envelope. No, two.

For Miss Magdalena Arber, in case of my arrest.
For Miss Magdalena Arber, in the event of my death.

17

> And Jesus saith unto him, Feed my sheep.[22]
> *The Gospel According to John*, 21:17

Harvest was long over; the wild geese had flown. Snow blanketed the village, a peaceful mantle absorbing all sound until the howling began. For ten days Siberian wind blasted the fields, beneath charcoal skies, driving snow and sleet before it. The children arrived at school wet through and numb with cold, or did not arrive at all.

In Magdalena's attic bedroom, the onslaught could be deafening. A layer of tiles separated her from the elements. And yet she learned to sleep through it. Nobody could insist on a meeting of the Band of German Maidens in this weather. Nobody could send her to bring civilisation to the primitives in what had been Poland and was now Germany. Nobody could march Magdalena and Marianne into Nasielsk, or Joniec, or – worst – Ploehnen, where she'd seen...

Don't say, don't say ... at least Dr Süsskind escaped that ... but where is Miss Heller? Don't ask, don't ask. Don't think about it.

Anyway, now you could sleep in. The weather sealed you in. Forget Ploehnen. Marianne had been sick in the gutter when she saw...

In Alt Schönbek, a sudden thaw brought torrents of melting ice.

Forget Ploehnen. Forget the tailor, Mr Goldberg, wearing the Star of David who'd been let out of the ghetto to pursue his trade by day. Magda and Marianne had been sent on an errand to pick up the Band of German Maidens camp leader's dress which Mr Goldberg was altering. Walking along the road, they'd seen that a row of houses had been boarded up. But from behind the fence, which did not quite touch the ground, they heard murmuring and movement, the babble of many voices.

Stooping, they saw beneath the fence ... feet. Countless soiled feet, naked, in slippers, sandals, shoes. They stood on tiptoe, looked over the fence and saw innumerable bald heads. They breathed in a rank smell.

And Marianne was violently sick in the street, she couldn't stop ... she went down on hands and knees ... but forget all that, there's nothing you can do about it, except wish you hadn't seen it.

In Alt Schőnbek the snow brought a purity. Magdalena lay in her attic room as a new freeze was followed by a fall of powdery snow, flakes drifting down gentle and feathery, snow on snow, building and building until the landscape was a desert of white dunes.

Skudde sheep blundered into sudden drifts, vanished, and came out frozen meat. Or were born again, scarcely able to bleat, when the shepherd waded through to deliver them. You might see a ram, just about alive, being hauled out by its immense curling snail horns. Cattle swam through snow, only their heads showing, making stately but urgent progress, prodigious horns curving wide. At Laulitz Farm, Alf carved skis out of planks of birchwood. He did nothing else. Night and day he worked on the skis, for the soldiers, farm workers, prisoners, and for Eva. This was an ancient skill at home in Norway, he said, teaching the craft to other prisoners: carve, plane, soak in boiling water, bend, oil, that's the way.

And the pigman said, *A Norwegian is nearly as good as a German. Same stem, see. Architect he is at home.*

Sleighs and sledges were preferred means of travel now. Over fresh snow the sleighs' runners purred past. On refrozen slush, they cracked the ruts with a musical sound like tinkling shards of breaking panes.

Dozing at weekends, Magdalena caught the sound of horses' bells in her dreams and let them lull her. The village carried on its tranquil pulse-beat of life in the Prussian heartland, as it had done for a thousand years. Planes throbbed high overhead but no bombs fell. She did not ask ... no, I won't ask that ... for what can I do? ... how the living skeletons in the Ploehnen Ghetto were faring in this freeze, with their shaven heads and their naked feet, and their shuffling murmur, and their smell. No, I'll sleep as long as I can.

I shan't ask what they have to eat or what warm clothes they have to put on, these *useless eaters*.

I shan't ask what this barbaric cruelty has to do with me or whether I am implicated in these crimes.

Beneath the mound of her quilt, a layer of warm air from the night sheathed Magdalena's lax Saturday morning body. But don't stir! Don't even turn over in bed – because the cold in the attic bedroom lurked, waiting up close, seeking a vent. You could feel it grasping at your skull, though your face was buried up to your hair in quilt. At the point of entry it would be all over with this pleasurable wallowing in the fug of your own stale breath, inhaling the animal smell of goose feathers. Magda's refuge was this weekend trance in which you could lie as long as you liked.

As she slept, snow mounted outside, scaling the house walls, layering the roof over her head. She'd learned to divine changes in the weather by hearing alone: in a thaw, snow slid down the tiles with a rush ... whereupon it might refreeze into icicles half a metre long. On Magda's water jug a film of ice formed every night. The face cloth froze to its dish, the dish to the cupboard top. Ink froze solid in the bottle.

Their poor bare feet ... shush, shush.

And Mr Goldberg, was he still there in his shop ironing trousers with amazing agility, spit – iron – spit – iron? We praised him for his skill, she remembered, and he smiled sadly at us, and we were glad to escape from Ploehnen, but what could we have done in any case? We took that ghastly woman's beautiful dress and ran to the station.

It's not our fault, Marianne had said when she had finished vomiting. On the train they'd closed their eyes but could not sleep. Their hands had stolen out and blindly clasped one another.

Roosting now in her eyrie, sound reached Magdalena muffled and distant as she relaxed under the handsome new quilt Ebba had sent: *keep warm, our darling, keep warm.* Julia had eyed it with envy. She was easy to find during games of hide-and-seek. She'd scamper upstairs and burrow down in the quilt's soft, dark cave.

Magdalena floated between asleep and awake, into ...

... a dream, languorous and exultant. What was that all about? She caught a wisp of the dream as she surfaced. Alf in the field, but in the dream the season was autumn, and misty. The mist seemed to steam up from the earth, a miasma: it enveloped and hid the two of them in its shroud. Alf's pale eyes, his height bending over her. If he would only... If Eva would only...

Up! She abandoned her bed with a bound, broke the ice film on the water jug, stripped the facecloth from its bowl with a sound like a zip fastener. Cold thrilled through flesh and bone to the marrow. Quaking, Magda pulled on trousers, two pairs, and several sweaters. Time to dive downstairs and bask in the warmth of the kitchen ... but first a brief pause, to take a view of Alt Schönbek by snowlight.

Ice patterns on the mansard window mimicked trees, branching out into a lace of crystalline forms. Your overnight breath had frozen into ferns and feathers, unfurling over imperfections in the glass. A rusted nail, left sticking out of the frame by some long-ago botching builder, sprouted and spiked like a cactus. Each day's frost experimented freshly. Today Magda's eyes made out an ice-pond crammed with squirming ice-tadpoles, on a map of an unknown continent, its tectonic plates on the move from day to day.

Huffing on the freeze, Magda circled with her finger, tracing a spy-hole. A skeletal beech tree came into view through the melt, solid, dark, but wavering, as though seen through running tears.

She fled downstairs to the kitchen, the domain of the tiled stove whose coal fire Ruth did not allow to die. Magda burst into the intoxicating smell of sizzling bacon.

An envelope ... no, two envelopes lay on the table. One was opened.

Ruth sat Magda down on the bench by the stove, putting hot chocolate in her hands. Her face was euphoric.

Real chocolate? They were celebrating? Where on earth had Ruth got hold of chocolate? Perhaps she'd hidden it from herself and forgotten its existence. (*Could* you forget chocolate?) If they ever came by any such luxury, it went straight to Julia as a matter of course.

'Has Julia had some?'

'Oh yes, plenty – don't worry. And I've some left over for her.'

The glimmer of a smile haunted Ruth's eyes as she sipped her drink. Magda wrapped her fingers round the heat, basked with her back against the warm tiles and breathed on the chocolate, which breathed its steamy scent hotly back at her.

'Did you sleep well, Ruth?'

'Like a top.'

'Well? Come on then? Out with it!'

She looked from the envelopes to Ruth, and back again.

'One for you and one for me.' Ruth handed it over. 'Here's yours.'

Magdalena read that Dr Vogel would be scheduling his visit to Alt Schönbek once the freeze had slackened. 'Oh lord. Visit from Zoo-man. You know – Mr Mushroom from the train.' She stuffed the letter back in its envelope. 'But what's in yours?'

Ruth handed it over.

'Little <u>FLORA DASCHKE</u> has adjusted well to the regime,' the typewritten message reassured her mother. 'She is always breezy and happy and shows no traces of homesickness. Dear little <u>FLORA</u> is eating so well that she has gained 1kg in weight. She is responding promisingly to the speech tutor.'

And a scribbled postscript: 'Flora's doll is a great favourite with the staff.'

'Adapted well! Eating!' Ruth burst out. 'Weight gain! See? Starting to speak!'

'That's wond—'

'Yes, yes, but the postscript – *handwritten!* The doll, you see – the doll, Magda! That is the salient detail!'

'Oh, Ruth ... I don't know...'

Sharply: 'You don't know what?'

'I only meant ... I don't know what to say.'

'Let me see it again.'

Ruth reached out for her message, read the typewritten words aloud, slowly, as if she might have missed something the first ten times, and it may be possible to wring out extra information. Progress reports had been arriving at intervals but they hadn't heard for more than a fortnight and Ruth had blamed the weather, the postal service, the railways.

The typewritten letters were obvious duplicates: Magdalena could see that the name Flora Daschke, in capital letters, had been inserted in a gap. What did that imply?

But after all it was not unthinkable that Flora might be eating better and learning some language, once she'd got over her initial homesickness – because hadn't Magdalena felt at one time and said to Ruth: *I think Flora's trying to speak, I really do. We just need to bring it out.*

Is it me then? Is my judgement corrupted? Has the infection spread so that I distrust everybody and everything?

Why would anyone serving the great machine of the wartime National Socialist medical service, stretched to its limits by the carnage of war, bother to bear witness to something so trivial as a child's toy, in the great scheme of things? The only answer could be that this off-the-cuff scribble represented a mother's hand reaching out to another mother?

At Gütersloh Ruth had met with more compassion than reproof, for challenging the rules. Surely the postscript had been inserted by the head nurse she'd spoken to there, who remembered Ruth and wished her well. What other explanation could there be? *Have faith in us,* that lady had said to Ruth.

Faith, whether in God or humanity, was a candle whose frail flame you had to shield, day and night: Auntie Ebba, holding on – sometimes by her fingertips – to faith in God and human goodness, had shown her that. Magdalena saw how much it cost Ruth – wryly sceptical as she was – to sustain her trust.

And surely Ruth was right. How could anyone be so cynical as to lie about an afflicted girl? And whatever would be the point?

Magda said none of this to Ruth, who wiped her eyes and blew her nose, saying, 'Well, that's enough of that. Breakfast. I hope you're hungry as a wolf.'

She turned the rashers and sausage in the pan; broke in a couple of eggs, scooped seething butter over them; dished up.

'How can I possibly eat all that?' asked Magda, receiving her plate, running with fat.

'I think you'll manage.'

Magdalena stabbed her fork into a yolk, slathering her bacon with it. To celebrate Ruth's birthday, the children had brought into her classroom meat and fish and over one hundred eggs donated by their grateful families. A hundred eggs! Officials from the Empire Food Corporation didn't bother to come round checking whether small market-gardeners were keeping more than the regulation share of what they grew and reared.

In Lűbeck Dad and Ebba were making do with tiny amounts of rationed oil, eggs and butter. And Clem: what about Clem, somewhere in Russia? How was he faring, what was he eating now?

As the army advanced into the teeth of the Russian winter, Clem's letters, few and short, took weeks to arrive. How could you write a proper letter bivouacking in a frozen ditch? Clem craved meat, cheese, chocolate, skin cream, mineral pastilles, vitamin tablets, razor blades, cigarettes, socks, gloves, cake, biscuits.

Surely it would all be over soon, he'd written: Kiev had fallen, and Kharkov, Bryansk and Vyazma. Moscow was in sight! But then had come the deluge. Columns of tanks sank swamped in roads that had never been proper roads in the first place, they were dirt tracks that had degenerated into bogs. Lorry-wheels, mired up to the axle, spun in a rich shit of mud; horses fractured their legs and had to be shot and eaten.

Then came November's freeze, the worst for many years: minus twenty degrees, minus thirty, and falling.

What Clem wouldn't give, he wrote, for a sausage. A hot meal. Fried potatoes. He dreamed of roast duck, smelt it in his sleep, woke with a mouthful of saliva to bread and watery soup. The soup that had started out hot arrived at your foxhole cold, or even frozen, and you ate it like ice cream. All the comrades talked about was food.

The peasants had been stripped of all they possessed. They had no food to share because they had no food.

Also: a hot bath with lashings of soap suds would be heaven.

One plus he could report: Clem had stripped a fur coat from a just-killed Russian. You have to skin them from the corpse without delay: otherwise clothes freeze to the bodies, no use to anyone. We do not have proper winter clothes.

We will bear anything for our Fatherland. It is comradeship that pulls us through, Lena.

Then in tiny letters, formed of faint dots, threading up through the lines of writing: *there are things we have to do, let it be over soon, please God.* As children they had sent each other secret messages on this principle: pinpoints of ink, only apparent to the pair of them.

Distances between the homeland and the front were immense; supply lines stretched to breaking. Fuel, food, armaments, tools ran out. Stalin poured in fresh troops, more materiel. The last letter Magdalena had received said, in that thin, scarcely legible ghost-writing, running athwart the lines of text, *It hurts, it all hurts, I can't describe, I miss you all, send what you can.*

It hurts: Clem would creep into her bed as a child, to be petted and comforted. A cut knee, a bad tooth. A dead father.

Nevertheless, what can you do? Magdalena tucked in to her breakfast, with appetite. Guzzle it while you've got it. Enjoy it.

She'd be going skating with Julia, Ruth said, on the lake. Why not come along? The team of ten-year-olds, just formed at Alt Schönbek school, would be playing ice hockey.

Julia, wanting to join in, had whined, *Why can't I be in the team? It's not fair!*

The answer to that was *Because you're a girl.*

To which Julia had replied, *I'm not a blooming girl!*

Ruth had expressed surprise, enquiring, *Oh, aren't you? I always thought you were. What are you then?*

After giving this some thought, chewing her lip, Julia had replied, *I'm a person, that's what!*

A good answer, they agreed.

'Where is she now?' Magda mopped up the remaining grease with the last of her rye bread. 'It's terribly quiet!'

'She's under the piano, reading a book to her animals.'

'Have you said anything to her about Flora?'

'Not yet. I think it's too early.'

'Yes, I'm sure you're right.'

'Do you think Julia has actually ... completely ... forgotten her sister?' Ruth asked in a bruised voice. 'I mean, forgotten she ever had a sister?'

She wanted to know, and did not want to know, the answer. Any possible reply must strike a nerve. She lit a cigarette, blowing out a stream of smoke. 'Want one?'

'No thanks. I don't know, Ruth. Sometimes we just bury things, don't we? I mean, all of us do. Or put them away in a sort of pocket. For the time being,' Magdalena replied, carefully. 'Things we don't understand. Things we can't do anything about. And a child...'

'But when Flora comes home ... *when* she does ... won't Julia wonder who this stranger is?'

'Well, just at first perhaps, love. And then she'll just accept her, and adapt, and be glad. Don't you think? It will never be too late. Shall we go and see what she's up to?'

Heat from the tile stove radiated throughout the ground floor, so that Julia could play in any room, without a fire, and still be warm as toast.

They peered round the door into the music room, where the child was sitting cross-legged beneath the piano, surrounded by four or five of her most favoured woolly animals, each equipped with a shred of paper. Less favoured toy animals were grouped at a distance: Foxy and Piglet were out in the cold. They had their ostracised faces turned to the wall and were not equipped with paper. Julia, her long hair pulled back severely in a bun, tapped a pencil on a slate for emphasis. She was instructing her class, in a professional voice, about *important matters you youngsters are required to learn.*

'Hallo, darling! – how is it going?'

'Please call me Miss Daschke! I'm a teacher, aren't I?'

'Oh yes, of course, Miss Daschke – sorry, Miss Daschke.'

'Anyway, yes, come into the school room, both of you – you're rather late for class. But never mind,' Miss Daschke said forgivingly. 'Sit down quietly in your places, Ruth and Magdalena. I'll excuse you this once.'

'I don't think we'll fit under the piano,' said Magda. 'Should we sit over here?'

'No! By no means! Not with the fox! That's not your place!'

'Oh. Why not?'

'That's where the dirty Jews sit.'

'What? What did you say?'

The shock penetrated you. Where had Julia got hold of that book on her lap, with its splash of scarlet on the cover, its bloated, swindling caricature of the Jew and the cunning fox?

I destroyed that damn thing, Magdalena thought, I burnt it. Told old Excorn it had gone missing. Now it's come back. Did he give her a replacement to pass on to us?

'How did you...?' she blurted, and stopped herself.

Magda had been bringing home such lovely children's books from Eva's private library at the rate of two a week. Julia's reading had come on in leaps and bounds. She'd lie on her back with her legs in the air, holding a book above her head, and read aloud from Kästner's *Emil and the Detectives* and Felix Salten's banned book, *Life Story from the Woods*, which she loved, even though the sorrows of Bambi and his mummy deer made her cry every time. Or *because* their sorrows made her cry, delicious tears.

Trust No Fox on his Green Heath and No Jew on his Oath.

Ruth was quick to react. She knelt calmly beside the piano and reached for the volume, which slipped from Julia's grip. Ruth handed it behind her back, to Magdalena.

Meanwhile she coaxed Julia: 'Come on, Miss Daschke, shut up the school for the day – time for the bell to go and all your little pupils to toddle off home to their mummies and daddies.'

'No! It's not home-time yet!' Sulky face; folded arms. 'And why are you taking my book? And leave Foxy where he is, please, Mummy! No, don't turn his face round – no! He is sneaky, he steals from nice good Germans, he guzzles all our dinner, it's not his dinner, it's ours, that's why the Jewboy's so fat, even his gobbling slobbering blubber-mouth is fat, his daddy is the Devil!'

'No, darling, Foxy is just an innocent creature, like all your other pets. We must love him and do him no harm. And people are just people.'

Julia looked confused, opened her mouth and closed it again, as if she wanted to claim that some people were not people.

'Anyway, let's not quarrel, angel,' said Ruth. 'Give Foxy a nice hug.'

Julia looked over at her toy fox and was silent.

'Come on,' Ruth coaxed, 'you were cuddling him yesterday when he hurt his ear. We don't want Foxy to be lonely, do we? It's not nice when people leave us out. And Piggie is a nice oinky porker, isn't he?'

'He's a runt!'

'In that case he needs all the love we can give him.'

'All right,' said Julia, grudgingly. 'But anyway, why have we got to go?'

'Skating, remember? On the lake. You've been looking forward to it. With your friends. Coming?'

Julia propelled herself from the piano schoolroom, on her bottom, using her hands as oars, and all the while issuing instructions to her class to do their homework in their neatest handwriting.

Magdalena ran upstairs and locked the book in a drawer. The bedroom's cold air clawed at her; she shook. And was afraid. What am I afraid of? This was just one of hundreds of such books. Its lesson was normalised, universally accepted. Who'd given Julia this copy?

Best, perhaps, to keep silent, allow the child to forget. Look blank if she asked after it. Julia had probably never even seen a Jewish person, for the simple reason that there were none in the village: laws forbade Jews to own farms or land. And now they were required by law to wear a yellow star, so everyone would have known if a Jew had so much as visited the village.

You could not say to Julia: *This book tells lies, it is vile, we forbid you to read it.* A child of seven cannot be burdened or trusted with a secret like that.

She'd blurt to someone: *You know what...?* Before you knew it, there'd be a knock on the door...

You could not counsel her: *Julia, don't tell anyone what we say about it. Or there'll be a knock on the door...*

Could you soften the message? – *It's just a story, like Grimms' fairy tales, and to be honest, not one we particularly like.*

Grimms' fairy tales were pretty nasty at the best of times: the stepmothers, for instance. The one in – what story was it, *The Juniper Tree?* – who decapitates a child, cooks him and feeds him to his father.

Magdalena rummaged in the cupboard and pulled out her skates. She hadn't skated in years: would they even fit? If not, she could just slide around on the ice in her boots. She packed an extra sweater in her rucksack. You'd be hot and sweaty when you were actually skating, but once off the ice, you'd be freezing again.

They were calling her from the bottom of the stairs. 'Come *on!* What on earth are you doing up there?'

'On my way!'

She felt giddy on the stairs, as if – which was ludicrous – the book was pursuing her. She slowed down, groping for the banister. There was a sense of being endangered.

And the anxious young man in the train that time, asking *Are you all right, miss?* On Königsberg Station he stopped for me.

And Miss Heller, her parents and grandparents, her violin, her seven-branched candlestick, her library, the lapwings on the heath. I must not cry for Miss Heller, who also stopped for me.

The Daschkes were waiting in the hall, in their thick winter coats, boots and scarves, Julia prancing from foot to foot with impatience: 'Where have you *been*? We're going *skating!* And don't be worried that you'll fall through, Magda, the ice is eight inches thick, eight inches! Or even ten.'

Magdalena looked at Julia's innocent, tempestuous face, bent and hugged her tight, wanting to cry.

And after all, I'm only a twenty-year-old know-all, she thought, with very little experience of anything except of being a born know-all. At Christmas she must speak to Dad and Ebba, laying the dark riddle of it all before them.

For she had been to Ploehnen; she had seen.

18

> It is forbidden to unnecessarily torment or roughly mishandle an animal ... It is forbidden ... to shorten the tail of a horse ... to force-feed fowl; to tear out or separate the thighs of living frogs.[23]
>
> *Law on Animal Protection,*
> Sections I–II, Berlin, 24 November 1934,
> Signed: Adolf Hitler

Christmas, despite the absence of Clem, had been peaceful at Lűbeck. Ebba and Magdalena had taken Communion; then home to share the half goose that Magdalena had triumphantly transported home.

At least Clem was alive and not freezing in a foxhole.

So Ebba kept reminding them all, and especially herself. Her son, after the fiasco of the Barbarossa offensive, was lying in a field hospital, with a foot that was only slowly recovering from frost bite and gangrene. *Don't worry about me too much, Mum – I'm safe here – only lost one toe! Being fed. Snoozing. On the mend. As soon as I can walk, I'll have some leave and we'll be together and you can cosset me all you like!*

Dad could talk more freely than Magda could remember, allowing them to meet as near equals, or so it felt. What had changed between them? She puzzled over this on the journey back to Kőnigsberg. Max had been no less Max, the rueful disciple of Voltaire in an alien world. Partly it must be to do with his acceptance that, just as Max was Max, so Magdalena was Magdalena, who'd proved herself – and would go her own way, which he recognised as a version of his way. And perhaps the affair of the socks! Her understanding and absolution.

But mainly, she concluded, it was something to do with Dad's new and secret writing project. No more nitpicking, he'd said, and learned footnotes, and recondite allusions, and sentences sagging under the weight of adjectival clauses. Oh the relief, to express the living detail of life in the pith of language! To try to do so anyway. It was like writing with his left hand, very hard and very good.

On Magda's last night he'd taken her out to show her, in the snowbound garden, exactly where he'd buried the first two books of his journal.

Just in case, he'd said. For safekeeping. As I finish each volume, I will add them to the cache. You will know where to look, Magdalena. They are for you.

*

March in Alt Schönbek: the ice melted away, not drip by drip but in gushing torrents.

The underworld opened; life surged from waterlogged ground. In the woodlands, marsh marigolds budded, amongst tangles of creepers, tussocky sedges and rotting timber. In ditches and around ponds, in marshes and meadows, their golden cups made ready to unfurl and track the sun around the day. All this deliquescence was full of latency. You couldn't help but feel it in the sunny but caustic spring air. Birds began noisily to nest.

Spring was coming, and Magdalena would see Dad, Ebba and Clem, all together again in the Easter holidays.

Meanwhile there was the long-awaited visit of Dr Vogel to prepare for. Forced labourers were drafted in to convert a barn, helped by the children of Alt Schönbek School. Magda worked with Alf on carving wooden eagles. They did not speak, not in words anyway. Occasionally her fingers touched his fingers and they both looked away. When Alf's eyes fleetingly met Magda's, they said: You will kill me if you come any nearer. It was literally true. And besides, the eyes added, I am married, I love my wife and children, I live in Norway with them despite being dragged so far from home.

Magdalena nodded to him curtly – it was the best she could do for him – and removed herself to help the children with their decorations.

The German guards mucked in. They were veterans, a bit past it, just relieved to be free of the hard graft of murder. The makeshift dais was resplendent with floral decorations, backed by sprays of evergreen. Flags at either side flanked a swastika and a portrait in oils of the Leader.

A volley of salutes greeted Dr Vogel as, accompanied by the welcoming party, he appeared on the dais. Since Magdalena had last seen him at Rominten Heath, Dr Vogel seemed to have clambered further up the Party tree. A new title – Chief of Animal Welfare (East) – now added lustre to his name. Amongst Vogel's entourage Magdalena recognised another scientist from Rominten. The name escaped her. You would not forget that maudlin, oily face: well-fed, satisfied with himself but perhaps less than satisfied with his lot.

Not to put too fine a point on it, Dad had said, the whole lot of them are eaten up by envy and balked ambition. That was one of the things that made bootlickers dangerous. They smarmed and smirked and deferred, but inwardly loathed one another. And here was the grandiose Dr Littmann, not seen in provincial Alt Schönbek for months. The zealous physician had discarded his rustic tweeds. His local-doctor days were well behind him. He wore the proud uniform of an SS medic, serpent crest resplendent on his collar patch.

Once on the stage, Dr Vogel performed an immaculate – and yet somehow agreeably modest – salute and wave, in response to Alt Schönbek's greeting. He smiled at the folk filling the barn, unassumingly, as if to say, *Aye, my friends, I may be flying with eagles, but for that very reason I do not forget my origins amongst the common pigeons like yourselves pecking around at ground level.*

But do feel free to admire my shiny new title.

Such an honour, the Area Group Deputy Agronomy Leader was

saying, to be privileged to welcome the Chief of Animal Welfare (East) to our corner of East Prussia.

On behalf of the Regional Education Service, the lowly Excorn rose to greet the distinguished guest. Light glinted on the lens covering his one seeing eye. He apologised for this improvised location (*Not at all, not at all!*) but Dr Vogel would like to know that the transformation of a barn into a reception hall had been effected with the corporate help of the village schoolchildren (*Bravo, children!*), with a view to welcoming their esteemed guest (*Too kind, too kind!*).

Magdalena, seated at the edge of the dais with Ruth and assorted wives, was conscious of Vogel's eyes seeking her out – and finding her. A crinkling smile and a nod. Dressed in the dark green tunic and riding breeches of a forester, he rose to greet with easy warmth the audience of local Party officials, agricultural ministry representatives, foresters and farmers, the Lutheran minister, and 'three of our most illustrious anatomists, Dr Hermann Voss of Posen Institute of Science, the great Dr Julius Hallervorden – East Prussian born and bred – and another eminent authority with whom you will be familiar – Dr Felix Johann Littmann.'

All too familiar, Ruth's expression implied. She emitted a faint snort.

Magda nudged her with her foot. Close the door of your face, her glance said. Lock it. She had resolutely closed hers, apart from an ungovernable tic under her left eye and a desire to sneeze.

Even so. Without the impression she herself had made on Dr Vogel, none of this would have come about. A woman can't rise in the world. Her place is to sit on the sidelines, and admire, and applaud. Women don't stand at lecterns and pontificate. In the end she's livestock, bovine in a byre with the other breeders, Magda thought to herself.

Bovine in a byre with breeders! That's it! The first line of a poem!

And yet here am I, she thought, Miss Magdalena Arber, a respected teacher! someone of account, and only twenty years old!

Be careful, be so careful, Dad would have said. *It just takes one word, one look, and you are finished.*

Magdalena closed the door of her face again.

Adjusting his tunic, Dr Vogel rubbed his hands together and placed them at either side of the lectern, at the front of which one of Alf's carved eagles stood ready to take off. The speaker had no notes and appeared jocular, expansive, in his element.

It went without saying that Dr Vogel was heartened to see so many loyal community leaders assembled to learn about the animal culture of the Third Empire, in which he himself had a modest part to play. But perhaps the adults would forgive him for saying that he was here, first and foremost, for the children of Alt Schönbek?

'Hands up, children, if you were amongst the honoured guests at Rominten Heath Nature Sanctuary! Guests of no less a personage than Imperial Marshall Goering – the President of Prussia – Master of the Forests! The knightly Siegfried of our times!'

Proud hands shot up. Vogel's smile swept the rows of young faces – the youngest girls and boys in their best clothes, the older ones wearing their Young-Folk uniforms, tan shirts and black neckerchiefs.

'I do not see your esteemed teacher's hand. Do you?'

Laughter – and: 'Put your hand up, Miss Arber!' from the children.

Magdalena raised her hand.

'I want to speak to you today about German animals in their *environment.* But wait a moment, what is the environment? A long word! It means the nature of the place where species have evolved over millions of years. We German zoologists call this study the science of *ecology.* Can you all say *en-vir-on-ment*? *E-col-og-y*?'

'Environment! Ecology!'

'Once upon a time, children – millions of years ago – which is to say, before even I was born! – primeval forest covered the entire continent of Europe. Some of you, I know, are the offspring of foresters and hunters. Perhaps that helps you to imagine a mighty

Aryan forest, teeming with wild animals – greater than anything we know today. The whole of Europe an Aryan forest! The – whole – of – Europe!'

Dr Vogel waved his right arm, to indicate the totality of the Aryan world.

'Now, who can tell me which Aryan animals lived in that primeval forest?'

'Please sir, bison!'

'Good answer, young man. And your name? Hartmut. And what noise did a bison make, do you think, Hartmut? Did bison bleat like little French lambkins who want their mummies? – No? You don't think so? Well then, boy next to Hartmut? – did bison moo like fat Dutch cows? – No? – Blonde girl with plaits, front row – Did they perhaps miaow like English pussycats? – Don't be shy!'

Dr Vogel mimicked the effete noises to be expected from these spineless creatures.

'Or,' he said, 'did bison *roar*? ... Everyone! – Louder! Louder! I can't hear you! And – what other ancient animals can you think of?'

'Mammoths? Mastodons?'

'Another good answer, little girl with the topknot. If I'm not mistaken, you were one of the party who visited Rominten Nature Sanctuary? Am I right? And I think you danced there for our great Master Forester. Is that not so? And perhaps your respected teacher Miss Arber can name another denizen of the Aryan forests? Well, Miss Arber?'

'You mean the auroch, of course, Dr Vogel.'

'And how, if I may pause to ask, is your own personal auroch faring? I mean of course, Miss Arber's trusty bike!' he asked, winking, and the children laughed. 'Is your own personal auroch still in one piece? Good! Well now, children, think about this, think very carefully. Those magnificent German animals are extinct. And what does extinct mean?'

'Gone?'

'Dead?'

'Gone off the face of the earth. Never, never to be seen again. Habitat destroyed by French farmers! Overhunted. Bred out in the service of so-called civilisation. The great crime against nature! Pure blood diluted. The wolf was weakened into the poodle. The auroch into the cow, by breeding only the feeblest specimens. So, how can we *bring back* animals that have died out, children? Any idea? And, by the way, what does a cow say?'

Wall-to-wall mooing.

'So what do you think an auroch said?'

Renewed roaring.

'And which would you rather be?'

'A wolf! A bison! An auroch!'

All but a leaven of girls joined this chorus. Their silence may have indicated that they'd rather be cows, and ruminate on grass and hay, and give nice creamy milk, and have a calf named Buttercup, and live on a nice, orderly farm near Alt Schönbek.

'But, boys and girls, these magnificent German beasts are extinct! Where shall we find them?'

'I know, sir! I know!' Julia's hand shot into the air. She had *that* expression on her face. Fanatical. She would not be gainsaid. 'I've read a book, sir, and I know!'

'Julia, please don't interrupt Dr Vogel.' Wincing, Ruth turned to admonish her daughter.

'Not at all, Mrs Daschke! Let the child speak. What would you like to say, dear little girl?'

'Well, what I say is ... what you should do is ... the fierce mummies and fierce daddies can have fierce babies. Then the fierce babies can have even fiercer babies. And they will get nastier and nastier ... and...'

Dr Vogel queried the term *nasty,* substituting *pure* and *Aryan* and *powerful*. But, yes, the little girl was right in principle.

And he had news for the class. The brothers Heck had already recreated the auroch! Yes indeed, they'd brought back the original beast, with mighty horns, powerful muscles and indomitable temperaments! The forests of what used to be called Lithuania and Poland were being populated with aurochs, bison and wolves. In the animal as in the human realm, feeble and degenerate specimens would die out, the powerful German specimens would return and survive, to rule the planet. For that is Nature's law.

And a postscript.

Having said all this, the Chief of Animal Welfare (East) must add – adopting a crooning voice – that the German nation could boast of being uniquely tender to our animal comrades on this earth. The Leader had signed laws to protect animals, Dr Vogel said, sacred laws.

'Woe betide,' he now cried ferociously, raising a hysterical arm above his head, punching the air, and slicing it, and fisting it, and startling his audience. 'Woe betide any man who inflicts pain on an animal! Never mind how big or small the creature is, be it a mouse, a dog, a sparrow! That criminal can expect the law's rigour. That man will wish he had never been born!

'But I know, my dear little German boys and girls,' he concluded, his voice softening – 'that none of you would ever dream of causing pain to our animal friends.'

*

'Excuse me, sir,' said Julia as Dr Vogel was helped to a second serving of roast duck, 'I'm worried about milk.'

Dr Vogel paused from shovelling what he'd termed 'your sublime East Prussian cookery' down his gullet. His face indicated surprise, given the fact that Julia and her friend had glasses of milk in front of them and milky moustaches on their top lips.

'Because,' Julia went on, 'there won't be any cows any more, will there, so will we have to drink auroch milk?'

Soothing smiles all round, and reassurance. Cows were for keeps. Without cows, no milk, no butter, no cheese, no culled bull-calves to roast. Dr Vogel had been talking about adding to the stock of the cattle species, not replacing it.

'Good, because I don't know how you would catch the aurochs to milk them if they're trampling round tearing up trees.'

Hearty amusement. Mention of babes and sucklings. Learned discussion of auroch milk and its probable taste, judging from the taste of the bison beef one of the zoologists had sampled. How difficult taste was to describe! You could only describe it in terms of other tastes. Savoury, faintly acrid, in a good way, a bit like Austrian smoked cheese, *Walder* and *Tiroler Almkäse* – and oddly sweet too, wouldn't you say? Garlicky. Barky. Resiny.

'What you are intimating, if I read you aright, Dr Hallervorden,' said Vogel, who, having swallowed his mouthful, was daintily wiping grease from his lips with his napkin, 'is that the meat tastes of the forest.'

Magdalena remembered snatches of conversation between the scientists at Rominten. *Smoked bison's lung! There's a treat!* That had been Hallervorden. For a moment she could understand why the Leader was a dedicated vegetarian, willing to consume only what had not been slaughtered. Hitler refused to eat suffering. He would not drink blood. Or eat lungs and livers and brains.

At Rominten horrid Dr Voss, pouring himself another glass of wine, had said ... what had he said about the brains? ... they were getting good brains from ... somewhere in the east. Buchenwald? Where was that? Animal or human brains? It had sounded as if... Well, that was what anatomists did, cut up dead human bodies, they couldn't be sentimental about it.

Time for the little guests to go to bed. Everyone said goodnight to Julia and her friend.

'And next time I come,' joked Dr Vogel, 'I shall bring you some auroch milk, little Julia! How about that?'

Julia pulled a face; disappeared.

Later again, talk and laughter and flowing wine. The guests were treated to anecdotes by the Party elite. It was like peering through a window into an unknown world.

Dr Vogel talked of the Imperial Marshall's magnificence. Vogel and Voss, with their wives, had been invited to a zoological get-together at the Goering mansion, Carinhall. A once-in-a-lifetime opportunity. The guests had gathered in a forest clearing, to be greeted by the Imperial Marshall himself, arrayed in an aviator's garment of India rubber, with top boots and a large hunting knife in his belt. The way he strode! And yet, you know, for a man built on a giant scale, Marshall Goering was nimble on his feet. Ah, but the humour of the man! The conviviality! The man of action!

Later on, when the guests entered Carinhall, Goering had appeared in spotlessly white drill trousers and tennis shoes, white flannel shirt and green leather jacket.

Later again, taking the guests on a tour of his art acquisitions – but Dr Vogel was unsure how to describe the glory of Marshall Goering's ultimate costume – he wore velvet knickerbockers, shoes with gold buckles, a coloured velvet jacket and ... oh yes, a silk frilled shirt ... and the Marshall had quipped, 'After all, I'm a bit of a Renaissance Man!' as he led the party past walls hung with Vermeers and Rubens, Van Dykes and Raphaels: priceless works of art gleaned from Italy and Holland, Poland and France. In a sumptuous setting. Almost too many paintings for the walls!

'Ah yes,' sighed Dr Voss. 'The whole experience was beyond imagination. And the food! Culled from all over the world. Caviar from Russia, duck and venison from the Schorfheide forests, Danzig salmon ... if only we could get food like this in Posen.'

'Not,' put in Vogel swiftly, raising his glass in tribute, 'that any of it came up to the standard of this East Prussian fare, Voss. Here we are dining, so to speak, on the countryside of Germany, planted, tilled and harvested since the thirteenth century by our own Aryan race. Blood and soil. Native food. Pure, healthy food ... can't beat it.'

'Oh, absolutely. No comparison. Although I have to say,' Voss responded, reaching his glass for a fill-up, 'the *pâté de foie gras* from France was out of this world. We only had to reach out and these rotten European countries dropped into our laps like ripe fruit. And the country that used to be Poland, of course, where I preside over the Institute. But the Poles, oh dear ... degenerates... I admit I yearn to return to Berlin from that godforsaken hole. Who wouldn't? Anyway, Carinhall. Remember the drink we were served, Vogel?'

'Vodka and claret...'

'Burgundy and bubbly...'

'And all the brandy we could drink!'

'I can tell you,' said Vogel, leaning back in his chair and patting his belly, 'I could hardly toddle or waddle after that! This is the kind of generous hospitality that can only be dispensed by a great man, acting, you see, on behalf of the Fatherland. So to speak, incorporating the body politic.'

Magdalena was tipsy, and Ruth was knocking it back as if there were no tomorrow. Against the walls, the hotel staff were mute, shadowy presences, flitting into view only to replenish a glass or offer more sustenance. They'd been picked for being ears rather than mouths. In the lamplight and the firelight, the scene appeared to Magdalena mysterious as a dream. The Gothic timbers met overhead, in brown gloom. There was something about being on the rim of this elite world that swept you away.

'A bit like the *Song of the Niebelungs*?' Magda heard herself say. 'The great feasts at the court of...'

Vanity flung Magdalena forward, and brandy, and the urge to make her mark. The room tilted, the table swayed, the guests' golden faces skewed and swam, only to right themselves before tipping the other way.

'Miss Arber draws our attention to great poetry, of course!' exclaimed Mr Excorn. He had evidently forgotten the chiding he'd administered about her foolish fad for archaic knowledge.

'And we have Miss Arber to thank for our gathering,' said Vogel. He began to recount the tale of their first meeting at Kőnigsberg.

'History is so important,' she heard herself blurting. 'East Prussia is just pregnant with history! For instance Labiau – the town hall, the castle, the museum ... the Teutonic Knights bashing the Lithuanians ... Napoleon and Queen Luise at Tilsit ... our children have no idea, they'd many of them never been on a train, never seen the sea! I've had it in mind to write a booklet for them about East Prussian history... Mrs Daschke and I took our classes to Kőnigsberg Castle and...'

She came to a halt, recalling little Hedwig peeing on the marble floor, poor lass –

but *don't mention this*, Magdalena's right mind admonished her left mind –

and how she'd been provided with a bucket to clean it up –

But do not say this! she ordered herself –

and the poor little soul had to go without pants for the rest of the day –

Zip your mouth up, for God's sake –

and she and Ruth had kept their eye on her, just in case –

I must not say the word pants.

*

'I didn't actually say ... anything awful, did I?' she asked Ruth as they sat over their non-breakfast of black coffee-substitute, with rancid mouths and bilious stomachs. 'Tell me I didn't.'

'Say what?'

'About Hedwig piddling on the castle floor? ... No? Thank God for that.'

'You did carry on a bit. And then you came to a sudden full stop and wouldn't say another word.'

'Did I?'

'Don't you remember any of it, Magda?'

'I remember quoting the *Song of the Nibelungs.*'

'You went on and on. I kept kicking you. You seem to have got the whole damn thing off by heart.'

Magda sank her head into her hands. 'Oh God. How embarrassing. Dad used to recite it to us and play all the parts. We used to howl with laughter. And learning by heart, he always used to say, would stand us in good stead if we were ever, for instance, in solitary confinement ... there'd always be something to read, even if you had no books... Was it the bit about Brunhild the mighty maiden hanging Gunther on a nail on the wall when he fiddled with her underclothes? It was, wasn't it?'

'No, I don't think so – it was something to do with four knights changing their sumptuous outfits three times in four hours – or was it four times in three hours? You linked it to Goering's changes of costume at Carinhall. As a heroic precedent. Quite intelligent really. For a drunk person.'

Magdalena swigged back the dregs of the vomit-tasting coffee-substitute. 'Oh god, my head. It's banging, is yours? My stomach's a sink. I think I'll go for a ride. Might help. There's a parcel to be collected. I'll pick it up on my way back.'

*

As soon as she was on the bike and taking off towards the trees, Magda began to feel better. The Auroch stuttered along the rutted path. Spring would not be long in coming, not long at all. You could feel it in the air. By the end of the month, the storks would reappear. They'd touch down after their ten thousand-kilometre flight from Africa. How did they know where home was? They knew.

Buds on these chestnut trees would soon unfurl, dripping with luscious sap. Come April, their leaves would uncurl. Like praying hands, like small wayside shrines. It would not be long before the delirium of the dawn chorus would awaken Magda in the attic bedroom.

If only Clem would come here and let her look after him for a while. He wouldn't be the same cocky boy she'd met at Kőnigsberg. He'd seen and suffered things she could only imagine.

If only Alf and I could ... at least speak to one another from our hearts in private. We only have today.

The storks paired, she knew, for one summer only. Males touch down first, to test out conditions; then females a few days later. Pairs would walk together through the moist meadows, up and down, waving their wings, exclaiming, creating their bond; then nest, breed, nurture their young. Their bond was not imperishable. Breast to breast they were joined for one summer only.

The Auroch bounced over ruts in the road and sloshed through streams of melted ice. She skidded to a halt at the post office, dismounted and stood the bike against the wall. Crocuses and daffodils made a bright parterre around the building, a sign of the new life that was due. She knocked and entered.

19

We put the urn aboard ship
with this inscription:

This is the dust of little
Timas who unmarried was led
into Persephone's dark bedroom
And she being far from home, girls
her age took new-edged blades
to cut, in mourning for her,
these curls of their soft hair[24]
      Sappho, Fragment,
      sixth century BCE

Mr Tadeuz, eighty-four years old, great-grandfather of two of Magdalena's sweetest pupils, signed the official documentation with slow care, and double-checked everything, his bespectacled eyes close to the page. He screwed the cap on to the pen, laying it down parallel to his ledger – and then, as if dissatisfied with the geometry of this arrangement, minutely corrected the angle of each. One could not be too exact in matters concerning the postal system. All appeared to be in order. He made as if to hand over the parcel but seemed to think better of it.

'It's a heavy weight for you, Miss Arber,' he said. 'And rather an awkward shape. How are you going to carry it?'

'Oh, don't worry, it should fit into the basket.'

'They should really have delivered this directly to Mrs Daschke's door. They normally would do so.'

Magdalena vaguely wondered who *they* were.

Mr Tadeuz insisted on carrying the package out for Magda and wedging it into the pannier. When you glanced into his pale blue eyes, there was a slight shock, as if they were looking through you, though in reality their pearly sheen betrayed the presence of cataracts.

'Thank you, Mr Tadeuz.'

'Take it easy on your steed, Miss Arber! And give my very best wishes to our good Mrs Daschke. And tell her…'

Magdalena waited, astraddle the bike. 'What should I tell her, Mr Tadeuz?'

'Tell her I pray for her.'

*

'He said … he prays for you, Ruth.'

Ruth was sitting on the bed in Flora's room, holding the urn on her lap, embraced by her arms, rocking it to and fro. Tears streamed down Magdalena's face, she could not stem them, she shuddered and sobbed, but Ruth's stunned eyes were dry. Magda, kneeling beside her, laid her broken face on the bed.

'Who did you say prays?' Ruth asked.

'Mr Tadeuz.'

'Mr Tadeuz?' Ruth hugged the urn closer to her body. Her breast partly rested on the lid.

'Mr Tadeuz the post-master, Ruth.'

'The post-master prays for me?'

'Yes. He wanted you to know.'

Ruth shook her head in wonderment, as if people's words and actions in these latter days were unfathomable.

'Read the letter, Magda,' she said. 'See if you think the prayers will help.'

*

The letter expressed sympathy with <u>MRS RUTH DASCHKE</u>. The hospital must regretfully report that <u>MRS DASCHKE</u>'s daughter <u>FLORA DASCHKE</u> had passed away, having unfortunately contracted inoperable appendicitis. She had not suffered. The death certificate was enclosed. Cremation had already occurred, to prevent the spread of disease. <u>FLORA DASCHKE</u>'s urn had been sent at no cost to the recipient, who was asked to complete and sign the enclosed form, and to return it, again at no extra cost to the sender.

*

The tale of Flora's life was soon told.

After all, how much could be gleaned concerning a child who had not ripened? What had happened of the slightest note in Flora Daschke's seven years on this earth? What deeds had she performed, what knowledge gained? Had she, for instance, learned to march in step and salute the flag? How had she justified all the food she'd ingested, when the health of the Fatherland was at stake? What had Flora Daschke ever said that was memorable?

White-haired Mr Poppendick, pastor of the Confessing Church, officiated. It turned out that he knew the answer to these questions. Despite being banned from public speaking, Mr Poppendick was free to perform such intimate ceremonies as this. Over the Daschke plot in the churchyard, he read from the Gospel according to Luke: 'Suffer little children to come unto me, and forbid them not, for of such is the Kingdom of Heaven.' He explained that the little girl was now in the arms of the tender Father of us all, and of her own dear daddy, who had gone ahead to wait for her in Heaven.

It was right, it was comforting, and they all – except the mother – shed tears. Ruth was very quiet throughout.

Spring flowers strewn over Flora's resting place made a lush counterpane of colour, blue and red and white and yellow. Poppies and roses, irises, tulips, daffodils, pansies, forget-me-nots.

'How are you faring, dear Ruth? What can we do for you?' asked her clustering friends and neighbours.

Ruth shook her head.

'It was a beautiful service,' they commented.

Ruth nodded.

'How is poor Ruth, Magdalena? In herself?' they wondered. 'At least now she knows.'

'And she has one healthy daughter left to her,' they chorused.

'Mrs Daschke will come to appreciate that it is for the best,' counselled the hard-nosed. 'After all, it can't have been much of a life for the child. Or the mother, come to that.'

*

The thing is, Ruth remarked later, my daughter had no appendix. It had been removed when she was five. So how did Flora die? And who or what have we buried today? What lies have we swallowed? What infamies accepted?

There was no restraining Ruth now, no reminding her that she had a surviving daughter, who needed her all the more, and that her first duty was public silence and conformity.

*

20

> But to us no resting
> place is given. As
> suffering humans we
> decline and blindly fall
> from one hour to the next,
> like water thrown
> from cliff to cliff,
> year after year, down
> into the Unknown.[25]
>
> Friedrich Hőlderlin,
> 'Hyperion's Song of Destiny', 1797/9

The persistent peace of Alt Schönbek was like a trance or reverie. When would they all be forced to wake up? Wild geese would soon alight and storks return; crops would be sown. While the world irrupted on the margins, and the margins shrank, Magdalena began to think of taking her pupils to play on the white sands of the lagoon. They'd swim in the azure water. Meanwhile she rode the Auroch through the woods in the moonlight. One unforgettable afternoon she and Eva exchanged memories. They spoke of those they'd lost – and their hopes of recovery. She watched spring break out in hedgerows and ditches. The lakes and sea continued rich in fish; the cows' udders swung, heavy with milk. Order prevailed in this magical, enchanted land, and the semblance of human decency.

Ruth was gone.

The last thing she'd said to Magdalena was, 'All wars are waged by men against women and children, Magda. All.'

A police officer had visited, accompanied by Mr Excorn. What did Miss Arber know about her colleague's dereliction of duty? Nothing? Really? Magdalena's heart had thundered. But Mr Excorn – oh, blessed Mr Excorn! – had vouched for his inexperienced young teacher, left high and dry with one-hundred-and-seventeen children on her hands. (After all, what was he supposed to do if deprived of both teachers?) Until a stand-in for Mrs Daschke could be appointed, he relied on Miss Arber to cope, without complaint.

I will do my absolute best, Mr Excorn, for the children. And for the Fatherland. The dangerous moment had passed. When Magdalena thought of her friend, it was as a receding figure travelling on foot across an endless heath. Smaller and smaller the grey figure became, moving into a universal twilight, never quite at vanishing point. Still searching for traces of Flora in an accursed land, either that or with the aim of holding someone to account for her abduction. Rosa House remembered Ruth. You stumbled upon traces of absence, in spaces where she'd sit with her knitting, plaining and purling away, not in the phlegmatic manner of the villagers, but *con brio,* so that the needles clicked and clacked, her tongue went rattling on, the chair shook slightly. Or in the music room, playing the forbidden Mendelssohn, a piano setting of the 'Scottish' Symphony adagio, with a complex look on her face, at once melting and defiant. The week after Ruth had left, Magdalena had opened, with profound misgivings, the envelope labelled *To Miss Magdalena Arber, in the event of my arrest.*

I leave my daughter Julia Daschke in the sole care of my friend and colleague, Miss Magdalena Arber.

21

I saw in the whole Christian world a licence of fighting at which even barbarous nations might blush. Wars were begun on trifling pretexts or none at all, and carried on without any reference to law, Divine or human.[26]

Hugo Grotius, *On the Law of War and Peace*, 1625

Palm Sunday 1942: Christ re-enters Jerusalem and East Prussia. Full moon over Alt Schönbek. A misty, phosphorescent glow arises from pools and rivers.

Roused at midnight – had someone called her name? – Magdalena did not turn on the light, for Julia in bed beside her was fast asleep, cuddled up to Foxy. Her love for Foxy, a creature previously spurned and disowned, was now a fellowship, all the more devoted for having been compromised. Julia's breathing told you that, for once, the troubled little girl was deep under. School was over for the Easter holidays: soon she and Magda would be painting Easter eggs together in intricate designs and hanging them on strings from the cherry tree. There'd be half a bar of hoarded chocolate for Julia, and outings on the Auroch.

Was the call that woke Magda just a dream? – or was something enormous going on out there? Slipping out of bed, she felt her way to the mansard window, eased aside the blind; looked out.

The stars!

Orion the hunter, stupendous, was astride the sky over the forest, his mighty club raised to despatch his enemy. Sword dangling from his bright belt, he lorded it in the black heavens. There was something terrible in the beauty of the night and the milky pallor that drenched the earth. Magdalena glanced down on the frosted streets. Was that a figure approaching the schoolhouse? Or not? A woman, returning? A warrior mother who had gone out in quest of revenge for the death of a daughter?

There was no one there: just a shadow.

*

Palm Sunday, 1942: Christ re-enters Jerusalem and Schleswig-Holstein. Full moon, hoar frost, calm sea. The River Trave glistened, a sheen silvered the canal, Lübeck Bay glowed, magical in soft light.

On this sacred night, British bombers incinerated the ancient heart of Lübeck. Magdalena woke to hear of the horror. She learned of bombs, incendiaries, mines, raining down on the mediaeval buildings, torching the timbers, plummeting into the harbour. Magdalena crouched with her ear to the wireless, heard of the mass death of her townsfolk in the firestorm, the displacement of thousands.

Frantic, she ran to Renate's house – 'The phone! The phone!' – and hours later, having lost all hope, connected with Dad.

'Thank God, oh thank God!' Her knees buckled, she sank to the floor.

'Well, I don't know about thanking Him, dear ... I'm not at all sure why He should single us out for special treatment! ... but let that pass for the moment!' was his madly characteristic retort.

The Arber home had escaped damage. Nothing to do with Providence, Dad thought fit to remind her. The disciple of Voltaire could never say *Thank God* ... for reasons he was starting to evince under headings, when Ebba grabbed the phone from his hand – 'For goodness' sake, Max!' – to reassure Magda in her quietly sterling voice that they were safe and their home was safe.

But then her voice unravelled. Safe, but the poor souls who'd lost their lives, Ebba sobbed, those poor souls ... and the British claim to be Christians ... and the bells ... the sacrilege ... the children ... the babies ... the churches ... mothers and children burning...

For a moment Ebba could not go on.

The twin spires of the Mary Church were smashed, their bells fallen. The Cathedral was destroyed; St Peter's reduced to rubble.

But these could be rebuilt. Jesus is not in the temple made with human hands, no, his home is the mortal heart, Ebba reminded herself, rallying.

The Arbers had taken in a family whose house had been bombed flat, lovely people, for luckily Magda's and Clem's rooms were free and ready. The little boy, Lutz, was thrilled with Magda's rocking horse and could hardly be lured off its back. He had eaten his lunch on horseback. The authorities had been very good, you had to acknowledge that. Oranges and apples were being distributed, as well as loaves, eggs, butter, cans and fish. Nobody would go hungry.

'Dad says he will call you this afternoon at Mrs Schmidt's, darling,' Ebba said finally. 'And I warn you, you may have to hear about Thucydides and the Peloponnesian War, and Max's old pal Hugo Grotius and what he said about war in 1620 or whatever. Bear with him, darling. It's his way. He is terribly shocked.'

Later, Dad filled Magda in on the relevance of these bygone thinkers to the bombing of Lűbeck in March 1942. In her mind's eye, Magdalena saw her father seated at his desk in the sepia gloom of his study, twiddling his fountain pen, poking the bridge of his glasses up his nose, madly discoursing of Philosophy whilst the world beyond his book-lined walls reeked of carbon and decomposition.

The British planes, he reported, had not returned to the scene of their crime to have another go (for crime it was, Dr Goebbels – *mirabile dictu* – was right about that). Indeed, what remained of Lűbeck to come back to? What had there ever been in the ancient heart of this city that was of the slightest danger to Britain?

Why bomb mothers and children and beauty and culture? Eh?

Why devastate a merchant city with few factories and munitions depots (and those not even hit)?

No doubt about it, Thucydides had it right, Dad concluded. All nations involved in war sink into a common barbarism.

And the beloved cats, Goethe and Schiller, he reported in a later conversation, had been drastically affected. They'd survived, but their minds had gone. While the city was a charnel, reeking of trauma, Dad submerged larger human issues in an obsession with the welfare of Goethe and Schiller.

'Goethe shrinks from every sound, he's a quivering wreck, while Schiller snarls and turns on his brother and rakes him with his claws. He's taken to filching Goethe's food and treats him as his mortal enemy – yes, I know, really hard to imagine, isn't it? Such good pals they were. Schiller chases Goethe into boltholes, where the poor persecuted creature gnaws at his own fur. And what are we going to feed them? The fish ration surely will be cut again – we give it all to our darlings, of course. We have their lives under our protection as a binding trust.'

Max was one of a detachment of frail older men called up to clear the ruins. He had the foreman's kind permission to take poor Goethe with him in a bag, to save him from the bully prowling their home.

After that came the bombing of Cologne, Kassel, Berlin. Kőnigsberg too was raided, somewhat incompetently, by the Russians. Otherwise East Prussia was more or less unmolested. Magdalena constantly begged Max and Ebba to come to the peace and safety of the countryside. There must be a way. Her guilt was heavy at living off the fat of the land, while they stinted themselves of the little that they had, for the sake of a couple of cats.

'We can't come to you, darling girl,' Ebba wrote, 'much as we'd love to. We have work to do here, important work, Max in clearing the bomb damage and myself at the church. I have a leading, I am called to be ordained a deaconess, since there's a need for people in the ministry, to minister in place of the absent men. Some called up, others in prison. But we're unspeakably glad you're safe. And that dearest Clem is coming to see you on his way back to the front. Take every care of yourselves. I hold you in my prayers. Your daddy of course doesn't pray, as you know, but he keeps you close to his heart.'

*

Hand in hand, they met Clem's train. Julia took to him at once. She sat on his shoulders and played pat-a-cake on his shaven head. She ran her fingers over the scars on his face. She offered him the best portions of her cake, or nearly the best. He took Julia on his lap and sang her to sleep in his arms.

'I want you to stay, Uncle Clem. Please stay,' Julia murmured, waking. 'Don't go away.'

'I can't stay, Chickabiddy, but I'll come back when I can, never fear.'

She stomped about in a paddy but he swung her up in his strong arms and whirled her round, calling her his poppet – and would she maybe marry him when she grew up?

No, she said, because he was nice but too ugly! And he'd only got nine toes!

Glancing from one to the other, Magda saw what Julia was seeing. Clem's face assumed a medley of compulsive expressions, a kind of rictus. The face had set hard and contorted, its boyish softness only a memory. In a year, he had aged a decade.

Four blessed days Clem had at Alt Schönbek. He wanted to be useful, in a banal, domestic way. Aided by Julia, he mended the rusty old pipe from the sink and cleared the drain. He took the Auroch apart, oiled the chain and brakes, married the parts back together, polished the chrome. Borrowing a bike for himself, Clem cushioned the crossbar so that the little girl could sit comfortably as he and Magda rode abreast into the forest, dumping the bikes to visit the wetlands.

They entered a world of deliquescence and wanton growth. And hubbub: the amphibian arias of the marsh frogs. Inflating their comical vocal sacs, in, out, in, out, clucking like hens, they cawed and chuckled and clicked, out there in the green sludge and slime of algae. Crazed oboists of the swamp. For a while you could hear but not see them. And then you realised that what you had taken for weed and slime was a mass of bodies. Green as the algae, massed males exhorted females: *Notice me, you froggy breeders – listen to how gloriously I gulp and burp, find me among the flag irises, seek me where the willows sink into the stream.*

Julia was beside herself at the preposterous racket, joining in with all her might, running wild in the squelch of oozing grass, imitating the belching rumpus of the frog symphony. Her spirit of happy fearlessness seemed to have resurfaced in the last few days. The light that had been quenched flashed.

'Come on, come *on*, Uncle Clem!'

Clem, relaxing in this world beyond his world, loved the marsh marigolds with their brilliant yellow faces and heart-shaped, scalloped leaves; the foam of meadowsweet with its medicinal, honey smell. Later they dried Julia off and lounged in the woods with a picnic, warm in a shaft of sunlight. He was the innocent Clem of Magda's childhood, chasing through the velvet pinewoods beside Lake Plön, boarding the boat at Fegetasche for a trip round the five lakes, swimming at Travemünde, climbing the beeches at Timmendorf and looking down together over the Baltic.

Julia returned from galloping round and round the clearing, to sit at his side as they reminisced, threading daisies. Very quiet.

And then: 'I was naughty to my mummy, Uncle Clem, and she went away, and nobody knows where she is.'

Julia put this to him, matter-of-factly. Magda listened, heart in mouth. Ruth's daughter never mentioned her mother.

'Angel girl,' Clem said, when he heard this confession, cupping her face in both hands. It was a moment of sheer grace. 'That wasn't why, you little goose. You love your mummy dearly. I've never met her but I'm sure she knows that.'

Julia shook her head. 'She's gone. I said nasty things to her. I went and rolled around in the coal hole. I said I didn't love her and she wasn't my mummy anyway, so there.'

'You should have heard what I said to my mummy.'

'What, Uncle Clem? What did you say?'

'I can't possibly tell you, it was too beastly.'

'Go on – tell. Whisper!'

'No, I can't even whisper it, Chickabiddy.'

'And what did your mummy say when you were horrible to her?'

'Well, she looked hurt. But then she just laughed and pinched my cheeks, like this, and said, *You don't mean that, Clemmy, what's the matter?* And I didn't. And you didn't. We were both having a sad sort of moment, weren't we?'

'Yes, but...'

'I'm sure your mummy will be able to come back before we know,' he said, brushing her hair back from her face. 'So let's hear no more about it, you little pickle. Mmn, I do like pickles! For instance, gherkins and pickled cabbage. You do remind me of a gherkin, Julia, come to think of it. A big fat gherkin. Come here, let me gobble you up!'

That evening the cousins sat beside the hearth, Julia being in bed and sound asleep, Clem's expression darker, his face closed.

He'd visited Lűbeck before stopping off here on his way back to the front. Taking his mother aside, he'd told her for God's sake to be careful. The pastor at the Luther Church had been arrested for calling the British bombing the judgement of God on Germany. He'd be guillotined, with three Catholic priests. Did Magdalena not know that? Did she not realise why his mother was being ordained? There were no men left to lead her own church, the Confessional Church.

'And, Lena, none of you have the least idea what I am holding off ... from you ... and let us hope you never find out. You're living in dreamland here. It's lovely but it's all delusion. You know how I got this leave?'

She shook her head; reached over to take his hand. Clem brushed her off. He'd crept right up to a Russian tank, he told her, and lobbed a grenade straight through the spy-hole, wiping out the whole crew. Their bodies exploded. He laughed a high-pitched hee-haw laugh. The rest of the column didn't hang around. It turned back.

'I did that off my own bat and frankly I enjoyed it. They gave me this special leave – plus there's a medal in the offing – and a promotion. So that's how I got here. Stop going round saying things like, *They're only human, we have to be sorry for them.* Guard your mealy mouth, Lena. You've already got yourself into serious trouble, associating with that demented schoolteacher, and landed yourself with her kid … yes, I know, Julia's a lovely girl, and you care about her – but even so. And the other kid by all accounts was a moron.'

'Don't say that.'

'Yes, Lena, she was. A useless eater. A leech. A parasite. Don't look like that.'

'You didn't know her, Clem. How can you say that? Flora was a little person. I loved her.'

Why was she using this pleading tone? Why did she feel she had no right to speak up for Flora? Ruth had abandoned them, leaving her with a catastrophe primed and ready to detonate.

Clem brought his scarred face close to Magdalena's.

'They'll be watching you. Some busybody will be registering your every word, ready to hand you in. Frankly, you are leaky – you're a sieve – and for someone who prides herself on being an intellectual, you act like a dope. Just like my uncle. I'm saying this for your own good, Lena. Do you really imagine they believe for a single moment that you're not in on your pal's plans? Are you soft in the head?'

'I will be careful,' Magda promised. 'Really, don't worry. But I wish you didn't think like that.'

'Well, I do think like that. It's how things are. A moron is a moron and a madwoman is a madwoman. And I am worried, Lena. Because I know you. And I know what's coming. And you don't. My comrades … I've buried two of my … buried them, Lena … with my own hands.'

He'd picked up Paul's body and hoisted it on his shoulders. He'd laid him behind a wall, opened his tunic and bloody shirt, broken Paul's identity disc, emptied his pockets of pay book, photos, matches and cigarettes, wrapped it all in a handkerchief to send back to Paul's parents, and finally he'd dug a grave, shovelled Ukrainian dirt over Paul's young face, planted a cross of birch twigs.

Once upon a time in Kőnigsberg a cocky lad of seventeen had insulted the irate Party chief and been lucky to get off. He'd been shamed. And Magdalena had shamed him too: *Stop showing off.*

She'd meant, *Survive.*

And this was what Clem, experienced now, was saying to her, and had some right to say: *Survive. Keep your head down. Your peace is an illusion.*

And then he was gone.

*

The temporary teaching replacement turned out to be Edith Struppat's youngest daughter Dagmar. Once the front door shut behind Dagmar, the newcomer confided that she was less than enchanted to be recalled to her native village. The back of beyond. Ghastly old women without teeth. Not that she was complaining, oh dear no. Dagmar was not now, and never had been, one to shirk her duty. And it was only temporary, after all.

'I do tend to tell it as it is,' she warned Magdalena, turning her flaxen head this way and that before the hall mirror. 'You'll have to get used to that. A German girl stands no nonsense, as our Band of German Maidens leader used to say. A German girl never lies. Is Alt Schőnbek still full of Christianity and that kind of Jewish thing?'

Dagmar's questions were mostly rhetorical. You didn't need to do more than mumble in response, for which Magda was grateful. It mitigated the consciousness of surveillance. Mrs Struppat's youngest daughter seemed a kind of machine. Wind her up and off she goes, in a mechanical frenzy.

Julia observed the newcomer, silently. Magda had trained her not to interrupt; not to make rude faces; not to cover her ears with her hands when Dagmar began ranting; never to answer back. To

Magda's surprise, the child effortlessly learned this discipline. She was intelligent enough to use reticence as passive resistance.

Dagmar's *sine qua non* was that she would on no account lodge with her mother. There was not room for the two of them in one house. Oh, her mother was exemplary, Dagmar acknowledged: you could not fault her patriotism, she was cleanliness incarnate, an ardent leader of the National Socialist Womanhood Guild.

But Mother had always blamed Dagmar for being a girl. And, for goodness' sake, Mother's *voice*!

Just between the two of them, she must acknowledge that Mother was *loud*, Dagmar complained loudly. With the best will in the world, you could hardly hear yourself think when Mother was in full spate, bellowing away. And she even moved like an elephant.

Dagmar explained that she had put this concern – tactfully, of course – to Mr Excorn, who'd been responsible for recalling her. After all, she'd said, I am twenty-three years old, sir, and have done the Leader good service! Oh, there'd be no problem, he'd assured Dagmar, in accommodating Miss Struppat at the requisitioned house known as the Teachers' Residence. He was sure Miss Arber would benefit from the company.

Magdalena and Julia helped Dagmar lug her cases upstairs and stow them in Ruth's bedroom, which Magda had had the foresight to clear of any sign of her friend and her heresies. Julia fixed her eyes on Dagmar and stared, beetling her brows. Happily, Dagmar was entirely innocent, not only of irony, but also of ordinary sensitivity. Her monstrous garrulity overrode her capacity to perceive. She simply remarked – fixing her favourite portrait of the Leader above her bed – that Julia Daschke (contrary to reputation) seemed a quiet little body, without much to say for herself.

'Are you always as quiet as this?' she asked Julia. 'Like a little mouse, squeaky squeak?'

Julia said nothing.

'Oh,' said Magdalena, 'she's rather shy. Aren't you, dear?'

Julia nodded.

When she'd arranged the bedroom to her taste, and fluffed up her white-gold hair, Dagmar came galloping down the stairs and filled Magdalena in on the work she'd accomplished for the Fatherland since her schooldays. Before she'd even left school, Dagmar had volunteered for a duty visit to Steglitz where she was accommodated in barracks that once belonged to a Protestant Kindergarten and had been requisitioned and converted by the Party.

'You should have seen us marching in, to take possession! I do wish you could have seen it,' she told Magdalena, taking a sip of coffee. '(This stuff isn't real, is it? Any sugar? No? Oh well.) We were marching in close formation. You know. Flags and song – and guess who held the pennon? Go on, guess!'

'You?'

'Little me! I was chosen to hold it! In these hands.' She turned her hands, palm upwards, to be admired. 'So proud I could have wept.'

Tears filmed Dagmar's eyes as she recalled this moment of beatitude.

'I can just imagine,' said Magdalena. Already she felt worn out. If Dagmar Struppat had been a wireless, she could have switched her off or pulled the plug.

'Yes, what an honour. *But*, oh dear, the mess! The nuns had left it in a filthy state...'

'The nuns?'

'Oh yes, Protestant nuns, Magdalena. You thought all nuns were Roman Catholic? Far from it. And the state of the place after they'd been chased out! Any self-respecting German girl would have thrown up rather than sit down there in the filth they'd left behind. The stink! It's a kind of Jewish smell, you know. Because this Christianity business is all tainted with Jewish hocus-pocus, isn't it? Well, of course we scrubbed every inch, painted the walls and decorated them with pictures of Great Men.'

'How lovely,' said Magdalena.

'Isn't it though? I'm so glad you see it like that, Magdalena. I thought maybe you'd ... well ... anyway, my next placement...'

As Dagmar droned on, Magda took Julia on to her lap. The child kissed Magda's face and laced her bare arms round her neck. Magda kissed her forearm, so soft. She felt the little lithe body slacken against her heart as her breathing deepened.

Dagmar stared. 'She seems very fond of you,' she said. 'I suppose she'd...'

To cut off any supposition on Dagmar's part, Magda replied that, yes, she and Julia were fond of one another.

'There isn't a blemish on *your* character, at least, Magdalena. And Julia seems quite healthy. After all, Mrs D always had a screw loose ... just between ourselves, she was never what you'd call reliable ... don't you think? ... and that retarded kid of hers, my mother told her straight, it was a deliverance, a blessing in disguise, and Mrs D would have been wise to accept that. Relieved of a problem, you see, like Mrs What's-Her-Name when her retarded son got taken off her hands, she was grateful – and better for the child, because, frankly, that was no life for a kid. Also if all these morons are let to live, it takes food out of the mouths of healthy children. Economics, you see. It's just common sense, after all. They can't be allowed to breed. We'd have a nation of morons!'

'That would never do,' said Magda with a straight face.

'And Mrs Whatsit, she showed my mother a letter of thanks she'd written to the Health Service. And a personal one to the Leader. But I suppose, well, you know, there must have been a taint in Mrs D's family, probably you could trace it back centuries...'

She went blasting on with her trumpet voluntary.

Magdalena switched herself off. It was the only way.

The SS police had examined Magdalena when they investigated Mrs Daschke's absence. In the event, no one had come forward to implicate her in Ruth's transgression and Mr Excorn had vouched for her. However, Dagmar was a plant. That was obvious, although Dagmar's qualification for the job of collecting information was a riddle, since she seemed to be big mouth, small brain and no ears.

Since Ruth's departure, Julia had been Magda's strength and stay.

Shouldn't it be the other way round? The tenderness Julia created in her and drew from her was unlike any emotion she'd ever experienced. Julia was her foster child now, and Magdalena swore to herself that she would do nothing, say nothing, to endanger her own survival, for both their sakes, and for Clem's and Dad's and Ebba's.

'The thing is, and this is something I have always prided myself on, Magdalena,' yacked Dagmar, 'I am not a Yid! I expect you feel the same. I could never stick the Yids. Even before I'd actually laid eyes on one. They are so fat, they all have flat feet and they can never look you straight in the eye. Luckily, my genes make me a splendid example of the Nordic woman – antecedents pure back to the sixteenth century. I am statuesque, you see, if I say it myself – my legs are long,' (she held them out from the chair) 'and my trunk is long,' (she reached her arms above her head). 'See? I am tall and I have the broad hips and pelvis built for childbearing which (I have to tell you this) made me do a great thing for our Leader!'

'Oh, really?'

Julia shifted her weight on Magda's lap, yawned, opened startled eyes and looked into Magdalena's.

'Did you drop off to sleep, darling?'

'No ... yes ... I don't know.'

It was bedtime, Magdalena decreed. She'd put Julia down for the night; it would take half an hour and perhaps, when she reappeared, Dagmar would have forgotten to recount whatever ghastly thing she'd done for the Leader.

*

Of course, Dagmar Struppat, now arrayed in Ruth's apron, rather small on her imposing figure, had not forgotten her theme. She was frying sausage in Ruth's frying pan.

She took up where she had left off. The thing was, with ancestry like Dagmar's, and valuable Nordic characteristics, certified free of contamination back to the Teutonic Knights more or less, no family history of dipsomania or imbecility – why not give the Leader a child? This had been Dagmar's train of thought, and, because German girls always act in accordance with their convictions, she'd wasted no time in presenting herself at the SS foundation 'Fount of Life' in Berlin.

'Gracious me, Magdalena,' Dagmar reminisced, while the sausages spat in the pan and smoke rose, 'talk about luxury! I had a bijou room to myself with flowers and pictures and handsome furniture. There was a library and a cinema, everything you could want. Is there any bread, Magdalena? Oh yes, here it is. Good East Prussian Pumpernickel, you can't beat it ... although the food at the home was the best I have ever tasted. Oh, it was sumptuous. We didn't have to work, and there were servants galore. And refined white bread. The prof in charge explained that Imperial SS Leader Himmler had been given the task by the Leader of refreshing the stock. At the Fount of Life, elite National Socialist women over five foot five tall – I am five foot seven in my stockinged feet, by the way, how tall are you...?'

'Five foot four.'

'You wouldn't qualify, I'm afraid. Oh well, never mind. If you don't slouch, you could pass for taller. Where was I? oh yes, we were partnered with equally valuable SS men, to lay the foundation of a pure racial breed! Here you are, I hope you like your sausage well done... Anyway, you know what I'm going to say next, don't you?'

'Not got a clue.' Magda reluctantly accepted the plate of burnt sausage.

'You don't know about any of this, do you? Well, Magdalena, I'm going to open your eyes. The Fount of Life. We had about a week to pick an SS-man we liked, making sure that his hair and eye colour and so on corresponded with ours. Then we waited till the *tenth* day after the *first* day of our menstrual period – you're following? – that is when one is *fertile,* you see – and then we were medically examined and allowed to receive the SS men into our rooms at night. One at a time, of course. There! I hope you're not shocked! You are a little bit, aren't you, admit it?'

'Oh no. Absolutely not. I'm beyond shock.'

'Oh good. Well, mine was quite a sweet boy, although he did hurt me a little, and I think he was actually a bit stupid, but his looks were stunning. He was so blond that he looked as if he had no eyebrows or eyelashes! You know the kind of look, I expect – hair almost white, freckles, a pinkish sort of face. Three evenings in one week I had him, and then he went on to help some other girl. I was very proud indeed at how fast my maternal function kicked in. I'm not bragging when I say that I won the race for conception hands down!'

'Really?'

'Yes. One girl must have been racially inferior as it didn't work at all. Could you pass the pepper, please? ... the pepper? Magdalena?'

Magda passed the pepper.

'Don't you want that sausage? Not hungry? Pass it over, I'll help you out.'

Magda held out her plate.

'Everything was very discreet. We were all called Mrs, to show that we were married to the Empire.'

'Of course.'

'And the baby was a boy! I suckled him for the first fortnight and then he was removed.'

Magdalena studied Dagmar's expression curiously. 'How did you feel about your baby being taken away, if you don't mind my asking?'

'He was not *taken* away, Magdalena. I *gave* him to the Leader.'

'Oh ... yes ... of course.'

'But how did I feel? I felt ... well, I felt ... yes ... satisfied! A man fights for the Fatherland in the trenches, a woman fights on her back in a bed, that's the maxim, crude as it may sound. And the chief surgeon, I have to tell you this, was so impressed that he asked me to come back in a year's time to give our Leader another perfect son! And he joked with me: *Maybe twins next time, Mrs Struppat!* But since then of course I've been called back to teaching so I'm only Miss Struppat again. Still, I've got years of breeding in me. After the war I shall undertake this work again.'

'I'm sure you will,' said Magdalena. 'Or you may marry, of course.'

'I may. And we can have a baby every year!'

'What is your son's name, if I may ask?'

'Oh, I don't know *that*.' Dagmar winced; her shoulders hunched; her head went down. She began to twiddle with a stray curl by her ear.

'Ah. Sorry. That must be painful.'

'Good God! Not at all!' Dagmar bounced back with a shriek of defiance. 'I had a pet name for Baby, just between me and Baby. Do you want to know what it was? I called Baby by the Leader's Name! There! What do you think? I felt this would be a blessing on him.'

'I do hope so, Dagmar.'

'I can see we're going to be the best of pals,' said Dagmar with an insincerity so flagrant you had to strangle a laugh. 'And by the way, Magda, you can tell me anything, even secrets! I'm very discreet. Only I have to be off on a course to refresh my teaching techniques,' she said with a yawn. 'But I'll soon be back in our den, all nice and cosy together.'

'Oh good.'

When Dagmar had departed for bed, Magdalena cleared up the pans and dishes. Her head rang. She thanked her stars that Dagmar had touched down only to refuel and take off again.

Grateful for the quiet, she poured herself a cup of herb tea; took it out into the garden and sipped it on the bench. Nobody was out in the streets. All windows were blacked out and nothing stirred, except moonlight glimmering on a spider's web.

22

Summer 1942

> I lived on earth in an era such as this:
> when the poet, too, simply kept his mouth shut,
> and waited until he might speak up again...[27]
> Miklós Radnóti, 'Fragment', 19 May 1944

She shot out of bed, stumbled downstairs, opened the door a few inches.

Behind the policeman the midnight-blue sky was already brightening, birds were chirping into wakefulness, but the planets still glimmered, and a three-quarters moon hung low over the village. The policeman was politeness itself. He apologised for getting Miss Arber out of bed at this ungodly hour.

Magdalena's heart stormed, although it was only Mr Rudat. A familiar figure, kinsman of Heini Rudat the Chief Forester of Alt Schönbek.

Uniformed police. Not Gestapo.

When he invited her to come with him, his manner was amiable, as if issuing a friendly invitation. Not wishing her to feel left out.

Magdalena tightened her dressing gown cord. The word *arrest* hovered in her mind. But he hadn't said it. Nevertheless she thought: *It's my turn now*.

'I'm looking after a little girl, you see, Mr Rudat,' she blurted 'Sergeant Rudat, I mean ... I can't leave her – her mother's not here ... and what about my classes? The teacher standing in for Mrs Daschke is away on a course.'

And in any case, she thought, over my dead body will Julia be given into Dagmar Stupid Struppat's tender care.

Mr Rudat suggested, in that same spirit of affability, that Magdalena leave Julia with a neighbour. And as to the school, a competent person would be asked to hold the fort, never fear. It was all being arranged.

'Arranged? Leave her?'

'Just for the time being, you know.'

Magdalena couldn't catch breath; clutched at her dressing gown collar. The shabby old garment was parting company with itself. Buttons were missing: she hadn't bothered to replace them. Ruth would have done that for her if she'd been here. In fact the whole garment was threadbare, it was falling to pieces, the skirts didn't meet, it wasn't decent. Beyond the sergeant's plump, kindly face, the sky was a dark turquoise, the milk cart clopped past, an owl hooted.

Was this it then? Was Magdalena about to disappear?

Mr Rudat seemed to be trying to reassure her, still standing well back from the doorstep. 'Don't you worry about the little girl or the school. Look, Miss Arber, I'll come in for a minute, while you get organised. May I?'

What wouldn't be for long? – and how long was long?

His palm cupped Magdalena's elbow, but not in an officious way. Shepherding her indoors, taking care to wipe his feet, the policeman perched on the bench beside the ceramic oven, its fire almost extinct. Since Ruth had gone away – and it had been several months ago now – Magda had failed to keep the fire alive, she hadn't the knack, or the time, or the will, although the nights and early mornings could be chilly. She was forever scurrying from pillar to post. But some warmth still lingered in the tiles. Sergeant Rudat took off his helmet and perched it on his knee.

'If you go and get ready, Miss Arber, I'll wait here. Bring overnight things, just in case, I should – toothbrush and so on.'

Her visitor was being mild and patient. So perhaps it was not serious? This was not the way people were arrested. She'd seen and heard assaults on doors in Lűbeck; folk dragged out into the street without coats or hats, or even shoes.

'And rouse the little lass,' Mr Braun said, folding the skirts of his long grey coat over his knees. 'But take care not to worry her. We'll settle her with a neighbour before we go.'

'Go where though?'

They were going to the State Police Headquarters in Kőnigsberg.

'Oh, and bring a book or some magazines with you to read, Miss Arber, I should, in case you have to wait around to be seen.'

On her way out of the door, she spun round: 'Am I under arrest?'

He couldn't tell her more but the sergeant expected, he said in his stolid way, that all would be well. 'Who would you like to leave the child with?'

'Oh, with Renate Schmidt, over the road, if she will...'

He'd go over now and alert Mrs Schmidt.

*

The bedroom was full of hush.

'Come on, my sweetheart, we've had a change of plan for today. Up you get! You're going to have a lovely special day with Auntie Renate. How would you like that? Take Foxy and Bunny. You can play with Karin, can't you?'

'No, I'm asleep, Magda, I'm fast asleep,' Julia muttered, her head burrowing into the pillow.

Finally she consented to get up; sat on the side of the bed, yawning and shivering, and allowed herself to be dressed.

'Why, anyway?' she asked, rubbing her eyes. 'I've got sleepy-dust. Look, Magda, it's on my eyelashes, and it itches. Aren't you going to plait my hair? I haven't even had my breakfast yet.'

'Auntie Renate will give you a lovely breakfast, I'm sure. Much better than boring old Magda's awful cookery.'

'It's not awful! I like your breakfasts,' Julia said loyally.

'Thank you! And ask her to do your hair, darling. Will you be an angel for Magda?'

Surprisingly, Julia looked into her eyes, read something there, and consented.

*

They were in the police car. Snarling along. Nothing much on the roads. The sky had paled to eggshell blue; the rising sun's rays caught stray clouds on the horizon and flushed them pink, but you could still just about see the stars and moon.

Go slower, Magda thought. *Gallop slowly, slowly, horses of the night.*

She sat with her bag on her lap, fingers looped in the handles as if they were reins. Her mouth was parched. In the whirlwind of preparation, she'd snatched in panic a handful of books from the drawer and stuffed them in her rucksack. Eaten a crust of bread, swallowed some water. Now half her mind stood aside, observing the scene and herself within it, as if viewing a film.

Blackened ruins of homes just outside Kőnigsberg flashed past, the prey of jettisoned bombs from the Russian raid. Pigeons perched on roofless walls. The mediaeval monuments of the city, auburn in the rising sun, still stood.

The sergeant's hands on the wheel were broad, stubby, pitted like craters.

Mr Rudat saw her looking.

'Carbuncles,' he said. 'Ever seen a carbuncle? Like a boil. Quite a crop I had. I took the law into my own hands – popped 'em with a pin! Big mistake. I swelled up like a big boil myself! What people don't realise is that carbuncles are not single. They all connect under the surface. Like a nasty web, see.' He flapped his hand at her cheerfully. 'I was in hospital with these, believe it or not. Had a nice cushy rest. Anyway, why am I telling you this? Now then, Miss Arber, we're getting near to headquarters. You might have to wait around a bit. But you'll take that in your stride, I'm sure?'

'I hope so. I'll try. May I ask you, Sergeant Rudat – is this anything to do with Mrs Daschke being away? Because they've already asked me about that.'

He could not say. But did his head nod faintly? Or not? She could not tell, and perhaps he did not know the answer.

The elegant, intimidating red brick façade with its stepped gable and ornate portal towered above her, as she got out of the car.

Once inside, hallway led to hallway, then a central staircase opening out into three other hallways, a maze. Up they went, up, then down to the rear of the building, past guardrooms, offices, men in uniform ascending and descending the staircases two at a time.

'Here we are,' Sergeant Rudat said just before they rounded the last corner. 'I have to hand you over now.'

*

A counter. Men. A long corridor with cells at either side.
  Sit there.
  No, not there! Where I'm pointing!
  Is she blind and deaf, or just stupid?
  Numb. Glazed.
  What is happening, please? What am I waiting for?
  You've been told to wait. So wait.
  Has she given in her bag?
  What's in your bag?
  Personal items.
  Right, I'll take that.
  Male hands rooting round inside her rucksack.
  Oh please, can I keep my books?
  No. And take off your watch. Also your belt.
  I'm not wearing a belt.
  It claims not to be wearing a belt!
  Is it wearing a suspender belt?

No.

Face flushed scarlet. Mortified.

Twinkle in the policeman's eye as he visualises the state of her underwear.

She tugs down her skirt, tucks its folds round her knees.

Your watch.

Pardon?

Hand – over – your – wristwatch.

Sign here.

Excuse me but I was told I could keep my books.

You were told wrong.

But...

No buts. Shut up.

She sits. Looks at her hands in her lap; at the two men seated opposite, heads low, muttering in a foreign tongue. Polish, maybe, or Lithuanian.

Shut your traps, you pair of gibbering apes!

They shut their traps.

Right. Come on.

You mean me?

Is she thick as well as deaf?

Move.

*

The door clangs shut behind you. You jump out of your skin.

Yes but at least I'm on my own here. Private. Nobody can see me.

Oh but they can see me. There's a spy-hole in the door, with a shutter on the outside.

What have I got in here? A pull-down bed or bench; toilet; tin table, with tin spoon and tin jug. Shelf with earthenware jug, thick with dust. Flickering electric bulb inside metal cage. Tiled walls. Opaque window high on that wall.

And noise. It's an echo chamber. Footsteps along the corridor.

Someone pacing overhead. Clamour travelling along rusty pipes. An inchoate shout.

Yes, but listen, Magdalena tells herself, you're on your own now. You can stop trying to control your face for a while.

Let go of your facial muscles.

As soon as she has relaxed, the seething need to pee announces itself. Suppressed since leaving home, it sings up from her belly.

Pee in that foul toilet ... in full view if they put their eye to the hole?

The lop-sided smirk of Suspender Belt Man rises in her mind.

But you have to go. Just do it.

Arrange your skirt like this. See, you can veil your ... intimate parts. She has never had any words for her intimate parts.

Her face burns.

The chilly steel of the bowl scalds naked, shrinking thighs. There you are, you are seated. Do the business.

Go on, go on, for God's sake. Or they'll come! Listen, they're coming! Can't let go. You can't if you're not private. You're a woman, it's different for a woman, skewered by lewd eyes.

Rapping and rattling on the door. No, it's not the door, just part of the horrible cacophony. But your bladder startles, winces, closes down.

Deep breaths. Shut your eyes, that's the way. She manages a few drops. Should help.

How do you flush the toilet?

There is no way.

Where to wash your hands?

Nowhere.

She sits down on the rackety bench or bed, leaning her head back against the grubby wall.

Waits.

There are raised voices down the corridor and crashing sounds.

Have I been waiting here an hour yet? But what am I waiting for? Nobody has told her anything. Fear floods the cell.

If only they'd let me have my books.

Someone once said to her, probably Dad, or it might have been Miss Heller: *Good idea to learn poems by heart so that you always have friends.*

But as time ticks by, or rather does not tick by because it's unmeasured, the poems she loves by Hölderlin and Werfel, recited aloud into the void, become lame and are overwhelmed. They cannot hold their own against the drumming of your heart.

Restless, she stands, stretches, decides to exercise, pacing wall to wall with short footsteps, then three strides, then several skips each way. Perhaps whoever is barging about overhead is doing the same.

She tries to pee again and succeeds better this time.

Thirst. The earthenware jug on the rickety shelf contains water. But is it clean? How long has it been there?

She decides not to risk it.

Waits.

Your hands reach for the jug; you stare in at the dark water. Is that slime on the surface? You slosh it about a bit and sniff it. Surely it's teeming with germs.

You replace the water jug untasted, to be on the safe side.

You wait.

You reach the jug down, put it to your lips, shut your eyes, drink.

Fear, intensified by tedium, sizzles in the palms of hands and soles of feet. Curling up on the bench, she closes her eyes.

*

Out!
    I said, out, you halfwit!
    She had somehow lapsed into a doze.
    Up! March!

*

She reels down the corridor between the cells. Has the idea that it is evening or even night, but how can you know? Don't bother to ask Suspender Belt. He's dangling her rucksack contemptuously from two fingers.

Interminable corridors. Then Suspender Belt halts and speaks to a guard, who raps on the door of a Captain M. W. von Stein.

Come!

A black-uniformed officer at the desk, a fug of blue-black cigar smoke.

Suspender Man, announcing Magdalena's name, hands over her identity papers and rucksack. Is told he can go.

The Captain surprises his guest with a display of immaculate manners and teeth ginger from nicotine. He is not an imposing figure, rather slender and compact, a narrow face, high forehead, thinning hair. Not old – but he has never been young. He gestures to her to take a seat, regrets keeping Miss Arber waiting; trusts she has not been discommoded? Does not wait for a reply. Goes through her papers in a cursory way. Yes, yes. Lűbeck? Ah yes! Enchanting Hanseatic city. He reminisces: has visited on several occasions, on his way to Kiel. It is always pleasant to stop off and wander the historic streets and sit for a while beside the Trave.

Anyway. To business.

Magdalena reminds herself to breathe.

I'll come straight to the point.

Von Stein aims Mrs Daschke's name at Magdalena, in the same smooth tone. The name glides towards her like a harpoon.

'This lady has been making a culpable nuisance of herself in Pomerania, to put it mildly. She has committed treasonable offences. What are you able to tell us about Mrs Daschke's aberrations, Miss Arber?'

'To be honest, nothing material, sir. She is – was – my fellow teacher, senior teacher, at Alt Schönbek School. And you will be aware, of course, that I lodged with her. Her younger daughter was ... she died and that was a terrible shock to Mrs Daschke, as I imagine it would be to any mother. I woke up one day and she was gone. I know that must sound lame...'

'Well, it does rather, doesn't it? There is Mrs Daschke going about her business as a responsible senior teacher – and the next day she simply departs with no explanation? And lands her child on you. You had no warning, no notion of her itinerary – no sense of her motivation or intention? Hard to credit. Especially as all witnesses agree the two of you were very close. Like sisters, I am told.'

'But truly, Captain von Stein—'

'And your colleague abandoned not only her professional responsibilities but also her other young daughter, just like that, without seeking your consent or discussing her plans with you?'

Careful, careful.

'Well, she did leave a note. And I knew – everyone knew – that she was upset. The note is in my bag with the books, if you'd like to check. But, if I may say...?'

'Of course, Miss Arber, that is why we have invited you here.'

The Captain leans back wearily in his chair, elbows on the arm rest, with an expression of invincible ennui. His fingers play a tune on the edge of the desk. His look says: you would hardly believe the imbecilities I have had to listen to in here. But carry on, let's see if you can divert me with some self-serving fiction of your own.

'It's not quite as odd as it must seem, Captain von Stein – although of course I was terribly anxious and didn't know what to do. But the thing is, I am like a second mother to Mrs Daschke's little girl. The remaining little girl.'

'I see. So you admit to being a good friend to Mrs Daschke? And yet you claim to have taken no part in her criminal actions?'

'Criminal actions?'

'Your friend has made accusations of infanticide against the State.'

'Oh no.'

'We are at war. Millions are dying. Every day our enemies incinerate German mothers and babies. Young German soldiers give their lives to defend those mothers and babies. And the deranged mother of an idiot child accuses the distinguished physicians of the National Socialist State of infanticide! What do you have to say about that?'

'I think ... perhaps ... Mrs Daschke is not well.'

'Not well in the sense that her moron offspring was not well? Is that what you mean? You feel that Mrs Daschke also belongs in an asylum? I'm inclined to agree.'

'Oh ... no ... I didn't mean ... oh dear, it must be *grief*, you see. That's what I meant.'

'And you failed to report her absence?'

'Oh no, that's wrong, I did report it, I spoke to my mentor ... Mr Excorn.'

She's over-breathing, she's panicking. They know. He said, *witnesses*. Who? Who ratted? (He is shuffling the papers again).

'You waited several days to report your colleague's absence.'

'The thing is ... I was terribly busy ... just me to manage the whole school ... I suppose I hoped she'd soon be back.'

Ruth had broken into an institution in Meseritz-Obrawalde and made treasonable accusations against the staff.

'Mrs Daschke was distraught,' Magdalena tells him, 'when her younger daughter died. A mother loves her child, she can't help it, it is nature. And it was because there was ... an unfortunate ... discrepancy ... in the official letter... Ruth's little girl, you see, was said to have died of appendicitis when she didn't have an appendix ... so she couldn't possibly have ... it had been taken out...'

'You say your friend left you a note? Not that a note proves anything. Let's see the note.'

'It's in the bag, with my papers.'

He opens the rucksack, decants Magdalena's books, locates the note, skims it.

The minute she sees the books, she thinks it's all over. What had she snatched up? Agnes Miegel's sentimental patriotic verse, yes, she recognises it on the top of the pile, that's fine, but what else did she grab from the drawer?

Eva's forbidden books concealed in brown paper covers? No, please no.

Beads of cold sweat stand on her forehead. She sits on her hands to kill the tremble.

The book in the interrogator's hands is that red and green horror, *Trust No Fox on his Green Heath and No Jew on his Oath*. Confiscated from Julia last year when she set up school under the piano and reviled her toy fox for being ... a fox.

Providence!

Thank God for that vile book!

Oh yes, Magdalena tells him eagerly, and assumes her teacherly persona, Miss Arber the literary brainbox:

'That is one of my all-time favourite books! Are you familiar with it, Captain? No? Well, it's a children's book so you wouldn't have come across it, I suppose. But anyone of any age can benefit from good children's literature, at least I always think so. Mrs Daschke and I love that book! And the illustrations are so powerful. The writer was only eighteen or so when she published it. It's a fable, you see, a story with a moral and political lesson...'

'Yes, Miss Arber, I do know what a fable is...'

On and on Magdalena goes, spouting filthy drivel, to cover her craven back, hiding behind the basest of lies, while von Stein leafs through the pages of *Trust No Fox*, pausing to grin at colourful illustrations that take his fancy. The fat malevolent Jew getting his come-uppance for persecuting the sweet little German kiddywinkies.

The Captain actually chortles.

Looking up, he closes the book: 'I see you are an enthusiastic reader and teacher, Miss Arber. You certainly have the gift of the gab. But may I give you some advice?'

'Oh yes, please do.'

'I have spoken with eminent acquaintances of yours, Dr Vogel the zoologist and Professor Littmann, the pathologist. They speak highly of you, with reservations, as does your mentor, Mr Excorn. He is impressed with your pedagogical dedication, as he puts it. But he suggests that you have yet to learn the spirit of true feminine obedience. For instance, Mr Excorn tells me that you will invent any excuse for failing to perform your Band of German Maidens functions. Your attitude is arrogant, lackadaisical and, in this regard slothful. A dereliction of your sacred duty. What have you to say to that?'

'Oh dear.'

'Yes, oh dear.'

'Mr Excorn has also told me that you consider yourself an intellectual.'

Heart in mouth, she acknowledges some faults of that nature.

'You may not be aware,' he says with a jaundiced smile, 'that in this office one develops a kind of second sight, or should I say, second hearing. One hears what is not said.'

What can you answer to that? She remains silent.

'You see,' von Stein says, 'personal loyalty is one thing.'

'Yes?'

'But loyalty to our great Fatherland transcends every other bond and duty. Of yourself, Miss Arber, you are not just a woman but a nobody.'

'I am a nobody.'

A shadow crosses his face and he half rises from his chair: 'Are you by any chance being flippant with me, Miss Arber?'

'No, oh no. I didn't mean ... I was just taking in ... what you said...'

She feels faint now, and blank. Wrings her hands in her lap and can't think of anything more to say to defend herself.

What is coming? Well, he is. Walks round the desk. Stoops from what now seems a considerable height. His cigar-scented mouth. Up too close. A gold incisor peeking from the general corruption in there.

What's he about to do?

He stands over her. Is he getting ready to strike her?

'May I just look at your hand, Miss Arber?'

'At my hand?'

'Your hand. If you please.'

She offers both. Tries to control the trembling. Shrinks back into her seat.

'And you are right-handed?'

'I am.'

'Then I shall require only your right hand.'

Now she is scared. He takes her right hand in both his own, comments on her long, slender fingers and asks whether she plays a musical instrument?

'The piano. The accordion.'

'And I gather you have aspirations to be a writer?'

'Well...'

'Yes or no, Miss Arber? Don't be shy. Admit it!'

'Well, I have sometimes ... thought...'

'Let us assume that you have the ambition to publish a book of your very own, shall we, like the juvenile authoress whose work you have – I must say, rather conveniently – brought along today? You have this ambition because you know a smattering of this and that, chiefly in the form of long words, and you want to make a name for yourself. So this is your writing hand? A strong, supple, young hand.'

He turns her hand palm-upward, rubbing his thumb suggestively round the flinching palm. Turns it over. Pauses. With the tip of his nicotine-ginger forefinger, he nudges Magdalena's forefinger upwards. Softly, gently.

She stares at her hand in his, then into his eyes, baffled.

'So this,' he says, face still much too close, 'is the digit that guides your pen?'

Faintly: 'Yes.'

'Let us see how pliant it is, shall we?' He pushes the finger up an inch.

What's he doing, what's he doing?

'Quite flexible,' he observes '– at least, so far. Let's see what happens when ... I ... do this...'

He presses her finger higher.

A yelp bursts out. Tears spark. Her elbows wince into her sides.

'Am I hurting you, Miss Arber?'

'Yes. Please...'

'Just a little more and you may hear quite an interesting snap, or pop. An anatomy experiment! Shall we try?'

'No, please don't ... no...'

'Now here's a lesson for you, Miss Teacher. They do say it is well-nigh impossible for a right-hander to learn to write with his left hand. There's a scientific explanation. You see, the brain is so configured that the dominant writing hand is ordained before birth, were you aware of that? Granted, there are some odd individuals who are ambidextrous, but I am assuming you are not one of these?'

'No.'

He presses the finger up further and pins it there.

Pain sears down into the underside of her wrist. She hears the pop.

He holds on.

He lets go.

Presses up harder and she screams.

He lets go; steps back.

She is shaking. She curls the helpless, damaged hand in her lap. Pain, searing hot pain. She hears herself whimper.

An interesting little experiment, he says. Wouldn't you say? Calm down now, Miss Arber, you're not hurt.

The sense of loneliness is overwhelming.

'Believe me, you don't begin to know the meaning of the word *pain*. Yet. Oh, and so good of you to explain to me just now, in case I was semi-educated, the meaning of the word *fable*. Perhaps you can see the glimmering of a *fable* here, in our little experiment. Can you?'

'Yes,' she whispers.

'Maybe you also imagine I am ignorant of the meaning of the word *irony? Ambivalence? Equivocation?*'

'No.'

Stein ambles back round the desk to his seat. Sometimes it's good for a schoolteacher to receive a lesson, he observes. And especially when the said teacher has worrying antecedents. For he is aware, he says, of her father's past deviance and detention.

He is also aware that her mother has been taken into protective custody.

'My *mother*?'

'Your mother.'

'What do you mean, my *mother*?'

'She was taken in by the Lűbeck authorities for questioning two days ago. This is news to you?'

'But no! My mother is dead! She's been dead for years!' Magdalena bursts out.

For a second, a lunatic hope rises: perhaps Mum is alive after all, they were mistaken about that, oh if only…

…as when the telegram addressed to Mrs Dorothea Arber was delivered a week after her death, to apprise the patient of a hospital appointment for the following week … and Magdalena happened to be at the door and signed in her childish hand for the telegram, and the hope soared that they'd been mistaken about Mum's death, mistaken, Dorothea Arber was alive, it said so here…

But they hadn't been mistaken.

Her mother is dead. She has died all over again.

The interrogator is turning over the papers and matter-of-factly correcting his error: Oh yes, apologies, I mean your aunt, of course. Not your mother.

Magdalena is mute. It's all over: she's about to be arrested. Names are extinguished like candles: Mum, Dad, Ebba, Ruth, Clem, Julia, Flora. This is the end for all of them.

She breaks down.

*

The Captain is stowing her books in the bag. He slides it across the desk toward her. Laces his hands. Nods to her to hurry up and take it.

Dry your eyes. You are free to go, Miss Arber.

Free to go?

Make sure you never give us the slightest cause to call you back.

*

A chained man with a black and bleeding eye is slumped against the wall, waiting with a guard outside Captain von Stein's door.

Magdalena is escorted through the labyrinth and down the stairs, with her rucksack on her back. She stumbles out into the dusk, still unclear as to whether it's today or tomorrow.

23

> Your beloved face has gone beyond my sight,
> The music of your life is dying away
> Beyond my hearing and all the songs
> That worked a miracle of peace once on
> My heart, where are they now?[28]
>
> Friedrich Hőlderlin,
> 'Another Day', 1798–1800

Overnight in the station waiting room, Magda's maimed hand – inflamed and swollen – lay curled in her good hand, which cradled it like a wounded creature. She shielded it from her own eyes.

By and by, sleep came creeping up. She thrust it back. It crawled up behind her again and swooped.

There was a confusion of past and present, sleep and waking.

Who was this? Ruth? Yes, Ruth was opening the door with a child in her arms, Flora it must be, shrunk back to infancy, but a baby not of our species, more like a little helpless monkey, and Ruth too had a simian look, her nose flattened, with wide nostrils, eyes liquid and soulful ... but, yes, it was definitely Ruth, murmuring in a language that might be Yiddish or Romany: *kushti kushti...*

For a second Magdalena surfaced with a jolt from sleep. Or did she?

Was she back in that cell with the jug of filthy water, was some thug about to burst in, call her a halfwit and drag her out ... or ... no, she was here at Kőnigsberg Station, a familiar place ... she'd got away from the ginger teeth ... she'd been exonerated ... told to clear off ... so that was all right.

Was it though? Swallowed again into sleep, Magdalena found

herself back in the bowels of the police headquarters. She seemed to be in a corridor, peering through a grille at – oh no – the hunched back of a woman in rags with a resemblance to Auntie Ebba, incarcerated in that same cell with the guttering light and the stained toilet.

She woke: only a dream. But no. Ebba was indeed under arrest. What in God's name had she said or done? And it would have been in God's name. The quiet woman had stood up and spoken out. And unlike me, Magdalena thought, she will not lie to save herself. She won't prevaricate or bear false witness. Ebba will never cower behind a filthy book.

And yet I thank God for the filth that saved me.

The book's lyrics rang in her ears, round and round, a worm sucking its own tail, located somewhere in herself: *Trust no fox on his green heath, and no Jew on his oath.* Waking and sleeping, the obscene earthworm burrowed in her brain, finding its nourishment in her own wish for a scapegoat: *lip hanging down and great red schnozzles ... The Devil brought the Jews to Germany...*

The Leader, staring down from his portrait in the waiting room, said, as the Captain had said, with weary contempt, *I know what you're thinking, I overhear what is not said, I hear it before you even think it, I have millions of ears and eyes at my disposal.*

At Sunday School in Lübeck they'd been shown pictures of the lidless Eye of the Almighty. It never slept. It tracked girls and boys, day and night. And God's angels, like clerks of the court, were kept busy writing down in a book the sins the Eye detected. Their speeding pens could hardly keep up with the trillions of foul acts committed by mankind with every passing second.

But Ebba had always said, *Don't worry, dearest – our God is nothing like that. He is all tenderness and compassion.* And Dad had always said, *It's what the still small voice of your own human conscience tells you that matters, nothing else.*

Where was the still small voice now? Magdalena could not hear it for terror.

She saw again the ashen face of the young man who'd stopped for her, here on Kőnigsberg Station. She saw him as if in close-up, with his paper collar and threadbare sleeves. And his dash into the dark. Long since, the young man must have been condemned to the yellow star and deportation.

The young man had the grace to stop for me. And yet, to save my own skin, I hide behind the book that condemns the young man in his goodness – and Miss Heller in her goodness, and Dr Süsskind in his goodness, and...

What else could I do? Magdalena asked herself, plaintively. I'm just one person.

Who was she pleading with? With Jesus, in whom she only intermittently believed? With Ebba? The worm only burrowed deeper as her conscience whined and wound and twisted. Forget the young man. And if I am a coward, so be it. *And after all, it was Ruth's fault!* said a nasty little vixen voice. *Ruth endangered me!* the vixen complained. *Ruth is to blame! Not me! I didn't ask for any of this.*

Oh, Ruth, dearest, forgive me, I love you, I miss you, where are you?

Magdalena got to her feet, stretched, shuffled to the toilet, washed the bad hand with the good hand and splashed her face. Stay awake, she advised herself. Think. Reason. Calm down. She returned to her seat and resolutely kept her eyes open.

On the opposite bench sagged the dark form of a rumpled stranger with a shovel-beard and arms draped over his paunch. His head lolled against the wall, mouth open, snoring slightly. An ordinary East Prussian labourer in everyday work clothes who came to with a start and a snort, asking *Whazzatime?* And they both laughed.

She must speak to Dad. As soon as she got back to Alt Schőnbek, she could use Renate's phone and find out about Ebba. Touch home. Talk everything through. Perhaps it was all bluff. Ebba would answer the phone, all would be well, all well...

Suddenly the shovel-bearded passenger was apologetically tapping her on the shoulder: 'Sorry to disturb you, miss, but the train's coming in. Let me take your rucksack for you. There you are.'

She thanked him and they boarded. The old crock of a train took its time, clanked and rocked along through the countryside, its unhurried gait assuring passengers that all was as pretty much as it always had been, not to worry, all would be well.

Magda was the sole passenger to disembark. The morning was still young and the station lay silent except for birdsong. Nothing moved in either direction along the road. She set off on foot.

Then the sky was throbbing with birds. The flock swept this way, it veered that way, it skittered and skimmed around its own ever-changing fulcrum, uttering high-pitched trills: *Sirrr! Sirrr!*

Waxwings!

Sirrr! Sirrr! – meaning, *Do we see the berries? Yes, yes, we see the berries, we all see the berries, let's go!*

What was it Ruth used to call them? *Bibulous birds!* An alcoholic minority would get drunk as lords on fermented fruit, keel over, waggle their helpless wings and die on their backs, singing. *Not a bad way to go either!*

They were long back from their winter in Russia, hungry for all that East Prussia could offer. They'd stay as long as the forage held out. Now the mob dropped down and began to strip the late-fruiting branches, swallowing berries whole, clambering from branch to branch. They were a touching, comical sight, festooning the trees, kings and queens with their spiky crests and peach-blush, black-masked faces. Magdalena sank down on the grass verge, to watch and listen. The waxwings took not the slightest notice.

Stay, stay, you wonders, Magdalena thought, stay with me.

For as long as they stayed, the spectre of fear drew off, until, with a rattling of wings, the flock abandoned the wood, having devoured every single berry. There was nothing left.

*

A force of nature flung itself at Magda through Renate's open door. Pain sang up her arm as the child leapt on her. She tottered back, lost her footing, nearly fell, and Julia with her.

'Hey, you little barnacle!' Magdalena gasped, struggling to right herself. 'You limpet! Let your poor old Magda breathe!'

'You *can* breathe anyway! Otherwise you wouldn't be able to say *Let Magda breathe!*' Julia retorted, still hanging on tight, claiming and mastering her. 'Would you? Because you'd be dead! And also you're not old, not really.'

Renate removed the child and the rucksack; drew Magda in gently. Noticed the injury. She placed one hand lightly on Magdalena's back, guiding her to the sofa and building cushions around her; and the caring hand spoke, saying, *Thank heaven you're back, dear young friend.*

'Thank you for holding the fort, Renate. Sorry you were woken at that unearthly hour. It was just – you know – a formal interview. All in order. I seem to have hurt my hand.'

'How did you do that, Magda?'

'Oh, I wrenched it on ... something.'

Renate made a sling and tied it on. She brought aspirin and asked Julia to be very, very careful as poor Magda had a nasty sprain – and when you have an injury like that, it gives you a shock. She set down a cup of steaming coffee on the side-table, and a plate of bread and butter. 'Try to eat something.'

'I'm starving but I don't think I can.'

'Maybe just a few bites, dear. Come on.'

'Thank you, I'll try. And when this little person lets me, I'd love that drink. Are you going to let me have my coffee, Julia?... How was she, Renate?'

'Oh, you know. Rather quiet, weren't you, love?'

'Actually Julia got in the cupboard,' Karin reported in a very audible whisper. 'And she wouldn't come out.'

'I didn't so!'

'You did so! And you were crying in there because I heard you!'

'Fibber!'
'I'm only *saying*!'
'Telltale!'
'Sorry. (But you did.)'

Magdalena sank back into the sofa cushions. She took a swig of coffee. Normal life was still going on here then? You'd been allowed to return from the underworld, having been introduced to a place of terror. How come you'd been released when so many were swallowed up in darkness? For reasons known only to the gatekeeper, you'd been discharged into the light of a morning of ordinary human blessedness. There was bread and butter, and two children were quarrelling.

But would you ever be quite the same again? You'd be looking over your shoulder, watching what you said.

As Julia guardedly confessed that maybe she *had* got in the cupboard, that one over there – a ton weight of ancient East Prussian oak, carved with leaves and birds – she glanced swiftly at Magdalena to make sure she wasn't cross about the fib, and Magdalena saw, not just Julia but a fleeting reflection of Flora. Something about the eyes snared her heart.

Her own eyes swam. Let me remember you always, little Flora. Perfect, as you were.

She set down the drink with a careful hand, put her good arm round the surviving twin and assured her that, in the great sum of things, it probably didn't matter too much about the cupboard. Did it, Renate?

'Of course not. Actually it looked nice and cosy in there. I felt like climbing in myself but decided I was slightly too big. Anyway, we had a nice game of hide-and-seek, didn't we? And then we fed Karin's tortoise.'

There was so much ordinary kindness in this house. And in the village, there remained an old-fashioned communal decency. It was as if the inhabitants of Alt Schönbek had for some time occupied a remote hamlet in a plague year. The rat-borne infestation of fleas had not yet succeeded in colonising the whole population.

Not quite yet.

Renate, sitting down beside her, took Magdalena's hand, rubbing the back gently with her thumb. Julia observed this language of solidarity and looked seriously from one adult face to the other.

'You came back, Magda,' the child said.

'Of course I did. May I use the phone, Renate, just to call home?'

*

Something was odd about the telephone reception: a clicking and buzzing when her father picked up.

'Dad. It's me.'

'Magda! Darling girl! Is everything all right?'

There was something peculiar about Dad's voice too. As if he were suppressing a cough.

'I'm fine. Have you got a cold or something?'

'Not that I know of. Of course there are plenty of germs going round.' He coughed again. '*Plenty* of germs. *Germs,* Magda, nasty ones. We all need to take care. How are you?'

'I'm all right, thanks, Dad. Just back from a meeting in Kőnigsberg. I was worried about you and Ebba.'

Silence. Then a rustling sound and a kind of hiccup. Had they been cut off? She heard him clear his throat.

'Dad! Are you still there?'

'Oh yes, nothing to worry about.'

'What's the matter with your throat?'

'Tickle in it. Probably a *germ*. I may have caught something.'

He was being very odd, even for him. 'Can I speak to Ebba?'

Crackle: '...not here at the moment...'

'Dad! what do you mean?'

'She's away, love, called away. Do you want me to give her a message when I see her? She'll be sorry to have missed you.'

'Only, to give her my love – and a big hug. Dad, I was told...'

He cut in briskly. 'Don't be concerned, nothing untoward. Ebba's just away briefly, sorting out a thing or two. Expected back before too long.'

'Church business?'

'Something like that. But how are you? Did I tell you about Goethe and Schiller?'

'The poets or the cats?'

'Well, the cats, of course, you goose! You are perfectly capable of interpreting the poets for yourself.'

Oh God, Magdalena thought. He's off again.

A long cat rigmarole ensued. Schiller, Dad said, was constantly lying in wait to pounce on Goethe. The bombing had turned the poor little animal's wits, and frankly Schiller had not been all that bright to begin with. So Schiller now saw his brother as the enemy. As soon as he heard Goethe meow he'd track him round the house, listening at doors, with his claws flexed, cats having very keen ears. You couldn't do anything about his behaviour, you just had to live with it and try to curb his worst excesses. And besides you could get mauled yourself if you weren't careful. Schiller was a law unto himself, he no longer trusted his poor little ginger pal at all.

'It must be worrying, of course – they were always such good pals ... but about Auntie Ebba, Dad—'

'Do pay attention to what I'm telling you, dear! Animals are also our kin. Creaturely life, Magdalena! Earthly creatures! We all exist on a continuum.' The disciple of Voltaire sounded mildly exasperated and was not bothering to conceal it. 'Think about it, Magda! You see, this works both ways, doesn't it?'

'What does?'

'Keep up now, keep up! This mutual awareness is what I'm alerting you to. Schiller is stalking Goethe – right?'

'Right.'

'But Goethe, on the other side of the door, is also *listening* to Schiller *listening in*. Right? So sometimes it's quiet in the household, and there's the appearance of peace and harmony. But this isn't real. The little chaps were fine until the bombing, and then *all hell broke loose*. Do you see now?'

'Dad...'

'Yes, dear.'

'It's you I'm worried about. You and Auntie Ebba. Not the cats, much as I love them.'

The line gave another crackle. A shuffling sound.

Belated light dawned. Code, she thought. Code.

'Sorry, Dad,' she hastened to say. 'I was being dense. Our Leader loves animals and that's so important to remember. Of course I want to hear about the little chaps! Tell them meow from me and Julia.'

A chuckle as he heard her catching on.

'How is our little Julia?' he asked.

'She's been staying the night with Renate, playing with Karin's tortoise Zippy, while I was away at a meeting.'

'Slow and steady with a pet like that, Magdalena!'

'And you, Dad – slow and steady.'

She put down the receiver. So the phone at home was being tapped. And Ebba was indeed in prison.

Quiet, contained and apparently biddable, Auntie Ebba was capable of hardening into steel. She would endure deprivation – hunger – even solitude – with stoicism. She'd be alert to the interrogator's every nuance. The still small voice would counsel Ebba, moment by moment. Magda hoped she'd been allowed to bring in her Bible, the scuffed old book that travelled with her everywhere.

Handed down the generations, its leather covers were bowed, its leaves flimsy and yellowing. As a child, Magda had liked the poppy someone had pressed long ago at the Twenty-Third Psalm. Its silken petals had endured through the decades. *The Lord is my shepherd, I shall not want.* The poppy had transferred a red-gold ghost of itself on the two enclosing pages. *He maketh me to lie down in green pastures, he leadeth me beside the still waters, he restoreth my soul.* A smell of age exhaled from the Bible's leaves, not unwholesome, rather like the bittersweet herbs that grew around Lake Plön. *Yea, though I walk through the valley of the shadow of death, I shall fear no evil...*

Being without her Bible would be hard for her aunt, but not the ultimate hardship, after all. Ebba knew the Gospels by heart, as well as her favourite passages of the Old Testament, especially The Song of Songs, The Book of Ruth, the Psalms – though she'd skipped, Ebba would admit with a grin, the interminable chapters in which so-and-so begat so-and-so, apparently with no contribution from the female of the species.

Still, without the physical book, it would not be the same. The object itself was a friend. A hand to hold. A voice to listen to.

*

The two of them played hopscotch – well, Julia did the hopping for them both – until evening brought a thunderous downpour of rain out of a clear sky. Water sluiced through the trees, made a river of the road, battered its fists on the water butt, and then stopped dead. The sky cleared. Soaked to the skin, woman and child took their chalks, fled into the house laughing and dripped their way upstairs to the bath. Magdalena removed the sling and Julia managed the taps. In they got together and basked in warmth. It was nearly as good as the lagoon, they agreed, well, not quite, because there was no nice fishy smell and no silky sand to wiggle between your toes.

Afterwards, Julia insisted on drying Magda and helped put on the sling. 'Poor hand,' she said. Kissed it. 'Soon be better, you'll see.'

And so the blessings we have given come circling back, Magdalena thought, inexpressibly comforted.

The two of them stood at the window, looking out at pools glistening in redeemed sunlight on pavements and roads, while Magdalena did her best to towel Julia's hair dry one-handed, and comb out the tangles. Long, luscious hair, which seemed to be growing thicker and darker and more mutinous by the day.

If Magdalena kept her attention on Julia, fear seemed to draw off. How unexpected it was, she thought, as Julia read aloud to her, that an adult took comfort and courage from a child's nearness. It was time to centre and focus her own life.

Was it just familiarity that made Magdalena fancy a likeness between her own face and Julia's? Of course it was, don't be ridiculous. I am just a stand-in, Magdalena thought, that's all I am. A useful bystander, a kind of auntie. She kissed the top of the child's head.

Well then, if I am a stand-in, I will stand. I will stand for you. I will stand by you. Surely I can do that.

They got ready for bed. Magda turned back Julia's quilt and they knelt to say their prayers. Julia climbed into bed and they followed up, as ever, with the Lovely Words. They said good night, sleep tight; they promised always to love and kiss each other; they asked each other to be best friends.

'You'll still be here, won't you, Magda, in the morning?' Julia asked, cutting into the ritual of the Lovely Words. As she turned her face up to Magda's, she again brought the gentle, puzzled beauty of her lost sister's eyes with her. Perfect, as she was.

'Of course I will, my angel.'

'Are you sure? If I wake up in the night, can I come into your bed?'

'My bed is your bed whenever you need it.'

They completed the Lovely Words, face close to mirroring face on Julia's pillow: 'Look forward to seeing you in the morning.'

Magdalena waited a moment on the threshold, listening to make sure Julia was settling down for sleep. She saw the little girl take the toy fox in the crook of her arm and heard her breathing deepen; turned and tiptoed to her own bedroom.

PART TWO

24

Summer 1943

> The Leader took the little blond girl by the hand and [treated her] to cake and strawberries with thick, sweet cream ... Then she made herself as tall as she could, put her little arms round the Leader's neck, and gave the Leader a long, long kiss.[29]
>
> Baldur von Schirach, *Primer for Elementary School*, 1935

The little girl was Magdalena's centre, the axis of her world. In a larger sense too, Magdalena belonged here in the village; she'd taken root. Villagers gathered round to celebrate their teacher's twenty-second birthday. Miss Arber was an East Prussian! Yes, you jolly well are, Miss, don't deny it! You even speak with an East Prussian accent when you're larking around! You do, you roll your Rs, you really do, we're not making it up! Flowers festooned her classroom, along with baskets of fruit, cake, vegetables, eggs.

Experienced and at ease in her profession, Magdalena loved the children and was fond of most of their parents, relishing the respect and affection in which she was held. But constraint had tightened, there was no denying it. The tide of war had turned against Germany. After the army's catastrophic defeat at Stalingrad, Dr Goebbels' raving 'Total War' speech in February had exacted from every citizen the sacred duty to give all for the Fatherland's victory over Bolshevism, hunting down the Enemy Within. *I ask you*, the minister had bellowed: *Do you want total war? Do you want it, if need be, even more total and radical than we are capable of imagining it today?* And the select audience of fourteen thousand in the Sport Palace had bawled on behalf of every man, woman and child in the nation: *Yes!*

In the rural world of Alt Schönbek, Mrs Braun redoubled her snooping campaign – the least she could do for her adored Leader – and denounced the blurtings of her next door neighbour, the eighty-six-year-old Mrs Hoffmann.

For Magdalena and Julia, long breaks in Lübeck were no longer permissible. Miss Arber must not desert her station. The noose was tightening. Clem, for the moment, seemed safe, with a timely flesh-wound, somewhere in the east. Where was Ruth? Nobody knew and her name was never mentioned. Auntie Ebba had been held in various prisons, still awaiting trial.

Over the phone Dad assured Magda, and the wire-tapper, of his certainty that his sister would be exonerated. National Socialist law was a golden system, he proclaimed: it mapped a new and truer Enlightenment. What were Voltaire and Diderot – those piffling, puffed-up, dandified Frenchmen – by comparison with our mighty-minded German colossi, Globke and Freisler? He had every confidence that his sister would be vindicated by this peerless body of law. Magdalena marvelled at the calm virtuosity of his lying. From the depths of fear and grief he brought irony, whose example added flair to her own fictions. Magdalena's hand would tingle, not with pain but with mute warning, reminding her of the danger of exposure. *Be on your guard. No rashness. Mind your stupid tongue. Perform the salute as if you meant it. Leave no paper trail.* Captain von Stein's thumb, intimately rubbing her palm, haunted her. She dreamed of him; winced at the memory of the popped ligament. After her interrogation, Magdalena had checked every drawer and shelf for evidence that might tell against her, destroying anything remotely heretical – apart, that is, from her diaries, for which she'd found a space beneath the floorboards.

Returning Eva's books, she explained that it was too dangerous to borrow from her library.

'Magda, there is no library. I've buried it,' Eva said. 'Everything. Safer that way, my young friend. The dopes will have to shift a whole lot of manure to find them.'

My young friend. Was that how Eva thought of her? Immature, junior? Of course it was. Eva felt a need to protect her, not just from the forces closing in, but from the Arber recklessness.

I could love you, Eva, Magdalena thought. *And I'm twenty-two, not that young – not young at all! Well, I do love you. But I came too late, your love is given to Leonie, and that's that.*

And yet, she counselled her mournful self, wasn't affection a kind of love, seeking the safety of the other?

In any case, I'll take what I can get, Magda thought.

On her visits to the estate she'd see Alf labouring in the fields: they'd smile with their eyes across the space between and then symmetrically turn away. Presumably she was also Alf's *young friend* and a dangerous one at that. There were occasional fascinating fleeting glimpses of Eva's kin as they came and went, the old aristocracy of Prussia, interwoven dynasties: officers like Henning von Tresckow or medical men like Hans von Wedel and Hans von Lehndorff.

Having returned her last loans to Eva's safekeeping, Magda went to the shelf and removed Goethe and Hölderlin, the defensive ramparts of the Laulitz literary fortress, still standing tall. Behind them: empty space.

'Be as careful as you know how,' Eva said, slipping her arm round Magdalena's shoulders. 'You've got Blondie sliming around.'

Magdalena rode home, ran upstairs, locked her door and performed the final sacrifice. She cleared the diaries from their hiding place and burned every last page. It hurt. Hurt too much. I can't not write, she felt, as the days and weeks went past and abominations in the public and private worlds mounted.

Then it came to her: an Anti-Diary. Of course. Write the opposite of what you feel and think. Release righteous venom on to the page. The spleen of satire.

*

Today Dagmar was to teach a lesson on racial science, which Mr Excorn – called up for army service, despite impaired eyesight, breathing problems, arthritic knees, age and diabetes – had required Magdalena to supervise on his behalf.

The poor old geezer would be no earthly use in action. Alt Schönbek, filling with evacuees from the bombed cities in the west, was emptying of the pitiful remnant of its menfolk, called up to bolster dwindling troop numbers in the east. What an opportunity for us ladies though, cried the Struppats. Showing our patriotism by filling in for the men! And final victory is nigh! they insisted, undaunted by Germany's apparent reverses.

The Leader's Wonder Weapon was about to be unleashed! It would smash the British hypocrites to smithereens! Mrs Braun volubly praised the Leader's genius in luring Stalin westwards by pretending to retreat. The Slavic hordes would be well and truly kettled: encircled and annihilated, once and for all!

Did believers privately tremble, Magdalena wondered, when they were awoken at night by Russian planes, and viewed fiery skies around Kőnigsberg? Although these poorly targeted bombs were supposed to have done little damage and the radio news was relentlessly upbeat, the Party faithful must surely be visited by qualms. Perhaps seeds of doubt made folk bluster all the more.

I wish I were deaf, Magda thought. I could just keep nodding and smiling at Dagmar if I were nice and deaf.

Into the schoolroom swept her colleague, with a robust *Heil Hitler!* – even though they had not long ago shared a bleary and monosyllabic breakfast. Unrolling a chart, Dagmar pinned it to the noticeboard. She set down a pile of books on the table. While they awaited the arrival of the children, she waved a volume at Magdalena.

'This primer ... is one that I particularly like, Magda. You don't know it? It is sheer poetry. Listen to this.'

In a throbbing voice, Dagmar read aloud a passage from a textbook composed by the famous Youth Leader, Baldur von

Schirach, showing how tender the Leader was to little girls. Although he's a mighty warrior, he takes time to serve a little blonde German girl with a bumper tea of cake and cream. The little girl knows not to fear him.

'She trusts him, and she stretches up and gives him a kiss. Not a little itsy-bitsy peck on the cheek. Not just a long kiss, even. But a long, *long* kiss, Magda. It's so moving.'

Pity she didn't throw up all over the swine, thought Magda. But she said, 'Yes, isn't it. He's a Man of Iron. And yet he takes notice of the little blonde girl. When he's so busy...'

...busy with his meat cleaver in his international butchery business, she thought.

Her right hand spasmed a warning. Its injury had moderated Magdalena's over-confidence. I'm not as brave as I believed I was, she thought. Frankly, I'm not brave at all. I'm a gelded woman. She liked to think that Captain von Stein might have been drafted to the Eastern Front – but if so, there would be plenty of black spiders still dangling from that web, alert for prey. Keep quiet, Magdalena told herself. Even so, the electric current of irony was hard to restrain when one lived cheek-by-jowl with the stupidity of a Struppat, who was now stating that the iron Leader would never rust. Or melt!

'Our iron man! You read my thoughts. That's just what I was going to say. Yes, really! Honestly, Magda, we really seem to understand each other, almost before we speak. Do you feel that too?'

Oh definitely, thought Magdalena, nodding and grimacing – especially when I hear you tiptoeing up the stairs and find you've been rummaging round in my room, truffling out secrets.

For the past month she'd been keeping a diary solely for the benefit of her clandestine reader. A kind of fictional diary. The journal had become an addiction. It wrote itself in satiric ink composed of venom. Sheer parody. Her hand raced across the page. She'd smother bursts of splenetic laughter as she scribbled. Occasionally she wondered if she should tone it down, but nothing seemed too insanely distasteful for her colleague to swallow. Magdalena wrote nothing meaningful about her inner life, or her anxieties about Ebba, still in custody awaiting trial – or about Ruth. Or Flora. Or Dad, Clem, Julia.

The children were late. Come on, for God's sake let's get started. When would Mrs Braun lead them in for their physiology lesson?

'I'll go and chivvy Mrs Braun,' Magda said. 'It shouldn't take this long to see to their ablutions.'

'The toilet's blocked,' replied Dagmar matter-of-factly. 'Give them another minute, and then I'll go and blow them all sky-high. My God, old Braun won't know she's born. These old women, eh? In many ways they're a decadent generation – don't tell anyone I said so... Can I tell you something in strictest confidence, Magda? Just between the two of us? But you must swear on your honour never to tell anyone.'

'That goes without saying.'

'Well ... but say it anyway, Magda.'

'I do.'

'No, I mean, say it properly, like an oath: I swear never to tell a soul what Dagmar Struppat is about to tell me.'

Magda repeated the formula.

Dagmar looked round at the empty classroom; lowered her voice. 'I was taken into custody once.'

'*What?*'

'Yes! ... Tell you later. They're coming... At *last*, Mrs Braun! What on earth have you been doing? Laying the water pipes?'

Glaring at Mrs Braun, Dagmar rapped on the desk with a pointer. Pay attention, because today would be an important learning occasion, she told the children. And this lesson they must remember all their lives!

'All stand! Boys here! Girls there! Quick now! ... Giddy-up! ... Fair-haired boys here! Fair-haired girls ... No, no! ... Flaxen boy, move along to the right ... Brown-haired girls, to the left ... yes, yours is brown, obviously – what did you think it was? Purple? Move along to the end... Now, eyes! Blue here, brown there...'

Dagmar dived at pupils she felt had cheated, until she was happy, or happy enough, about the provisional order. Provisional because German racial science was rigorous and complex. And confusing.

'Brown eyes with brown hair at the end... I said, at the *end*! ... Don't argue, please ... and if I hear one more stupid, ignorant word out of you, Heini, I shall take the stick to you, I would have hoped you'd have learned from your last thrashing...'

Oh, how Dagmar had enjoyed beating Heini, who really could not help his compulsions and tics.

'So! There we have it! A demonstration, approximate of course, of the gradations within our Nordic race. And we can view the unique *boldness* of that race, in the flat, backward-tilting forehead of the male, the straight or straightish nose from high nasal roots...'

High nasal rot, thought Magdalena childishly. She dared not look at Julia, who she knew was staring at her, eloquent eyebrows raised.

Furtive jostlings: nobody wanted to be labelled dark, or accused of having a crooked nose, a snub nose or, worst of all, a hook nose. There seemed to be a worry about where red hair stood in the league of blondness. Julia and Karin were standing halfway along the girls' rankings, Julia having for some time failed to qualify as a peerless strawberries-and-cream Aryan prodigy. Magdalena risked glancing at her. Julia's lackadaisical expression said: what do I blooming well care anyway? When will I be able to go and fish in the river or climb a tree?

The blondest children preened. The darkest hunched their shoulders. And now Magdalena put her foot in it. Up to the knee.

Stationing herself at the dark end of the row, she looked over at Dagmar, nodding to her to take a place at the blond end, while she went on to say, 'Remember, children, that Teutonic characteristics are a spectrum – and our great Leader, bearing this out, himself has brown hair.'

Dagmar looked aghast: this was not something you *said*. Ever. She reddened with embarrassment.

The undersized, dark-haired, pigeon-chested gods of the Aryan race strutted and raved: the myopic millions revered and swooned.

'Isn't that right, Miss Struppat? Scientifically speaking?' Magdalena asked.

'Miss Arber!' Dagmar gasped.

The classroom was silent as the children scanned curiously from one end of the row to the other, as if watching a tennis match.

'Oh, I only meant that it's acknowledged by the experts that hair colour can darken with age.'

Dagmar, flushed, stammered out something about the Leader's electric blue eyes.

Backtracking, Magdalena praised the Leader's eyes, eyes which had been called mesmerising and compared with the legendary Blue Flower.

Dagmar mentioned that when the Leader looked into your eyes, his gaze pierced deep into the soul – and we could see that in the portrait, couldn't we, children?

'Yes, Miss Struppat!' they chorused, and, taking their cue from her, they all saluted the Leader's portrait.

Dagmar went on to read to the class the Primer episode in which the mighty Leader feeds cake, strawberries and cream to the little blonde girl, who then stands on tiptoe (for he is very big and she is very small) and bestows on him that long, *long* kiss.

*

'Whyever did you *say* that, Magda?' asked Dagmar.

'Say what?'

'About the Leader having dark hair. I was shocked.'

'Did I say *dark?* I thought I said *brown?*'

'You said *dark.*'

'Ah. I meant to say *brown*. There is no way I would ever cast the slightest aspersion on our Leader. I am devoted to him. You know that, Dagmar.'

'Even so, don't you see, we can't say such things to *children*.' Dagmar paused, and then blurted, 'And in any case I was supposed to be leading the class today, not you.'

'Which you did, very effectively.'

'Yes, but you weren't meant to meddle and make me look like...'

'Like what?'

'Well, undermining my authority. The children all love you ... and...'

So that was it. Dagmar's creamed face and blonded hair shone in the lamplight. She'd come down in her dressing gown to fetch a glass of milk. She looked like Julia in one of her sulks.

'But, Dagmar, I was required to supervise, wasn't I? Children need to feel acceptable, whatever colour their hair is. After all, every family in Alt Schönbek has impeccable racial credentials. All our children can boast certificates of racial purity going back to 1750.'

Dagmar piped down but she was not happy. Perhaps she also reflected that Magdalena, deputising for Mr Excorn, had the upper hand, at least for the time being.

'I'm sorry you were upset,' Magda temporised. Dagmar was pouring milk with an unsteady hand.

'Oh, I wasn't upset,' Dagmar lied. 'Why would I be upset? I always want to get everything *correct*. That is my nature, Magdalena.'

She turned away and said no more.

25

I could kiss you a thousand times and still not be satisfied ... I am having keys cut for you to my front room ... I would like to make you my little puppy, my dear, my eternal, my lovely Adolf ... I kiss the letters of your name and do it without a blouse so that you feel how I love you...[30]

Excerpts from *Love Letters to Adolf Hitler*,
sundry penwomen, 1931–1945

'Can I help you?' Julia wheedled. 'Oh please, Magda?'

She clasped Magda's waist and, swaying the pair of them from side to side, reminded her how she loved baking and loved Magda, and really *really* wanted to help, because Magda looked tired and frazzled and had a poorly hand, even though she *said* it was fine now.

Magdalena laughed and handed over the bowl and a fork. Last night she'd dreamed harrowingly of being arrested and separated from Julia, never to see her face again. Waking, she'd known that Dagmar was within an inch of denouncing her. Perhaps she had already done so. But there might still be a way to woo Dagmar: see what *she* needs, feed her.

Julia rolled up her sleeves and washed her hands, as bidden. With all her might she thrashed the butter in the bowl, sieved in the sugar, beat again till the mixture stood up in peaks, then paused to taste it on her fingertip, sucking off a blob of yellow goodness.

As they worked, Dagmar was heard to bang in through the front door. They both froze. Listened as Dagmar went upstairs. A few minutes later she came down again. Exited without a word to anyone.

Where was she going? This had better work.

'Julia,' Magda said. 'I want you to listen to me now. Listen carefully.'

'Mmn?'

'And stop licking the fork. It's unhygienic!'

'I was only testing.'

'Yes, well don't test. Listen now.'

Julia listened; nodded grave assent.

One at a time they added the precious eggs; folded in the flour and almonds; dolloped the mixture into the baking tin; slid it into the oven. While Magda whipped the cream, Julia was allowed to rinse and hull the strawberries. And, yes, she'd done a first-rate job and – *Oh, go on then!* – earned the right to eat these two baby ones.

When Dagmar arrived home again, Julia in her red satin dress, a matching ribbon in her hair, skipped into the hall to waylay her, and dropped a curtsey.

Beaming, she ushered Princess Dagmar into the fairyland of the dining room.

Dagmar stared, incredulous. Candles on the table. Blue irises in a tall vase. Ruth's fine china and cutlery had been removed from the glass case in which they'd been kept for best, and laid out on a newly ironed, snow-white tablecloth.

Cold cuts of ham and sausage. A lavish serving of contrition. Luscious cake, fruit, cream, such as the Leader had served to the little blonde girl. A bottle of wine.

The guest of honour tucked in with relish to this feast of hypocrisy.

*

Replete and a little bit tiddly, Dagmar confided later in the evening that nobody had ever put on such a lovely spread for her before. Ever! Not even when she was a child. Well, of course one had always had a birthday cake and presents and so on, but (just between herself and Magda), Dagmar's parents had not wanted another girl. Seven daughters in a row was not a tally to be proud of. The family name would die.

It was bad luck. Dagmar was bad luck.

She'd drunk most of the bottle of wine. She became maudlin and tearful; said it was disappointing to be a disappointment.

'Oh but I'm sure your mother doesn't think of you like that.'

'Mmn. Well. Perhaps not now. Anyway, I've got something to show you. It's secret. Never shown to anyone before.'

A bundle of papers, tied in pink ribbon, emerged from a box. They were exact copies, Dagmar said, of letters she had sent to the Leader when she'd been very young.

'Has it never crossed your mind,' she asked, looking at Magdalena with liquid eyes, 'that our Leader has no child to inherit his mantle? How can he have a son – or sons – when Germany is his bride? Who will succeed that greatest of men?'

And this had been her motive, Dagmar confided shyly, when she sent these letters to Adolf Hitler. Of course, it was normal in her house to write letters to the Leader. Her mother was always at it, sending him advice about Woman's Mission, which generally got a gracious acknowledgement from his office. Edith never failed to send the Leader a handmade birthday card, and often a gift, such as a handcrafted tapestry with a portrait of the Leader on one mountain top and a lonely stag on another peak, baying.

And when Dagmar, aged sixteen, had taken to composing her own private missives to her beloved, it was not girlish nonsense and fantasy! No, it was actually an attempt to address a genuine political problem – in the way that only a true German girl could do. Would Magdalena like to read copies of the letters and cards she'd sent to the Leader?

My darling sugar-sweet Adolf, Magdalena read, *wouldn't it be possible for us to spend a few hours together at Christmas or New Year's Eve?*

Pitiful comedy. The poor girl had been fed from the cradle on a diet of drivel. She was suckled on Edith Struppat's tainted milk. The Band of German Maidens. The wireless. The newsreels. Her teachers. Festivals. And it had all fermented in the vat of her body until puberty unleashed it.

Sweetest love, favourite of my heart, my truest and hottest beloved, my love for you is endless, so tender, so passionate and so complete...

Oh my sweetheart Adolf, please let me be the gateway for your heir to enter into his rightful inheritance, I do not ask anything for myself, only the glory of being useful to you and the Fatherland...

And perhaps when you hold your sacred baby in your powerful arms, you will sometimes think of your little Dagmar...

'Oh dear. What happened?' asked Magda.

'If he'd had a chance to read them himself, everything would have been different.'

The official replies had been signed not by the Leader but by his minions, and latterly by Mr Bormann. If the young lady did not desist, there would be consequences. But how could Dagmar desist? She was a girl in love. She had a vision, a sense of destiny. In the end, she whispered, the Gestapo had arrived at the door and taken her into protective custody, to administer a short, sharp shock.

The awful thing was that they'd been issued copies of the letters, and Dagmar could hear the policemen sniggering outside the cell door.

'Laughing at me!' she wailed. 'I hate being laughed at! And I am not funny, am I?'

'Not at all.'

'But I found another way – as you know – to give the Leader a baby. I still think of him – my Adolf – in the night.'

Which Adolf did she mean? – Great Adolf or Baby Adolf, whom Dagmar had delivered at the *Lebensborn* home and donated to the great German gene pool? Magda did not ask.

She learned that Mrs Struppat had been outraged with her daughter. To have two Gestapo agents turn up at her virtuous door, arresting her offspring like a common criminal – in plain sight! In front of the village gossips and the Jew-loving non-Party members – and all the rest of the gormless rustics of Alt Schőnbek! Even worse, in front of Edith's fellow Party members jockeying as ever for precedence!

On Dagmar's return from Kőnigsberg the following day, her mother had yanked her through the door, slammed it and struck Dagmar in the face, two terrific slaps. She would have denounced Dagmar herself, she'd screamed, if she'd had the least idea what her slut of a daughter had been doing up there in her bedroom all that time, writing dirty letters, and stealing her stamps too, oh yes, did Dagmar think she didn't keep a tally? Dagmar had been sent off to Steglitz where she'd been at school, to lodge with her aunt and do a course in childcare.

'Which was completely beneath my abilities, Magda ... but then when I rose in education and so on, and I had the *Lebensborn* certificate, oh yes, she was happy enough to welcome me back then, wasn't she?'

*

Moment by moment, Dagmar could be mollified. The effect never lasted. She snooped, prowled, burst in upon Magda and Julia if she heard them laughing and demanded to know what the joke was. As the months passed, Magdalena did her best to pacify her colleague in her baffled search for mastery and advancement. Envy, humiliation and disdain stoked Dagmar's suspicions.

As often as they could, Magda and Julia escaped for the day. Summer was almost over when they took the stopping train to the Vistula Spit, to bathe in the green, crystal waters of the lagoon and the blue currents of the Baltic.

Still and pure, the water seemed lit by the whiteness of the sand at the bottom. Julia, swimming like a little porpoise, would hold her breath to dive, rising to burst up above the surface in a splash of joy. She'd found a piece of amber! Look, look! Thirty million years ago, this had been resin in a tree. The smooth, wave-washed remnant had waited here, drifting golden amid the Baltic seaweed, for young Julia Daschke to find.

We'll come back next weekend, they promised one another, whilst guessing that time might be short.

'I want to ask you something, Magda,' Julia confided as they slithered along the dunes towards the shadow of the forest. Hand in hand they navigated the slippage of the hot white sand, one step forward, half a step back.

'Go on then. What is it, love?'

'But will you say yes?'

'Well, I don't know. I'll try to. Ask away.'

'I don't want to ask you until I'm absolutely sure you'll say yes.'

Magdalena, caught by the rawness in the child's voice, put down the bags and knelt in the hot sand. She took both Julia's hands. 'Come on now, love, don't turn your head away. I can't imagine denying you something you really wanted or needed – if it were in my power. You can talk to Magda, can't you?'

But Julia's face was closed, her jaw was clamped, she lurched ahead out of reach, kicking at the flotsam on the shore.

Probably nothing much, just a whim. Julia would have forgotten whatever it was by tomorrow.

26

Summer 1944

> δαὴρ αὖτ' ἐμὸς ἔσκε κυνώπιδος, εἴ ποτ' ἔην γε
> There was a world ... or was it all a dream?[31]
> Homer, *Iliad* III. 180

Lithuania seemed to have abandoned Lithuania. The nation was trekking westwards on foot, on horseback, on carts pulled by oxen, through East Prussia. Baltic languages being close cousins, inhabitants of Alt Schönbek could make out the gist of what the refugees meant when they cried: *Alkanas, alkanas! Duona, duona? Pieno, pieno?* In any case, you could translate from their haggard faces and grieving voices:

We are hungry. Bread and milk for our children?

The Lithuanians thanked you in broken German with their ravenous mouths.

Back there, they warned, pointing the way they had come. *Bad things. Terror. Red Army. Run, run now. Ivan raping, murdering, looting, burning. German army kaput. Lithuania gone. Latvia gone. Estonia gone. East Prussia soon to go.*

You looked in the direction they pointed. Your heart misgave you.

But this could not be our destiny. After all, we are Germans, they are Slavs. We have Wonder Weapons, they have blunderbusses.

And what if a bunch of English and American troops had landed in France? Our mighty armies were preparing to encircle them. There would hardly be an Englishman left standing, if you could call them men.

And besides, in East Prussia the sun was still burnishing a generous harvest-to-be. Its rays sheened the lakes that were rich with fish. Immense blue skies blackened with flocks of birds. There had never been greater abundance of wild deer in the forests. Hunting parties went out and never returned empty-handed.

But look, whatever were those?

A meander of strange animals passed along the river valleys, ownerless cattle in ones and twos, straggling westwards blindly through the ripening blond fields and moist meadowlands. These breeds were unfamiliar. The animals did not seem to belong together in herds but roamed separately, away from forces unseen.

Late July: Dagmar came bursting in with shocking news.

'Traitors, traitors!' she bawled. 'Aristocrats, so-called! Filth – scum of the earth! The swine laid a bomb to assassinate our precious Leader in the sanctum of his own Wolf's Lair! A bomb! In a briefcase!'

Her face was livid with shock. 'Turn on the wireless, Magda! Turn it on! Oh, for goodness' sake, I'll do it myself! ... Why is it set to this station? What have you been tuning to?'

'Someone must have been fiddling with the knob,' said Magdalena neutrally, looking up from her book. 'But what is it, Dagmar? What has happened?'

The radio waves washed in, curled over and fizzled into foam, then they came billowing at you and crashed against your eardrums. In your mind's eye you could see families all around the Empire sitting around their sets with downcast heads and bated breath, leaning inwards to hear the announcements, which now came thick and fast.

Yes! Our Leader was alive! Praise be! Dagmar was ecstatic. Her mother came dashing in, and Mrs Braun. They'd all heard the beloved voice attesting to his miraculous survival, albeit hoarsely and tonelessly.

Mrs Braun wept copious tears, drenching her handkerchief and flailing it around the room like a fly-swatter. She wailed about sacrilege and impiety: this atrocity was far worse than the Jews crucifying the so-called Messiah. That was nothing compared with this villainy, nothing at all! After all, the fellow was a Jew himself! A Jew claiming to be God, don't make her laugh! The Leader was Mrs Braun's Messiah, and only He, and she would do anything for Him, anything in the world.

Edith Struppat shushed her incensed friend's quasi-theological outburst but shortly worked herself up into an equivalent frenzy. She snarled that she would gladly kill these beasts with her own hands. She wrung their imaginary necks as she would have throttled chickens. And, in fact, she had done so only yesterday to a fowl that was at this very moment roasting in the oven, so she should remember to get home and baste it.

Mrs Struppat repeated over and over that she was speechless.

Then she bolted to baste the bird, shortly reappearing.

Dagmar leapt to her feet and saluted the wireless as her beloved Leader's voice sounded. She gazed up into the eyes of his portrait. She was comforted by her Leader saying that it was a 'small, a very small group of ambitious, unscrupulous, criminally stupid officers' who had tried – and failed – to eliminate him. Any German who knew of accomplices to this crime, the Leader said, had a duty to arrest them or just go ahead and slay these elements on the spot 'with no further ado'.

Edith Struppat would gladly slay them, she said, if she found any in Alt Schönberg. Mrs Braun, still sobbing, turned and ran out of the door. Was this with a view to arresting and slaying suspects?

Dagmar was still on her feet, testifying. Her mother was also standing to attention.

Magdalena, shaking her head, said – in a quavering voice – that her legs had gone to jelly, she felt faint and that it was the saddest, most appalling thing in the world. Which was nothing but the truth. She sat with her elbows on her knees and head bent, sorrowing. How the hell could a bunch of army officers botch a simple execution? Yes, it was the saddest thing in the world.

And how could she have left the wireless indicator tuned to the forbidden BBC news?

She hung her head between her knees, so convincingly that Dagmar, taking pity, went and fetched a glass of water for her. Patting her on the shoulder, Dagmar encouraged her, 'Bear up now, Magda. Our beloved Leader is safe now, safe.'

'Thank you,' murmured Magdalena.

The radio kept them informed of the justice meted out to the July criminals. Once the Gestapo had started to pull on the threads of the clandestine network, thousands of conspirators were revealed, arrested, tortured, hanged, guillotined, shot. Their names and titles, Mrs Struppat predicted, would go down in the history of infamy. Of odium! Of opprobrium! Of obloquy! They and their children's children would pay dearly for this, she said. Aristocrats were forever under suspicion.

'Mark my words, there will be a cull.'

As these names began to be broadcast, Magdalena's sinking feeling became deeper: she'd been introduced to Henning von Tresckow at Laulitz Farm – and von Stauffenberg – wasn't he connected to Eva in some way?

*

Even so, summer persisted, golden and balmy. In Kőnigsberg folk going about their business through the ancient streets or asleep in their homes, were intermittently disturbed by a droning thrum in the air above them. Reconnaissance planes circled. Sirens sounded nightly. No bombs dropped.

Area Leader Koch wanted women.

Never mind your puddings and darning. Never mind gossiping over walls and fiddling with laundry! Get out here and defend your country! You've been mollycoddled long enough. All adult females under fifty without small children were to man the flak towers, supervise the bomb shelters, join the Marine Help, Airforce Help, Nursing Help. Get busy.

Rural women had been fully occupied for years as farmers and foresters. They followed the seasonal cycle as normal.

But time seemed to accelerate. The sudden rising of the stork battalions startled Alt Schönbek, for surely it was too early? Don't leave us, blessed spirits. Too late. The birds clattered their big bills, clapped their wings, circled the ancient land of their nativity one last time and decamped in squadrons for the south.

Hospital trains carrying injured German soldiers flowed west through Königsberg from the Eastern Front. Mortal wounds went unaddressed.

Unease and scepticism spread, muffled but constant. Magdalena caught the resonance everywhere. Doubt. Murmuring. Who nowadays greeted you with *Heil Hitler*? Most folk recurred to a quiet, neighbourly *Good morning*. German refugee families from the bombed-out cities who'd been evacuated to safety in East Prussia had long since scurried home, to escape the horrors looming... *over there*.

*

Phone communications remained unimpaired. One September morning Dad reported good news: he'd been permitted to visit Ebba in custody in Kiel, prior to her move to Berlin. Eleven minutes the authorities had been gracious enough to grant, supervised of course. Dad's heart had been eased, although Ebba was rather gaunt and he was not permitted to kiss her. His sister had seemed, in some strange way, taller. Odd, wasn't it? Very calm, contained. Sent her dear love to Magda and Julia. Asked if Max had heard from Clem and when he said no, her lip quivered, that was all.

'And oh, darling, I ought to mention,' said Dad, as if this were an afterthought, and quite inconsequential, 'I may be out of touch for a while.'

'Out of touch? What do you mean?'

'You are not to worry, Magda.'

'Not worry about what?'

'Actually, my main concern is what to do about Goethe and Schiller while I'm away.'

'Away *where*, Dad?'

The Leader had decreed that Max Arber be drafted to renovate and fortify the West Wall, that crumbling bulwark against oncoming Allied armies, along with young lads and older men incapable of bearing arms. But how, Magda panicked, could her frail father, with his gammy leg and the signs of a heart murmur, be of the slightest use in building bunkers?

The Empire Labour Force had summoned him from the bottom of the barrel of manpower, and that was that.

Dad's voice was measured: as long as Magda was safe, that was the main thing. But also Goethe and Schiller. How would they fare without him?

'Dad, they are cats! They'll manage! Never mind them. It's you I ... you need to appeal...'

'Oh, my dear, I wouldn't dream of it,' Dad said, for the benefit of any wire-tappers who might be listening in. 'When the Fatherland calls, we must all joyfully obey. But now, my Magda, listen carefully. If by any chance you don't get letters, don't panic. There may not be means or leisure to write and civilian post may be held up, as is only right and proper. My main concern is always for you. And remember – you are my life and that life continues in you, Magda. That's just how it is. If you care for yourself, you care for me.'

They hung up. She must escape home to Lübeck. At once.

She broke down.

No. If she left her post, she'd go the way of Ruth. Shot, maybe, for desertion. And what would become of Julia then?

*

The ground shimmered in baking heat. Were the stressed trees beginning to turn? Surely not.

At Eva's farm, Russian prisoners were maddened with fear. They'd seen and heard the Eastern European refugees pouring westward; knew what was coming. They needed to flee. Now. They meant: flee west, not east into the arms of their oncoming brethren. But why, if you believe your comrades are coming this way? They won't be liberating us: they'll cut our throats as collaborators or send us to Siberia, you haven't a clue what's in store for us. You are our family now! Leave, leave with us!

Area Leader Koch proudly donated a trinity of statues of East Prussian intellectuals to the Albertina University of Königsberg: Immanuel Kant, Nicolaus Copernicus, Adolf Hitler. *And the greatest of these ...* Koch was understood to have proclaimed ... *is Adolf Hitler! He may not have been born in East Prussia but Adolf Hitler is local everywhere on German soil, he is not constrained by space or time!* Thunderous clapping.

Then, in two nights of British incendiary bombing it was goodbye to the Albertina University and its philosophic statuary.

Goodbye to the seven-hundred-year-old Teutonic Castle.

Goodbye to bridges, churches, homes, warehouses.

Goodbye to most of the Cathedral.

And in the firestorm that raged all day and the next night, burning civilians jumped into the river; were asphyxiated in cellars and swallowed in craters; wandered with babes-in-arms over the boiling streets.

Goodbye.

From the mansard window Magdalena observed on the far horizon the flaming sky and plumes of towering smoke. The following day, Alt Schönbek was swathed in a pall of wind-blown ash. Scraps of blackened paper drifted down. She caught one in her hand: the remnant of someone's shopping list. The tenement on the island of Lomse where her mother had come into the world lay in ruins with the rest.

And now the movement of strange species of cattle from the east had become a stampede. The traumatised animals had lost all sense of bonding or community. Wild creatures now, they would have no truck with one another, let alone with the feral human species.

Once upon a time Julia had asked Dr Vogel whether, if cows were bred backwards into aurochs, children would have to drink auroch milk? And if so, how would you catch the aurochs to milk them? Wouldn't they trample and gore the milkmaids? Wouldn't their milk taste disgusting? And old Vogel, the back-breeding fantasist, had unctuously reassured Julia that German children would always have access to cows' milk to drink. It was just that they would have aurochs as well.

The marauding cattle broke down hedges and fences, shredded bushes and charged at children, bellowing. Their sole instinct was to flee or fight humanity with its cremations, smoke, slaughter. Terror had undone domestication, scattered herds and driven the creatures from their burning farms ... *over there*.

The eastern horizon lit up blood-red; flashed with bombings and flak. The Red Army had reached the border of East Prussia. All night the earth rumbled. What was the army doing to protect Memel and Eydtkuhnen? Where were the Leader's Wonder Weapons when needed?

There were no Wonder Weapons, folk murmured behind their hands. It was another lie.

All the whispering furnished a field day for informers.

Autumn, veering to winter. The desiccated trees had long lost their emerald green and the sweet chestnut was studded with spiky burrs. A line of silver birches shivered their last tinkling leaves in gusts of wind. Light mellowed, shadows softened, and there was a musty smell of decomposition. *We need to go, we need to escape while we still can.*

Area Leader Koch forbade any German civilian evacuation, on pain of death. Officials put up posters to reprove and rally the faint-hearted: 'Our walls may be broken but our hearts are unbroken.' Not one inch of East Prussian soil, they claimed, would the population concede to the subhuman horde. Defeatism will never be tolerated.

And as for schoolteachers: be aware, Miss Arber and Miss Struppat, wrote Mrs Excorn, deputising for her absent husband, that it is deemed desertion to abandon your post. The penalty is execution. A teacher is also a soldier.

*

Renate tapped on the front door. She came into the sitting room, glancing warily behind her before shutting the door and asking if Dagmar was out. Yes. And Julia? Yes, in the garden.

Renate had been to see her friend Ursula. They'd had quite a talk. Ursula was getting out of East Prussia, taking whatever she and the children could carry, and making for her cousin's family in Bavaria. Ursula had told Renate, in confidence, that German radio was lying about how far the Russians had penetrated into East Prussia. Our army was being decimated. It was only a matter of time. And not much time either.

Ursula had told Renate what the Russians did to women.

No?

Yes. Yes. Yes.

Ursula had shared her supply of ... this stuff ... with Renate.

She drew out a phial from her bag and showed it to Magda. Ursula's friend was a pharmacist and had set it aside for her. Worth its weight in gold, this stuff. Everyone wants a supply but no one admits to it of course. So generous of Ursula to share it with Renate. She was a true friend. They'd been at school together. Very quick-working. You won't feel pain. Did Magda want some as a stand-by? For her and the little one. If it came to it.

A swooshing sound as Julia shot up from her play-space behind the couch. 'What do the Russians do to women, Auntie Renate?'

A moment's shocked silence, and then Renate came out with, 'Oh, it's just that ... just ... they like to dance ... it's their ... culture.'

Julia shook her head. 'What's wrong with dancing?'

Magda came in quickly with, 'Oh, it's not what you would mean by dancing, Julia. You wouldn't understand. But more to the point, what were you doing there, skulking? It's rude to listen to other people's conversations – you know that.'

'Skulking? I wasn't skulking! I was here first. You were skulking if anyone was skulking. Anyway, what is skulking?'

'Well, Magda,' Renate said, getting to her feet. 'Come over this evening and we can...'

'Yes, I will, thank you.'

*

Without flinching, Magdalena accepted the phial, stowing it in her first aid box, packed around with cotton wool. Then she locked the metal box in a drawer.

Standard medicine for the new world. You kept it as a stand-by. A safeguard. She remembered how Veronal had saved Dr Süsskind from Aryan predators; saved his dignity and freedom, allowing him to remain himself and control his life up to the moment of departure. She could not imagine administering this to her child. But it might come to that. It might. Whatever happened, she and Julia would go together.

How generous people were to share this cordial with their friends.

Magdalena and Julia sat together with a book, as they did every evening, Julia reading aloud. She was always allowed to choose the book. Fluent and versatile, Julia was a superb reader, way beyond her years. She performed all the voices. Hansel and Gretel were not having an easy time of it, given that their stepmother was bent on making their dad abandon them in the forest, on account of the famine raging in the land. *We can't afford to feed the brats*, croaked the stepmother in Julia's nastiest voice. *It's either get rid of them or cook the little beasts for dinner.*

Magda held the book in her left hand. The injury to the right had long healed; its pain was just a phantom. And yet the wraith was real. The hand hung back from any transaction, reluctant to lead. Her left hand was now dominant. Did muscles have memory? She thought they probably did, from the way her fingers knew how to play piano pieces by Liszt and Chopin, learned in childhood.

These days Julia tracked Magdalena closely, keeping her under surveillance. By night the house was restless. The little girl had bad dreams, awakening heartbroken and clingy. But dumb.

What did you dream, darling?

I don't know.

One night the household was awakened by howls and screams. Magda raced into Julia's room.

Fast asleep.

No, it was Dagmar, having a nightmare. By the time Magda got to her, she was walking repeatedly at the mirror and attempting to clamber in. She didn't seem to be awake although her eyes were open. Guided back to bed, she allowed Magda to pull the covers up to her chin. In the morning there was a bruise on her forehead.

Magda dreamed too. Officer Rudat drove her to Kőnigsberg. *To the von Stein Abattoir*, he explained ruefully, for he was fundamentally a decent man who had not chosen to have carbuncles all over his hands: *That's where we collect heads, you see.* The dream-Magda objected, *But, Mr Rudat, I'm not an animal: there must be some mistake.* To which Rudat shook his head: *Unfortunately, Miss Arber, you've been ratted on.*

Julia had reached the part of the tale where Hansel and Gretel are out of the frying pan and into the fire, for the wicked witch in the gingerbread house in the forest plots to cook and eat them. Julia, knowing that the girl saves the boy in the end, was unperturbed. She rendered the voice of the witch as an ear-splitting cawing.

Closing the book and shelving it, the little girl returned to the couch. She picked up the string she liked to play with, knotted the ends together and began the first stage of a cat's cradle. Looping the cradle-to-be around the fingers of both hands, she drew the string taut and slipped the middle finger of each hand through the loops.

Now you take it from me. Magda plucked the shape painlessly on to both hands, weaving a new pattern with thumbs and forefingers.

She held out her hands ready for Julia to transform the weave as she received it back.

Julia paused; then came out with the question that had been hovering between them for so long: 'I want to ask you, Magda. Can I call you Mummy now?'

What could Magdalena say? What should she say? It was many months since Ruth had been heard of. Ruth, who had – even in her madness – loved and trusted Magdalena and named her as her daughter's guardian. Who else did the little girl have?

Magdalena said yes.

And if you are a mother, that comes first. That is your profession. You do not abandon your post. Ever. Nothing is more important than your child's safety.

Julia just nodded. She did not try out the word.

Magdalena began to make lists. She packed two rucksacks full of essentials.

*

Autumn was turning to winter. Terror spread like influenza. Order was breaking down. Villagers melted away, mostly without a goodbye. For who would you dare to confide in? You could be shot for trying to abscond, although surveillance in the countryside had declined, with the loss of remaining manpower. Families packed up and decamped in wagons and vans for Bavaria and Schleswig-Holstein, to get as far away as possible from the Russian advance. Pupil numbers dwindled; the school system was crumbling.

This morning it was abnormally still in the house apart from Julia's cough.

Magdalena grumbled, 'You're all snotty, don't wipe your nose on your sleeve,' and Julia said, 'I wasn't,' and Magda said, 'What do you call this then, if not snot?'

Julia replied authoritatively, 'The correct word, Mummy, is phlegm, I think you'll find,' and they both laughed.

There: Julia had said the word. Mummy. There was no going back.

'Blow your nose and go and wake Dagmar, love, will you?'

'Oh, do I have to? It's so nice and quiet in the house.'

Again they both laughed. Dagmar was loud but Julia could be louder, so for Julia to praise peace and quiet was a novelty.

'She's usually up and about by now. Just go and put your head round the door and tell her the time – *politely* – there's an angel.'

Julia sloped off, sighing, went upstairs and came clattering down again, saying, 'She's not there.'

The bedroom was a chaotic mess. Magda's first thought was that there'd been a burglary. They stood on the mat and gaped. The thick quilt was gone, and all the bed linen. Belongings were strewn around the floor. Ruth's bureau stood open, empty of Dagmar's treasures and documents. The walls were still swathed in swastikas, posters and flags. The portrait of the Leader sat skewed above the bed. Dagmar's wardrobe door stood ajar. Only winter clothes seemed to have been taken – and Dagmar's boots. Underwear and sweaters had gone from the drawers.

She'd left no note, as far as one could see.

'But however did we not hear her leave? She must have lugged her packing case down the stairs.'

'Well, I don't know, but good riddance to bad rubbish, I say,' said Julia.

She got up on the stripped bed and bounced, but rather feebly. The springs twanged and she timed her coughs to her bounces.

Where the hell had Dagmar gone?

Barbara Grawert, not quite sixteen, had been recruited last week to man a watchtower. Anything with hands and legs and half a brain was required to serve the Empire in its peril. So perhaps Dagmar had been called away to exercise her gifts. A top-secret mission. But then she would hardly have left her bedroom in chaos. Also,

Dagmar being Dagmar would have bragged about having a secret: *...something special I'm doing for Our Leader.*

Renate was at the front door. 'Did you hear? The Struppat has bolted.'

Magdalena went to the head of the stairs. 'Come up. *Mrs* Struppat, you mean?'

'Who else?' Renate ran upstairs two at a time.

'What do you mean, Renate: *bolted*?'

'Taken off. Gone west. Left all her Party junk behind. Old Braun is off her head with fury. *Funk!* she says. *Blue funk!* Does Dagmar know?'

'Dagmar's not here either. Come and look at her room.'

'The rats,' said Renate, looking round the bedroom, 'have left the sinking ship. Alt Schönbek is Struppatless! Get all that muck down from the walls, Magda, I would. And we need to leave.'

They began to tear down the posters. It was time.

*

But...

That day, and throughout the night, all was still, apart from Julia's hacking cough.

No more blasts and bombings *over there*. No more cannon fire. The silence of the night was complete, the sky resplendent with stars. Fields and meadows glimmered with frost in the moonlight. And again the next night. And the next.

Renate came and said, 'We're leaving, Magda. Are you coming?'

'How can I, Renate? We can't take Julia in this state, can we?'

Julia's temperature was sky high. She soaked the sheets with sweat. Her lungs creaked and gurgled.

And then she seemed to have some sort of seizure. Her body spasmed, her lips were blue. It lasted perhaps a minute. There was no doctor to call.

Magdalena bedded down with the child, sponged her forehead,

opened her nightshirt to cool her, listened to her chest, coaxed her to drink water. Come on, darling, come on. Just tiny sips. That's the way. Another? Fight, fight. The little flushed face was hot to the touch of her palm, as Flora's had been in that other world, and when Julia opened her eyes, they were Flora's eyes. Which was unbearable. No, you can't go. You can't leave me. Magdalena talked to her, whispered, sang, to keep her daughter in the world.

When Julia seemed to be sleeping more comfortably, Magdalena turned on the radio. The broadcasts were triumphalist. So much for the Russian army! In full retreat! An army of ants! Back to their antheap they were said to be fleeing.

And perhaps the radio was, for once, telling the truth? Maybe the Leader's Wonder Weapon was real? Perhaps he had launched the technological miracle at Moscow?

A handful of absconded villagers, taking heart, reappeared, to feed their deserted livestock or to fetch something from home. Unlocking their doors, they stepped into an abandoned familiarity. A tap dripping. Mouse droppings on the carpet. Look, the grandfather clock has stopped. They sat down gingerly on their own chairs, like guests. How cold it was in here, and musty. Let's light the fire. Look, that patch of damp has spread. They drew their fingers across a patina of dust on an old oak table.

But how delicious to lie down on your own bed! They took the chance to wash their filthy clothes and eat their fill. The temptation was too great. Let's stay, surely it's pretty safe now. We'll keep our ears and eyes open and our stuff packed up, and at the first sign we'll bolt.

So said Mrs Happke, meeting Magdalena in the street, with the little Happkes in tow. The Leader, her blind father felt, had successfully lured Ivan into his trap. She asked anxiously if, in their absence, Magda had noticed any officials knocking on her door to check whether the family was still at home.

No, because the Party leaders had been amongst the first to cut and run, in their official cars, full of petrol, crammed with choice provisions. You could be sure they'd turn up in the west wearing civvies, new-minted members of an underground resistance that never was.

The swine! the two women agreed, in relief.

Mrs Happke, trained as a nurse, came in and listened to Julia's chest. She thought maybe pneumonia.

'Do this, Miss Arber. Every hour or so.'

She turned the child over on to her front and lightly tapped her back, then her front, then her back again, to release the congestion.

'The more she coughs out, the better. And get her to drink. It will bring the temperature right down.'

Taking Magdalena's hands, she said, 'Julia is a strong girl, Miss Arber. Have faith. You are a godsend to her. She knows that.'

Magdalena fed Julia from a teaspoon like a baby. She kept the rucksacks packed and the Auroch oiled and ready, with an old raincoat wrapped round the crossbar for Julia, when she should be strong enough to travel.

One night, soon after, Magdalena crashed down through her exhaustion into a deep sleep. Waking, she saw a beautiful face suspended inches above her own, looking down at her.

Was it Flora or Julia? A dream, a hallucination, a living girl or a real ghost? Impossible to say. But it was a turning point.

Several peaceful weeks had gone by. Julia breathed more naturally. She sat swaddled at the window, watching winter deepen and darken. Magdalena, having mastered the secrets of the tiled oven, was able to keep the house warm, though November gales flayed the land, leaving not a blade of grass.

Still the silence held in the east.

The alien cattle, skeletal, stood motionless on the frozen ground, udders shrunken, bellies distended, spines protruding. They bellowed in their extremity of hunger, like calves separated from their mothers. Their bodies swayed, their legs splayed and, one by one, the animals fell.

27

> She froze up, curled in a ball,
> Like a little animal.[32]
> Aleksandr Solzhenitsyn,
> *Prussian Nights*, 1947

Magdalena latched the door behind them: no point in locking it. The barrage of noise had been massing on the horizon, like a huge sheet of metal being beaten, louder and louder. Sheet metal that hung from the sky all the way to the earth. She turned to face the wind and follow Julia, a swaddled bundle in as many clothes as she could wear, topped by a pixie hat inside a furred hood. They slip-slid down the icy garden path to where the laden Auroch waited.

You are outsiders now, said the voice within.

There is nothing between you and the murderers.

Out into deep snow and a yelling wind. Out.

The past was a sealed world. There would be no going back. Over in the east, Alt Schönbek's sister villages were burning in the dark dawn. The snow was red around their pyres. Villagers flooded the highways, fleeing west.

It would not be possible to pedal the Auroch over this rutted ice, jostling in this stream of refugees. But it was worth its weight in gold. The machine was a beast of burden, the most valuable thing Magdalena owned or had ever owned. She'd push it. So, here we go, she thought, sit the child on the seat, wedge her tight, that's the way, in her multiple layers of sweater, coat, trousers, scarves, sheepskin mittens. Secure your rucksack to your back.

The precious phial was wrapped in cotton wool within a small metal box, secure in one of the rucksack pockets.

Julia smiled down, she smiled into Magdalena's eyes, she smiled, how come Julia could still smile? The panniers were stuffed with food.

Are you all right, my darling? Magda will push you along.

Heads down, they joined the trek. There was Mrs Happke and her brood; behind them the Brauns. The Rudat brothers and their families could be glimpsed ahead, a two-horse forestry wagon, piled high with forage for the animals, loaded with goods and furniture and there, seated in a chair like a throne, perched Grandma Rudat, who had seen it all before and survived. You are all one creature now, like segments of a single earthworm, Magda thought.

...And do you know what an earthworm is? Dr Vogel had genially enquired, plump hands linked over paunch. *Well, let me enlighten you. It's an in-and-out tube! If the ladies will forgive me ... nothing but a giant eating and defecating machine! Simple as that!*

A fleeing neighbourhood bent cowled heads into the storm, with carts, horses, bikes, trolleys, sleighs, sledges, prams, and some with cattle roped to their carts. Anything was better than the uproar pursuing them. Can't we go faster? – why are we creeping at snail's pace? Once you'd struggled through the avenue of leafless silver birches, you found out why: there on the main road journeyed a toiling mass of folk from every village, hamlet and farm east of Alt Schönbek, the young, the old, the halt, the lame, they were all slogging westward ... as far as the eye could see in each direction.

The crowd wasn't going to let them in willingly, so they sidled in where they could. The snow had stopped but the air was so icy that it carried minute crystals that pricked your eyes like pins.

Just keep going. One hour, two, three.

And, no, Magda thought, no ... there are ... they can't be ... frozen ... by the roadside ... skewed in grotesque attitudes ... like statues or pillars of salt, dead women like Lot's wife in Exodus, who fatally lagged behind.

But what was this ... on the verge ... the statue of an ice-woman with an ice-baby in her arms ... a *pietà*?

Darling, don't look ... shut your eyes when Magda says.
The silent child obeyed.
That's it, my sweetheart ... you can open them now.

What was the point? The dead were littered everywhere, there was no looking away. You stopped noticing. Stopped thinking.

*

Then ... a searing roar from above and behind. Magdalena swivelled her neck, to glimpse a grin up there behind shadowy glass...

Wrench her off the Auroch.

Slam down the bike.

Leap into this snow-drifted ditch and throw your body down on top of hers because you will not ... you will never ... countenance ... never ... one hair of her head to be harmed. Your violence had terrified the child, she shrieked and struggled with all her might beneath your pinioning weight ... and you bawled in her ear, *It's all right, it's all right, I've got you*, but you could not be heard because the roaring thing was directly above and firing indiscriminately, and folk were falling over there on the road ... they were falling but you were spared.

It's gone. Or has it? Is it coming back? No?

Those who can get to their feet do get to their feet.

Let the dead bury the dead.

Magdalena hauled Julia up, her angel, her one-and-only, dragged the Auroch back on to the icy road, kissed her, brushed the snow off her coat, gave her this little piece of biscuit, restored her to the saddle, continued through the wailing storm.

*

Night was about to fall, heavily. Her feet plodded on, of their own accord. She couldn't really feel them. The freeze intensified. Julia's eyelashes were white. She slumped; was bound to be dangerously colder than Magdalena because she wasn't moving. Must stop, find shelter, must, there's no option, must.

All were thinking the same thing. Where, where?

The abandoned farmhouse was crammed with desperate wayfarers. But there was an immense threshing barn. Occupied already but they found a corner. Straw to lie on, and not filthy straw either.

Auroch propped against wall, chained and locked.

Rucksack open.

They could hardly see one another. Magdalena pulled off Julia's boots and chafed her feet. Slowly, feeling seeped back into their bodies. Magdalena divided a portion of rye bread between the two of them and the taste was beautiful, earthy. There was a square of cheese each. Milk for Julia, water for Magdalena.

They snuggled up in a blanket.

They did not forget to say their prayers and the Lovely Words.

They slept in one another's arms.

*

Morning broke.

Magdalena wakened, having dreamed of Flora, left behind in her grave at Alt Schönbek, under a mound of snow.

If I forget thee, O Jerusalem, may my right hand forget her cunning.

 On the road again.

  Or rather, off it.

   Swept aside by hellhounds.

Move, move! Out of the way or be crushed, we are the Centurions of the Empire, officers, heroic warriors etcetera etcetera, tanks, lorries, official cars, big hats, bright black boots, medals, sneers, cigars, booty, plenty of petrol – oh no, not *retreating*, we don't know the word *retreat*, it's not part of our vocabulary – what's the French for it, General? – *reculer pour mieux sauter?* – that's it, a tactical withdrawal in order to take a leap forward! Saving our skins? – Perish the thought!

The whole corpus of refugees formed one single mighty ear. Its reverberating tympanum registered the lie of the hellhounds. The community cursed the cowardice of the officers escaping ahead of civilians it was their duty to protect.

East Prussia had been brainwashed but the wash had washed away, on a black, bitter tide of reality. Very late.

When the official cars blared their horns, you dived off the road as fast as you could. What did the bigwigs care if a few carts and wagons overturned? These cynics would be in civvies tomorrow, their SS medals offloaded into a handy lake.

*

Mummy, I'm hungry.

I know, sweetness. Hang on for just a bit.

What's a bit?

Not long now.

I'm cold.

I know, it's very cold.

My nose hurts.

Put your scarf over it, that's the way.

They swerved to avoid a dead cow, legs stuck up in the air. It had starved to death but there must surely be some meat on those bones. Folk hacked out ribs and shank before the carcase froze hard.

Fires had been lit at the roadside.

I want to go home.

We can't go home. We're going to a nice safe place.

But I want to go home.

Someone was carrying a ... what is it? ... partridge? ... can't be ... some bird anyway ... out of the wood?

Mummy, I'm hungry. I'm freezing. I want to go home.

*

The monstrous hydra toiled forward.

Where were they heading? No one seemed to know. Marienburg, said Mrs Happke. No, the lagoon. We can cross the ice. Pillau. Take ship. It's the only way. Danzig. Westwards.

The roads wound, carts upended. The snail colony crept forward. Don't try and mount on the verges to get ahead. You will sink in a ditch like that donkey over there, those carts with the wheels off the axles.

A fellow eyed Magdalena with a look of lust. Not for herself but for her assets, her wherewithal, her treasure. Who didn't covet a bicycle? A bike conferred advantage. Magdalena hung on tight to the Auroch's handlebars. Nobody else possessed an Auroch, she thought: it is unique, Clem built this hybrid to last, he built it powerful, from army surplus, he created it with an engineer's imagination. The Auroch might have been made for this terrain and this time.

Where are you, Clem?

The voice within forbade such questions but they could spurt up through a burst pipe in the mind.

Dad – where?

Ebba – where?

Clem – where?

Ruth – where? Eva – where? Renate? Marianne? Alf?

Magdalena forbade herself any intimate thoughts whatever, then she closed down and became an automaton, her mechanism ratcheted up for the sole purpose of tramping forward, feet blistered from endless slog.

Three days now they had been on the trek. She never let the Auroch out of her sight, chaining and padlocking it nightly and resting her head against the wheel.

*

Suddenly: a fug of warmth.

Julia nibbled a triangle of rye bread, topped with a scraping of grease, which she licked off, while they all waited for the miraculous potatoes to bake. Fighting her own impatience, Julia ate daintily, to relish every morsel and make it last.

What a pretty house. Tasteful. Clean. Your dazzled eyes admired the polished curve of a grand piano, gilded by lamplight; oil paintings, including both martial and sacred scenes, and ancestral portraits. Porcelain gleamed on the dresser: three Meissen figurines; a dinner plate bearing the Königsberg coat of arms. The plate may have been one of the most precious items in the house, worth a mint of money. The martial eagle's ireful beak gaped and extended an outsize tongue as if flying a flag or looking for food to lick.

Those who'd taken refuge here had agreed to share, cook and eat what they'd found. A bag of good potatoes had been brought from the cellar – swedes – turnips. There was even a burble of conversation in the fug of the monumental tiled stove.

The family must have left in a hurry this morning, for the stove still held some heat when the refugees entered. Several very old women and one ninety-year-old granddad who hadn't a clue what was happening – and that was the best for him – huddled in blankets. There were several children. Julia worked up enough energy to teach a clapping game to a boy of perhaps four.

Good boy, Franz! You're doing well, Franz! Let's go and sit under the piano!

Pale adult faces glimmered with wan amusement at the remnant of the children's zest.

For the first time in days, people had been able to remove a couple of layers of clothing. Marvel of marvels: there was running water to wash and a proper toilet.

And, would you believe this? – the electric lights still work! But be careful to check the blackout – and we only need the one lamp on. A pinkish-golden glow suffused the room. There was a green velvet-upholstered couch with tapestried cushions, where the oldest fugitives could rest.

Look what I've found in this buffet! Cherry brandy!

Never – I don't believe it! Everyone can have a snifter. How on earth did they manage to leave that behind?

On the dining table lay plates from the last meal the family had consumed, with crumbs scattered on a lacy and pristine tablecloth. Five place settings. Julia licked her forefinger to harvest the larger crumbs.

And in this corner ... what is it? Let's see ... oh look, it's a doll's house! So beautiful! Do look at the beds with frilly pink quilts. And, oh my goodness, the windows open and close and everything is to scale! Minute saucepans in the kitchen, with lids you can take off. There are tiny peg-dolls in home-made dirndls, and hand-carved model furniture. And everything the peg-dolls need for a comfortable life is here.

The visitors ate until they were full.

They lay down for the night on quilts and cushions.

And then.

*

And then.

*

The officer's arrival at the bedroom door spared Magdalena and the blonde girl the attentions of the rest of the queue.

The officer addressed his men rather quietly, and it was a wonder they heard him amid the bedlam. Or that they took the slightest notice, given that they were on fire and reeling drunk and the fucking Fascist filthy bitches were paying the price. That's for my sister, that's for my aunt, my child, my wife, here you are, this one is for the parents and grandparents you burnt alive...

But the men did hear the officer's voice.

He said something like, *Brothers, that is not the way.*

The men halted in their tracks. But they did not disperse.

Comrades, I would hate to have to shoot you.

The disappointed queue dispersed, growling like dogs.

The officer – *I am Alexander, I regret* – ordered two soldiers to pick up the screaming blonde girl from beside Magdalena on the big bed. The adolescent was carried downstairs to her mother.

Alexander-I-regret (as she would always think of him) helped Magdalena to her feet and cupped her elbow as she hobbled down the stairs, retching, into the living room, to find Julia in the arms of a bearlike Russian comedian, a jolly, playful soldier who was encouraging her to play with the doll's house, which Julia was shrinkingly loath to do.

He put her down as soon as he saw *Alexander-I-regret*. Lumbered to his feet and stood to attention.

The crashing and smashing ceased, the moment *Alexander-I-regret*'s foot crossed the threshold. A small, squat soldier quit his work breaking the windows with his rifle butt. Another, having hurled the priceless antique Königsberg plate like a discus at the wall, was reaching for the Meissen. The Meissen survived, for now.

Julia ran to Magdalena, wrapped her arms round her body, which winced and spasmed under the onslaught as she cried: 'I thought you'd ... gone ... Mummy ... what are you doing? Why is your mouth all swollen, ugh, your mouth looks like a blue plum, it's bleeding, why?'

They huddled behind the couch. Magdalena swabbed the blood off her legs, she was glacial, she felt nothing.

The sofa was removed, to be carted out. Mother and child retreated to a corner.

'That man didn't hurt you, did he?' Magdalena mumbled out of her swollen mouth.

'No. He wanted me to play with the dolls, he was singing, he threw me up and down, he smelt, he had eight watches on his arm like bracelets and one was *gold*.'

'Listen. Julia. If a soldier asks you your age, stick your thumb in your mouth, act as babyish as you can.'

Julia nodded.

'If they grab me, you just stay quiet, with your thumb in your mouth, and hide until I come back.'

Julia nodded.

'And always wait for me, I will come back. Always. Have you got that?'

Julia nodded.

'What have I just told you?'

'Always wait, thumb in mouth, always remember.'

'I will keep testing you on that, Julia. If you forget everything else I've taught you, make sure to remember that.'

Julia nodded.

Russian men claimed to love children. The fellow who'd been dandling Julia had not molested her, Magda was sure. He'd jounced the little girl on his lap. Perhaps he had daughters of his own back home in Uzbekistan.

Now the Russians were busy with removals, all hands on deck, everything in the house was worth plundering, stick that table on the truck, legs in the air, you can put this old bike on top, that's it.

A good haul, their faces said – for we don't have such houses at home, we have hovels, or we did have hovels... until you Nazi scum burned them down and shot and tortured and raped and starved peaceful Russian peasants... so did you honestly imagine that you would not have to pay?

Alexander-I-regret said apologetically, in very good German, that he regretted that he'd have to take the women into custody for interrogation, for possible transportation to the Soviet Union.

Why, why?

For labour. To expiate the crimes of the fascists.

Manifestly there were some things *Alexander-I-regret* could control and others he could not. His young, thin, triangular face was a mass of complex wrinkles, its decency under constant siege.

The things he could control were limited, although it was not nothing, in the great sum of things, that *Alexander-I-regret* had been able to call off his men from the queue for female flesh.

He could not hold them off from shooting the unnecessary old people on the couch as they departed. Or from setting fire to the house.

Magdalena and Julia got to their feet, wound their long scarves round their faces and heads, held hands, lined up with the others.

Spasibo, Magdalena had the presence of mind to whisper as they passed *Alexander-I-regret. Thank you.*

*

A transit camp. Mass sickness struck like a deadly blessing. Fever that made her feel she was out of her mind, they were soaked in sweat, both of them.

*

A makeshift hospital in an old Nazi army camp. They were lying on pallets with four thousand other sick German prisoners, distributed between barrack blocks and cellars. Captured German doctors and nurses were employed to care for them and German orderlies to remove corpses.

Still together.

Once in a while there were bits of something in the watery soup – millet or corn husks perhaps. Occasionally the soup would be quite warm.

Julia was said by one of the prisoner-doctors to have scurvy as well as the infection and the communal infestation of lice.

A little bag of bones, she lay with bleeding gums and bruised skin in a state of torpor.

Magdalena roamed in and out of consciousness. She seemed to recognise the German doctor but couldn't place him ... tall, austere, narrow horse-face, low eyebrows, a grave and gentle look. Ascetic, intellectual, speaking with the fruity brogue of the German aristocracy. He picked his way between recumbent bodies, indicating to his team of orderlies those patients who had died in the night and whose corpses should be removed and stacked outside for the waggon to collect.

Perhaps we shall be next but I must not go first, she will be left alone. And I no longer have the blessed poison.

Magdalena fell asleep holding Julia and wakened holding Julia.

Dr von Wedel had begged, borrowed or stolen pails of porridge for those in their barrack block capable of eating. Magdalena coaxed Julia, begged her to try, a little, just a little. The skin-and-bone girl did try.

The doctor squatted beside them and whispered, *Act sicker than you are, Miss Arber. Don't be in a hurry to recover.*

Miss Arber? Who was this Miss Arber? She was carrion, infected and infested, but a presence from another world addressed her as Miss Arber.

The German Sister, Perpetua, an evangelical Christian, administered a precious teaspoon of cod liver oil to Julia. As precious as the Eucharist. And the miracle was that Julia swallowed it.

It stayed down.

Next day there was a tablespoon of malt – and then later, a helping of rhubarb which Dr von Wedel had come across in a waste allotment. *Vitamin C,* the Sister said. *Don't leave a morsel, little Julia.*

Anyone showing signs of being or becoming able-bodied was separated from her children, if she had any, and transported to a work camp in Russia, Magdalena knew that. But dysentery, typhoid and tuberculosis had taken hold, providentially – for the Russians were not eager to catch it. The administrators of this hellhole therefore permitted the introduction of some hygienic practices.

Female patients, Hans von Wedel confided, are so much more practical and intelligent than the men. 'You don't give in as quickly as the men,' he said. 'You have powers of organisation.' He spoke about his various escapes and recaptures. A member of the Confessional Church, Hans led impromptu Christian services for small groups of staff and patients. Magdalena asked if he by any chance knew of her aunt. Yes, he'd heard of Ebba Arber-Thiessen's arrest. Did not know what had happened to her.

We are little dung beetles, Hans said, who've just been run over by a steam roller and can't quite grasp why we're still alive.

Then he grinned and said, *Got it! I know where we've met before!* He recalled Magdalena and Julia riding to his cousin Eva's estate on their bicycle for the harvest... He didn't know what had happened to Eva.

'The Auroch,' Julia said. 'That was the Auroch. It was stolen. The Auroch is our bike.'

'You have to understand,' Hans explained, 'that the Russian people have been born and raised in poverty – pauperdom – such as we can hardly imagine. They've never in their lives seen possessions such as we Germans take for granted. Their deepest desire is to loot these luxuries and send them home to what remains of their families. A form of compensation for the evil we visited on them. The means of transporting the furniture has run out but they loot it anyway in their rage.'

*

That night small fingers stroked Magdalena's temples in soft circles. Ice melted, tears welled, they flowed, they flooded, the little girl held the woman's head in both skinny arms. The two of them curled up in a ball, like one little animal.

*

Recovered prisoners will be marched at gunpoint back down the road.
Where are we going? Not to Russia?
In Mother Russia they will be able to expiate their crimes.

Crimes? What crimes? Prisoners? Why? What are we supposed to have done? Sirs, we are just women. Wives and mothers. Women have no say. We were never members of the Party or of the Nazi Women's Organisation, no, we never owned a great farm or kept Russian forced labourers, no, we were poor and humble people, with one pig and a couple of chickens, we lived hand to mouth and we hated the swine Hitler, in fact we were underground members of the Resistance, we always voted for the Left, we never approved of the war, we loved the Jews, the Jews were our brothers, we sheltered them, we used to be members of the Communist Party ... no, we aren't strong enough for work, look at us, we are meagre and starving, you can't deport us to work camps...

The women were to be marched to a transit camp in the east for selection. The official leered as he described the conditions the German workforce would experience. Absolute luxury, he said! We'll pull out all the stops for you! Just as you did for us! Nothing too good for you! Fifteen to a cell, so you will have plenty of company. Standing room only, so if you want to sleep, you'll have to do so sitting back-to-back, in shifts. Communal bucket for piss and shit. Interrogation leading to transportation on the trains. Siberia perhaps.

Mothers and children will be separated.

No, I will die first. And she must die with me, I cannot leave her to the wolves.

*

She waylaid him as he passed, hand on his sleeve. Could Hans spare some Veronal, her supply having been lost along the way? Enough for the two of them.

He looked – not shocked – but discountenanced, and besides he was in full sail, his grubby white coat flapping out behind him. No, he could not give her Veronal, Dr von Wedel said, and he was the physician now, not the genial Hans: no, under no circumstances.

'Hans, I cannot leave her. You must understand that.'

He was out of the door. But within five minutes he was back, looking relieved.

He brought his head down close, pretended to take Magdalena's pulse and breathed, 'So why not vanish with me?'

'Vanish?'

He'd been denounced to the Russians for theft of their supplies and was on tomorrow's execution list. The office staff had been overheard working out how to spell his name. Time to disappear.

'You two come with me,' he said briskly. 'Never mind the Veronal. Come into the storeroom when you see me signal. Carry Julia over, Miss Arber, as if she needed urgent treatment.'

'Dress as a boy, can you do that?' he asked Julia. 'Here's a cap, here are some dungarees, a bit too big but roll up the trouser bottoms, that's the way. We'll shave your head. Your name will be ... what do you want your boy-name to be?'

'Emil? A good name. So don't forget, you are Emil. You have been very ill, little Emil-Julia, but you are a strong person, you have spirit and courage, and you will need every ounce. Miss Arber, you'll be my nurse, here's an armband. Here's my rucksack, with provisions, here's my Bible, here's a torch and medication we'll need. Be ready at dawn.'

Her head shaven to foster the lie, Julia gazed at the pile of heavy, dirty curls on the floor. Her face worked as if about to cry. Instead she cackled with laughter, put both hands on her bald skull and explored it curiously.

'Are we really leaving this stinky place?'

'Shush. Yes.'

First thing in the morning, they vanished into the welcome fog and rain.

Creeping past yesterday's pile of corpses, they broke through festoons of spiders' webs, sidled along the narrow gap between the perimeter wall and the outbuildings, past a mountain of rubbish and a heap of ash, through a shed and out, into the forest.

By-roads and cart tracks. Hans knew the terrain intimately. It was the country of his childhood. He used to hunt in these forests, fish in these lakes, climb these trees.

A day and a half's trek. Who was this lumbering towards them? A Russian soldier – giant of a man, not sober. Just keep walking. Sing, Emil, that's the way. Oh God, he was stopping. But only to ask the way to a village for he'd got lost. The soldier grinned at Emil and off he shambled.

Keep walking. Emil was asleep on his feet. But he refused to be carried.

You didn't think, you didn't chat, you just plodded.

How many days? Seven? They slogged through an occupied town, strangely silent, the townsfolk fled or dead. A gaggle of Russian soldiers at the town cross stood about smoking, nobody taking the least notice of the ragged wanderers.

German lorries and tanks, burnt out. Oh Clem, don't be that charred skeleton sitting bolt upright in the cab, as if awaiting orders.

A lift from German workers in a cart carrying logs for the Russians.

A night in a fire-blackened, gutted house, where there were proper beds.

Beds! The comfort of beds! Emil flung himself on to one and cuddled a pillow. He fell fast asleep. Magdalena lay down beside him but was so tired, she couldn't sleep and maybe never would again. She heard Hans across the room murmuring prayers and passing out in mid-sentence. The night seemed long. But Emil slept and that was the main thing. Magda heard tanks on the road, saw lights, heard voices and gunfire, but nobody appeared in the house.

In the cellar Emil discovered potatoes, mostly gone to mush in the freezing winter but edible, just.

Many days of walking. Hans shot down two woodpigeons with a catapult. They cooked and ate the gamey grey flesh. Why, given that they were famished, did Magda retch at the first sweet, fatty taste that flooded her mouth? Her stomach wasn't right. Her body was a nest of horror. Don't think about that. Don't think about the Russians queuing in the refuge that had been no refuge at all. Why in God's name had *Alexander-I-regret* not arrived earlier to disperse those animals?

Later Magda's cavernous stomach demanded more, more. Emil foraged for chickweed and wild leek, but only meat would do.

Was this spring hitting the woods? Drumroll of woodpeckers threatening one another from different trees. Territorial disputes between squadrons of songbirds. Chestnut buds spearing the air, bright with running resin. Whitethorn blossom breaking its green buds.

They lay in the wreckage of last year's bracken while squads of troops passed by. Shots. Explosions. Screams.

At night they built a fire, baked the last potatoes, dried out their shoes.

'Do you want to see something?' Emil opened his hand, where something golden glowed in the firelight.

'Whatever's that?' asked Hans.

'Amber. I found it when I was a girl. Would you like it, Hans?'

'No, my brave darling. You keep it safe in your pocket.'

They circled past Danzig toward Marienburg, swerving to give the town a wide berth. March, April. They'd been walking for nearly four months. Their blistered feet bled. One moonlit night they entered the von Wedel estate. The mansion, partly black and ruined, spoke of archaic privilege and wealth. Hans took them into the trees and tapped at a cottage door. Someone opened the door a few inches. One alarmed eye peered out.

'It's only me, Kathryne – Hans von Wedel.'

The old woman yelped with shock, drew them in. She broke the news of the fate of the von Wedel family.

'In my heart I knew,' said Hans steadily. 'How could it be otherwise? How did it happen?'

'Oh, it was quick, sir.'

Hans' mother and younger brother had been shot, for the crime of aristocratic lineage, when the Russians took over the mansion. The enslaved estate workers worked the land for the conquerors. Hans crept out alone one night to kneel and pray at the mounds that covered them. Magdalena never saw him weeping.

Kathryne hid the three of them, gave them her dead sons' beds and they slept, and they slept, and were fed, and they washed the filth from their faces and bodies, and there were chickens in the loft which had not been detected by the Russians. Emil sat up there with the hens and clucked with them as he fed them seeds.

He found a wad of paper and began drawing masterly portraits of his favourite chicken, Marie Antoinette, with himself depicted as a huge egg rolling around in the straw.

Something was happening to Magdalena's body, something she would not name. A foreign species had taken root in her innards, it had claws and suckers and ate her alive from the inside. She could not digest the little food available; she herself was food for the parasite within. But then suddenly she was ravenous, the world would not have been enough to sustain her.

Magda stared at Emil's plate with avid envy.

Hans saw her staring and handed her the remainder of his bread. He said nothing but he knew the signs. And that was surely why he kept insisting she must try to get home to Lübeck sooner rather than later, with him or without.

When every crumb of their breakfast had been consumed, Magdalena sat down beside Emil who was drawing – and began, feverishly, to write. The more she wrote, the more she wrote. Details of their journey and then a description of Emil feeding the chickens. A journal, fragments of a travelogue, a trace of truth.

April turned to May and Hans was out on his rounds most nights. News of the doctor's presence had raced round the surviving community: mainly women and children, a few old men, many of them sick, skeletal, infected, wounded, half-starved. In need of medical care. Between houses across the estate and beyond ran a web of whispers, passing along information someone somewhere had gleaned from a rare and prohibited wireless. The Soviets were in Berlin. It could not be long now. The British and Americans had occupied the west. There were zones of occupation. The Allies were partitioning Germany.

'And Lübeck, what about Lübeck?'

'In British hands.'

'But my God! Just heard! He's gone!'

'Who's gone?'

'The Leader. Died a hero's death. Or a lemming's. Anyway we've got a new Leader now. You won't guess. Dönitz.'

'Who?'

'You know, the sailor. Admiral. Plans to carry on saving the homeland from Bolshevism.'

A week later the whisperers reported: 'We've capitulated. Unconditional surrender. Signed and sealed.'

Magdalena could not bring herself to cheer. She felt nothing.

'Magdalena, if you are ever going to make it home, you have to leave now,' Hans told her.

'We're going together though?'

It was out of the question. Hans must stay here to take care of his people. A cart was carrying produce westwards for the Soviets. He'd made it worth the driver's while to take them, in workers' overalls, towards Rostock; walk the rest of the way, taking their chance.

Hans had drawn a careful map of highways and byways, especially byways. 'I will pray for you and perhaps in some other world we may meet again.'

28

Lübeck, Summer 1945

> I had a lovely homeland long ago.
> The oak trees grew
> So tall; softly the violets blew.
> It was a dream.
>
> Germany kissed me, and spoke
> (Unimaginable joy
> To hear) the phrase: *'Ich liebe dich!'*
> It was a dream.[33]
>
> Heinrich Heine,
'Ich hatte einst', 1834

The thunder of hooves jolted her awake.

She must have dreamed. But no, the ground reverberated; the bed quivered; there was an onrush as of animals in flight. Where was Julia? Where was the warm comfort of her small body alongside? She'd gone. Back into the charnel house?

Where in the world had Magdalena ended up? She could make neither head nor tail of where she was. At the foot of this bed was an open door into a passageway bathed in dingy light and ending in a distant shaft of foggy brightness. Racking her brains to identify this foreign space, Magdalena levered herself upright only to be plunged into vertigo.

Deep breaths now, Magdalena.

There's nobody here, she thought. I am alone in the world. Have I been apprehended? If so, by whom? This may be a prison – or a hospital perhaps? There seemed to be other beds over there in the gloom – or perhaps they were pallets for the horses' hay?

Julia has gone into the dark with all the rest, she thought. Perhaps she has realised I'm too ruined to give the kind of love she deserves.

I'll get up and have a look round, Magdalena decided: everything will fall into place. It always does. You've obviously been dreaming. But then she found she couldn't get off the bed. Her sagging belly. Her unhealed leg. How did I do that, she asked herself? Ah yes, she must have fallen off one of the *Trakehner* mares at Eva's farm. That's it! She sensed now where she was.

In the adjacent stalls, dairy cattle must be quartered, the Holsteins cared for by the Polish and Russian Prisoners of War, black pied thoroughbreds, whose shiftings-about assured you of a life going on as it had immemorially done. Their udders swelling overnight with the delicious fatty milk. You could even smell their droppings. A good shit smell, mingling hay with grass, herbs and meadow flowers. Quite unlike human ordure.

Now that Magdalena had located herself in a single place, the panic began to subside. You can't inhabit two places at once.

But the horses? Pell mell they flowed past in what must be a vast herd, over there, out of sight. However many? Eva's farm doubled as a stables and stud. So perhaps the *Trakehners* were galloping round and round a track of some sort. As a child, you had not been allowed to see the stallion mount the mare. By hook or by crook you'd managed it anyway, excited and impressed.

Yes, Magdalena told herself, but this is not your memory! You have appropriated a memory. This must be Eva's memory. How can that be possible? Your body has memory. Your hands remember the piano keys, your feet the ice skates, your centre of gravity remembers the Auroch.

Still, Magdalena had no idea how one can share a memory and there was nobody to consult ... I am a conduit for others' memories, she thought, and I shall write them all down. Perhaps that is the use of me, to remember Alt Schönbek and record all the details so that it will be less lost. Without Julia, I have no other use.

Perhaps, she thought, I can be a conduit for a land that no longer exists. East Prussia has been emptied and rolled up and divided by the victors, a giant carpet of green and yellow and blue, forests and lakes and marshes, and the expelled people, good people most of them, salt of the earth.

I got to know them so well, Magdalena thought – the villagers, farmers, foresters and especially their children – and where are they now? Her memory began to call the register of the hundred children she used to teach ... name after name, and she saw them all. One after another, their faces passed before her and she counted them off against the register she kept in her mind.

A stream of fearful questions came pouring into consciousness, and it was as if it was all happening again. Dam the flow, but no, you can't – you're running away but the questions keep pace. Who else got out when the Russians came? Who was discarded, a raped and bloated corpse on the roadside? How did her children – for, yes, they were all of them Miss Arber's children – fare? What became of the farm? What happened to Rosa House, did they burn it to the ground? Did Magdalena's precious books, which she'd been forced to leave behind, go up in smoke? But what did that matter? Oh, Eva, Renate, Ruth, she cried silently, I hope you did not suffer. Of course you suffered. But I hope you suffered in such a way that there might be an afterwards for you, as there may be for me, in which you could still to some extent be yourselves.

What Magdalena needed was the comfort of those fat old feather quilts they had in East Prussia. Once you snuggled under one, drawing the luxurious mound close around your neck, the smell of goose feathers filling your nostrils, cold never stood a chance. And of course, she acknowledged, beginning to make sense of her surroundings, I am not in Alt Schönbek and never shall be again, I know that now.

The thing is, I am still myself, Magdalena thought, even though I haven't the foggiest who that is.

She was back in Lübeck, that was clear. But not in the Arbers' own house, which was down. They'd made it to the safety of the British Zone. There were no horses: put that out of your mind.

Hamburg was ash. Dresden was ash. Lübeck was still to some degree Lübeck, despite the destruction. You are home, Magdalena instructed herself, watching the flickering light in the passage outside the unknown room. Or rather you are staying in a haunted house, and through the wall is … well, never mind. You are in your own city, the war is over. That's right, and they'd come a long way, with bombs falling all around and the screaming horses, and – blessings upon his head, *Alexander-I-regret* – and later the two of them had trekked with Hans through the forest. Hans von Wedel to whom she and Julia owed their lives.

She was one of tens of thousands of fellow German refugees from East Prussia, now living – if you could call it living – in Lübeck, where children ate from bins. The stench. The looting. The violence. The controlled chaos. You scarcely dared enter Moltke Street, made over to foreign Displaced Persons, Polish, Estonian, Dutch, crowded in their rabbit warren, flying their flags, playing their patriotic songs on accordions. Spitting at us. Why wouldn't they hate us?

Along the thronged streets stumbled liberated concentration camp inmates, still wearing their striped uniforms. Haunting us with our obscene guilt, she thought. Which we deny, consumed with self-pity.

This is your patch of earth, your haven. So … you know perfectly well where you are, she scolded herself, resting back against the pillows. There are no horses. Of course not.

She had imagined she'd outrun the horror: against all the odds the pair of them had reached the British zone, and safety, only to confront the fact that the horror had plunged inside her body and seeded itself. It had bedded deep within her like a growth: from day to day she'd swollen with the foreign presence.

Magdalena had said nothing to anyone. But compared with so many thousands of women, she'd been lucky and the foetus had aborted itself.

Gone now. Expelled now. And yet it had been an innocent

creature, I might have learned to love it – him – as I love Julia and Flora. Should I be glad it's dead?

I won't say it's dead. I'll say it – he – never came to anything.

She slid the conflict down into the depths of her brain, sealed the door on it. Survival was everything. I am quit of the stigma but I'll never love a man after this, I'll never marry, Magdalena recognised, her gorge rising. The thought of a man's intimate touch ... no, don't think of that ... it revolted her, her own body repulsed her. I shall never have children of my own. Does that matter? It needn't. I shall find work. Somehow. A life. Meaning. And clarity. I shall love again but in different ways.

And perhaps, perhaps, those I care for and who love me will come back, take me in their arms and give me their counsel. Maybe Dad is alive. And Clem. And Auntie Ebba. Don't give up.

And yet all this while, the stampeding animals had continued to pour in one direction. It occurred to Magdalena that their pace had slackened and that there must be far fewer. It was as if the going were more difficult, not to say impossible, for while some had dropped out, others seemed to be foundering. The animals may not have eaten for days. Those that were left seemed to slither ... on ice? ... and their frozen corpses would be left where they fell, no doubt, with their legs stuck up in the air, steaks would be hacked out of their bellies and haunches by the mass of refugees.

For the world was running away from itself into a final silence.

*

The next thing she knew was that a chatterbox was kneeling on the bed, bouncing a little so that the bad-tempered springs twanged. Gently Julia shook Magda's shoulder. She insisted that Mummy must wake up this instant.

'It's time,' she said. 'And when you have got up I will show you what I've found and there's plenty more, so you'll have to help me dig it all out. If you're well enough today. Are you feeling better now?'

'You should have woken me,' Magda scolded, propping herself on her elbows. 'Don't go swanning off on your own, Julia, don't.'

'Well, honestly! You are the absolute limit,' Julia scolded in return. 'In actual fact – you wouldn't wake up. I shook you and shook you. You kept saying weird things.'

'I must have been dreaming,' Magdalena reached out her arms to Julia. 'Sorry – did I scare you? I thought ... there were horses ... and cows ... in here ... and you'd gone. Where have you *been*?'

'Cows in here? That would have been all right! We could have milked them. I've only been next door. To look at our old house. Is your tummy still hurting? Are you getting up?'

'Yes to both. But can we have a cuddle first? After that I'm definitely getting up. How are you?'

In the mornings Julia seemed her old energetic self but, thin and malnourished, she tired easily and by the afternoon all energy had drained away.

'I'm all right. Do you want me to rub your tummy?'

'No, love. You haven't been climbing on the ruins again, have you?'

'Well, no ... not exactly climbing.'

'Julia! What did I tell you?'

'Well, I did just need to have a look round.'

A sepulchral voice intoned from across the room, 'You never know what they're getting up to.'

'I beg your pardon?' Magda had forgotten that they lived check by jowl with another family. Camping in the corner of what had been the main bedroom in Dr Süsskind's old home, Magdalena and Julia shared space with a traumatised East Prussian mother and three sad and angry, but enterprising, adolescent children. Mrs Kondritz's children cleared off during the day, leaving the mother to languish for long periods on her bed, head in hands. They would come back in the late afternoon and feed their mother portions of whatever they had managed to cadge or steal. *Open your mouth, Mum! Open it. Now swallow. I said swallow, for God's sake.*

The mother hardly seemed to hear her children when they yelled at her.

'I'm just saying, they're out of control, there are no standards any more,' croaked Mrs Kondritz. 'It was all so well organised under the Leader, you knew where you were, the young were kept busy and disciplined – but the Leader's gone – he was betrayed – and this is what we're left with, this havoc, this lack of decent standards, it's beyond a joke.'

Magdalena offered no reply.

The dolorous voice repeated, 'Beyond a joke...' and then was silent.

Julia pulled a comical face, raising an eyebrow and mouthing, 'Beyond a joke.'

'Your children will be all right, Mrs Kondritz – you'll see,' said Magdalena. She had got up and was pulling on her jacket. 'They've been through a lot, we need to ... put our wing over them. They're doing their best for you.'

No answer.

Could Dr and Mrs Süsskind really have slept here, in that quiet, earlier world, under the great lemon-yellow quilt which now, filthy and noxious, covered Magda and Julia at night? Beneath this quilt, draped in a British Army blanket, she and Julia whispered the Lovely Words at night, adding a phrase of thanks to Hans von Wedel for his loving kindness.

Magdalena longed to know if Hans had survived and, if so, where he was. And Alf: had he made it back to Norway? Had Eva managed to cross to Switzerland and find her friend?

Dr Süsskind's house, reduced to squalor, was crammed with refugees, like every other intact house in the city. No running water. No sewerage. No electricity. No coal for cooking, except what the Kondritz children managed to filch at the railway sidings. Minute rations. Mothers sobbing in the night for their dead children. Quarrels. Need preyed upon need because compassion in a world of stint and near-starvation can seem hard to afford. And always the fear of gangs looting.

Nevertheless, there was compassion too, fellow-feeling and generosity of spirit; even at times, laughter.

Julia's hair was growing longer. It kinked and curled. Of her own accord she was returning from Emil. I ought to have insisted, Magdalena thought. And yet she had not insisted. Her child had been in hell and found means to adapt. Nobody had seemed to guess at the time that Emil was not a real boy. Even the boys hadn't guessed. Emil, even half-starved, was bossy and brave.

But then he'd always been that when he was Julia.

Magdalena remembered, in that white world of the East Prussian winter, Julia objecting to being barred from the ice hockey team as being only a girl: *I'm not a girl – I'm a person, so there!* Which had been such a good answer that Magdalena and Ruth had wanted to cheer – and Magda remembered the look that passed between them, tender and amused. Ruth came vividly to mind. The melting look in her brown eyes as she tended her remaining child.

Hand in hand, Julia and Magdalena went out into the bright day, taking with them the remnant of their bread ration. How strange it was to look up at the Arber home and see its partial collapse, the outer wall down and the private rooms open to public view like chambers in a doll's house or sets at a theatre. It hadn't been directly bombed: the blast had caused it to part company with itself.

Magdalena squatted to Julia and grasped both her hands.

'Never go up there again. Do *not*. One day the whole edifice will come crashing down. You would not stand a chance. Did you hear what I said, Julia?'

'But wait till you see what I found.'

'I'm not interested. Look me in the eyes. You haven't promised.'

'All right then. I won't. Anyhow I found leaves,' said Julia. 'Not tree-leaves. Pages. All dirty and raggy and torn. Some of them burnt. There are books everywhere, all torn up, look. Do you want to see? Shall we do some collecting and then go and search for Uncle Max and Auntie Ebba?'

She showed Magdalena the trove she'd stashed under fallen

masonry. There were disbound books and single pages of old manuscripts. Many of the leaves were covered in handwriting, smeared but often legible. Dad's hand. Ebba's. And wouldn't this be Dr Süsskind's, for the language must surely be Hebrew? Shopping lists. Memoranda. Formal letters with the imperial eagle riding on a swastika. Some of Magdalena's own writing, from four years of letters home from East Prussia.

> *and Flora said a word! I know she*
> *because she kept repeating it and gurg*
>   *! We tried to work out*
> *meant and she meant her doll*
> *won't go anywh*
> *doll*

*

The writing was perishable. It testified. It must be retrieved, all of it.

At dawn the next day when the household could be counted on to be asleep, and curfew was still in operation, Magdalena slipped out of bed and went into the garden to count the paving stones.

It must be this one.

Magda levered it up. A slither of earthworms. A blue ground beetle scuttling for its life. Webs of white root. She dug down. Nothing here.

Ah but yes, the edge of a box.

Carefully Magdalena disinterred the wet and rotting box; held it against her chest, slipping into the house, hearing a baby cry on the second floor, her heart throbbing with the kind of expectancy you feel when, round the next corner, you are about to encounter a beloved face – at last, at last.

Julia slept on. The bedroom soughed with communal breathing. Nothing was private here.

Sitting on the bed beside her daughter, Magdalena removed the lid.

Nine or ten volumes. She took out the top volume: Dad's diary for 1941. Moisture had seeped in, rippling pages and sticking them together. Dad's ink had run ... not too badly, it was all right, she'd still be able to make out the writing – Dad's familiar and characterful italics rather than the spiky old Sütterlin.

She held 1941 up to her face. Max had taught her: books carry traces, they are constellations of living or once living things. Books change their meanings, he used to say, over centuries, as new generations read. But they help us to think back over the decades or centuries to search out the original meaning. They are letters we post into the future, testaments. There is nothing more personal than a manuscript.

The book smelt of loam: the grave from which it had been exhumed. Of damp. And perhaps a whiff of tobacco? She saw Dad quite clearly: laying down his fountain pen, lighting up a 'gasper' in his study. Leaning back in his chair, he'd drag the nicotine into his lungs and exhale with relish into the permanent fug of smoke. Or he'd tamp down his pipe with his index finger, leaving a stain that never washed off. The nerves in that finger were half-dead from daily contact with hot embers.

There was a small round hole in the margin of the second page: a cinder perhaps? Crossings-out. Additions in red ink. A doodle!

Magdalena called upon her heart not to dissolve in grief but to accept the gift, in the hope that it would not turn out to be all that remained alive of him.

*

By day she suppressed the grief, searching for work to generate an income and food to supplement the ration. Just get on with it, was Magda's watchword. They foraged for fag ends to create cigarettes for use as currency on the black market. Julia was (as she herself pointed out) a genius at tracking English soldiers with a cigarette in their nicotined fingers, waiting for the butt to be jettisoned. She'd pounce before it could be trampled or any rival opportunist could scoop it up. Later they'd extract the remnant of unburnt tobacco from the butts and roll it all together in clean papers, then trade their creations for black market food. They negotiated their way through the crowds of Displaced Persons, refugees, concentration camp survivors and ex-slave labourers with crosses painted on their backs.

At lunch time the two of them made their way to the river, to eat the bread saved from breakfast.

Then they both saw him. Quite clearly. He was wearing his shabby old raincoat, collar turned up, a hunched figure shambling as he dragged his injured leg.

Letting go of Magdalena's hand, Julia dived past the woman ahead, grabbed the skirt of the man's raincoat and shrieked, *Uncle Max!* The stranger cried out in shock; wheeled round. Nothing like.

It was the first of today's sightings. Of Dad and Ebba. Of young ex-soldiers who were the spitting image of Clem and were never Clem.

To Magdalena's guilty horror, in the thick of the crowd, she spotted Ruth.

'Changed my mind.' Stopping dead, she snared Julia's hand, twisting round. 'We need to go...' She couldn't think where. 'Somewhere else.'

Magdalena rarely thought of her friend, she'd buried her name – and suddenly the name had thrust up above ground. Ruth, Ruth.

'We're going to ... the market place...'

'Why? I don't want to go to the market place ... I'm still going to the river to eat my bread and there might be swans ... let me go, stop pulling my hand, you're hurting me, Mummy...'

'Oh do stop grizzling, for goodness' sake, Julia.'

'I'm not *grizzling* ... don't be mean... I'm hungry, Mummy, *hungry,* and I'm so tired, and I want to sit down and eat my bread, and I want to go the river, you promised, and see the swans.'

Magdalena halted in her tracks. It was no good. In the end they trace you, she thought. And anyway Ruth knew the Arbers' home address. And do you actually want Ruth to be dead? Magdalena asked herself. And is this the kind of vile person you have become? A stranger to all vows and loyalties? A cheat willing to steal your bereaved friend's one remaining child?

Capitulating, Magdalena turned to face the meeting with Ruth, her heart melting with remorse.

It was not Ruth. The stranger trotted past without a glance.

Magda stooped to Julia, caressing and kissing her hand, apologising, saying that of course they're going to the river. Apologising also to the lost Ruth, who had become her family and whom she'd grown to love, and did love like a sister, over the border, in that other world.

She didn't know what had come over her, Magda said to Julia, sorry, sorry.

At the riverside, Julia asked, 'Where are the swans?'

You flinched from telling your child, who had already seen far too much reality, that the swans and ducks would have been killed and eaten. Magdalena gave Julia her share of the bread, saying that funnily enough she was not at all peckish, eat it all up, don't waste a crumb. And here was some water to go with it. Maybe the swans are on their nests, she suggested, and Julia asked where the swans' nests were, could they go and see them and maybe see the cygnets too?

'The nests are a long way away, I think,' Magda said.

She watched litter glide down on the surface of the water, which was pocked with spots of drizzle.

The time had come to clarify for Julia exactly what had happened to divide her from her real mother and sister. Or at least, a version of the truth. A sensitive version, fitted to a child's understanding, an account Julia could bear to receive.

They sat dreamily at the edge of the river, carrying the detritus of war to the sea.

Once Magdalena had been out on the heath with her teacher.

Forests of buddleia, purple and mauve, blossomed as far as the eye could see. The ecstatic scent had made you giddy. Drunk on nectar, flocks of peacock butterflies had roamed the blossoms, rising and falling, spiralling up in pairs perpetually changing places, digging their proboscises into the heart of the flowers. Magda must have assumed that because there were so many of these beauties, it would be all right to collect one. One out of tens of thousands. She'd had no net but somehow had managed to trap a peacock in the cave of her hands, where its fluttering tickled thrillingly, in the dark cave of its mortal panic.

But Miss Heller had seen and said, 'Let go now, Magda, open your hands and let her go, or you will rub the powder off her wings and she will die.'

Magdalena had opened her hands.

If I make it clear to Julia that I am not her biological mother (which she obviously knows perfectly well at some level), this does not disqualify me, it doesn't make me a false mother, Magdalena thought, but rather confirms me as a true friend.

Truth is very hard. So take your time, she counselled herself.

Deferral lightened her heart at once. She knew herself too well not to understand that deferral breeds deferral.

*

Like thousands searching for missing persons, Magdalena scoured shopfronts, doorways, signboards. Messages were pinned everywhere: *I seek my wife Irina, aged 36 and my son Rudolf, aged 13 ... I reside now at 55 Fischergrube.*

She and Julia posted their own messages: *I seek my father, Dr Maximilian Arber, and my aunt, Deaconess Ebba Arber-Thiessen, and my teacher, Miss Miriam Heller ... and my friend Mrs Ruth Daschke.*

She spotted an advert on the newspaper office in Königstrasse, calling for writers with journalistic experience and languages.

29

> The man who has become free spurns the contemptible sort
> of well-being dreamed of by shopkeepers, Christians, cows,
> women, Englishmen and other democrats.[34]
>
> Friedrich Nietzsche, *Twilight of the Idols,
> or, How to Philosophise with a Hammer*, 1889

The khaki Captain's plain, pleasant face was rather shiny, as if he'd just come out of the bathtub, which was more than Magdalena could say for herself, with her greasy hair and ragged clothes. His uniform was crumpled but clean. He was clearly well fed. As Magda and the emaciated child waited in the antechamber, she overheard Captain Dickens complaining to some unseen typist that he and his fellow officers were nicely lodged but in urgent need of a woman to do the cooking and ironing – and of course the War Ministry didn't allow you to employ a German cook, and why not, eh? In case she was a diehard Nazi and poisoned you? He chuckled whilst saying it was no blooming joke. What he wouldn't give for a plate piled high with roast beef, Yorkshire pudding and three veg, lashings of gravy – yes, and steamed pudding and custard to follow!

He'd been a Boy Scout so he knew how to heat baked beans over a paraffin stove, ha ha, but that was his blooming limit!

A youngish man in RAF uniform carrying a sheaf of papers passed through as Captain Dickens continued to lament his privations. Julia's legs were stuck out in the airman's path. Having started the day full of beans, she was already lethargic. Cold sores bloomed in the corners of her mouth. She was crooning listlessly to herself, one of the English nursery rhymes Magda had taught her.

Vitamins were what Julia desperately needed, Magdalena

thought – never mind roast beef and Yorkshire pudding. She squeezed Julia's hand. If I could only get some kind of income from the British, she thought ... I could feed her from the black market.

The airman stooped to the child and joined in with 'Humpty Dumpty'. Wakening from her lethargy, Julia sang up. He asked her name and age. He had a little girl at home, he told her: Ruth. Younger than Julia. Lived with his parents.

'You must miss her terribly,' Magdalena said.

Something in her tone arrested him. 'My Ruthie is seven. She lost her mum. You're here for an interview, Mrs...?'

'Magdalena Arber. Yes, with Captain Dickens.'

'Very best of luck.'

He seemed to want to stay and chat but Captain Dickens bustled through, patting his pockets, apologising for keeping Mrs Arber waiting. 'Now, where did I leave my...? Ah, here it is.'

Pipe wedged in mouth, he cleared a space on his desk. The airman dumped his files and left. The British didn't seem to do much saluting. What a mess the office was, with tottering piles of books against one wall, rearing up nearly to the ceiling.

Magdalena liked Captain Dickens at once. Liked him rather urgently. He was no fool. Informal and friendly as he appeared, there was a canny vigilance in his face as he waited to see if or how you would betray yourself. Every German is a Nazi until officially denazified was the British watchword. Well, Magdalena had the certificate. Was it showing on her face, how desperate she felt, how empty and violated and ill, and how she would do anything, say anything, to gain an income, however minimal? They had nothing. Just the clothes they stood up in.

But everyone was desperate. In this hungry, angry Babel, the streets were jammed with Displaced Persons competing for jobs with the British occupiers. Magdalena had encountered so many languages – French, Dutch, Yugoslavian, Italian, Latvian, Polish – and perhaps it was language and writing that would give her advantage, and Julia security and vitamins.

You heard the East Prussian dialect in the streets. There was no East Prussia now. It had been abolished. Julia's homeland was being chopped up and divided between Russia and Poland. You could hardly take it in.

Captain Dickens must be besieged by persons with nothing to sell but their pens. She hoped the odour she and Julia had brought into the newspaper office was not too rank. You couldn't wash properly. Perhaps the smell was masked by the tobacco smoke.

'And you speak English, Mrs Arber?' Captain Dickens asked in flawless German.

'Yes, sir, I do,' she replied in what she hoped was flawless English. 'And some Russian which I learned as a child – well, the grammar – but I have added to it in terms of colloquial Russian ... let us say, in my travels. Also some Lithuanian. And, of course, French. And I have some Latin and a bit of Greek, not that this will be much use. My father...'

Her lips trembled.

'Your father?'

'Is – or was – or, no, is – a scholar ... specialising in the philosophy of the Enlightenment. Voltaire, Diderot, the French Encyclopaedists. I wonder, could my little girl sit down, please, she's not been all that well?'

'Oh, of course, of course.'

Mr Dickens drew up a chair for the child and hunkered in front of her, asking her name; smiled as he brushed her hair gently back from her forehead. Would Julia care for a sweetie? He had some rather tasty American candies, if she would like to choose two? He confessed to having a sweet tooth himself and his wife often told him off about this.

'Thank you,' said Julia, trying out her English as she dipped her hand in the bag. 'How are you today? The weather is quite nice.'

'I am well and indeed the weather is lovely and warm! Take another, dear. Go on. Put it in your pocket for later. Oh, for goodness' sake, here you are, have the whole bag. Shall I give it to Mummy to keep for you?'

'Yes, please.'

And maybe the little girl would like a piece of paper and a pencil to draw while she was waiting?

Julia's face lit up.

'It happens that we have plenty of paper, despite the shortage,' Mr Dickens told Magdalena, reaching into a desk drawer. 'A positive glut – though it won't last forever. We managed to confiscate a ton of the stuff on its way to Dr Goebbels, who won't be needing it any longer.'

Captain Dickens turned out to be an intent listener. A benign but shrewd paternalist, he was an Oxford graduate (as he evidently liked you to know), who had been sent to set up a new and ethically palatable news sheet in Lübeck, to teach the German public the difference between journalism and propaganda. Of course, he'd recognised at once why Magdalena went out of her way to emphasise French philosophy over Kant and Hegel and Nietzsche.

'You are searching for your father, Mrs Arber?'

'I hope he is also searching for me.'

'A philosopher, you say?'

'He published two monographs on Voltaire, Mr Dickens. Long before the war, obviously. You might be acquainted with his work? ... I mean, my father's work ... Max Arber? No? He had the distinction of being arrested and detained in Dachau in '33; released after some months. Permitted to continue his work at the college in a, well, menial capacity. As a porter. He'd been a prominent member of the Social Democratic party which made him suspect.'

Mr Dickens clearly liked her phrasing – *had the distinction* – but otherwise didn't look particularly impressed. Of course they all laid claim to clean hands, the ex-Brownshirts and the Party lackeys, the jumped-up jacks-in-office, the Gestapo weasels: *Oh no, I was a Social Democrat ... never a Nazi, God forbid, here are my forged papers to prove it.*

'And you are an authoress yourself, Mrs Arber?'

'Since I could hold a pencil, it was all I wanted to be. My war-work was a teaching position in a village in East Prussia and I kept writing in my spare time. I'd be most grateful, sir, if you could offer me an opportunity to … maybe show you what I am capable of?'

'You have publications?'

'No,' Magdalena confessed. 'Who in Germany – in my lifetime – would publish the work of a young woman – a humanist – who thinks for herself? Thinking for yourself is – was – a crime.'

She described the elderly Mr Excorn, his left eye shooting coded threat at his minions, his right eye blacked out. Excorn who'd been co-opted into the People's Storm militia at the end of 1944 and sent to fight on his one working leg against the muscular bipeds of Russia. She told him how Mr Excorn used to preside behind his Prussian desk with its antler horns and carved dog heads like a beast that had lumbered in from the forest. Excorn who was now, if not dead, extinct.

Excorn's round face, his balding head like an egg – but why at this juncture did Magdalena inwardly acknowledge a twinge of scornful pity for the old geezer who'd set her on her path as a teacher by informing her in his pompous way, rolling his 'r's and hissing his sibilants, *There is no such thing as knowledge?*

Mr Dickens was entertained by this comic vignette. That was the posthumous use of Mr Excorn in present circumstances. Mr Dickens' laugh rumbled out.

Julia, sucking her sweet rather than chewing, to make it last, leaned forward and flapped her paper at the adults, to show off her sketch. A chap with an owl's face and a rumpled jacket was seated at a desk opposite a glamorous lady modelling a stylish outfit quite unlike the patched and frayed jacket Magdalena had on. A fur collar and a rakish hat with a plume and a ribbon.

'This is you, Sir Dickens. And this lady is Mummy.'

'A fine portrait, my dear. May I keep it?'

'It is for you, Sir Dickens.'

'*Mr* Dickens will do fine, dear,' he said, with a smile. 'Have another sheet of paper – here you are. And keep the pencil.'

'Thank you, Mr Sir Dickens. Oh, and by the way, I am not a girl. Not always, anyway. When I am a boy, I am called Emil.'

'Ah?' He glanced at Magdalena.

'I was advised to dress Julia as a boy when we escaped from the Russians ... safer for her.'

He paused; reflected; comprehended; frowned. 'Ah, yes ... yes, I see. Of course. Would you write down your address, Mrs Arber? And your husband is ... not with you?'

'I don't actually have a daddy,' Julia chimed in, saving Magdalena from the necessity to improvise. 'I have an uncle but he's not here. And an auntie but she's not here either. And also Clem who is somewhere else. But we are looking for them and we will find them. And I did once have a sister. And another mummy. And also my Auroch was stolen by nasty men and my rocking horse Blitz has been burnt. I can draw them for you though.'

He nodded sympathetically, warily. He must surely see that Julia was too old to be Magdalena's daughter. This could be explained in due course, if he could offer them work.

Magda told Mr Dickens their address; explaining that they were lodging next door to her old family home, which was partly in ruins.

She burrowed in her bag and handed over a sample of her diary, the jottings made on the flight from East Prussia at the von Wedel estate. Captain Dickens received without comment the papers, concealing any surprise at this home-made submission. He held it carefully, aware of its fragility and perhaps of its precious uniqueness. *Amateur* was probably the word that came to mind. Magda hoped Captain Dickens would see that she could write about what she called *real things, in a real way*. And catch these moments on the wing, at vanishing point.

He would of course read the sample with interest, he assured her courteously, and would take great care of it. Perhaps Mrs Arber would come back the day after tomorrow? He stood to extend his hand.

'And also,' Magdalena added, reaching into her bag, 'I have one of my father's journals if you would care to see it? He left them buried in our garden and we dug them up.'

One man's truth, sunk in the soil and disinterred, its cover still stained by the earth which had preserved it, was handed over. Magdalena relinquished it with a qualm of misgiving: it was a unique manuscript, a survival from the universal bonfire. What if it never came back?

A hankering expression suffused Captain Dickens's face. He opened his palms to receive the volume; laid it on his desk. He really needed to use those white cotton gloves to handle this, the Captain remarked, as you would in an antiquarian library. For this was treasure.

'How did you come to find it?' he asked.

'My father wrote telling me where to look for his journals. And when I came home for a break, he pointed out the second flagstone from the end of our garden. If he didn't survive, his testament might be there, a legacy for me, a memorial. So, as you can imagine, these mean the world to me.'

'These?'

'Yes, there are eight other volumes.'

'No? Eight? Really? Great Scott. I shall take the greatest care, I promise you, Mrs Arber. If you come back the day after tomorrow … no, tomorrow morning, first thing, I can give you my answer.'

*

It was a *Yes* from Captain Dickens. A hearty *Yes, Mrs Arber, we can use you*.

He sketched out his idea for a weekly contribution to the news sheet from the angle of the thousands of East Prussian refugees in Lübeck. Flight Sergeant Owen would conduct her to the various bunkers where these refugees were accommodated, to see for herself their difficult situation. They were chiefly women and children. Mrs Arber should concentrate on advising them to put up with their regrettable conditions for the time being, locked up every night in the bunkers, behind a grate like a mediaeval portcullis. And there were also special camps set aside for German refugees from the eastern provinces, where she would be driven. The more patient these displaced Germans were, the sooner their needs could be addressed. It would be important for Mrs Arber to reassure them that the British authorities were doing their resolute best to find them more appropriate lodgings.

He handed back the two diaries, wrapped in brown paper and tied with string, and watched his new-minted contributor stow them carefully in her bag.

'Oh, and before I forget, Mrs Arber, cash in advance of your first piece. It's not much – but better than nothing.'

'Oh, thank you. Thank you so much, Captain.'

Weak at the knees, and dizzy, she leaned back against the wall. Relief overwhelmed her.

Captain Dickens settled Julia in a cubby-hole with a glass of milk, a story book about Emil and the Detectives, a notepad and a pencil.

'You will sit still, my dear, won't you, and be very, very quiet? I know you love reading, like your mummy. You need to be like a little mouse because this is ... well, rather irregular, to say the least.'

'I will be a mouse.'

Julia proved her good faith by not stirring except to put up her hand to ask the secretary if she might go to the lavatory. Magdalena had never envisaged Julia learning the art of sitting still and keeping quiet. In their travels, the little girl had absorbed the lesson. Something of the old light in her eyes had faded months ago.

The Captain showed Magdalena round the offices and the printing press, explaining procedures and outlining a role. Having read her diary fragments, he'd seen – or believed he'd seen – her heart. He'd be a razor-sharp reader, trained, sceptical, the opposite of Dagmar Struppat, lapping up the weasel words of Magdalena's decoy diary.

'And that mountain of books over there, Mrs Arber,' he said, 'is a hundredweight of Nazi filth we found in one of the old newspaper offices, stacked in the loft. I need to go through when I've a moment, before we burn it. Maybe you could give me a hand with the children's books?'

Magdalena knelt beside the stacked books that reached up the wall. Yes, she had met them all in her past life. Ernst Hiemer's *The Poisonous Mushroom*: ten copies: 'The Jewish nose is crooked at its tip. It looks like the number six.'

To the fire.

The same author's *The Poodle-Pug-Dachshund-Fox-Terrier-Mongrel*: twenty-three insane copies. The Jew is an amalgam of all the animals you detest: hyenas, locusts, snakes, bedbugs, tapeworms, chameleons, all mixed in a farrago of germ-laden cells.

To the fire.

Elvira Bauer: *Trust No Fox on his Green Heath and No Jew on his Oath: A Picture Book for Young and Old*.

Ah, so you've turned up. Magdalena sat back on her heels.

How alien the familiar blood-red cover and the forked tongue of the Gothic lettering appeared as the book delivered itself from concealment into this khaki, monochrome world. An obscene fantasy of miscegenation that had imprinted on young minds the plan to slaughter who-knows-how-many-millions of innocent people? The stack aborted a couple of copies into Magdalena's lap.

I didn't write this book, I didn't teach it. But it saved my skin.

Thirteen copies. To the fire. Again. Finally.

*

She could hardly believe it. Doleful Mrs Kondritz had actually arisen from her bed, dressed in a navy frock, brushed her hair and held in her hand a miracle.

'A letter for you, Miss Arber,' she said.

'For me?'

'From Switzerland! Sorry, not being nosy! Well, I am, but, well, you know, I couldn't help noticing! Here you are. By the way, we're leaving. Staying with my sister-in-law in Plön. Ta ta!'

There was no postal system. In the devastated city, the nomadic thousands had no fixed address. So this really was a miracle. Ah yes, Magdalena saw that the letter had been sent via the Red Cross. She recognised the dashing handwriting, each word chasing the tail of the next. Sinking down on her bed, she held the miracle in both hands, turned it over, kissed it, carefully prised it open with her thumb because she might be able to reuse the envelope.

Excuse my frightful scrawl, my dear Bookworm. Just to say I'm safely here in Zurich with Leonie and to give you our address. <u>Please let me know how you are faring.</u> We are working with the Refugee Council and they will pass on letters. Are you safe and well, is Julia well, can we send you anything? You will like to know that Alf got back to his family in Norway. Said he passed Lübeck on a bus and thought of you. Your Renate and her little girl made it to Stuttgart. <u>Leonie wants to meet you, Bookworm!</u> Hurry up and write soon! Ever yours, Eva.

Magdalena brought her makeshift desk to the window. There was a sheen on the street, the light refracting through a rolling mist. Passers-by floated in and out of view.

Dear Eva,

I am overcome to have your letter. Can't quite take it in. Still shaking. And to know that you and Leonie are together is the most beautiful news. Please give Leonie my heartfelt greetings and thank her for lending me her library of good books!

My address is as above (actually next door to our old house, which is unstable and has been marked for demolition).

Firstly, yes, Julia is with me, I'll tell you about our journey when I see you. What a fierce little wonder she is. I think she saved my reason on many occasions and my heart from breaking. The Lübeck schools, which were requisitioned for use as hospitals, have just begun to open and Julia is so glad to be back and making friends. Your cousin Hans von Wedel helped us on the journey west, we could not have managed without him. He stayed on at the family estate, said he could not leave his people without a doctor. I have heard nothing of him.

Not sure if you ever met her but my good friend Marianne (teacher) made it back to Köln, travelled on the very last trains.

I've found work with the local British news sheet so we have a small income – can purchase small extras for Julia on the Black Market. I've encountered nothing but goodwill amongst my English colleagues.

My darkest news I will tell you without comment. My father died of heart failure as a forced labourer at the West Wall. My cousin Clem, whom you met briefly, deserted and was on his way home when the SS caught and executed him – wearing a placard reading, 'I am a coward who betrayed the Führer and Fatherland' or words to that effect. Ebba (my aunt) has not come home. The last I heard was that she was imprisoned with a few other Christian resistance women in the Berlin Moabit prison, partly bombed in the final days of the war. Did she escape? I don't know. I have no news of Ruth. I fear the worst.

Better by far just to tell the direst news factually. But, of course, the tears that fell to the page were perfectly legible. The sight of Eva's writing had conjured the hand that held the pen – Eva riding out with slack reins across her green land in an East Prussia that was now abolished, partitioned between the Soviet Union and Poland, its entire German population expelled.

Magdalena read through her letter. Was there more information she ought to convey or request?

Perhaps finish there. She signed and folded the paper. The link was made.

*

No, it was not the end of the letter, far from it. Magdalena unfolded the page to add a postscript and her pen ran wild.

PS Eva! Eva! I wrote that the day before yesterday. Everything has changed! My darling darling Auntie Ebba is asleep on my bed, Ruth is looking over my shoulder and whispering that I should send you and Leonie her very best wishes, she is overjoyed to know that you made it. Julia has said very little, she just sits and stares at each face as we take it in turns to hug and caress her and each other – she has three mothers now, poor mite! – each as opinionated as the other – she can hardly take it in, surrounded by our love – and Julia has just murmured what's for tea, she's absolutely starving?

EPILOGUE
Palace of Justice, Nüremberg, Winter 1946

> Not that fair field
> Of Enna, where Proserpin gathering flowers
> Herself a fairer flower by gloomy Dis
> Was gathered, which cost Ceres all that pain
> To seek her through the world...[35]
> John Milton, *Paradise Lost*

The perishing cold. Magdalena had pinned a Grand Hotel towel under her coat, warm clothes being in short supply. Beneath Nüremberg's ruins bodies still lay unredeemed, eighteen months after the war's end; their stench tainted the air, despite the icy conditions. A diminishing number of diehard Nazi terrorists remained crouched in catacombs beneath the mediaeval walled city, emerging at night with guns and grenades. Snow and ice compacted in the all-but-empty streets, where charred skeletons of hundreds of buildings rose, black against the snow, and a few stunted trees clung on.

Magdalena looked down from the International Press Gallery at the judges, defendants, attorneys, military policemen, interpreters, court writers – an aerial view. The accused physicians filed in and sat in a tightly packed row. Dr Littmann with haggard face and sparse grey hair, was wearing a tweed jacket and a sickly, martyred air. He held his elbows in to his waist as if chary of contamination by the known malefactors at either side.

The white-haired woman in the witness box stood dwarfed in the immensity of the courtroom, with its marble pillars and mahogany panels.

'You are a survivor of Ravensbrück Concentration Camp, Mrs Daschke?'

The Prosecutor's microphone emitted a rustling interference, for the lawyers would pack their suits with crumpled newspaper in the attempt to keep warm.

'I am.'

This was Ruth's time. Flora's time. Julia's time. And therefore, my time, Magdalena thought. Time for the voiceless, murdered multitude of the elderly, the mentally ill, the afflicted children, to be heard. Time for a mother to have her say.

The Prosecutor opened by asking the witness to describe her relationship with Dr Felix Littmann. Ruth rapidly got into her stride. They'd asked for her story and by God Ruth Daschke's story was what they were going to get.

'In an earlier incarnation, Dr Littmann was a decent family physician. A shabby, comfortable, slouching sort of man – no airs and graces, liked a drink. But from being a provincial nobody, Littmann saw he could impress the Party grandees and rise in the medical hierarchy. He selected my children to help make his name in science – so-called science – and labelled my younger twin defective. Subhuman. A threat to the Aryan gene pool. Not viable. A useless eater.

'My beautiful Flora ... who you kidnapped and murdered! Don't you shake your head at me! You came after her sister too, the so-called viable twin – and finally you had me sent to Ravensbrück – where I survived against all the odds, to point my finger at you...'

'Witness,' intervened the Prosecutor, 'you may not address the accused directly. Or threaten him or point at him.'

Ruth nodded and continued. As she spoke, the map of their lives together unfolded in Magdalena's memory. The removal of Flora to the asylum. Ruth's agony and defiance. Her search. The cynical lies of the nursing staff at Gütersloh. The urn purportedly containing Flora's ashes. The falsified cause of death. Ruth's journey to, amongst other murder centres, the Hades of Meseritz-Obrawalde.

'Littmann waged war on women and children. I am his external conscience – he has none of his own – and I shall be with him all the way. This is the sacred oath Littmann has broken: ἐς οἰκίας δὲ ὀκόσας ἂν ἐσίω, ἐσελεύσομαι ἐπ' ὠφελείῃ καμνόντων ...'

'What on earth?' asked the Prosecutor.

'Ancient Greek. The Hippocratic Oath.'

'The witness must testify in German, French, Russian or English, or in a language for which we have translators.'

Ruth translated.

Magdalena felt a helpless rush of tenderness for her friend. She gripped her pencil and notepad and reminded herself of the work she was there to do. Out of the morning mist Ruth had materialised. And Ebba too. With ingenuity born of shared need and old loyalties, the three women had woven a web of sustaining love around the surviving twin. A family.

*

Littmann's testimony was shrewd and plausible. Modest and thoughtful in choosing his words, chastened in demeanour, as if he too desired to get to the root of what had happened in his corrupted nation, he spoke from the heart, or so it appeared. Aghast at the charge of euthanasia, which he utterly repudiated, Littmann acknowledged failure on the human level. He'd sorrowed for women like the brave and formidable Mrs Daschke and done his resolute best – or so he'd felt at the time – for all the mothers and children in his care.

But, Littmann added, after a pause, this had not been enough. He saw that now. He had allowed himself to become overwhelmed by the demands of his profession and forfeited something of the respect he owed his patients.

And, yes, he had been vainglorious about his achievements.

For these human failings, he would never forgive himself. Dr Littmann bowed his head. But as to the accusations, there was not one shred of evidence. In any case, all documents had gone up in flames during the Soviet invasion of East Prussia.

*

The Americans put the witnesses and reporters up in a style Magdalena and Ruth could hardly have conceived of. A bomb had split the Grand Hotel in two, so that to access one half you had to exit into the snow and re-enter through a revolving door. But the building was warm, or warm enough; the electric lights worked; there were thick quilts on the beds and cloths on the tables, soap in the dishes and towels with few stains.

Unbelievable luxury: food such as you had dreamed of and craved and talked about obsessively, eking out your tiny ration of calories. Magdalena's fork punctured the egg yolk; yellow goodness seeped out on to the bread. White bread. The taste was the taste of health and plenty. She'd tried to hang on and wait for her friend to come down for breakfast, but now she'd given up: it was either begin to tuck in or start drooling. Arrayed on the table before her were pancakes, powdered milk, canned fruit.

A luscious coffee scent permeated the refectory, where famished Germans waited on the top brass of many breakfasting nationalities. Magda could imagine them licking the plates that were returned to the kitchens.

How often had she licked her own plate?

She caught the name Littmann. Talk was all of yesterday's verdict. At the tables of the Grand Hotel, groups of diners – Americans, Russians, Britons, Belgians, French, Czechs – compared their own extempore verdicts.

He'd seemed on the whole a decent sort of chap. At least, by comparison. Magdalena heard someone remark on how oddly English he seemed – yes, really, you could take him for an Englishman – one couldn't exactly say why except that the fellow didn't hector with that frightful clipped, shrill Teutonic manner so many of these ruffians had, looking down their snouts at you. A tall, modest-seeming and intelligent man. How did someone like that get mixed up in all this evil? Didn't he remind you a bit of Albert Speer?

'They all had their trotters in the filth, just a matter of degree.'

'Oh, I agree, but this guy at least seems more … human.'

'A matter of presentation, surely?'

Littmann at least, they could agree, was small fry compared with the monsters in the dock alongside him, who had more than earned the death penalty.

'But what about this skull collection he's supposed to have had?'

'That was not proved, Harry. The witnesses had never seen it. Hearsay.'

'Listen, they all had collections.'

'Really?'

'Don't be naïve. Hallervorden, departmental head at the Max Planck Institute – he was boasting that he had 697 brains! 697! Heard that from a colleague of his. Where do you think he acquired those? And Voss too – he's touting his collection as we speak! Those skulls will have been Littmann's babies! All the mad neurologists had collections. He'd have transported it west before the Russians came and, you mark my words, it will be stored in some laboratory somewhere behind a locked door. Worth a mint to science! Believe me, those vultures will all retreat with their loot into the fog of respectability. They'll sell themselves to the Allies. My guess is, Littmann was killing his patients at the asylum by lethal injection.'

'But there's no proof…'

'No, there's no proof…'

'Even so … acquitted!'

Magdalena got up to leave, pocketing the remains of the buttered bread for the trip back to Lübeck. This man had stripped the dear gentle face from Flora – and liquidated who-knew-how-many others. It was not impossible that one day the law would catch up with him. But the task now was to persuade Ruth to relinquish her search, settle down with her family, return to teaching.

Magdalena imagined Felix Littmann, carrying his shabby luggage, emerging from the Palace of Justice, a free man; and how he must have glanced around, breathed in lungfuls of icy air, ducked his head and hurried into the crowd, absorbed into the body of the new Germany.

CODA

Note on the fate of
HISTORICAL CHARACTERS ...

**Captain Arthur Geoffrey DICKENS (1910–2001) returned to England in Autumn 1945 and was demobbed. In 1949 he was appointed Professor of History at the University of Hull, later at London University. Dickens, who published his *Lübeck Diaries* in 1946, enjoyed 'a deep love affair with Germany' and was a moving force in the establishment of the German Historical Institute in London. He was decorated by the German government. Dickens died in London at the age of 91.

**Hermann Wilhelm GÖRING (1893–1946) was a veteran World War I fighter-ace, early supporter of Hitler, morphine addict, charmer, who created the Gestapo and rose to the rank of *Reichsmarschall*. Amongst his many vainglorious titles, Göring was named Commander in Chief of the Air Force, Prime Minister of Prussia, Chief Forester of the Reich, Chief Liquidator of Sequestered Estates, Supreme Head of the National Weather Bureau. Convicted at the Nüremberg War Crimes Trials of (amongst other charges) crimes against humanity, Göring eluded hanging by committing suicide with potassium cyanide.

Marianne GÜNTHER (later **PEYINGHAUS) taught at a village school in East Prussia, from 1941 to 1945. She escaped the Soviet invasion in late January 1945, travelling home to Köln by stages. Marianne collected the letters she had sent home to her parents, both of whom survived, and her brother (who did not), and published them in 1985 as Marianne Peyinghaus, *Stille Jahre* *in Gertlauken: Erinnerungen an Ostpreussen* (*Quiet Years in Gertlauken: Memories of East Prussia*). As yet there is no English translation of this beautiful book.

****Theodor HAECKER** (1879–1945) was a writer, philosopher and author of the incomparable diary, *Journal in the Night*, a testament of implacable Christian resistance to the Nazi regime and all its values and deeds. Haecker was connected with the Scholls' 'White Rose' resistance group, in whose gatherings he read excerpts from the diaries.

****Dr Julius HALLERVORDEN** (1882–1965), physician and neuroscientist, born in East Prussia, active in the Nazi T4 euthanasia programme, collector of the brains of the executed, never paid for his crimes: on the contrary, he benefited from them. He became President of the German Neuropathological Society and pursued his researches at the Max Planck Institute in Giessen.

****Dr Ludwig Georg Heinrich HECK** (known as **'Lutz'**), (1892–1983), was Nazi director of the Berlin Zoo, hunting pal of Hermann Göring, back-breeder of the 'Heck cattle' and 'Heck horses', plunderer of Warsaw Zoo.

****Dr Friedrich Percyval RECK** (calling himself **RECK-MALLECZEWEN**) (1884–1945) was an anti-Nazi royalist and Conservative and the author of one of the most powerful journals of his era, published posthumously as *Diary of a Man in Despair*. In this magnificent work, he elevated political invective to the level of high art. The Nazis arrested Reck, who died just before the end of the War at Dachau Concentration Camp.

****Dr Christian Heinrich Emil Hermann VOSS** (1894–1987) became professor at the University of Jena. His anatomy textbook, based on experiments with Jewish and Polish skulls at his laboratory in Posen and at Nazi execution sites, became in the post-war period (for forty years) the standard manual for German medical students. In retirement, Voss moved to Hamburg and died in January 1987, aged 95 years. In his flight from the Russians in January 1945, Voss inadvertently left behind his incriminating diary covering the years 1932–45. It is the diary of a sentimentalist and a predator.

... and the afterlife of
FICTIONAL CHARACTERS

Magdalena Dorothea ARBER worked as journalist and editor for the British Occupation press and went on to freelance for newspapers in Europe and America. She travelled extensively. Magdalena edited her father's diaries as *The Good We Did Not Do*, published during the 1960s and reprinted, to acclaim, in the 2000s. Magdalena's origin owes something to the character of ****Marianne PEYINGHAUS,** as revealed in the letters of *Quiet Years in Gertlauken*, but radicalised.

'**Alexander-I-Regret**' is an imagined glimpse of ** **Aleksandr SOLZHENITSYN,** world-famous novelist and Soviet dissident, who commanded a battery of Russian soldiers in East Prussia. Arrested there in February 1945, he was sent to the Gulag. Solzhenitsyn recorded the atrocities committed by his men in his poem, *Prussian Nights*, composed in his head while serving his sentence of forced labour. One of the most powerfully telling things in *Prussian Nights* is the poet's anguished recognition of his own complicity.

Deaconess Ebba ARBER-THIESSEN became a Quaker. She spoke frequently for female spiritual and social equality and the duty of Christian resistance, and against racism and German rearmament. She died in 1973, aged 71.

Ruth DASCHKE worked as a teacher in Lübeck until her daughter left home, when she retrained as a Classics lecturer. Ruth's monograph on the poetry of Sappho was published in 1965. In 1998, Magdalena, Ruth and Julia, together with a group of friends from the village formerly known as Alt Schönbek, visited their old home, to be welcomed with generous kindness by the Polish families who now owned the houses and farms. At the grave marking the last resting place of the ashes purporting to be those of Flora Daschke, Ruth laid flowers in memory of 'every victim of Nazi atrocities'. Ruth died in 1999.

Julia DASCHKE studied Politics and Philosophy at the University of Zurich. Radicalised in the 1960s, in 1968 she was briefly arrested for daubing graffiti on the wall of a medical laboratory. In later life she became a Green Party activist. Married and divorced, she has a son and a daughter, Max and Flora. Julia retired to Plön in Schleswig-Holstein, where she remains active in the Green movement.

Walther EXCORN is thought to have fallen in his first engagement with the *Volksturm* against the Red Army in December 1944.

Eva von LAULITZ successfully led the Laulitz Farm Trek in 1944 over the frozen Vistula Lagoon out of East Prussia. She and her lifelong friend **Leonie WEISS** worked for the United Nations Relief and Resettlement Administration. They made their home in Zurich, where they died in the same year, 1979.

Alf HANSEN, a Norwegian Prisoner of War, is loosely based on the character of ****Odd NANSEN** (1901–1973), Norwegian architect and humanitarian, co-founder of UNICEF, son of the famous explorer, ****Fridtjof NANSEN**. Odd kept a hidden diary throughout the years of his concentration camp incarceration at Sachsenhausen and other prisons. After the War this moving and revelatory testimony was published as *From Day to Day: One Man's Diary of Survival in Nazi Concentration Camps*.

Miriam HELLER died at Auschwitz Concentration Camp in 1942 with her parents, grandparents, brothers, sisters and cousins.

Dr Felix Johann Helmut LITTMANN, acquitted of Crimes Against Humanity, went on to gain an international reputation, working with ****Dr Julius HALLERVORDEN** at the Max Planck Institute. Littmann had secretly smuggled out his valuable brain collection, which he donated to Hallervorden's research collection at the Institute. In 1990, after the fall of the Berlin Wall, the brain collection was buried in a Munich cemetery. Dr Littmann died, full of honours, in 1974.

Dagmar STRUPPAT escaped from East Prussia to Berlin with her mother (to whom she liked to refer to as 'a noose around my neck'). Dagmar married SS Lieutenant Siegfried Beck who was taken into custody by the US authorities in 1945. Although Dagmar never renounced her National Socialist ideology, in 1946 she bigamously married an elderly Jewish man just liberated from a camp. It is not known what became of her – or him – after this. My ghoulish portraits of Dagmar and her mother are both rather closely based on the account of herself given to the Jewish writer **Louis HAGEN** (1916–2000) by ****Hildegard TRUTZ (née KOCH)** and published in English in 1951 under the title *Follow My Leader*, republished in 2011 as *Ein Volk, ein Reich: Nine Lives under the Nazis*. (The nine were people whom Hagen, a Jew who had suffered in a concentration camp before absconding to join the British army, had known before the war. Of Hildegard he recorded: 'everything she had absorbed during the Nazi years of triumph came out parrot fashion and completely intact.')

Dr Herbert VOGEL settled in Wiesbaden and worked as a researcher alongside ****Lutz HECK**, ex-director of the Berlin Zoo, on whose behalf he had scoured the Eastern Reich zoos and helped plunder Warsaw Zoo. After the War, Vogel attempted (without success) to locate the 'Heck Aurochs' for further back-breeding experiments. In 1958 Vogel accompanied Heck to South Africa. He died there of malaria in 1959.

Dr Hans von WEDEL remained in hiding on his East Prussian family estate, covertly giving medical support to the neighbourhood until his presence and aristocratic lineage became known to the Russian occupiers, whence he escaped to the west in 1946. The depiction of Hans owes something to the life and Christian testimony of ****Hans, Graf von LEHNDORFF**, one of the greatest diarists of the era.

REFERENCES: EPIGRAPHS

Translations from German are my own unless otherwise indicated.

1 Adolf Hitler to Hermann Rauschning, 1934, in Jost Hermand, *Old Dreams of a New Reich: Volkish Utopias and National Socialism*, tr. Paul Levesque and Stefan Soldovieri, 1992.

2 Aleksandr Solzhenitsyn, *Prusskiye Nochi*, translated by Robert Conquest as *Prussian Nights*, 1977.

3 Gerrit Ernst Manilius Engelke (1890–1918), '*An die Soldaten des grossen Krieges* 'To the Soldiers of the Great War', posthumously published in *Rhythmus des neuen Europa*, by Jakob Kneip in 1921, tr. Merryn Williams.

4 Walter Flex (1887–1917), '*Wildgänse rauschen durch die Nacht*' in *Der Wanderer zwischen beiden Welten,* 1916.

5 *The Jewish Prayer for the Dead (El Maleh Rachamim).*

6 Baldur von Schirach, '*An den Führer, Adolf Hitler*' ('To the Leader, Adolf Hitler'), in *Die Fahne der Verfolgten, (The Flag of the Persecuted People), 1939.*

7 Tu Fu (712-770), 'Dreaming of Li Pai', in *Selected Poems of the Tang & Song Dynasties,* tr. Rewi Alley, 1983.

8 Johann Wolfgang von Goethe, '*Mignon*' ('*Kennst du das Land, wo die Zitronen blühn*'), *Wilhelm Meisters Lehrjahre, 1796.*

9 Bertolt Brecht, *Kriegsfibel, War Primer* (composed 1940–47, published 1955).

10 Voltaire, *Questions sur les Miracles, Questions Concerning Miracles*, 1765.

11 Georg Trakl, *'Im Osten'*, 'On the Eastern Front', 1914.

12 Erich Kästner, '*Kennst Du das Land, wo die Kanonen blühn*', in *Herz auf Taille*, 1928.

13 Johann Wolfgang von Goethe, '*An den Mond*', revised version, 1789.

14 Ernst Jűnger, *First Paris Diary,* 1942, in *A German Officer in Occupied Paris: The War Journals, 1941–1944.*

15 Anon, *Das Nibelungenlied*, c.1200, translated as *The Nibelungenlied* by A.T. Hatto, 1969 edition, Ch. 16.

16 *The Hippocratic Oath,* estimated to have been written 500–400BC: (ἐς οἰκίας δὲ ὁκόσας ἂν ἐσίω, ἐσελεύσομαι ἐπ' ὠφελείῃ καμνόντων, ἐκτὸς ἐὼν πάσης ἀδικίης ἑκουσίης καὶ φθορίης, as translated by Professor Ceri Davies in private correspondence).

17 Dr Julius Hallervorden, recalling his own words at his interrogation in July 1945, quoted by Götz Aly in Aly, Chroust and Pross, *Cleansing the Fatherland: Nazi Medicine and Racial Hygiene,* tr. Belinda Cooper (1994).

18 Theodor Haecker, *Journal in the Night*, April 1940, entry no. 173, 1950 edition, translated by Alexander Dru.

19 Johann-Erasmus Freiherr von Malsen-Ponickau, Head of Munich Auxiliary Police, *Motivational Address* to SS Guards at Dachau, April 1933, quoted in Christopher Dillon, *Dachau and the SS: A Schooling in Violence (2015)*, p. 37.

20 Ernst Jűnger, *First Paris Journal*, 1941, in *A German Officer in Occupied Paris: The War Journals, 1941–1944,* translated by Thomas Hansen, 2019.

21 Anon, *Homeric Hymn to Demeter*, seventh/sixth century BCE, lines 66–68, translated by Gregory Nagy.

22 *The Gospel According to John*, 21:17, *King James Version of the Bible*.

23 *Law on Animal Protection*, Sections I–II, Berlin, Nov 24, 1934, *Reichstierschutzgesetz*, in Boria Sax, *Animals in the Third Reich: Pets, Scapegoats and the Holocaust* (2000). Appendix II, pp. 179–183.

24 The original epigram (*Greek Anthology* VII. 489), attributed to Sappho, was translated by Mary Barnard in *Sappho, A New Translation*, 1958.

25 Friedrich Hőlderlin, '*Hyperions Schicksalslied*', ('Hyperion's Song of Destiny') in *Hyperion; oder, Der Eremit in Griechenland* (1797/9).

26 Hugo Grotius, *On the Law of War and Peace (De Jure Belli ac Pacis)*, 1625, edited and translated by Stephen C Neff, 2012.

27 Miklós Radnóti, '*Töredék*' ('Fragment'), 19 May, 1944, translated by John M. Ridland & Peter V. Czipott, in *All That Still Matters At All: Selected Poems of Miklós Radnóti*, 2013. One of the greatest Hungarian poets of the twentieth century, Radnóti was murdered as a Jew in the Holocaust. His final poems were found on his body in a mass grave exhumed after the war, inscribed in pencil in a small exercise book.

28 Friedrich Hőlderlin, '*Wohl geh ich täglich*' (1798–1800), translated as 'Another Day' by David Constantine in *Friedrich Hőlderlin: Selected Poems*, 1996.

29 Baldur von Schirach, *Fibel für die Grundschule (Primer for Elementary School)*, Gütersloh, 1935.

30 Excerpts from *Letters to Adolf Hitler*, composed by sundry Nazi penwomen, 1931–45, edited by Henrik Eberle, 2012, from a cache discovered in the KGB Special Archive in Moscow.

31 δαὴρ αὔτ' ἐμὸς ἔσκε κυνώπιδος, εἴ ποτ' ἔην γε/ 'There was a world ... or was it all a dream?', Homer, *The Iliad* III. 180, as represented by Robert Fagles in lines 218–19 of his expansive translation, 1990.

32 Aleksandr Solzhenitsyn, *Prusskiye Nochi*, 1947, translated as *Prussian Nights* by Robert Conquest, 1977.

33 Heinrich Heine, *'Ich hatte einst'*, 1834.

34 Friedrich Nietzsche, *Twilight of the Idols, or, How to Philosophise with a Hammer,* 1889.

35 John Milton, *Paradise Lost*, 1674 edition, IV. 268–272.

ACKNOWLEDGEMENTS

I thank the brilliant Dr Eda Sagarra, who introduced me to Hölderlin's poetry as an 18-year-old student at Manchester University. Eda's students hung on her every word. She predicted, 'You will be known for two things: as someone who takes everything to heart and who cannot spell Nietzsche.' I am confident that I have made progress in one of these fields.

I am constantly grateful to the late Professor Idris Parry who taught kindness and Rainer Maria Rilke. In the 1990s I attended the Goethe Institute, Manchester, and would like to record my debt to Dr Heinrich Stricker and Mrs Ursula James.

Professor M. Wynn Thomas is a dear friend and eminent Swansea colleague who has supported me during five years of research and went out of his way to acquire rare books for this project. Professor Ceri Davies gave me generous help with translation and interpretation of Greek literature. I thank my distinguished friend, Mr Glyn Pursglove, for memorable discussions of poetry and history.

According to the joyous principle of serendipity, I crossed paths with various people whose families had links with East Prussia and could confide details of their family history: one of them turned out to be my dentist, Dr Renate Prells, with whom I enjoyed many one-sided conversations. I also thank my colleague at Swansea, Dr Marie-Louise Kohlke, and my good friend in Australia, the author Evelyn Juers.

I am grateful to novelist and poet, Dr Gayathri Prabhu, for an exchange going back twenty years; to authors Julie Bertagna and Frances Hill; to fellow Germanist and novelist, Anne Lauppe-Dunbar. I thank my bookworm friends, Jeff Russon and Stuart O'Donnell, for their encouragement. My greatest debts of gratitude are to poet Andrew Howdle, for a unique writerly collaboration over many years and to my husband, the late Frank Regan, for not less than everything.

I thank my agent, Euan Thorneycroft of A.M. Heath, for his support and guidance. I am grateful for the skills and empathy of the staff at Honno – and, not least, to the laser insight of my editor, Caroline Oakley.

Any mistakes of fact or interpretation in this work are attributable solely to myself.

Finally, I record a kind of dark gratitude to my late father, Harry Davies, who had fought in the War in the Western Desert and Europe, and never got over the inhumanity he had seen. He took my teenage self to visit Dachau when we lived in Germany, asking me not to forget and to bear witness to my generation. It is late.

Stevie Davies, Swansea 2024

ABOUT HONNO

Honno Welsh Women's Press was set up in 1986 by a group of women who felt strongly that women in Wales needed wider opportunities to see their writing in print and to become involved in the publishing process. Our aim is to develop the writing talents of women in Wales, give them new and exciting opportunities to see their work published and often to give them their first 'break' as a writer.

Honno is registered as a community co-operative. Any profit that Honno makes is invested in the publishing programme. Women from Wales and around the world have expressed their support for Honno. Each supporter has a vote at the Annual General Meeting. For more information and to buy our publications, please visit our website www.honno.co.uk or email us on post@honno.co.uk.

Honno
D41, Hugh Owen Building,
Aberystwyth University,
Aberystwyth,
Ceredigion,
SY23 3DY.

We are very grateful for the support of all our Honno Friends.